The Devil's Kiss

The Devil's Kiss

John Geerer

ISBN Paperback: 978-1-7353654-1-1
ISBN eBook: 978-1-7353654-0-4

Printed in the United States of America

Book Cover and Interior Design: Creative Publishing Book Design
Cover Art: Bogdan Maksimovic

For My Muse

CHAPTER ONE

The Arrival

Wednesday, June 16, 1999

And then the window shattered. It was the damnedest thing he ever saw. He was looking out at Doliber's Cove from the upstairs bedroom window, when it broke with a sudden crack. Yet the entire pane stayed intact; not a shard went flying. What was a moment ago a clear, single sheet of glass now resembled a completed jigsaw puzzle of dozens of dagger-shaped pieces of promised pain. The window that had recently displayed a beautiful view of the cove beneath the cerulean summer sky now looked like an abstract work of Picasso from his blue period. Tom Stone was not happy about the window. He didn't care much for Picasso either.

"What the hell?" Tom cautiously lowered a defending arm from his face. He stared in dumb perplexity at the sight before him. His eyes flashed down at the floor beneath the window. The hardwood was clean. Not a sliver had fallen from the frame of the shattered pane. There was no focal point of the break—just a hodgepodge

1

of stubborn glass pieces of like size and shape. They reminded Tom of a Saracen sword, the kind he'd seen on a Knights of Columbus bumper sticker. *How could all the pieces look so similar?* He shook off his confusion and reached for the small spiral-bound tablet and carpenter's pencil sitting on the third step of the ladder. With the stubby, tooth-mark-pocked pencil, another task was added to his to-do list. Tom slipped the pad into the pocket of yesterday's shirt that still clung to his back. His list was getting longer, not shorter. *Damn.* The room was hot as the sun mounted the late-morning sky. The air in the room, still and heavy, left Tom feeling a little claustrophobic. If only he could open the window. *Yeah, well, that's not gonna happen.* Tom wiped the moisture from his brow with the short sleeve of his shirt. He caught a whiff of himself in doing so and added yet another item to the list: laundry.

He was off to a poor start. The morning was almost gone, and he was walking listlessly, if not aimlessly, through the early hours, unwashed and unshaven. This in itself was atypical of his behavior and a growing cause for concern. Before he had moved into Stonecroft Inn just two days ago, he was a very different man.

Tom stood square-shouldered at six feet and one inch. Recently retired from the US Navy after twenty-six years of service, he maintained a fit and trim physique that reflected an incredible amount of self-discipline. Clean in habits as well as in hygiene, he found joy and comfort in order and discipline. As his best friend, Jake Brean, often said, Tom *owned himself.*

He attributed his sense of order to his upbringing in Bismarck, North Dakota. Life in Bismarck had been hard and the winters extreme. He was the only son of a loving mother and a broken home; the two of them had rationed most everything—from food to clothes to electricity—as if there was a war on. And to Tom's way of thinking, there was. The war of survival.

His mother died on a Tuesday, in their small house on West Avenue B that lay in the morning shadow of the Cathedral of the Holy Spirit. Tom was sixteen years old. Two months later, on his seventeenth birthday, he left Bismarck High School, walked into the armed forces recruiting office on Main Street, and joined the navy. As so often happens when the disadvantaged enter the military, Tom made the most of the opportunities presented to him. After getting his GED, he pursued a bachelor's degree in health science, completing his coursework as his duty stations would allow: correspondence courses while at sea, and classroom participation whenever he had shore duty. It was a long, tough haul—all the while moving up the enlisted ranks. He never missed an advancement, never knew the pain of receiving the mark of PNA—passed but not advanced—which is the navy's way of saying you're not good enough, try harder. By the time he was twenty-nine years old, Tom had ascended from seaman recruit to chief petty officer. One year after they'd tacked on his chief's anchor, Tom walked in his San Diego State University commencement ceremony, having graduated with honors. The following day, he was off to the Officer Indoctrination School in Newport, Rhode Island. After six weeks of officer training, it was on to grad school, following which he received his license to practice as a physician assistant.

Throughout his naval career, Tom's foremost virtues were strengthened through overcoming challenges and a zealous devotion to discipline: Courage. Duty. Honor. He was an exemplary sailor and a tried-and-true shipmate—but it was also said he had a heart as hard and cold as the haze-gray steel hull of the USS *Kitty Hawk* upon whose deck he served. The fact that his eyes were of a similar gray color was understandably lost on them, but it wasn't lost on Carol.

Tom never thought of himself as a romantic person, but that began to change the night he met Carol Stevens. Sitting next to each other in a philosophy class one evening, the two enlisted service members—Tom was a first-class petty officer at that time; Carol, third class—exchanged doubtful looks as their professor drew questionable parallels between the works of Aristotle and the Who. Over a post-lecture cup of coffee, they both swore it was a class they'd never forget. Each secretly knew why. And it had nothing to do with Greek philosophers, eccentric associate professors, or classic rock and roll bands. After a brief courtship, they were married six months later—an eternity in military dog years.

Tom remained a serious man even after they were married. The regimented, organized life was not only how he lived, but part of what defined him.

But he changed in other ways in his life with Carol. Whereas the discipline required for a successful military career came naturally to Tom, the vulnerability of being in love—relinquishing control of his emotional life—did not. In fact, it was more frightening to him than the thought of facing down an enemy armada. But he loved her. He trusted her. And he learned to let go. He lost nothing in doing so, and in the fullness of time, he freely showed himself to be an understanding and compassionate man with infinite patience for those who did their best. He began to see life as something more than battle-readiness exercises recorded in a ship's log in military time. He looked beyond a life in uniform and saw what it could be with Carol. They shared their thoughts and dreams and began to make plans.

What they struck upon was settling down and running a little seaside inn. Quaint. Comfortable. Safe. They found magic in its simplicity. Soon, or so it seemed, Tom's retirement loomed large. Through detailed planning, extensive real estate market research, and the aid of a small fortune Carol had inherited years earlier from a grandfather she'd remembered meeting only once as a small child, they landed the perfect little place to start a new life, in Marblehead, Massachusetts.

They'd had contractors, craftsmen, and inspectors hard at work months before Tom stowed away his uniform in his seabag for the last time. They wanted all the heavy lifting to be done by the time they moved in, and their excitement grew with each passing day. It would be life as it should be, Tom thought, with Carol serving as the center of his universe—everything would revolve around her. But then Carol died, and Tom's world spun out of control.

Thinking back, Tom had a vague recollection of someone talking about something in the Bible that referred to faith, hope, and love. It went on to say that the greatest of these was love. Tom disagreed. He disagreed with that and just about every other deep, mystical saying, slogan, motto, or mantra that organized religion had to offer. *Hope. Having hope, that's the greatest. And that's what I need right now. Having a reason to live, a reason to just stay alive and not kill myself.* Even after Carol was diagnosed with glioblastoma multiforme and endured the torturous treatment triumvirate of surgery, radiation, and chemotherapy, he clung to hope. It was there. Distant. Dim. But still there. And it gave him the strength to keep going.

With Carol's death, he was introduced to a new life partner. A soul-crushing pain that was his constant companion. It promised never to leave him. It had a name, and it wielded that name as if it were a weapon in itself, which, of course, it was. Despair. The absence of hope. Tom's most ruthless adversary. Bold and unrelenting, despair was a far more sinister and evil enemy than hate could ever hope to be. Hate might make you want to kill someone, but despair made you want to kill yourself. *That fucker.*

Now the shattered window became another notch in the gun belt of the bizarre and inexplicable. He had hoped for better, especially after another night of strange, disconcerting dreams. At first, they seemed nothing more than the natural ventures of his subconscious, a vehicle for his doubts and fears to break free from their confinement and hurl themselves into the spotlight of the ethereal stage for one final curtain call. But the dreams began to build, one upon the other, night upon previous night, creating a dangerous dreamscape, an unstable emotional tower, teetering, threatening collapse. It had taken a violent turn last night, if not in its actual outcome, certainly in the intent of its subject. Tom tried to recapture the sequence of events in his dreams. But it seemed the harder he tried to cut and paste them into place, they'd just as quickly slip away, like trying to grab a fistful of smoke. Then, slowly, when he finally gave up his pursuit, a few of the scenes quietly emerged from some dark space on a dusty shelf of his memory.

He remembered the old woman—that was easy enough. She stood darkly, clad in a blanket of thick fog, her narrowed eyes attempting to pierce the gray veil that surrounded her, as if anticipating the arrival of a loved one. As Tom stepped into his dream, he approached the woman, the dense fog swallowing the sound of his footfalls. He asked the old woman, "Who are you looking for?" As with his footsteps, his voice was lost in the mist. The words formed on his lips, but he could issue no breath to carry them. The old woman shifted her eyes to Tom for only a moment. It was a brief but knowing look laced with contempt. Just as quickly, she caught sight of something over Tom's shoulder, and her eyes widened in joyous recognition. He recoiled and turned away from the fetid breath that seeped through her jack-o'-lantern smile, and Tom found himself facing down the approaching figure. He knew it was a man, but the features were drawn and gaunt and remained indistinguishable through the fog, even as he came closer. And closer. It seemed as if it were a corpse, stiff with rigor, being moved upright on some hidden cart pushed toward him. Then Tom saw the eyes. The eyes were alive. Or at least they had an energy to them. They didn't glow, exactly, but they were able to pierce the veil of the relentless fog. And Tom recognized something else. He didn't know how, and he didn't know from where, but Tom was certain he *knew* this man. He then felt the presence of the woman behind him. She was nearly on top of him. He tried to turn to fend her off but he couldn't move. It was as if he were paralyzed. Tom felt as though thick leather belts had been strapped around his neck and chest. He couldn't draw a breath. He was suffocating.

Panic snapped Tom out of his daydream. His breath came back quick and deep. He gulped the air. Downstairs, the grandfather clock in the gathering room measured out the final death throes of the morning in somber ticks and mournful tones. Slowly, the room, the heat, and the shattered window returned to him. But the melancholy residue clung to Tom like a wet, sticky blanket. The need to get clean seemed a desperate act of reclamation. He cast a wary eye behind him as he stumbled out of the empty bedroom.

* * *

After a shower and a shave, Tom lifted the typical pocket paraphernalia from a crudely woven basket atop his dresser. The basket was the product of an entire semester's worth of work for Carol back in their San Diego State days. She'd needed an elective. So, wanting to cultivate her creative side, she decided to take an art class. She chose basket weaving for two reasons. First, she didn't want to take a pottery class because she couldn't stand the thought of being up to her elbows in clay for a whole hour, three times a week, for an entire semester. Second, she had no aptitude whatsoever when it came to sketching, drawing, or painting. After seeing one of her attempts at a seascape done in watercolor, Jake, Tom's best friend, said that Bob Ross would've kicked her out of class. So basket weaving it was.

The basket was a gift to Tom from Carol. In truth, it was as artistically unsound and visually unattractive as her watercolor seascape had been. And just as true, it was one of Tom's most treasured and precious possessions. It sat between two pictures. One of Carol and him on the beach at Waikiki; the other of the two of them with Jake and Marie Brean, laughing in the afternoon sunshine on Ocracoke Island later that same summer. *That was a great trip.* It was the first trip the two couples had taken together. *The first of many,* Tom remembered as he continued his routine.

Each item was inspected for readiness before being billeted into a pocket of his cargo shorts—wallet with license and credit cards, money clip with bills in a descending denominational sequence; twenties on the inside, then tens, then fives, with only the ones showing on the outside. A cleaning cloth for his sunglasses and reading glasses. Lastly, he snapped a chronometer into place on his wrist.

With his morning routine reestablished and completed and his friends, the Breans, arriving tomorrow, Tom wondered if things might soon start turning around. He took a few deep, cleansing breaths in an attempt to rid himself of any malingering melancholy from the cheerless morning and went down the squeaky back staircase that led to the gathering room.

He padded through the house, conducting a walking inspection and making small adjustments on recently finished projects—placing protective felt pads on the feet of kitchen chair legs, removing the last of the painter's tape found hiding on the tops of window frames and doorjambs, swearing under his breath as paint, still not completely dry, clung to the edge of the tape with far greater tenacity than it had to the wall. After tossing the wad of crumpled blue into the kitchen trash bin, Tom slid open the windows. The ocean breeze poured into the house and stirred the stale, stagnant air, and for the first time that day, he was able to feel the beauty that surrounded him. Carol had told him that Marblehead was a place of dreams and magic. He'd managed to hide his eye roll from her when she said it, but in time, Tom saw the town in much the same way, if perhaps for different reasons. In Tom's mind, much of the small seaport's mystery and charm remained intact because, at its heart, Marblehead had stayed true to its colonial seaport origins. *To thine own self be true,* Tom thought. *Where's that from? Oh God, not from the Bible, I hope.* Tom took in a lungful of sea air and carried on with his inspection.

In the gathering room, a name commonly applied to the main room of the house back in the day, Tom slowed the pace of his examination. He felt the uneven firmness of the ancient planked floor beneath his bare feet and the cool of the blue-gray slate hearthstones of the magnificent fireplace that commanded the room. As impressive as the fireplace was, it sorely begged for the ministrations of a skilled mason. The mortar around the stones on the left side was breaking away in chunks. Tom took a thumb and forefinger to a particularly large piece and moved it as easily as a first grader's tooth. He looked around the room. Rough-hewn support beams rose from the foundation and joined at right angles with the horizontal ceiling beams. The blackness of the wooden beams and the wide-planked floors gave the gathering room the old seafaring atmosphere that Tom had hoped for. It was an ambiance he knew he could not have created himself; the house possessed these vibrations on its own. It had lived it—and was living it still. It had, Tom thought, good bones.

He was starting to feel a rhythm, a lightness in his chest and shoulders, and a slowly rising optimism. There was still a lot of work to be done. But Jake and Marie would be there tomorrow, and many hands make light work. Besides, he knew that all he needed to do to get Jake motivated was to provide as many historical references to the place as he could. He had quite a bit of factual information on the house's history and, more importantly, much of the folklore that was still whispered throughout the town. There were even rumors of ghouls, ghosts, and other things that go bump in the night. At any rate, he knew he had the stuff that history teachers live for. He would be able to keep Jake working for days on end.

As Tom reviewed the story of the house in his mind, he was once again reminded of the genuine affection that he'd already developed for the place in the short time he'd been there, at least when weird things weren't happening. He was the owner of a seaside inn on the rocky New England shores of Marblehead, Massachusetts. And it was important that he know, and play, the part.

Built on a small, craggy outcropping, Stonecroft Inn commanded a sentinel view of Doliber's Cove to the north and opened to the Atlantic Ocean to the east through a mouth formed by Peach's

Point, Marblehead's heavily wooded northeastern tip, and Brown's Island just to the south. Brown's Island was a small scrap of land, not much more than a wooded sandbar, that sat directly off Stonecroft's seawall about a hundred yards away and impaired the inn's otherwise-unobstructed view of the Atlantic beyond. You could walk to the island in knee-deep water at low tide. A quarter of a mile to the south of the inn was Little Harbor, the original harbor in Marblehead, the heart of seafaring commerce going back hundreds of years, which now served only as a calm and friendly place for boaters to drop their anchors and enjoy a floating picnic lunch.

The original inn was built in 1690, when it served as a tavern, but only the gathering room, central fireplace, and back staircase remained largely undisturbed from that early period. A smaller fireplace was added around 1750. Tom had heard most of the local lore, dealt out by the townsfolk for consumption by the hungry ears of visitors in search of stories of maritime adventure. Through the years, such fables were told and retold, with new twists and turns, leaving one to wonder whether any truth echoed in them at all. Most had to do with the sea and the sailors who loved her. There were tales of Homeric shipwrecks and heroic derring-do, of alluring barmaids and murdering cutthroats. But those were just old sea stories that, to a seasoned navy man like Tom, were taken with a grain of sea salt. Tom usually discounted them as complete fabrications, just like stories of Santa Claus, the Easter Bunny, and ghosts.

Tom would even have trouble telling such stories to Jake and Marie, but he clearly understood that this lore, especially the history of the inn, would serve as the very enticement to bring his future customers to rest at his hearth. They would listen to the tales and try to recapture some of the old New England that was long past. Even if Tom couldn't see himself spinning the yarns he'd heard in town, he could feel their pulse as he walked through Stonecroft Inn, and he began to wonder if some of them just might be true.

Tom stepped out the back door to complete his inspection, the patio stonework warming the bottom of his cool feet. His eyes searched for problems around the windows, gutters, and chimneys. The paint on the outside trim was in surprisingly good shape—not that there weren't opportunities for improvement. His concerns were more with the condition of the masonry and stonework on the windward side of the house.

Stone had been used instead of wood for extra protection against the weather and salt air. The inn derived its name, Stonecroft, from having been built of the abundant stones quarried from the rocky ground it rose upon. An impressive stone patio extended fifteen feet out from the east side of the house and wrapped around the southern corner, then extended another twenty feet from there, where Tom had plans to develop an outdoor dining area. He studied each patio stone and its border. The cement appeared sound as he traversed the patio, his head swinging like a pendulum as he examined the ground.

At the southern side of the house, a chimney rose from the stone deck like the mast of a ship, tall and slender, a bony finger pointing skyward. It was the chimney for the smaller fireplace in the gathering room. The one that sat unused and unnoticed across from its considerably larger older brother. Still, every inch of Stonecroft required time and attention, especially in terms of safety. Upon closer scrutiny, he discovered a network of fine cracks. Tom picked at the cement around the bricks. It seemed ready to break loose in some places, just like the mortar around the central fireplace. Tom cursed under his breath. *This should have already been fixed.*

The man with whom he had contracted to do the masonry had, at first, been a difficult person to deal with. He was a meticulous man who worked off a schedule and would not deviate from it for all the fish sticks in Gloucester. He was, in many ways, a man whom Tom could admire, were it not for a rigidity that sometimes served no purpose other than to piss people off. His name was Mr. Goddard. That's how he introduced himself, and, by God, that's what you called him.

Tom had pressed the man to start immediately, without effect. It almost seemed to Tom that the more desperate he became, the longer it was going to take the contractor to get there. Then one morning at five o'clock, Tom was awakened by a shuffling sound outside, coming from the patio below. When he got up to investigate, Mr. Goddard was up on a ladder just outside Tom's bedroom window, inspecting the chimney with a flashlight. When it came time to start a job, Tom realized, this guy was too impatient for the sun to rise. One thing was for sure, the son of a bitch wasn't lazy.

But that was two days ago, and Tom hadn't seen him since. He stared at the rotting chimney and started to sweat. This job had to get done, and it had to get done soon. Because until it was completed, Tom couldn't even call to schedule a building inspection. And if the inn wasn't inspected or didn't pass the inspection, Tom wouldn't be able to open. If Tom didn't open, the bank, not to mention the patrons, would want to know why. He had to give Mr. Goddard another call. Tom wiped the sweat from his brow with the heel of his hand and squinted into the pale-blue summer sky. It was going to be a hot one.

CHAPTER TWO
Ol' Navy Buddies

Thursday, June 17, 1999

Jake Brean walked out of the Dunkin' Donuts in the Newtown Center at 7:05 a.m. He wasn't alone. The name on the other man's forest-green work shirt, stitched in cursive gold lettering above the left breast pocket, read *Tim*. Over the opposite breast was an embroidered patch with the company logo in lowercase letters, *tim buckley co*. And if anyone looked toward the row of trees that lined the northern end of the Big Y Shopping Center parking lot, they'd have seen a big plumber's truck that displayed the same company logo on magnetic signs that straddled both sides of the green vehicle.

"So," Jake asked, "from a plumber's perspective, what kind of problems would you be looking for if you bought a three-hundred-year-old house?"

"From a plumber's perspective?" Tim confirmed.

"Yeah."

15

"I wouldn't buy a three-hundred-year-old house."

"No shit? Oh, OK," Jake said in mock appreciation. "Thanks a pantsload, pal."

"Seriously," Tim added, "there can be problems everywhere. It all depends on how old the plumbing is and the quality of the upkeep it's received. Any idea of the condition of the place? How old the pipes are? Was it properly winterized when no one was living there? If your friend's opening a B&B, I'm assuming he'll have installed a high-capacity water heater, a new sump pump, that sort of thing? Maybe even a new water-softening system. I'm guessing he's got a well, right?"

Jake looked dumbly at Tim.

"Well," Tim said with a shrug, having made his point, "if you come across any problems, give me a call—maybe I can talk you through 'em. If not, well, at least you'll know you've done all you could."

"All right. Thanks, man," Jake replied. "Glad that fucking conversation's over with," he added to himself.

Arriving at the Breans' car, Jake slipped into the driver's seat and passed the coffee and doughnut holes to Marie. Tim bent down and looked at Marie through the driver's-side window. "Hi, gorgeous," he said. "How's my favorite science teacher?"

"Good, Tim. How're things with you?" Marie asked.

"All is well, I'm happy to say. Gonna be caretakers for the summer, I understand?"

"Yep, a friend in need . . . ," Marie said.

"Gotcha," Tim replied. "Well, I've told the old man here to give me a call if he encounters any problems."

By the time he'd settled in and buckled up, Jake was already bored with Tim and Marie's conversation. It was nothing but white noise to Jake. He'd had enough.

"All right, get the hell away from my car," Jake said with feigned irritation. "I've got places to go, things to see, people to do."

Marie rolled her eyes but held her tongue.

Tim took a step back and held up a hand in parting. Jake put the car in drive and slowly rolled to the parking lot exit.

He was silent as he pulled out onto Queen Street and remained so as they waited for the light to turn green at Churchill Road. Marie wondered where his thoughts had taken him—were they on baseball, the school year that had just ended, or the potential plumbing problems that awaited them in Marblehead? When they turned onto the eastbound I-84 on-ramp just beyond the Blue Colony Diner, Jake still hadn't spoken. Marie looked at her watch. *Three and a half minutes. A new record. Something's coming.* Ten minutes later, as they were passing through Southbury, the new record was set.

"OK. So who the fuck is gonna want to stay in a bed-and-breakfast that's run by a middle-aged single guy? I mean, how fuckin' creepy is that?"

And there it was. *A good question, actually, even if indelicately phrased,* Marie thought.

"That's why we both need to be there," Marie stated. "To provide a welcoming environment that will make the guests feel comfortable." She added, "So could you please try to remember that, and watch your language while you're at it?"

Jake cast a sideways glance at his wife, then turned his attention back to the road. "I don't know what the fuck is wrong with saying something's creepy," he said quietly to himself. Marie stared out her window.

Jake set the cruise control at seventy-five in the sixty-five-mile-an-hour zone and slipped in an old Steely Dan CD. With one eye on the rearview mirror, Jake settled back to enjoy the ride as they wove their way through the Nutmeg State, both lost in their own little worlds while enjoying the early-morning sunshine on a brand-new summer day. Donald Fagen was at the mic, and to Jake, the boys never sounded better.

Marie was getting excited and looking forward to helping put the finishing touches on Tom's new place—*Stonecroft*, she heard it was called. *Stonecroft Inn.* Some last-minute antique shopping in Litchfield earlier that week had secured some period pieces that even Jake had to grudgingly admit were "kinda cool"—six silver candleholders with light deflectors, which would sit on sconces around the main room of the inn. Marie couldn't help but think of her friend when she saw them. Carol would have loved them. Tom, on the other hand, well . . .

"When Tom called last night, how did he sound to you?" Jake's question brought Marie back to the here and now.

"Um, OK, I guess," she said, trying to recall. "He was getting a little edgy with the opening being so soon, but other than that, he seemed fine. He really didn't say much before I handed you the phone." Marie studied her husband. She could see him thinking and sensed concern in his voice while his eyes never left the road. "Why? Do you think there's something wrong?"

Jake drew a deep breath and slowly shook his head. "I don't know. When I was talking to him, he mentioned some of the jobs that still needed to be done." Silence. Three seconds. Five seconds. Seven seconds.

"And . . . ?" Marie prompted.

"And he didn't mention one job that was any big deal, outside of some masonry work that he's contracted out. He seemed distracted, as if he were looking over his shoulder while he was talking to me. Like someone else was there." Jake held a questioning palm upward, his elbow resting on the padded console between the two leather bucket seats.

"Tom's in his element when he's doing that kind of work, and he seemed fatigued when I was talking to him, completely deflated. It almost seemed like he doubted he did the right thing by buying the place." He paused and glanced out the window as bushes and trees rushed by in a blur. "I don't know," he concluded, "maybe it's because he's pursuing a dream, and Carol isn't there to share it with him."

Marie knew that he wasn't really talking to her; he was just worrying out loud about his friend. She looked at him, pleased that he cared so much. But something continued to scratch at Jake's brain. "Nah," he said decidedly, continuing his reflection. "There was something more to it. Tom wasn't just distracted. He was . . . scared."

* * *

In the navy, many friendships are forged. But in living such a transient life, few of those friendships last. Those that do are the stronger for it. Tom met Jake fifteen years earlier when the two were stationed at Naval Hospital, San Diego. At the time, both were respiratory therapists with completely different long-term goals. It was this contrast, along with a mutual respect they had for each other, that served as the foundation of their friendship. Whereas Tom was serious and somewhat reserved, Jake was the quintessential extrovert. When the two brought their wives into their social circle, it was as if the four had known each other for years.

These were the thoughts going through Tom's head as he heard the muffled crunching sound of car tires rolling up the long gravel driveway and a blaring horn. He opened the door to see his friends waving to him from the car. Well, Marie was waving, anyway, Tom noted. If Jake was waving, it was only with one finger. The car rolled to a stop, and Jake sprang out.

"Little help!" he shouted, popping open the trunk of the car. A soft smile lit Tom's face as he approached the couple.

"Hey, good to see you," Tom said to Marie, hugging her in greeting. "Go on in and take a look around; I'll help Jake with the bags."

Marie headed toward the house as Jake grabbed Tom in a back-slapping embrace. "Good to see you, Tommy Boy!" he said, honest joy in his voice. "By the way," Jake quickly confided as he watched his wife disappear beyond the threshold, "on the way over, Marie said the thought of an old guy, like yourself, running a bed-and-breakfast is really pretty creepy."

Tom paused, doubtful and curious. "And what did you say?"

"I told her to watch her fuckin' language."

"Yeah, I'm sure that's how the conversation went," Tom said, wondering why he'd taken the bait to begin with. "C'mon—let's get your bags inside and get you squared away."

Jake stared at the open trunk, more than a little irritated. "Look at the amount of crap she packed." Tom nodded. He remembered the days when his own exasperation at car trunks and back seats filled beyond safety limits with Carol's "necessities" left him hopelessly frustrated, and he envied Jake his discontent.

Tom grabbed the bags and cases from the deep trunk and noticed Jake surveying the property with an admiring eye. "Go ahead—take a look around," Tom suggested with an encouraging toss of his head. "I'll take care of this." As he continued to unpack the car, Tom allowed his friend to drink in the scene. Enchanted by the beauty of his surroundings, Jake treaded noisily over the gravel drive, across a close-cropped patch of healthy crabgrass, to the low stone wall that stood sentry over the north side of the property, where the rocky hill began to give way to the small, secluded beach of Doliber's Cove.

As he looked down the shallow hill on which he stood, the tide lapped leisurely on the pebbled shore of the cove. Larger stones that spent half their lives below the waterline boasted a thick, almost fluorescent, green moss upon their crowns. The calm water of the cove opened to the wide expanse of the Atlantic, canopied by a clear blue sky, a canvas smudged only by streaming traces of titanium white. A steady breeze came in off the ocean and carried with it the smell of the sea. *Ah, salt air,* Jake thought as his olfactory senses embraced the memory. He'd forgotten how much he loved that smell. He'd forgotten how much he missed the ocean.

Jake filled his lungs with sea breeze and turned away. Seeing his host standing by the empty car on the long gravel driveway that divided a well-manicured lawn, Jake strode slowly back across the grass as the sound of the gentle tide died away. Other than the occasional soft ping of his car engine cooling off, the only sound Jake heard was the offshore breeze as it brushed through the leaves of the trees that shielded the inn from Beacon Street. "What a setup," Jake said, sincerely impressed. "Almost total seclusion from the street, with a three-sided ocean view. Man, I gotta say, Tommy Boy, when you do something, you do it right."

"Thanks," Tom said, forcing a smile. He would forever hide from Jake the near-fatal financial exhaustion that came along with *doing it right.*

On crossing the threshold, Jake found himself transported back in time. The smell of ancient wood and a faint hint of pine tar mingled with the scent of the sea. In front of him stood a large staircase. Off to his left was a nearly empty room. The few pieces of furniture and the ornately tiled fireplace suggested that, someday, this room would grow up to be a fine formal living room. Following in Tom's footsteps, he moved off to the right and entered what he instantly recognized as the focal point of the inn. And in the middle of that room sat the most massive table Jake had ever seen. The heavy, dark oak table measured twelve feet long by five feet wide. And as big as it was, there was still plenty of space for additional smaller tables to seat more guests. When his eyes struck on the immense fireplace, he found himself taking a quick step back. It was cavernous, as wide as it was deep, and were he to have hunched over just a bit, he would have been able to walk into it. Jake stood amazed.

"This is the gathering room," Tom said, snapping Jake out of his trance. "This room was part of the original house built over three hundred years ago." The ceiling was typical for that period—low, only a little more than seven feet, with exposed beams overhead, giving men as tall as Tom and Jake the feeling that they had to duck their heads as they walked. Floor planks, each two and a half feet wide, were held in place by large iron nails, which may have been more appropriately called spikes. The deep grooves in the floor spoke to its strength and age. "When this was a tavern," Tom went on to explain, "it served as the social center, where travelers and guests would eat their meals, smoke their pipes, and drink their rum." Tom spoke the last part in his best pirate voice, which wasn't very good. In fact, it was terrible. Jake looked at him as if with a bad taste in his mouth.

"Never speak in that voice again," Jake said. "Forever."

Tom hesitated. "Yeah. Well, this is where they ate their meals," he said flatly.

"Better," Jake admitted with an approving nod. "Much better."

"Speaking of eating meals, Tommy Boy," Jake added, suddenly remembering, "not only did we make great time, but we even made an unscheduled stop in Saugus." Jake bent down and picked up a cheap Styrofoam cooler and lifted the lid for Tom to see.

"Rib eyes, fresh from Hilltop Steakhouse!"

"All right!" Tom returned with equally matched enthusiasm. The men high-fived each other as if they had just climbed Mount Everest and returned with all their fingers and toes.

After Tom had provided a detailed, room-by-room tour, Jake reviewed the current list of projects that Tom had scribbled in his notepad. The two conferred as to the best way to make short work of them. Jake volunteered to change the faulty light switch in the kitchen; that was a quick and easy task. Then he'd take on the sizable interior painting job, as Tom had hoped he would. In his years after the navy, Jake had spent a couple of summers as a commercial painter back in Newtown to supplement his teacher's salary; he knew how to knock down a job like this quickly and cleanly. And he drew a smile out of Tom when he got started immediately.

It was strange, Jake thought as he unscrewed and removed the cover plate from the light switch, how so often the living looked for ways to bridge the gap between the material and the spiritual worlds. And is that what Tom was doing in having a go at getting this place up and running? How much sense did it make to spend one's life trying to hang on to the dead? Waxing philosophically was a particular hobby of Jake's. And his waxing was painfully interrupted as 110 volts of "wake up" shot up his arm from his index finger and buried themselves deep in his brain. He jumped back with the speed of a startled cat and stared at his finger. A slow, baritone "Whooaaa" rolled from his dry mouth. He looked accusingly at the unit. "Well, you've just seen your last day," he declared to the switch as he shook his finger in the air. It was a helluva jolt. He immediately resolved to leave the electrical work for someone else, like Tom. He felt a little funny, kind of like a firefly. As Jake left the kitchen in search of a safer occupation, he wondered if his ass was lighting up.

He thought he'd initiate painting operations in the upstairs bedroom at the north end of the hall that looked out onto the cove. He described his painting plan of attack to Tom, who struggled to show interest while he wrestled with a light fixture in the hallway, just outside the bedroom door. "I always like to start by cleaning the walls with a bucket of hot water and just enough Lysol so that you can smell it, to get rid of the freestanding dirt and grime. I ought to be able to knock out a couple of these rooms today."

Tom looked over his shoulder and nodded. *And when Jake's working, he's also talking.* Tom turned his attention once again to the new light fixture he was hanging in the hall.

Jake liked the sound voices made in an empty room with hardwood floors. There was a resonance, almost an echo, and it brought him comfort. To him, it was how a room sounded on its way to becoming beautiful. "It's all right, baby," Jake whispered to the walls. "Daddy's gonna make it all better." Then Jake took a careful look at the large window that showcased the view of the bay and realized that his initial impression—that it had some sort of strange treatment or surface application—when he first entered the room was incorrect. It was broken. But not just broken. Shattered. He cautiously approached the window, dumbfounded, and wondered how the glass could possibly have stayed in place. It was so curious. It was as if it had been made of windshield glass, the way it had splintered but held. But the pieces seemed almost uniform, like someone had designed it. "Tom, how the *hell* did this happen?" he called out.

Tom came down from the ladder. "I have no idea," he replied from the bedroom doorway. "I was in here yesterday morning, looking around, when it just . . ." Tom shrugged and pushed an open hand toward the window.

Jake slowly shook his head as he studied the sight. "Well, I'll mask it off just to be on the safe side," he said, doubt lacing his voice.

"Probably a good idea," Tom agreed. "I called Mr. Goddard yesterday, and he said he'd be here tomorrow to fix that window and get to work on the masonry." Tom paused and grinned. "Wait till you meet this guy. He's a real piece of work." The uneasy smile on Jake's face faded fast as he watched in muted fascination as the window undulated within its wooden frame. He stood, tape in hand, wondering how best to secure the window—it seemed that the slightest touch might trigger a dangerous crystal avalanche. Yet it was moving in an easy rhythm, like the gentle rise and fall of a sleeping man's chest. Jake studied the movement with a dubious eye. *Well,* he thought, *if there's a gusting breeze outside . . . and if the glass has significant tempered qualities, and if . . . Yeah, and if my aunt had balls, she'd be my uncle. There's something really fucking weird going on here.* Jake was mesmerized by the movement. He suddenly felt a cold, clammy hand grip the back of his neck. He wheeled around with a start.

"Steady, sailor," Tom quipped as he entered the room, stepladder in hand.

"Yeah. Sorry," Jake said, reddening with embarrassment. "You just startled me when you put your hand on my neck."

Tom looked at him from across the room. "Uh, do you see where I'm standing?" he asked with mild indignation. "I didn't touch your neck."

Jake stared at Tom for a long, lingering moment, then fixed his gaze back on the window.

"Tom, what the hell's going on here?"

Tom didn't know what to say. He didn't have the words because he didn't know himself. Then something clicked in his mind. It was as if a light switch had been flipped on and sudden illumination pierced the dark veil that cloaked his memory.

"That's nothing," he finally said as the previous night's dream came back to him in full. "Wait till I tell you about the old woman who tried to kill me a couple nights ago."

CHAPTER THREE
Salem

September 1692

The boy scurried about in an almost frenzied state. With his pale-blue eyes never leaving the ground, he came dangerously close to running into a tree on several occasions. A surge of excitement came over him as he uncovered, with dirty, eager hands, what looked to be a perfect stone. As he began to dig, it quickly became apparent that it was much too large for easy removal, and the excavation was aborted. Momentarily daunted, he stood up slowly; swiped the long, sandy-blond hair out of his eyes; and once again scouted the surrounding grounds. It was strange that in the rocky earth of New England, it now seemed so difficult to find stones that were just the right size. He sought one small enough for a strong twelve-year-old boy to carry but large enough to be helpful in such a just cause. His father and the villagers were counting on him—or at least, he let himself believe they were. So his frantic search continued.

In his heart, he knew that they didn't actually need his help. They had all the rocks they required to complete the job. Small rocks, big rocks, and some in the middle—they had them all. What he really wanted was to show them that he was part of the town. He wanted to attest to everyone that he belonged. It was *very* important that he prove his usefulness. In the few short years that he had lived there, he had never felt so much a part of the small village as he did now. Neither had he known such peace and pleasantry at home. Not until the hangings had started.

Father had been a very stern man all his life, as far as Israel knew. He couldn't remember many nights when his father didn't beat his mother. But things were better now—Mother was dead. Father didn't hit anyone anymore, except on certain nights when he stunk of rum. On those occasions, when his father's wrath turned on him, Israel thought he must have done something to deserve it. He knew his father loved him; otherwise he would not hit him. And on this glorious morning, Israel Hands was determined to make his father proud.

As he walked from shade into sunlight, a steely glimmer about twenty feet away caught Israel's eye. He crouched slightly and approached the object with breathless, boyish anticipation, hoping he had found his prize. He could see a large portion of granite protruding from the dark New England soil. The stone shimmered with Israel's movements as the sun sparkled off the specks of mica. Israel knelt in front of it and fingered the ground around the rock, creating a dry moat. He dug furiously. It was easy to handle because of its size and shape, but its weight made carrying it a considerable task. Israel would pick it up and walk only a dozen paces or so before he had to set the stone down and rest a moment. He was half a mile away from his destination when he first shouldered the stone and an hour older by the time he delivered it.

The sun burned directly above Israel's head when he reached his father and the other men of the town. His pains were rewarded, for upon his arrival, he saw in his father's eyes a look of satisfaction that he had never seen before. As Israel turned his prize over to Sheriff Corwin, he looked up as his father clapped a warm hand on the boy's tired shoulder. "Good lad," he said with an approving smile. Israel's heart sang. With stone in hand, the sheriff again demanded a plea from Giles Corey on the charge of practicing witchcraft, a plea that would never come. So on went Israel's stone, adding to the already-considerable pile pressing the life out of Corey. As it landed, Israel heard air escape from the chest of the suffocating man. He also thought he heard bones breaking. Had his stone finally crushed the man's chest, he wondered? Maybe it did, or maybe, he cautioned himself, it was just his false pride. A sense of shame fell upon him, and Israel rebuked himself for the thought, for he knew that pride was a sin.

He stood at his father's side for quite some time watching Corey die under the late-summer sun. It was the devil that was being crushed out of Corey. That's what Ezekiel Hands had told his son. And Israel knew that his father never lied. So there they stood, watching the devil leave Salem. It was odd, Israel thought as he observed the blood flow freely from the mouth, nose, and ears of the dying man, how bright red the fresh blood was, whereas the blood that had come out yesterday was now almost black. Israel scratched his head. There were lots of things he didn't understand, but it was all right by him. The important things in life were loyalty and faithfulness. A lot of people said they were the same thing. Israel didn't know. He liked the way it sounded when he said it. A lot of people also said it wasn't a good thing to kill people. He didn't know about that either. They'd been hanging people since the corn was small, and everything seemed all right, so he reckoned it wasn't always a bad thing to kill people.

Israel tried his best not to laugh, but with his eyes and tongue bulging out of his head, Corey looked more like a fish brought up from deep waters than a man. And when Sheriff Corwin stood on the pile and pushed the man's swollen tongue back into his mouth with a stick, Israel had to turn away to keep from laughing out loud. Shortly before he died, Giles Corey swore an oath, breathlessly cursing and damning those around him. This time, Israel did laugh out loud.

"As a plea was not pressed out of the man, then we pray that we pressed out the devil." Israel made no response to his father's statement. He saw it for what it was, a declaration of righteousness that required no blessing from a twelve-year-old boy. As they made their long way home down dusty lanes and cobblestone streets, the two walked in communal silence. Ezekiel was lost in his thoughts on the day's deeds well done. Israel knew well enough not to interrupt his father's musings. For he was at his father's right hand, and that was his strongest hand.

Before reaching their small carpenter shop down on the wharf near the customs house, Ezekiel drew three silver coins from his leather purse and purchased a ham hock from a farmer who had come to town to cater his pork and mutton. The smoked meat was a welcome change for Israel, and it served as what would likely be his only meal for the day. In the wooden confines of their shop, Ezekiel set two bowls out on the planked table and deftly stripped the bone of meat with five swift passes of his knife. After filling the two wooden cups with freshly drawn water, Israel joined him at the table. If the two shared their meal in silence, then it was also shared in companionship. Israel went so far as to allow himself to believe he detected a faint smile on the face of the man seated across from him. That night, Israel slept well. It had been a good day.

He was back up with the sun, as was always the case, and dutifully set himself to work. As he shaved off the remnants of rough wood and smoothed the harsh lines from the face of a goddess that would soon adorn the ship the *Vindicator*, the first mate of that ship, James Barry, entered the shop with a mulatto deckhand in tow.

"Ah, and did I not tell you that Isr'l Hands would bring both luck and beauty to our fine ship?" James Barry asked his silent comrade. "And did I not tell you, and tell me true if it not be so, that young Isr'l here would be havin' the most skilled hands of any cutter that ever took up the wood carvin' trade?" James Barry leaned heavily on the plank, resting on two barrelheads that stood as the only barrier between the boy and the big sailor. He regarded with mild humor the nervousness with which Israel eyed the even bigger mulatto. Barry tossed his head over his left shoulder in reference to his associate.

"Don't pay him no mind, Isr'l. He can't talk. Got the tongue ripped out of his head when he got caught lyin' to his master on the plantation in Jamaica. Can't hear, neither, I suppose," Barry surmised, studying his attendant with doubting eyes. "I don't rightly know. He ain't never said!" A thunderous roar of laughter came from the sailor as he slapped a happy, heavy hand on Israel's shoulder. Israel knew in that instant that beneath the mirth was a formidable fellow. The sea did that to a man, Israel thought as he shared a timid smile with his customer.

It took both sailors and the aid of an oxcart to carry the magnificent carving out of the shop. As the mulatto gripped the cart handles,

Barry looked down with growing admiration at the piece—the bust of a young maiden breaking through the laced bodice that so tightly held it captive. Long, flowing hair streamed back as if already blown by the wind. Her face displayed both softness and strength, with a single tear resting upon the maiden's right cheek. A full-lipped mouth, devoid of emotion, set the face resolute against all those who would seek to come against her. Israel had hewn it from the trunk of a large ash tree. He had been commissioned for the job after the captain of the *Vindicator* discovered that Israel had carved a similar figurehead for the ship the *Nancy*. After seeing what the young boy was capable of doing with carving knives, the captains and crews who lumbered arduously over the hard, flat seas of the streets of Salem considered Israel Hands to be well named.

Before departing, James Barry paused for a final word. "If you ever get the notion to follow the way of the sea, Isr'l, you be tellin' me first, that I might find you a billet aboard a proper vessel, where you will be sure to be treated like the man you already be." James Barry left Israel with a wink and a gold doubloon. At the time, Israel didn't know the value of the coin, but it was big, heavy, and gold. It shimmered as he moved it in his hand; its brilliance struck his eyes as sharply as the noon sun reflecting off a rippling pond. He'd never seen another coin like it.

Israel stood in the doorway of his father's carpenter shop on that warm September morning and watched as Barry and his shipmate wheeled their prize back to their floating lodge. Through the crowd, Barry moved with an air of strength and purpose—a man-eater, silent and deadly, swimming among a school of lesser seamen and two-legged wharf rats who pooled on the docks, prey unworthy of the attention of the predator.

Israel unfurled an admiring smile and wondered if, one day, he might indeed become one of them. They didn't act like the sailors from the other ships. The crewmen of the *Nancy* and the *Vindicator* were different. They walked differently and even talked differently from the other sailors. They dressed in colorful clothes and sometimes wore tall boots and carried short, heavy swords called cutlasses. They had bright-colored scarves that they often wore on their heads and had many various shades of crewmen as well. They were, as Israel had heard the townsfolk say, privateers.

Out of the corner of his eye, Israel noticed a familiar form moving toward him with quick and deliberate steps. It was his father, on his way back from wherever he was coming from. Israel certainly didn't know, and he knew well enough not to ask.

"How much for the ship's head, lad?" Realizing that his father had seen the two seamen leaving the shop, Israel answered by showing his father the coin. His father's eyes widened. Israel had never seen so much white in his father's eyes and feared that his skull would not be able to hold them in. Suddenly mindful of his enchantment, Ezekiel quickly regained his senses and snatched the doubloon from his son's fingers.

"Ye best stay clear of their kind, lad," his father warned him with a wagging finger, "if ye don't care to find yourself in a pact with Beelzebub."

"Yes, Father," Israel replied, greatly disappointed, having just discovered how well Beelzebub pays.

"Quick with ye now, lad, back to work. There are a great many tasks to be done before we gather in two days' time at Gallows Hill."

Oh yes, Israel remembered, *the hangings.* He smiled and picked up his carving knife.

* * *

As dawn broke on the morning of September 22, Israel leaped from his cot and went straight to work, saving his morning bread for later. There was plenty to be done, for the *Katherine Jane* was to weigh anchor with the morrow's morning tide. The *Katherine Jane* was a magnificent ship, perhaps the largest Israel had seen. It was a Spanish galleon that had just been overtaken by His Majesty's navy and now flew the flag of home. With mallet and chisel firmly in his hands, Israel was fast at work, smoothing and finishing a dozen wooden cleats for the great ship.

Israel had met the ship's carpenter a week ago. He didn't like him very much. Once in a while when such men came into the shop for additional supplies and saw a boy with carpenter tools, they'd give Israel a scornful eye. In some instances, he had been paid with the back of a hand instead of a shilling, but mostly they greeted him with acceptance. Israel thought that the cleats he had fashioned would do nicely to replace those torn from their moorings during battle. He was hopeful that the carpenter of the *Katherine Jane* would think so too.

At exactly twelve o'clock, Israel had finished the work. At that very instant, Job Tabor, the *Katherine Jane*'s carpenter, pushed open the broad oak door with startling force and stepped inside the cramped quarters of the carpenter shop. With a cold, baneful glare, the sailor shifted his gaze from Israel to the finished cleats, then back to Israel. Eyeing the boy with doubt and suspicion, the sailor stuffed the pieces in his ditty bag and turned for the door. Israel swallowed hard.

Almost as an afterthought, the man stopped, turned only halfway toward Israel, and tossed two gold coins into the sawdust-covered dirt. Israel scampered to pick them up. *Two pieces of eight.* Actually, he corrected himself, they were wholes of eight. Israel hated when they were in pieces; they broke away so easily. The young wood-carver couldn't believe his good fortune: two more gold coins! Not of the weight or size of the doubloon, but gold all the same. Fingering the coins mindlessly as he returned to his feet, Israel watched the gruff seaman as he rambled out of the shop, wondering what adventure lay ahead for the ship's carpenter and the rest of the crew of the *Katherine Jane.*

Israel's imaginings were cut short as the memory of time drifted back to him. He pulled his carpenter's apron off over his head and slipped the neck sling onto the wooden post on the back of the door. Latching the door behind him, Israel ran all the way to Gallows Hill with an eager boy's limitless energy. He was fraught with disappointment to see so many people occupying the good ground. He would not be able to sit where he had positioned himself when they hanged Goody Nurse and Sarah Good. At that time, he was close enough to hear Sarah Good curse Nicholas Noyes when she said, "I am no more a witch than you are a wizard, and if you take my life, God will give you blood to drink."

Well, he doubted very much that he would be able to hear anything today. He looked about the shrinking space, hoping he could find an advantageous spot from which to watch. His eyes came to rest on a young but hardy maple tree. Israel smiled. *No one up there—yet.* He made his way through the growing number of Christians who had come to see the devil's whores receive their due.

Israel scampered up the tree. For a moment, it became the tall, straight foremast of the *Katherine Jane,* and he was racing up the rigging to search out the enemies of God and the king. He felt the sea breeze buffet the smock against his chest and tasted the briny spray pruning his lips as the sweet scent of salt air filled his head. From the crow's nest, he shimmied out onto the fore-topsail yard and looked out over the open sea and down into the multitude of fish swimming there. Once secure upon his perch, the world quickly returned; the tall pine mast was a maple tree once more, and the yardarm he straddled, a sturdy branch.

From his position aloft, Israel looked down to search out those he knew. He saw Thomas and Nathaniel Putnam standing over a barrel, talking to Reverend Parris. Every few minutes, they would cast an uneasy glance toward the back of the crowd that had gathered. Israel turned in his perch to see what they might be looking at. Nothing appeared to be out of place. He did, however, observe Samuel Nurse, Peter Cloyes, and John Tarbell in a state of decided agitation. They were the family of Rebecca Nurse, who had been hanged back in July, and today they would lose another member. Mary Easty, the sister of Rebecca Nurse, would be hanged today. The family had removed themselves from the church soon after Rebecca was hanged. *Heretics.*

The presence of the Nurse family members was causing quite a stir among the multitude. The only one Israel recognized who seemed unconcerned by their presence was the minister of Salem, Nicholas Noyes. Israel watched him as he coolly read aloud the death sentence of the convicted witches. Israel didn't understand most of what he was saying; it was hard to hear, but what he could discern sounded quite bad. The sun was beating down angrily on the throng, and the sweat rolled freely from Israel's brow. As the wind shifted, he could smell the horse shit that littered the streets to the east.

He was surprised to see how brave the witches looked as they were brought to the gallows. Israel knew *that* would soon change, and he smiled. He didn't know most of the people who were about to die. He had really only heard their names since the town had told them they were witches. But he knew Martha Corey. That is to say, he knew her well enough to be pleased to see her die. It wasn't that he didn't like her; she had always been nice to him. It was just that, well, it was more fun for Israel to watch someone he knew die than it was a perfect stranger. To see the chest heaving for air; the body wrangling in spasm as the feet searched hopelessly for solid ground; and the eyes, first wide with terror, then slowly changing to a pair of glazed, sightless orbs—it was so much more exciting when they belonged to a neighbor. He liked it best when they were looking in his direction when they died.

Israel's senses heightened as the nooses were slung over the heads and around the necks of the witches. The entire world was just what was now framed before him, nothing else. Most of the condemned looked straight ahead or down at their feet. Israel heard they had all declared their innocence before the magistrates and the court. He wondered why they said nothing now, moments before they would be killed. It was a small matter, he reckoned. A final prayer was recited by Reverend Parris, which was followed by a single jeer from someone in the crowd. Israel wasn't sure if the person was angry with the witches or with the reverend.

He turned to see. It wasn't any of the members of Mary Easty's family, for they were nowhere to be seen. Israel was looking into the crowd when he spied his father. Swaying as with the wind and standing on unstable legs was a drunken Ezekiel Hands. Israel shot a horrified glance at the Putnams and Reverend Parris. They had paid Ezekiel no attention. But Israel noticed that Minister Noyes glared spitefully at his father. Ezekiel had always supported the trials—why was he behaving this way now? Even after they had killed his friend,

John Proctor, he held fast to his belief in the righteousness of the court. This would not bode well for his father.

With nothing left to say, the hangings began. Standing on the rock ledge jutting from the side of the hill that served as the gallows, with a rope tied around her ankles, Martha Corey was first to have her feet pulled out from beneath her. Israel smiled as she danced a lively dance. Before she had stopped moving, the feet were pulled out from under Mary Easty, then from under another witch, and then yet another. *No!* Israel wanted to scream. *Too fast, too fast! It's much too fast!* He could not recognize the bloated, purple faces anymore. Most of the victims had released their piss onto the ground. Some had lost control of their bowels during their dances. Israel was angered by the quickness of the executions, feeling he had been denied some small pleasure owed to him. Down on the ground, a boy Israel recognized from town sitting directly in front of the dead witches started to vomit. The smell prompted the boy next to him to vomit as well. Despite his displeasure with the speed with which the victims were hanged, the entire scene brought a giggle up from Israel's throat.

It was soon after Wilmot Redd stopped twitching that most of the townspeople began walking away. Israel didn't know "Mammy" Redd, as the sailors had called her. She was from across the harbor in Marblehead. Israel could hear some of his retreating neighbors calling on almighty God to protect them from further attacks from the devil's minions. Israel didn't leave. This was his favorite time. Almost completely by himself, he was able to just sit and watch them sway. Back . . . and forth. Back . . . and forth. Slowly. So slowly. So silently. Israel smiled at Mammy Redd. She was looking at him.

Israel's walk home was a quiet one. His head was pounding from sitting in the hot sun for two hours with the smell of piss and vomit pouring into his nose. It suddenly occurred to him that he didn't see his father before he started off for home. He'd lost sight of him once the hangings had begun. Instinct told him Father would be waiting for him when he arrived at the shop. He had two gold coins that his father would be wanting.

As he quickened his step down the dirt road, Israel heard a faint squeaking noise. He turned an ear to the sound. It was the cry of a small bird. He slowed his pace and searched the ground ahead. A frightened, injured sparrow lay stranded in the middle of the lane a few paces ahead. As Israel approached, the bird's cry grew more desperate. Israel looked around. He was alone on the road. He picked up a stick from one of the wheel ruts in the old road and snapped it in two. Standing directly over the helpless bird, Israel bent down and slid the two sticks beneath the sparrow, then lifted the bird. The shrill barks of the sparrow grew in tandem with its fear as Israel carried the bird to the edge of the woods at the side of the dusty road. Kneeling at the shady base of a mature pine, he set the bird gently down on a soft bed of the tree's fallen needles. Then he stood up, tossed the sticks aside, and walked home.

* * *

The boy wasn't overly concerned when his father didn't return home that evening. It wasn't uncommon for him not to come home at all after a night of hard drinking, much to Israel's shame. But when he didn't come home the following evening or even the day after that, Israel grew worried. There was something very different about this absence. Something was amiss, and he now knew where his father was. More precisely, he now knew where they held his father. Lightheaded with anxiety, Israel tripped clumsily down the uneven streets of Salem and sensed the accusing stares of his neighbors upon him as he made his way through town. He caught the unmistakable whiff of treachery in the air.

Still some distance away from his destination, Israel spied Sheriff Corwin standing outside the jail, speaking to Minister Noyes. Their conversation ended abruptly as Israel entered their line of sight. The two men glowered at his approach. For the first time, Israel wondered if he himself might be in danger. Although he'd done nothing wrong, the suspicious gazes of the minister and sheriff made him feel as if he might have.

"Good day, Sheriff Corwin," Israel opened a bit timidly. "I seek my father."

Minister Noyes stepped forward and put his face inches from the boy's. "Seek ye first the Kingdom of God."

Israel was taken aback by the ferocity of the minister's delivery, much more so than by the message itself. The minister pushed by Israel so brusquely that he knocked him off balance. Israel glared at the back of the departing man of God. He felt the fear inside him melt away and was conscious of a growing calm, cold and comforting.

Israel turned to face Sheriff Corwin. Corwin considered the lad carefully. He saw before him a boy of only twelve years, albeit large for his age. Yet he also knew the skill this boy possessed with a carving knife. This, coupled with the fact that the boy, at times, seemed to display an unholy fascination with death, made the sheriff uneasy. "Here now, lad," Corwin said, holding up a calming hand to keep the boy steady. "Spectral evidence against Ezekiel Hands has placed him in the company of those bewitched by Satan, and he is to be kept within these walls until his guilt or innocence be determined by the magistrates."

Israel shifted his weight. He understood only half of what Corwin had said. He looked at the door that stood between him and the sheriff. "Can I speak to my father, Sheriff?"

Corwin looked the boy up and down. A loose cotton shirt hanging untucked over baggy knee breeches was all the sheriff could see. What concerned him was what he couldn't see. Was there a knife tucked neatly beneath the belt that was covered by the smock? Relying more on gut instinct than on sound judgment, Corwin consented.

The sheriff opened the door. Israel stepped down several feet into the earth and entered the one-room jail. He searched through the cool darkness for his father. There were more than twenty men in the room, or so Israel guessed. He hadn't the time nor the inclination to count them all as he moved in the dark. A sense of hopelessness accompanied the darkness. He could feel its heavy presence in the silence. In the far corner, slumped in the dirt, lay the ill-treated form of his father. Israel rushed to his side while trying to keep from trampling on other men lying about the dirt floor.

"Father," Israel whispered tenderly as he cradled Ezekiel's battered face with a cupped hand. Ezekiel strained to see his son through blackened, swollen eyes.

"Israel," he managed to whisper through bloody lips. Israel's eyes pooled with tears. It was as much for the affection with which his father had spoken his name as it was for the devastation wreaked upon his father's face. Israel swallowed hard and tried to steady his voice. "Father, who did this to you?"

"Nay, lad, do not pursue them." Ezekiel winced from the pain of broken ribs.

"Father," Israel continued in a firm, measured cadence, "who are they?"

"The sons of the devil," came the answer, with weakening breath.

"Who, Father, who?" Israel felt the rage rising within him. "What are their names?" His father could only shake his head now, but Israel pressed on.

"Was it the sheriff?"

Ezekiel shook his head.

"Then give me another name, Father," Israel demanded in a voice that intoned, "someone must die for this." So it might as well be the right someone. Finally, with the last surge of his ebbing strength, Ezekiel Hands condemned a man: "Seth Barlow." Then, succumbing to exhaustion, he slipped into unconsciousness.

"Yes, Father. Sleep. Rest."

Israel's thoughts, like his eyes, flitted about in the darkness of the room. He tried to place the name as he stood up and wiped the dirt from his knees. *Seth Barlow? That makes no sense. The innkeeper?* Israel drew from his mind's eye the face and form of the man his father had accused. Barlow was a man no taller than Israel himself, although certainly of greater age and weight, but was commonly known for his cheerful nature. Israel would not have thought the man capable of such action. A small matter now, he decided. Israel made a silent vow to his father: Seth Barlow would die. He tried not to think of the fate that awaited his father and made another vow that he would not see his father hanged. And indeed, he would not.

Israel knew where to find Seth Barlow; like Mammy Redd, whose death had given Israel some pleasant moments just a few short days ago, Barlow was from Marblehead. And Marblehead was but a quick pull of the oars across Salem Harbor. Israel stormed away from the jail without so much as casting a backward glance at the fat little sheriff. He would be back to deal with Corwin in the Lord's good time, but first he needed some tools from his shop. Israel's steps became quick and light with purpose. He remembered an old sea ditty that he'd heard the sailors sing, and he started to whistle as the gathering storm within his soul grew ever darker.

* * *

Having rowed a borrowed skiff across Salem Harbor, Israel tied up in a small cove just beyond John Doliber's property on the windward side of Marblehead's northern point. He'd walked the narrow lane unseen and had been waiting quietly in the woods across from the tavern since shortly after nightfall. The incessant chirping of the crickets was interrupted only when he swatted a hungry mosquito. The welts left on his body served as itchy reminders of how often he silenced the crickets. Israel tried counting the stars to pass the time. He'd counted up to thirty-seven before he had to stop. Clouds rolled in to block the stars, so he turned his attention back to the tavern.

It was just before midnight when the last drunk stumbled out the door of the Gold Crown Tavern. He had to be sure that Barlow was alone before he acted. Israel picked up the tools that lay beside him, wrapped tightly in a small sack, and crept, hunched over, across the narrow road. The heat from the day had not retired for the evening, and his shirt clung to his shoulders, heavy and damp. He searched the black sky above and sniffed the air like a dog at a stranger's approach. The night was changing fast, and the boy could smell rain. It would be coming soon.

He leaned hard against the stone tavern and peeked in through the window to spy his target. Seth Barlow, with his back to the door, was cleaning up the remains of the evening. The creaking of the wooden sign that swung from an iron rod above the tavern door announced the arrival of the storm. With the aid of the light streaming from the window, he watched the first large drops of rain speckle the faded image of a gold crown on the sign. As Israel reached for the door latch beside him, the heavens opened up. He lifted the clumsy iron latch and slowly elbowed the heavy door. He winced as the moving door whined on rusty hinges, but the power and suddenness of the storm proved enough distraction to mask his entrance.

Peeking around the door, Israel saw Barlow working intently at the table at the far end of the room. Israel drew a tool from the sack and stepped cautiously into the room. Without a sound, Israel set the bag down just inside the door. With his eyes never leaving the back of his intended victim, he took his first steps toward Barlow. Israel improved his grip on the handle of the tool he held. He could feel the blood flowing hot in his veins and was unsure if he was hearing the crash of thunder outside or the terrible, thrilling pounding of his own heart. And yet in the excitement, a peculiar calm fell over him as he continued to step, undetected, toward the innkeeper. A sudden flash of lightning and crash of thunder startled Barlow and caused him to look up, but not back. Israel Hands stood behind him and raised the two-foot chain hook above his head. "Close by," Barlow said out loud to himself, peering out the back window.

"Aye, just above you," a strange voice announced.

Startled, Barlow whirled around only in time to see a dark form plunge a heavy metal hook into the base of his neck. The pain—so immediate, pure, and exquisite—was like a lightning bolt ripping him in two. So intense, he couldn't scream. So electric, his knees could not give way. With bulging, disbelieving eyes, Barlow saw the boy smile as he tightened his grip on the handle. In a single motion, Israel pulled back hard on the hook and propelled Barlow across the room and into the window near the door. Barlow shattered the glass panes upon impact, shards slicing deep into his face. Israel moved quickly to the door, where he removed the next weapon from his sack. The innkeeper spun away from the window with scarlet rivulets streaming down his shredded face and gored neck. The man tried to scream, only to receive a marling spike directly into his chest. Unable to breathe, Barlow sunk to the floor, looked up, and saw death, as a boy, standing in front of him.

"You accused my father of witchcraft, Mr. Barlow?" He could only stare at Israel, pulling hard for air that would never reach his straining lungs. Against the silent defense, Israel continued. "My father thought you to be a friend. What made you turn to see him undone?" With glassy eyes, the dying man looked on as if he could not hear the questions. The hook had been set deep in the left side of his neck, and the point had come out from under the collarbone. A deep, dark-red stream of blood flowed freely from the wounds. Israel became momentarily mesmerized by the smooth, velvety flow until he shook himself free of its enchantment and found himself again. "You received favors from one who would have my father dead. Who would that be?" Israel put his ear close to the man's mouth in an effort to capture a name. None was gained. He'd run out of patience.

Israel began to lean on the marling spike as the clock struck midnight. The point buried halfway into the chest of Seth Barlow carried the pulse of life to the end of the iron shaft on which Israel cupped his hand. "If you will not talk to me, go talk to the devil." With one fierce thrust, Israel drove the last two feet of the marling spike through the body of Seth Barlow. With the exception of the lightning-quick widening of the eyes, the man made no movement at all. He was dead.

Israel stood and stepped back to observe his handiwork. He looked down at his hands, bloody to the elbows, and started to shake. His breathing came to him in fitful shudders as he stood in the middle of the tavern. He began to turn in counterclockwise circles, slowly, staring at his stained hands. Round and round, he turned. Slowly. So slowly. Round and round. He let his hands fall to his sides, and as he turned, he let them glide smoothly away, like wings outstretched in flight. Israel dreamed as he flew through the black night of his mind. His dreams flew with him—to his father's release and to the cleansing rain outside, to the sea beyond the horizon and beyond the reach of men, and back again to his father, but never to the dead man in the room with him.

He stopped when he could spin no more. His breathing came easy now, but his head was still whirling. His dreams exiled, the boy was filled with emotion; the realization dawned that he could never go home. He could not even return to bid his father farewell. Israel thought he should cry but didn't know how. He looked down at the corpse of the man he held responsible for what would soon be the death of his father. For Israel now understood in his heart that his father would not live through his ordeal. As the innkeeper had not lived through his.

Israel felt only cold satisfaction when he reviewed his work. If he carried any regret, it was in the knowledge that Seth Barlow was not the only man who had accused his father. They would not have abused him so on the word of only one man, especially if that man was merely an innkeeper. And so another man carried an equal share of the guilt, whoever he was.

Israel vowed that if he were ever to find him out, he would apply the same measure of justice as he had with Barlow. Knowing he was doomed if he stayed in Salem, there was now only one way for Israel to turn. He entered the storm as he left the tavern, slogging his way back up the muddy lane to the little cove where his skiff lay moored among the moss-covered rocks on the Marblehead shore. His only hope was to make it back across Salem Bay, to the docks and the sea beyond. He knew what he needed. He needed to find James Barry. Israel Hands was now running from a society that would seek to destroy him. With only a carving knife tucked beneath his belt, he would wage war against the world.

The Visitor

Friday, June 18, 1999

"The house," Tom explained as he removed the light-switch faceplate near the bedroom door, "is a lot like the rings on the inside of a tree. The center rings are the oldest, right?" Jake eyed him sternly, sincerely hoping his question was rhetorical.

"Go on, Paul Bunyan," Jake said and resumed rolling pale-blue paint on the thirsty white walls.

"Well, as years go by, rings are formed," Tom continued. "Same thing with this house. The very center of the house is the gathering room. The central fireplace and the staircase that went up to a loft or a bedroom or something were part of the original structure, dating from the late seventeenth century. Over time, it fell into near ruin and had been all but forgotten through the rest of the colonial period, until the early 1800s, when it was brought back to life as a tavern, where drunken sailors and weary travelers could rest for the night. Marblehead, at that time, was one of the busiest ports in the country."

Jake watched with growing concern as Tom removed a new light switch from its box.

"Hey, watch it, buddy," Jake warned. "Those things can put a nasty snap in your shorts if you're not careful."

Tom lifted his eyes, an amused smile creasing his lips. "Yeah, that's why I flipped the circuit breaker downstairs before I changed the light fixture in the hall. Just like you should've done yesterday."

Jake rubbed the back of his neck absentmindedly and allowed Tom's commonsense safety tip to sink in. *Oh. Yeah. That would've helped.* "OK, great," Jake said quickly, eager to get the conversation back on track and away from any electrical faux pas. "Sorry, you were on a roll. Pray continue," he added with an encouraging smile.

"Well, that's when they started adding more rooms. They added two rooms upstairs and the sitting room downstairs so female travelers would have a comfortable place to rest without being in the tavern. Now the only room left from that renaissance is the sitting room," Tom explained, pointing with the screwdriver in his hand to the sitting room beneath them on the first floor.

Jake smiled. *Renaissance? I wonder who at the chamber of commerce used that term in front of him.*

"Then all four upstairs bedrooms were reconstructed in 1926 when it officially became a licensed inn. It prospered for a few years—until October 29, 1929, after which nothing much prospered at all. And for a long time, it lay in disuse. Since then, its owners have come and gone sporadically, none of them truly able to garner the full complement of treasures this house has to offer. The admiral we bought the house from, the last in the succession of titleholders, never actually lived here." Tom paused for effect and looked around the room admiringly. "Such a great house, with much of its history still untapped."

"Yes!" Jake shouted in approval as he dropped the roller in the paint tray and burst into applause. "Now that's what I'm talkin' about!" The history teacher was thrilled by Tom's well-rehearsed—albeit overdramatized—presentation. He clapped until his hands turned red. "I gotta tell ya, man, that was great! How'd you learn all that? Wait," Jake quickly added, not giving Tom a chance to take a breath before answering. "Lemme guess, the Marblehead chamber of commerce, right?"

"No," Tom rebutted, shaking his head like an insulted schoolboy. "I spoke to a local historian." Tom didn't sell it well, and Jake didn't buy it.

"Oh, really, and where did you find this local historian?" Tom ignored the question for the moment and ran downstairs to flip the circuit breaker back on. Jake waited patiently as he listened to the tramping of Tom's footsteps back up the main staircase and down the long hallway until he breached the bedroom doorway. Jake held his gaze and would continue to hold it until he got his answer. Both knew that Jake could outplay Tom in the waiting game. For the only thing that could unnerve Tom more than a Jake who could talk for hours on end was a Jake who could remain perfectly mute for even longer. It was just so . . . unnatural. Tom flipped the switch on and off. It worked. *Great.* He looked at Jake with a guilty smile. "The chamber of commerce."

* * *

Marie had worked diligently in the gathering room all afternoon. At the end of the day, a large beeswax candle that served as the centerpiece for the grand table burned softly in a silver candleholder of colonial design, sturdy and simple. The yellow glow of the small flame reflected dimly off the pewter tableware.

Over the fireplace, which was whitewashed many moons ago, Marie had placed a decorative display of greenery, primarily made of small pine cones and holly branches. The stones themselves gave the appearance not of white painted stone but of milk-soaked charcoal briquettes. A grandfather clock, nicknamed Ol' Sentry, stood guard in the far back corner; it had been privy to all that happened there for almost two hundred years. The fireplace itself was now equipped with a large copper kettle, not yet properly blackened by flame, hanging from an iron swing arm. Eighteenth-century andirons were set in place, flanked by an array of fire-tending tools—a small coal shovel; large tongs; log-carrying chains; staying hooks; and a large straw broom with short, blackened-tip bristles.

On the smaller side tables that surrounded the large center table, Marie had placed wicker flower baskets that displayed the natural ornamentation of the season; bright, colorful flowers lay in splendor, a celebration of new life from the earth, along with the dark greens of the New England countryside, strong and deep. Marie was pleased with the look. In the corner, a half-dozen feet beyond the bottom of a staircase whose curious history carried with it the moniker "the ladder" because it was so narrow and steep, Ol' Sentry tolled six o'clock as the two men descended the creaking stairs into the gathering room.

"Lookin' pretty good, babe," Jake said as he surveyed the room.

Marie smiled. "Are you and Tom done upstairs?"

"Yeah. Well, for today, anyway."

"How much did you get done?"

"I finished the two empty bedrooms up at that end," Jake said, pointing upward to the north end of the house, "and Tom finished a lot of the electrical work."

"Wow, not bad," she said. "What else do you have to do?"

"A lot more of the same," Tom interjected. "The biggest job, I suppose, is the masonry work on this monster," he said, patting the heavy stone fireplace and eyeballing the trouble spots as he spoke. "Then there's the broken window upstairs. I also want to change out a few more light switches and a couple of wall outlets, and there's a bunch of loose bricks at the top of the chimney on the patio," Tom droned on, his voice diminishing until he stood completely silent.

Jake stared at Tom for a good ten ticks from Ol' Sentry. "You know what, Tom?" he finally concluded. "*You're* a loose brick. Now take your black cloud and your Eeyore ass into the kitchen and clean up." Jake cracked a smile. "It's rib-eye time."

The gas grill had been set up on the patio outside the gathering room, far enough away from the chimney so as not to be struck by falling debris. Tom likened it to patrolling the Alaskan coastline, being able to watch a glacier break away and fall into the sea from the safety of the ship's deck. He fired up his trusty Kenmore grill while Marie, wrapped in a light sweater against the cool rush of evening air, sat comfortably at the new patio table, her face to a sun that was lining up to take its last bow for the day. Jake walked across the scant backyard of mixed-grain grass and down the long aluminum gangway that sloped away from the land to a ten-by-ten floating dock. From the vantage point of those up on the patio, it appeared that Jake's head was detached and resting on the seawall ledge.

Down on the rocks, the gulls had gathered to involuntarily share a small meal the sea had so sparingly served them. The few got some;

the many got none. And the many voiced their displeasure with the frenzied, high-pitched protest of those unjustly wronged. To Jake, the sound was pure melody playing to the underlying rhythm of the gentle surf tapping out its beat on the pebbled shore.

A call from behind invaded his momentarily perfect world. Or as Jake would have put it, *fucked with his zen.* Without turning, he shouted in reply, "Medium rare!" He came back to the sea, if only for a moment, and with one deep, cleansing breath, spun on his heel and headed up to join the others. Climbing back up the long gangway, he performed a visual survey of the southern chimney, which stood with all the stability of a drunken sailor over the patio. He could see where some bricks had loosened and appeared to have shifted at the very top. Some were missing altogether. Tom was right; guests couldn't be out here with shoddy masonry looming over them. Too dangerous. He scanned the length of the house and made a continuous visual assessment as he moved. As his eyes flitted past the chimney, Jake caught sight of someone in the upstairs window, just to the right of the chimney. He shot a quick eye up again, but whatever he had seen was gone.

Jake halted on the gangway and stood motionless, halfway between Stonecroft Inn and the sea. He fixed his gaze on an empty window that framed only the blank bedroom wall beyond the glass. What was it he saw? Or more specifically, he asked himself, what was it that he *thought* he saw? A man in a white shirt, looking down on Tom and Marie. No, not a shirt—it was more like a smock. *Yeah,* Jake thought to himself, *something like that . . .* and suddenly shook his head and snapped himself out of his absurd imaginings. It was just the reflection of a passing cloud mirrored against the window glass. That's all it was. Jake recalled his Poe: "'Tis the wind and nothing more!"

"Did you see it?" asked Tom with obvious concern.

"Yes!" Jake said with a flicker of hope and a wealth of surprise. "Could you see it from there? What was it?"

"Hell yes, I can see it from here," Tom insisted, pointing at the chimney with the long barbecue fork. "I'm missing so many bricks up there it's beginning to look like Mount Rushmore." Jake's excitement cooled instantly. Tom hadn't followed the line of Jake's question at all. *Must have been the clouds.* Too embarrassed to let on that he was seeing things, Jake turned his attention back to the steaks. "How we coming along on these babies?"

The announcement of "steaks are ready" served as the starting gun for the parade back into the house to begin. Shouldering complete responsibility for the entrée, Tom took the lead with the serving tray of beef. The Breans hurried behind, grabbing glasses, bottles, and sweaters on the way. Too bad it was so chilly, Marie thought, looking heavenward; it would have been a perfect evening to eat outside under a cloudless blue sky. Pulling up the rear, Jake followed his wife's gaze upward, yet he felt quite differently about the cloudless sky.

Sitting at the head of the table, Tom opened the bottle with a sharp twist. The first Bud Light of the day, and because it was a special occasion, he emptied the beer into a frosted pilsner glass. Jake shadowed his host's action with a nonalcoholic brew. He used to be a "real beer" man, as Tom would say, but set it aside years ago and discovered he didn't miss it in the least. Tom asked him once why he'd quit drinking—if it was because he'd had a problem. "Nah," Jake had replied casually, "I never abused alcohol. I only abused myself." And that was the end of that. Before picking up their forks they raised their glasses and toasted to the success of Stonecroft Inn. And until the candle flame buried itself deep in beeswax, the only noise that was heard was the clatter of silverware on pewter and the clinking of glasses.

With plates empty and bellies full, the men hoisted themselves from their seats and began clearing the table. It was a quick and easy cleanup, really, but Marie appreciated not being the presumptive busboy. Once the dishes were rinsed and put in a large commercial dishwashing unit that Tom had been anxious to try out and the coffee was brewing in the kitchen, it was time for the evening's entertainment to begin.

Jake was excited to show Tom something he had recently picked up. He ran upstairs and was back in less than a minute with a cardboard shoebox. Tom and Marie watched in mild amusement as Jake removed the cover of the box. It really didn't matter to Tom whether Jake was about to be entertaining or boring; he'd make fun of him either way. Jake set the box on the mantel. With his back to them, Jake fumbled around for a moment or two, then struck a match. Lit match in hand, he turned around. With the stem in his mouth and the bowl in his hand, Jake touched the flame to the tobacco and puffed gracefully on his new pipe. "It's from the Sherlock Holmes collection," he boasted.

"No kidding," Tom quipped. "How many box tops did that run you?" Marie looked on with a small, approving smile.

"What? You don't think it makes me look scholarly?" Jake asked Tom.

"Scholarly? Let me put it this way: you'd look more scholarly if you put soap in that thing and started blowing bubbles." Tom made himself laugh with that one, a slow, pleasant baritone roll of notes that fell softly on the ears of those around him.

"Well, I like it," Marie said, defending the pipe more than her husband. "I've always loved the scent of pipe tobacco. When he first got it, I tried to complain, but the smell was so pleasant," Marie confessed. "I really like it."

Tom could see that Jake was starting to eat this up. They stared at each other—Jake with a scholarly air of self-importance and Tom with an expression that said, "Enjoy it while you can; I'll bring you down a few notches later." Dirty looks spoke volumes.

As Marie continued to admire the aroma of the tobacco, Jake struck a thoughtful pose, amaretto clouds swimming about his head. Using the corner of the fireplace as a prop, he leaned easily against it.

"Whoa!" They jumped as a team as Jake sprang away from the wall of slipping granite. The heavy sound of stone grating against stone caused their hearts to leap into their throats. The stones had shifted, but only that, and by the time they had braced for the rockslide, it was evident that the stones had buttressed themselves against each other.

They all stood in silence for a moment, watching . . . waiting . . .

"Son of a bitch!" Jake finally exclaimed as he and Tom approached the fireplace to examine the stones that had broken loose from their moorings. The stones had only shifted, but they were *big* stones. They would have caused considerable damage were they to have fallen on someone. "Well, now we know for sure just how unstable this section is," Tom stated rather matter-of-factly.

"I hope this Mr. Goddard is a good mason, Tom."

"Actually, Mr. Goddard has a guy named Vince who does most of the masonry work for him. I've never met him, but he's supposed to be the best around." Tom's eyes held on the stonework. "We'll see."

They continued to visually examine the mortar and stone borders and moved all the fire utensils away from the troubled corner where the stones had shifted. "He'll inspect the entire fireplace," Tom commented as he viewed the mortar at point-blank range, "and hopefully he won't find any other problems, but I'd rather he find them now instead of a guest making the discovery with his big toe a month from now." Guardedly satisfied that the stones would hold their positions, the men joined Marie at the table, Jake with his extinguished pipe clenched firmly between his teeth and Tom tapping a mindless rhythm with his fingertips on the heavy oak tabletop. In time, the conversation grew quiet and easy, with only an occasional sentinel glance cast toward the impaired stonework.

As the night drew nearer, a cold northeast wind began to blow. The chilled air streamed unchecked through the open windows of the inn, bringing the men from their seats to close them throughout the house. The stiff breeze raised gooseflesh on the bare arms that turned the wind away with the latching of the windows. Still, by the time the house had been shuttered, the chill had settled in for the night, providing Tom with a reason to prepare the ample fireplace for use.

"Do you think that's a good idea with the stones being so loose?" Jake asked as Tom began stacking logs onto the grate. Tom looked up from his crouched position at the monster's mouth and assessed the risk of getting bit.

"Yeah, it should be fine. It's five feet from here to that corner." He looked directly above him. "The stones up front here are secure." A long, undulating bass note of thunder rolled in from the black, burgeoning northeastern sky as the first drops of rain tapped loudly against the windows at the back of the house.

"Do you lose power during storms here, Tom?" Marie asked nervously, standing behind her chair at the table, watching the windows as she gazed warily out at the onrushing storm.

"Sounds like we're about to find out," he answered as he touched the match to the ruffled edges of crumpled newspaper stuffed between the heavy metal grate and the kindling. He watched stiffly as print and picture faded behind a veneer of fluttering orange and yellow tendrils. When yesterday's edition of the *Marblehead Reporter* had been reduced to leafy flakes of carbon and the kindling had taken flame, Tom handed the matches over to Marie, who began to light the many candles in the room, a shield against the threat of sudden blackout. In a few short minutes, the room was transformed into a warm haven bathed in the soft glow of firelight from hearth and candle. Gathered before the fireplace, the three sat transfixed for some time, staring into the light of the crackling flames, awakened from their trances only when the fire snapped its fingers, sending sparks dancing up the chimney.

Although it was tranquil and warm inside the house, the mood outside had changed considerably. Tom and the Breans were becoming more aware of just how very different this night would be in contrast to the day with which they had been blessed. Jake tapped out the burned pipe tobacco onto a makeshift pewter ashtray, which had been intended by its maker to be used as a bread plate. A question came to mind as he continued rapping his pipe on the dish of tin, copper, and antimony.

"So, Tommy Boy, what's the story with the old lady who took a fuckin' shot at you?" Jake asked, a bit distracted as he tooled the unused tobacco out of the pipe bowl. *What a waste.*

Tom looked puzzled. "Where'd you get that? I never said the old lady took a shot at me. I just said the old lady tried to kill me."

The statement hung in the air for anyone to take a swing at, and Jake gladly stepped up to the plate.

"Well, I was going to give you the benefit of the doubt that she didn't take you in a knife fight. And I figured that if it was hand-to-hand combat, she'd have beat the crap out of you, and you'd pretty much be black and blue from head to toe. So you tell me where I'm off track, Rambo."

Tom laughed. He knew he would be able to laugh again with Jake around; he had just forgotten that a lot of the laughs would be at his expense. Now, he remembered.

"Well, it was Tuesday night," he began, the smile on his face quickly wearing thin until it wasn't worn at all. He stared into the fire as he spoke. "It started off like the same dream that I'd had the previous two nights. I'm walking through a fog when I come upon this old lady; she's really kind of creepy, but she doesn't do anything. She's just standing there, looking around, as if she's waiting for someone. I even ask her who she's waiting for, but she doesn't answer me. All she does is look at me and smile. What's been changing is that every night, her smile has a bit more of an angry edge to it." Tom's eyes narrowed as he recalled the intensity of her expression. "It's like I've pissed her off, and she's gonna get her big brother to come and stomp my ass," he said with a shake of his head. "Her smile," he admitted, "*that* was the really creepy part."

The fire was slowly dying. Tom rolled out of his chair, took the cast-iron poker from its holder, and shifted the logs. The flame sparked back to life, dropping newly born charcoal into the growing bed of white-hot embers on the floor of the firepit. The heat pulsed outward, and Tom felt its sting on his face as he placed the poker back in its rack.

"So Tuesday night after I had the dream again, I woke up. I tossed and turned for a while but eventually fell asleep," he said as he settled back in his chair. "At least, I thought I fell back to sleep. I was lying in bed, and I looked over at the alarm clock on my nightstand to see what time it was. It was twelve midnight, exactly. And I heard the grandfather clock downstairs start to chime."

"You mean Ol' Sentry?" Marie questioned.

"Yeah," Tom confirmed, "Ol' Sentry. Anyway, I counted out twelve chimes. I counted out loud. It was one of those things that you do that makes you realize you're really awake."

"OK, so you were wide awake. So what?" Jake asked.

"Well, after the clock sounded . . ." Tom paused and shook his head, embarrassed to continue. "After I heard the clock, my eyes were drawn toward the foot of the bed, to the far end of the bedroom. I saw this very dull . . . light. At first I could barely see it; then it began to grow. It looked like a small grayish ball. I thought my eyes were going bad, until I noticed there were no lights on in the room, but I could see other objects in the room just fine." Jake and Marie nodded like bobbleheads. "Anyway, the ball begins to grow bigger and I realize that it's getting bigger because it's coming closer." Tom's wide-eyed look said *You know where this is going, right?*

"Then, the gray spot is about the size of a fuzzy basketball and five feet away from the foot of my bed when I see the back of it waving, kind of like a cloudy snake. The ball in the front comes closer still and then it starts to roll up." Tom tapped his right index finger nervously against his lips and stared blindly at the flickering flame while recalling the moment. The Breans sat in breathless anticipation.

"As it rolled up, it became a face. The face of the old gray woman from my dreams. And I mean her skin was gray, like a gray powder." Tom's eyes narrowed. "Like burned charcoal. Her eyes were just black holes but not clearly defined; they had very diffuse margins. The lips on this thing were just like black leather strips. No frown and, sure as hell, no more smile. It just kept coming at me like some ugly, vaporous snake until it was right on top of me. Its face was only inches away from mine. I couldn't move. And I couldn't breathe." Tom turned, his eyes locking on Jake. "The damn thing was suffocating me, man."

Jake and Marie exchanged looks of mounting concern. "Surely you've noticed that the stairs on that ladder creak?" Tom asked, tossing his head toward the narrow staircase behind them. Jake nodded, wondering where Tom was going with the question. "Well, I can't do a thing about it. I've tried. Hell, I've replaced the steps that made the noise, but I can't get the creak out," Tom said with a small, helpless smile. "I heard them creaking last night." He poked an accusing finger at the ladder. "Someone was walking up those stairs as the old lady was choking the life out of me." Jake did a complete about-face, and with his eyes, he traced the path Tom's phantom might have crept.

"When the stairs stopped creaking, the thing above me looked over at the bedroom door, as if she expected someone to walk in. Then she looked back at me and whispered something. It sounded like she said, 'He comes.' Then she floated up, away from me, and sort of vaporized. And that was it."

"That was it?" Jake asked incredulously. "What the hell do you mean, 'that was it'? She's choking the fuck out of you one minute and then decides that, what, 'Gotta go, it's quittin' time'?"

"Jake, calm down," Marie ordered solicitously.

Jake ignored her but settled slightly. "OK, so what did you do then?"

"Hell, I was choking," Tom reminded him. "I sat up, gasping for air and coughing so hard, trying to catch my breath. About a minute later, I think I rolled over, and, well, I might have puked on the floor from coughing so hard. That's what I did. What would you have done?" Tom asked hotly, trying to deflect his shame.

Jake nodded. "That's probably what I'd have done."

"He comes?" Marie mused quietly, almost to herself but loud enough to draw the attention of the men. "The whole thing could certainly be explained away as a nightmare," she ventured aloud, "which I'm sure it was," she was quick to add. "But what the old lady said: 'He comes.' That has the air of the prophetic." Jake considered the statement for a moment, but Marie's line of thinking was a hit-and-run accident to Tom, and it blew completely by him.

Tom was an intelligent man. But in matters of the spiritual, preternatural, or supernatural, he was clueless. And in all things religious, Tom was a faithful nonbeliever. "What do you mean, prophetic?" he asked.

"Simply that this dream suggests that someone"—or some*thing*, she thought, although she didn't say it—"is coming." Marie pondered her own words as she explained. "Someone worthy of this pronouncement." Tom chewed on the words, the look on his face an amalgam of doubt and fear. He glanced at Jake, who, behind shifting eyes, still searched for an alternative meaning of the dream and the secret identity of its subject.

"Someone worthy?" Jake repeated, mystified. "Who in the hell would that burned-charcoal bitch consider to be worthy? I can't imagine she'd set the bar very high."

Tom could hear the tension in Jake's voice. It was a little puzzling to Tom until he realized . . . "You! You think it's real, don't you?" Tom asked, forcing a short, mocking laugh at his friend's expense.

Jake glared at him. "Listen, dickhead, I'm not the one who got scared and shit the bed."

"I puked," Tom stated defiantly.

"Yeah. Whatever."

Outside, the wind howled, and coming in off the sea, the rain buffeted the eastern side of the house. The night had become angry and bitter, an ugly, jealous sister of the beautiful day that came before it. On several occasions, the three had paused in uneasy anticipation as a violent gust slapped the windows with a force that would prompt a creak or thump somewhere in the house.

For every action, there is an equal and opposite reaction, the science teacher thought to herself.

I hope I don't lose another window, the innkeeper thought to himself.

Fuck, was all that came to Jake.

A new sound entered their world as marble-size hail began to pepper the windowpanes. The ice struck crisp and distinctly singular at first but quickly intensified. They were merely the opening notes to the discordant symphony that soon followed. All three inhabitants winced as the incessant rat-a-tat-tat of hail accosted the glass mercilessly. They sat in a silent, almost meditative, state, willing the glass to hold, praying the glass to hold, until the ice storm finally passed and the drumming hail ceased with the suddenness with which it had started, sowing the ground with its frozen white seed. Moments later, the deluge arrived. It was a hard, heavy rain that gave the windows a drive-through-car-wash look, but it was a considerably more favorable offering of nature's abundant gifts than was the hail. A single bolt of lightning ripped across the sky over Brown's Island, a shocking blue skeletal finger pointing at them through the translucent, water-covered panes.

A tremendous thunderclap accompanied the flash, and for an eternal second, Stonecroft Inn lost all electrical power. Tom, Jake, and Marie shared a quick, bewildered glance. In that brief expanse of time, the gathering room changed. Although the fire burned bright, the warmth it provided was gone, vanished as if through a vacuum. The firelight was cold illumination, with no comfort to offer in its melancholy hue. It carried in its inimical light an essence devoid of all things good.

In that solitary moment, as if a snapshot had been taken, the four people sitting in the room were utterly drained of energy, drained of life, and looked on the scene as if from outside themselves. It was placed before their confused eyes for but an instant and then ripped away from sight. And like the hailstorm before it, as suddenly as the warmth had left, so it returned.

Jake stared at his hands. A small patch of pale-blue paint on the side of his right index finger caught his attention. He slowly scratched away at it with his thumbnail. He scratched until the skin beneath it was red, long after the paint was gone. He turned his hand over and searched for more pale-blue patches and applied the same remedy to each, leaving crimson where once there was blue. He brought his eyes up and looked over at Tom, who sat motionless, his attention fixed on the flames as if hypnotized by the flickering tongues of fire. Jake shifted his gaze to his wife, who sat back heavily in her chair and shot quick sideways glances at the empty chair at the far end of the table.

Tom disrupted the unsettled silence as he raised himself sluggishly from his perch. He approached the fire and poked weakly at the remnants of the last burning log, set the poker back on its stand, and squatted there, staring into the fading glow in thoughtful rumination. Marie lifted herself from her chair and muttered inaudibly to no one in particular as she took herself into the kitchen on some trivial, mindless mission. Jake remained at the table, thinking, questioning: *Four?*

By ten o'clock, the storm outside had diminished to a stiff breeze and a light drizzle. The mood in the house rose marginally with its departure, and by the time good-nights were being said, all was outwardly back to normal, although no one questioned or commented on what they had experienced but could not explain. Besides, they were all tired. It had been a long day, Jake surmised; they were simply exhausted. *"Once upon a midnight dreary, while I pondered, weak and weary"* . . . *No,* Jake admonished himself, *no need for Poe tonight.* One by one, each with a stabilizing hand on the hemp-rope banister, the three trudged up the ladder from the gathering room, every other step creaking beneath skittish feet.

Alone in their room, Marie was able to debrief her husband on the findings of the day. "What do you think is going on here?" she asked.

"No, now come on," Jake said, waving her off. "Don't start this."

"Start what?"

"I know what you're gonna say. You're gonna say that there's some malevolent spirit in the house, and we need a priest to come over and bless it and yada, yada, yada." As soon as he'd said it, Jake knew he'd stepped on a land mine. One of those Bouncing Bettys, he told himself—not the kind that kill you but the kind that fly up about crotch high and rip your balls off when they blow. Jake heard it click when he stepped on it; now he was just waiting for the explosion. He was just waiting for the pain.

"As a matter of fact, I don't believe there is any malevolent spirit in this house," Marie began. "I think Tom is dealing with a lot of unexpressed grief over Carol's death, and it's now taken the form of nightmares. Nightmares that are seemingly very real to him. I can't tell you what his dream meant. All we can do is to try to support him. I thought that maybe you two talking and spending as much time together as possible would help him the most. I was only going to say that if you needed me to pick up a little bit more of the jobs to free up some time for you and your friend, I'd be more than happy to do it. *That's* what I was going to say." Marie turned away.

Ah, Jake realized, the explosive device came in the form of the guilt trip. The most reliable weapon in a woman's voluminous cache of munitions. It was a direct hit. Jake searched for the exact words that would help apply pressure to the wound. But it was too late for his balls; they were gone. They were probably bobbing up and down somewhere in Salem Harbor at that very moment. He tried to read his wife's face by staring at her back. When she was ready, she'd whirl around and stare him down. He knew it. She'd stare down the man with no balls. More precisely, the man whose balls were bobbing up and down somewhere in Salem Harbor. She turned, and he met her icy glare with the only weapon a man has left at a time like this.

"OK," he said meekly, with a slight shoulder shrug.

She looked at him in a way that somehow made him feel pathetic. "OK? That's all you've got to say?" Marie questioned.

"What?" he responded, with a look that spoke more of idiocy than of innocence.

"I don't believe you," she said, trying to be angry but losing the smiling battle in front of the man she loved. The man with no balls. She shooed him away. "Oh, just go and brush your teeth or something while I finish up in here." Jake smiled to himself as he strutted into the bathroom. Another victory, snatched from the jaws of defeat, for the married, and happily harried, man.

* * *

Jake fell into bed, and night entered the room with a twist of the switch on the nightstand lamp. Almost immediately, sinister and

67

threatening images conjured themselves from out of the gloom and sifted into the open spaces between his thoughts. They did not attack. They did not retreat. They held their ground and watched him, unmoving, knowing that their time was coming, and it was near.

Still awake almost an hour later, Jake lay motionless in the darkness and stared unseeing at the ceiling. He tried to dismiss the demons that squared off against him in his mind as they prepared to unfurl their battle flags. He turned his head toward Marie and whispered, "What did you see down there?"

The gentle, rhythmic breathing of a sleeping woman was the only answer he received. And it was answer enough. Jake let it go and closed his eyes. He bid the demons to do their worst, and they scattered. Somewhere in the night, he fell asleep.

In the room across the hall, Tom sat up in bed and listened. Awakened by a steady, deliberate knocking, he tried to place the location of the sound. It came from outside his room—not on the door, but through the wall. He speedily reviewed the short list of possibilities in his mind. The plumbing was old but sturdy, and it didn't sound like rattling pipes, anyway. It couldn't be the boiler, Tom reasoned; a new one had recently been installed, and all the thermostats in the house were buried at the lowest settings on the dial. It would have to be forty-five degrees inside before that sparkling-new beast kicked on. He looked at the clock on his nightstand: 10:37 p.m. *Well, it's not Ol' Sentry.* Whatever it was, Tom surmised, it felt no further introductions were necessary. He had walked through the house on previous nights to track down the source of various auditory anomalies and had found nothing more than the typical vital signs of an old house—the drip of a leaky faucet; the creak of an old wooden joint; and the occasional, inexplicable draft that brushed by his ankles. But night had since lost its innocence.

Tom turned on the reading lamp that stood at his elbow on the nightstand. He sat listening as the knocking grew louder. He sat until he could sit still no longer. The strength of his anger at the unwarranted intrusion surpassed that of the fear nesting in his heart. Tom sprang from his bed in defiance of his fear, and immediately, the banging stopped. His heart hiccuped at the sudden cessation of sound.

He considered, for a fleeting moment, waking Jake, then rejected the notion almost immediately. What would he say? *Hey, Jake, would you come downstairs with me? I'm afraid to go by myself.* That simply wasn't going to happen. Tom grabbed the flashlight he'd stored in the top drawer of his nightstand, the same one he'd taken with him on the previous nights' fruitless investigations. He liked this flashlight, and for a good reason. It contained four D batteries in the handle, lending weight to the piece and making it a potential and effective weapon. Not that it would be much use against this particular uninvited guest, he suspected. The forty-watt glow from the reading lamp cast a moving and diminishing shadow on the wall as Tom approached the bedroom door.

The silence was more terrifying than the banging. A sound has a point of origin. Silence is all around you. Engulfing you. With a slippery grip on the newly antiqued doorknob, Tom twisted it slowly, grimacing with the squeaking of the cramping hinge. *Damn, I gotta fix that.* He peered out into the dim hallway, his ears sniffing the air. Something had changed. The sound had returned, not coming through the walls this time but from down the hall, and down the stairs, and from somewhere beyond that. Tom stepped out into the hall, shooting a final thoughtful glance at the door to his left, behind which his friends slept undisturbed. With quick and shallow breaths, he trod lightly toward the ladder. Somehow, as he advanced closer to the sound, asking for company didn't seem like such a bad idea, but he decided against it and pushed on.

As he edged forward, alone, the fear swelled within him. Standing at the top of the ladder, Tom could see the faint glow from the light he'd left on in the kitchen, spilling out onto the wide-planked floor of the gathering room and at the feet of Ol' Sentry. His heart pounded in his ears, and moisture gathered in the lines of his palms. Tom breathed slowly and deeply, for he found he could exchange large volumes of air without making a sound. Were he of the belief that the visitor down below was of flesh and blood, he would be down the stairs like a shot. And so he remained, for the moment, at the top of the stairs, frozen with fear, flashlight wrapped in his uncertain grip.

Tom began his first step with a dry swallow. His heart sank as his foot came to rest with a loud creak. A reminder, as if he needed one, that this was no dream, not even a nightmare. With that one step, other sounds arose, new sounds—voices. Tom strained to listen, and for a brief moment, fear yielded to curiosity. He could hear men shouting, arguing. It seemed very far away—the voices were angry, yet muffled and indistinct. The exchanges grew into those of a spirited brawl, the scraping and clashing of metal against metal, the curses now flying, sharp and fearful. Tom pressed hard against the staircase wall to shelter himself from the unseen blows of the fight. Cries of anger and virulent profanities rose to a crescendo when a disembodied scream tore across the room, up the ladder, pushing past Tom, still bracing himself in fearful wonder against the wall, and then . . . silence.

From deep within the sudden emptiness of that silence, the pounding broke in once more. The sound began to change in tone as Tom, descending the stairs, drew closer to its source. It was less thunderous and yet more fearsome. Tom could now detect the thud of flesh on wood. Flesh striking wood, or wood hammering flesh, with such ferocity that Tom found himself wincing with each blow. There was no rhythm to it as there had been earlier. Now it seemed to come sporadically, as if at the end of an angry thought. Tom hesitated only momentarily as he neared the bottom of the ladder. He took a final breath before quickstepping down the last few stairs and wheeling to his right to fully view the gathering room.

Seated at the far end of the table, in the chair that might typically be reserved for the master of the house, was a presence that seethed with a malignity that Tom could scarcely have imagined. The man sat with arms outstretched, resting white-knuckled fists on the table. With his chest heaving under a white linen smock and his head bent slightly forward, he looked up through wisps of graying hair, shaken loose from the shoulder-length crop that had been pulled back and tied with a dark strip of cloth. It was a look that struck with the speed and ferocity of a bolt of lightning, a piercing gaze that cut as deep and sharp as a knife through Tom's soul, and he felt his knees about to give way.

Shockingly pale-blue eyes set in deep, black sockets peered out from beneath the stray locks. The skin was pure white and stretched thinly over the skull, devoid of any wrinkle or mark. The hell-born gaze held Tom in horrified fascination. Nostrils flared with every labored inspiration; rotten, yellowed teeth were exposed when the taut, sneering lips parted. It spoke not a word, and yet the specter made its intention clear. Its bosom heaved with the warmth of the dead, and its eyes flashed with the compassion of the damned.

Tom could perceive no sound save for the whirling of the hurricane that encircled him, holding him captive. He reached for the end of the rope banister to steady himself as he felt the world around him slipping away. The coolness at his temples and his brow, the sweat on his upper lip, and the waves of nausea that washed over him told him it was time to shut down. As the flashlight slipped free from his clammy grasp, Tom's six-foot-one frame fell hard against the wall and crashed to the floor with a sickening thud between the bottom step of the ladder and the feet of Ol' Sentry.

The tremor that reverberated up through the walls was enough to rouse the soundest of sleepers. Jake was out of his bed as if propelled by a springboard, sensing the worst. Pulling a T-shirt over his head as he ran down the short hallway past Tom's bedroom, Jake flipped on the staircase light from the top of the ladder. Marie followed close behind and screamed when she saw the blood on the floor where Tom lay facedown. Jake bounded down the ladder, knelt by Tom, and was instantly relieved to hear him breathing. He palpated Tom's neck and shoulders, checking for any obvious fractures.

"OK, Marie, get up here at his head," Jake instructed his wife. "As I turn him on his back, you turn his head. Got it?"

Marie nodded nervously.

Supporting his head and neck, they turned him to keep his spinal cord aligned.

"Oh my God," Marie whimpered, the sight of Tom's bloody face unnerving her.

Tom came around with an aching groan and brought an unsteady hand up to his salt-and-pepper hair. To the relief of his rescuers, Tom began to move his head slowly from side to side, without any signs of discomfort. Marie ran into the kitchen to get some damp towels to clean his bloody face. Tom moaned and brought his legs up in a feeble effort to rise.

"Easy there, champ," Jake cautioned. "How do you feel?" He studied Tom carefully as he spoke. "You want to try to sit up?"

"Yeah, I'm OK," Tom was able to mutter past a fat upper lip. Slowly, they helped him to a sitting position and spoke to him in even tones, knowing it was important to keep him calm; the possibility of Tom going into shock still loomed. As Marie wiped away the blood, it became apparent that it had come exclusively from Tom's nose and upper lip. Jake continued to talk to him, assessing his mental status through a series of simple questions. Although he responded with monosyllabic answers, his replies were appropriate.

"What's your name?"

"Tom."

"What's my name?"

"Jake."

"How many fingers do you see?"

Tom managed a smile. "One."

Everything seemed to check out, but Jake held one concern that he did not voice to Marie. The blood had stopped flowing from Tom's nose, and after the cleanup, he looked remarkably well for someone who'd fallen down the stairs. Jake and Marie watched Tom a few more minutes before they let him stand, with their assistance. Even then, it was to move him to a chair at the table. Jake continued to monitor him closely and was pleased to see his level of awareness return so completely, so quickly. He had no doubt suffered a concussion, but thankfully, it was apparently a slight one. They sat up and talked for more than an hour. Marie made some coffee, which only Jake drank as the interrogation continued.

"But you had a flashlight?" Jake clarified.

"It slipped out of my hand."

"It slipped out of your hand, so you fell down the stairs?"

"It slipped out of my hand because my foot slipped off the lip of the stair step," Tom replied, making up the answers as he went along. "When the flashlight hit the deck, I was still falling, and in the dark, I couldn't see anything to grab hold of."

"Well, you were lucky," Jake assured him. "Your face broke your fall." Tom tried to join him in a smile but winced with pain instead. Jake looked at Marie. Cold stare. No smile. Time to go to bed.

"So, then, the noise you heard was coming from down here?" Jake asked Tom as they rose from the table.

"Yeah."

Jake saw Tom's anxiety level begin to rise.

"And you never found out what it was?"

"No, I told you—I slipped on my way down to look for it." Jake wanted to accept this simple explanation, but he just couldn't.

"You look disappointed," Tom said with mild curiosity.

"A little," Jake conceded.

"Why?"

"It's not important," he said and changed the subject. "You sure you don't need to get checked out at the hospital?"

"My nose hurts and I've got a fat lip, that's all." Tom waved him off. "Let's call it a night."

Jake offered Tom the staircase with an open hand. "After you."

The three tired souls trudged up the stairs, with Jake at the rear of the pack to watch Tom. *He did it again,* Jake noticed as Tom started up the stairs. At that moment, Ol' Sentry struck midnight.

"Twelve o'clock and all is well," Tom said musically.

"Yeah, right," Jake added. "Everything's just ducky." He took one last look before heading up. *Better wake the fuck up, Ol' Sentry.*

CHAPTER FIVE

Rockport

Saturday, June 19, 1999

Mother Nature often does the pruning of the New England landscape, but seldom does she clean up after herself. Looking from their bedroom window to the front yard below, Marie measured the strength of last night's storm by the amount of debris strewn around the yard. It was mainly wispy cords of willow branches and the thick, knuckled fingers of aging red maple trees that littered the ground. She could probably complete the job on her own in less than an hour, but then, what would be the fun in that? To watch Jake try to stutter and stammer his way out of yard duty was well worth the wait. Marie smiled into the morning sky. Even with the storm's residue scattered across the grounds, she saw the burgeoning promise of the new day. Everything seemed brighter to her. Birdsong filled the crisp, clean air. Robins hopped merrily about, relishing the buffet at their feet. Goldfinches flitted here and there as if drops of brilliant sunshine were given wing. A more subdued yet still beautiful female cardinal extended a morning greeting to Marie with a cordial nod of her head. Marie glanced over at Jake, who snored quietly on. The clock on the nightstand next to him read 7:15 a.m. She'd give him until eight o'clock.

After a quick shower, Marie tossed on some tan shorts and a pale-yellow cotton blouse. As she shod her feet with a pair of well-worn canvas slip-ons, an eerie moan emanated from beneath the bedcovers. Marie at first ignored the thing churning under the blankets as she walked across the room, but she turned when she reached the doorway to face the bed creature head-on. "Get up—we've got yard work to do."

"Nooo," came a low, grumbling wail from a voice buried deep in linens. Marie was prepared. "If you're dressed and downstairs in thirty minutes, you won't have to do any weeding. All I need you to do is help pick up the small branches that were knocked down by the storm last night." It caused her no hardship to mention the weeding that Jake would not have to do—in fact, there was no weeding to be done. She watched from across the room as Jake emerged from the sea of covers, a pillow crease running diagonally across his face. He was quick to seal the deal.

"No weeding? All right, I'm up." The crafty smile of a Mississippi gambler etched the corners of his mouth. *Do I know how to play her, or what?*

Jake was downstairs with time to spare and surveyed the scene out back from the safety of the kitchen window. He moved from the galley out into the gathering room, sipping his morning brew, to monitor the progress his wife was now making in the front yard. *Impressive.* He was calculating how long he could hold out before

Marie came in looking for him when the front door opened and Tom entered with his car keys in hand.

"Morning," Tom said with a smile as he took off his sunglasses.

"Looks like you got the makings of a real shiner there," Jake observed. Tom waved it off.

"Not near as bad as I thought it would be." Jake sensed that an exposed nerve lay behind the thin veneer that Tom fronted. He smiled and attempted to shrug off the events of the night before, but Jake saw clearly through the smoke screen. He was about to question Tom when they heard a sharp rapping at the front door.

"Should be Mr. Goddard," Tom said over his shoulder on his way to the door. "You'll want to meet this guy." Tom shoved the keys into the pocket of his jeans as he opened the front door.

"Hi, Mr. Goddard."

"Morning, Mr. Stone." (Which actually came out as, "Mawnin', Mista Stone.")

Jake took in the view over Tom's shoulder. Mr. Goddard was everything Jake thought he would be. Midfifties, five foot six, *maybe*. Dark hair, probably brown, but it looked black, greased straight back. *Had to be Brylcreem,* Jake guessed by the smell. *Do they still make that shit?* His thin face was shaved so closely it glistened. Standing to the right and a step behind Mr. Goddard was a big man. A very big man.

"Mr. Stone, this here is Vince." (Which sounded like, "This he-ah is Vince.") He continued, "He'll be tendin' to your masonry concerns." Vince stuck a big paw out beyond Mr. Goddard and shook Tom's hand.

"Nice to meet you, Mr. Stone," Vince said with a startlingly soft voice.

"Hi, Vince," Tom returned. "Thanks for coming out."

Vince smiled shyly and nodded.

"Mr. Goddard, I want you to meet a friend of mine. This is Jake Brean."

"Hi, Mr. Goddard. Nice to meet you," Jake said, coming out from behind Tom with an extended hand.

"Hello, there," Mr. Goddard replied, giving Jake a firm grip. "I'll be back to get Vince about suppah time," he said to Tom as he turned to leave. "His truck's in the shop." And that was the end of the conversation. Tom and Jake stood silently and watched as Mr. Goddard walked away in his starched and pressed khaki utilities, his black, spit-shined, steel-toe boots snapping the gravel driveway underfoot. He turned the key in the ignition of his truck that, save for a slight loss of tread on the original tires, looked as it must have when he first drove it off the lot some seventeen years earlier and slowly backed out of the driveway.

"Ain't he a piece of work?" Tom said to Jake. Vince stood there, smiling, watching the two men watching Mr. Goddard drive away.

"Well, Vince, inside fireplace or outside chimney today?"

"Let's take care of that chimney," Vince said, looking up at a clear blue sky. "Nice day to get rid of an outside safety concern, isn't it?"

"There you go, my friend," Tom said with honest enthusiasm. "Weather can change fast. Get the outside work done when you can." Every so often, Jake noticed, Tom showed signs of possibly becoming his old self again. Jake hoped it would continue but suspected it wouldn't. There were still too many questions yet unanswered.

Tom and Jake were watching Vince set up for the day's work when Marie came around the corner to check on the progress. With the three onlookers craning their necks to observe the top of the chimney, Vince politely explained what he had in mind and patiently fielded a number of questions with good-natured grace. Confident in Mr. Goddard's choice of masons, Tom let Vince get to work and headed back inside to tend to his own tasks. He didn't have much time. Apparently, Jake and Marie had made plans for the day.

Just before midday, with the yard work complete, Tom and the Breans waved their farewells to Vince as they piled into Tom's Ford Expedition and rolled out of the driveway for an afternoon of home-decor shopping. They had decided to dedicate the day to finding all the little things they needed to complete the look the house demanded and thought they'd try their luck in the tiny seaport village of Rockport.

Marie was anxious to show Tom all around the small town situated about twenty miles northeast of Salem. It was one of Marie's favorite places to visit this side of the Yankees–Red Sox line. Despite an almost phobic aversion to shopping, Jake couldn't argue against it being an interesting spot as well, and he also thought it would be a productive diversion for Tom. But his mind was somewhere else as they motored through downtown Salem, across Bridge Street into Beverly, and up Route 22 on their way to pick up 128 for Rockport. For three solid weeks, Tom had been doing nothing but repair work on the inn, with only trips to the local home-improvement and hardware stores to interrupt the routine of his days. He needed a break from all the work and, Jake believed, a break from Stonecroft Inn.

There was something not quite right with the place. Jake didn't know exactly how to tell Tom what he thought of the inn. The guy had poured everything he had into it, and Jake was now going to throw a monkey wrench into the whole thing? He couldn't do that to Tom, who needed a friend, not a critic. *But what the hell happened last night?*

"Isn't this cute?" Marie asked as they approached the outskirts of Rockport and slowly drove past the small seaside homes of the coastal village, nearing the end of their thirty-five-minute drive. Both men gave the cottages a nonchalant obligatory glance and nod before returning their attention forward without a word. As they rolled into town, they started looking for the elusive parking spot that was bound to show itself to a hunter's eye. They took the curve at Dock Square at Bearskin Neck and found a spot a couple of hundred yards up Main, just across from Jewett Street. No small miracle on a beautiful summer day.

South Road was more like a paved wharf than a street. Barely wide enough for a car to pass through—no two-way traffic here—the street was straddled by small shops and eateries. Art galleries and T-shirt shops tempted dollars from wallets and purses. Fresh lobster tail sold itself for just a few bucks and kicked in the melted butter and plastic forks free of charge. At the end of the street, the jetty pointed out to sea. Lovers and families sat on the rocks and watched the sailboats breeze by as a man played Beethoven on an electric violin.

A carnival of scents in the air greeted Tom, Jake, and Marie as they approached South Road—corn dogs, cotton candy, popcorn, and something being fried that they couldn't identify but smelled great. With stomachs growling and mouths watering, they wondered if they would make it to where the lobsters were waiting for them or if they would simply eat their way down the street. The wharf teemed with people weaving busily through the shops and galleries. Marie ducked quickly into a candle shop to see if anything would catch her eye. Jake and Tom walked about aimlessly, rudderless ships on a crowded blacktop sea.

With hands in pockets, they peered incuriously into shop windows; it was too crowded to go into most of them, and frankly, they wondered where they were hiding all the guy stuff. Tom was interested in purchasing several hundred feet of hawser, the heavy rope typically used as mooring lines for ships, the same that formed the banister of the ladder back at the inn. He wanted to create stanchions, which would be made of creosote-treated telephone poles cut to order by the local lumberyard; secure them in place around the driveway perimeter; and use the hawser to link the stanchions, creating a dockside feel for the parking area. The marine supply store in Marblehead could get it on order, but it wouldn't hurt to do a little price-comparison scouting. Besides, it gave him something to do.

In between shops, they looked up and down the street and tried not to stare at the seemingly endless parade of sun-drenched Barbies who strolled the wharf, ostensibly unaware of both the admiring and the disapproving looks they drew. Their holey denim mini-shorts covered little more than the fluorescent thongs that peeked out from beneath at the beltline, while their bronzed, surgically enhanced breasts were proudly displayed in a minimalist fashion setting.

"Why didn't girls look and dress like that when *we* were young?" Tom wondered aloud. Jake could only shake his head. And stare.

After twenty minutes of aimless wandering and hopeless lusting, Jake and Tom saw Marie emerge from the candle shop. "What'd you get?" Jake asked Marie as he grabbed the edge of the bag to peer in.

"Stop," Marie said, slapping his hand. "They're just some candles for the house." Jake's interest quickly turned to his stomach.

"Is anybody hungry?"

"Let's get some lobster," Tom commanded.

"I'm as thirsty as I am hungry," said Marie.

"*You're* thirsty? When you were in there buying wax, Tom said he could *smell* beer."

"Bud Light," Tom added, sniffing the air.

They moved with a collective purpose to Roy Moore Lobster Co., just an art gallery and a fudge shop away. Tom and Jake placed their order with the friendly, bearded owner, who stood behind a case of fresh steamed lobster, while Marie searched out an empty table in the shade. The food and drinks were on the counter just as fast as Jake could pay for them, and almost as soon as Marie sat down, Jake arrived with three Diet Cokes. Behind him, Tom carried a tray with three steaming lobsters in red-and-white paper baskets that were usually partnered with french fries. After glazing their meals with melted butter, the group ate voraciously, the quiet interrupted only by the sound of cracking lobster shells. "Anybody want another one?" Tom asked, breaking the comfortable silence as he wiped his buttery hands on a paper napkin. One nodding head sent him back to the counter for two more, and soon the men were enjoying their second order.

When they'd finished, Tom found he was able to appreciate their surroundings in far more comfort now that his stomach had stopped rumbling. He looked around in quiet ease in the shade of the wooden lobster shack. The breeze was deliciously cool as it came in off the ocean. Sitting in post-meal bliss, he watched the seagulls in the sky as they circled overhead, waiting for some inattentive air-traffic controller to drop a french fry and bring them in for a landing and refueling. Sitting soon became too much of a chore, and with a momentary surge of energy, they gathered and disposed of soggy paper baskets, buttery napkins, and empty soda cans.

Back in the sunshine, they resumed their trek up the seaside lane. In the course of only a few minutes, the distance widened between Marie and the men. It wasn't that Marie ran ahead so much as Tom and Jake lagged behind, and it wasn't that they were captivated by the scenery, as beautiful as it was. They were two men with full stomachs on a warm summer day, and they were shopping. Their energy level couldn't have been lower. Jake stopped in front of an art gallery, Maggie's of Chatham, to view the original works of some of the locals. Tom was about to enter a leather-goods shop when Jake hailed him. Tom watched with a questioning grin from across the lane as Jake looked at him, then at a painting, then back at him, and again at the painting. Jake's positioning brought Tom's attention directly to a framed piece in the front window of the store. The curious smile on Tom's face vanished in one heart-skipping beat when he arrived at Jake's side. Tom felt as if he had just had the wind knocked out of him and dropped to one knee, desperate to maintain the outward appearance of control.

The name of the artist was R. A. Putnam, and he called his work *The First Mate*. The artist had captured on canvas, in startling realism, a sailor of old, weathered by battle with both man and nature. The lean sailor faced the wind and the setting sun, his age-worn shirt pressed hard against his muscular chest. Long brown locks, once tied back by a ribbon, were now loosed from their tether and flowing wildly in the wind. One hand held the rung of a rope ladder while the other grasped a long knife sheathed in the sailor's wide belt. The tanned, leathery face with features as sharp as the knife's blade told the story. The Roman nose with flared nostrils spoke of ensuing action. A pair of strikingly pale-blue eyes screamed with rage above a firmly set mouth while the sailor's strong chin jutted out defiantly against his enemies. The overall countenance of the man cried ferocity and hatred. But there was something more.

Jake and Tom stared at the painting in dumb fascination. Although masterful, it was not the artist's brush technique, use of color and light, or positioning of spatial relationships in the portrait that unnerved the two. A subtle, indefinable quality was at work that somehow laid bare the character of the man in the portrait, as if the outer layers of his being had been peeled back to reveal his true nature. There was a disturbing genius in the artist's hand that captured the essence of the sailor's soul and not just his likeness alone. There was life in the painting—more real than the colorful oils hardened on the canvas or the heavy wooden frame that held it bound. It was almost as if they could reach through the frame and touch the angry seaman. Or more alarmingly, that the seaman could reach beyond the frame and touch them.

An eerie stillness surrounded them among the throng of noisy tourists, as if someone had pushed the mute button and silenced the rest of the world.

"Is this who you saw last night?" Jake asked, breaking the silence.

Still on one knee, Tom cast a startled glance up at Jake, who stood above him, haloed by the afternoon sun. Jake saw the fear and shame in Tom's eyes and stood as confessor to his kneeling friend, who looked away, still uncertain of what he was willing to say.

The sun, so recently a happy and welcome companion, now beat harshly on Tom's slouched back, a heavy yoke, hot and damp, weighing him down. The kneeling Atlas with the world on his shoulders. The heat lay as evenly as a blanket of needles against the back of his bowed neck, and he felt the first temporal pangs of a besieging ultraviolet headache. Tom wanted to answer his friend and searched fruitlessly for the magic words that would explain it away. What Tom found was not answers but questions. Questions that would take him in a direction he could not possibly go, far deeper into himself than he was willing to dig. Jake sensed the struggle within Tom, and in that, he received his answer. He turned his attention once again to the painting.

"Last night, when the lights flickered for an instant," Jake said, pointing at the portrait, "I think I saw this guy in the room with us. I don't know exactly where he was." He paused, then said with a shake of his head, "He was just . . . there."

Tom quickly regained his composure and stood beside Jake.

"How did you know I saw him?" Tom asked, his tense, pinched features washed smooth by the floodwaters of relief.

"After you fell down the stairs, you kept looking over at the table, as if you had seen someone, or some*thing*, sitting there. Even when we were going upstairs, you looked back. It was like you thought someone might be following us."

"I did," Tom said, now resigned to a full confession. "I saw him when we had the blackout, too, just like you did. Only . . . he was older," Tom said, looking down at the face on the canvas, "and angrier. If you can believe that."

"There's not much I wouldn't believe right now," Jake replied. "I wonder if Marie saw him?" he asked, scanning the crowd for his wife. "We need to find out if she did."

Tom went on to tell Jake the whole story of the night before: the knocking sounds, the invisible battle that played out all around him, and the menacing fiend he found seated at his table.

"So then, last night was the first night you actually *saw* him?"

"Yeah. Before last night, it was just some strange noises, but they were, like, house noises, maybe not even related to this stuff."

"What about that broken window?" Jake asked, seeking to make a connection. "How did that happen?"

"I don't know." Tom shrugged. "But I swear nothing touched it. I mean, I was standing right there looking through it when it shattered." His voice trailed away as he spoke; his thoughts were stuck, snagged on something just below the surface, and seemed to spin around some central point that eluded him, a connection he could not join. It hung just out of reach at the edge of his mind. Tom looked at the portrait that stared back at him. "Wait a minute! The old lady in my dream. She said it. She said, 'He comes.' Do you think she meant this guy?" Tom asked, hoping he was wrong.

"You know, when we were barbecuing last night," Jake recalled, "I was down on the dock when you guys called for me, and as I was walking back to the house, I looked up and thought I saw someone in a white shirt in the window."

"What window?" Tom inquired.

"The upstairs window. Your bedroom window." Jake added the final piece. "The window near the chimney, where Vince is working." The two stared at each other.

"Where Vince is working," Tom repeated, the words sinking in. "Time to go."

"Tell you what," Jake urged, "you go find Marie. I'm going to ask someone about this painting." Tom nodded, happy to put some distance between himself and the artwork, and ricocheted from shop to shop in search of Marie as Jake entered the gallery.

Five minutes later, Tom and Marie were in view of Maggie's of Chatham when Jake stepped back out on the street. Jake could see by the look on Marie's face that Tom had told her of their find. Jake held up the painting as she approached and saw her jaw drop when she was still twenty paces away.

"See anyone you know?" Jake asked.

"Oh my God," Marie gasped, eyes locked on the painting.

"Not even close," Jake said flatly.

Marie looked to the others and asked, "What do we do now?"

"We go home," Tom said, displaying the quiet confidence that had once defined him but that had recently been plaintively missing. Holding the picture by the top spar of the sturdy frame, Jake slipped it into a large white plastic bag.

"Where the hell are you taking that?" Tom asked.

"It's going with us," Jake said defensively, instinctively shielding *The First Mate* from Tom's reach. "I bought it."

"You gotta be shittin' me," Tom said, his eyes flashing with anger. "Are you serious?"

"Tom," Jake replied, "has it occurred to you that not only is this the guy we all saw last night during the storm, but the simple fact that this painting exists means that at least one other person has seen him as well?"

The thought was fresh to Tom's mind, but it made all the sense in the world. "The artist?"

"Bull's-eye, Sherlock. We need to speak to R. A. Putnam. And I know where he is," Jake announced with an unmistakable note of triumph in his voice. "The owner of the gallery told me."

"Only if you bought the painting, right?" Marie asked pointedly. "I'm not going to ask how much you paid for it," she added, irritated. "Well, where is he? Where's Putnam?"

"Maggie said I could find 'R. A.' at a little place called the Cat and the Cauldron," Jake replied, then waited for the coming fury.

"The Cat and the Cauldron?" Marie asked, with equal measures of suspicion and disapproval in her voice. "Where is that?"

Jake fumbled to find the right way to break it to his ultra-Catholic wife. "Um, well, it's in Salem, as a matter of fact. And if that's where

Putnam is, then that's where we're going," Jake proclaimed, regaining confidence in stating the necessity of their mission. Marie remained quiet for the moment, but Jake could feel the frosty chill coming off her. It would be a cold drive back for Jake, whereas the heat continued to pound away in Tom's head like a baseball bat against an empty metal oil drum.

"Well, we can stop there some other time," Tom said, rubbing his fingertips over his brow and temples, kneading the pain in his head and seeming to know, or feel, something else the others did not. "I really need to check on how things are going at the inn."

The ride back to Stonecroft was a tense one. For Marie's sake, Tom retold the story of the knocking he'd heard the night before. He recounted how the thumping had intensified as he had moved toward it. From a gentle tapping on the door, as if coming from a welcome guest, to the pounding of a pulverizing mallet in the hand of a madman. He spoke of the anger displayed in the being's countenance. He saw the rage and the hate. But what had scared Tom the most was that the ire seemed so personal, as if he had, himself, done something to offend this man. His story was met by silence.

The drive from Rockport to Marblehead wasn't a long one—about thirty minutes, give or take an hour, depending on the traffic and the route taken. Tom got off Route 128 at the exit that would get them back to Marblehead the fastest, through Salem. Like a dog recognizing the familiar turn in the road as it senses home, Jake began to fidget, shifting restlessly in his leather seat. He turned around and watched Marie, who, lost in her own thoughts, was oblivious to his gaze. He looked beyond her to the white plastic bag that leaned against the left wheel well. A corner of the cardboard frame protector was all he could see from the open end of the bag. But with the vibration from the road, the bag began to slowly creep down along the sides of the frame. Inside the bag, a piece of the puzzle had been found, and Jake knew that this piece wanted something. *What's your story, then, matey? Someone else knows you too. Did you know that? Oh yes, apparently, he knows you very well. And frankly, what I want to know is: Who are you, and what the hell do you want?*

"Comin' up on Salem, Jake," Tom said as they passed the metal road sign at 45 mph. The sign read Welcome to Salem above the silhouette of a witch with a pointed hat riding a broom. Jake looked at the street signs as they rolled cautiously through the crowded downtown lanes. As they motored down Hawthorne Boulevard, Jake mapped out in his mind the approximate location of the Cat and the Cauldron as he passed familiar street names.

"There's Derby Street; we'll need to go down there when we look up Putnam," Jake said in tour-guide fashion. Marie was looking to her left at the same time.

"There's Immaculate Conception Church," she said. "You'll need to go there first."

Jake said nothing. They were going in a direction that left Marie very uncomfortable. When it came to all things supernatural, Marie's conviction that they should be dealt with only by those empowered to handle such matters was unwavering. Jake understood. And although his sense of adventure screamed at him to move forward, he thought it prudent to respect his wife's sensibilities, and he did what he could to put her at ease.

"Hon, we just want to ask Putnam some questions. Aren't you interested in finding out what sort of contact he's had with the man in the painting? I mean, how does he know him?" Jake asked sincerely.

"Will you listen to yourself?" She looked at him with imploring eyes. "We don't even understand how *we* know this thing. Was it a vision? A shared phenomenon? A dream? We don't know. I don't think it's interesting at all. I'm scared out of my wits." The tears began to pool in the lower lids of Marie's eyes. Jake reached his hand back to comfort her. She managed a weak smile, but Jake could see how terrified she was. Looking at his wife, and hating himself for her tears, Jake wondered if buying the painting might not have been such a good idea after all.

As they came into Marblehead, Tom crawled up the left-turn lane on Lafayette and waited to complete a turn onto West Shore Drive. His fingertips tapped urgently on the steering wheel; the line of oncoming traffic seemed endless. The day had turned decidedly melancholy. The high clouds gave the aging afternoon an edgy orange glow. The drumming of fingertips was replaced by a white-knuckled grip on the wheel. The oncoming traffic finally cleared, for the most part, and Tom stamped down hard on the accelerator. The Ford's front end leaped forward as if it had its own sense of urgency, causing Jake and Marie to grab at whatever their hands could clutch in a nanosecond. An oncoming motorist with his own designs on the yellow light was forced to brake hard to avoid a collision. Fortunately for everyone, he hit his horn only *after* he hit his brakes. Tom didn't see the looks he received from people outside or inside his vehicle. He didn't hear the other guy's horn or his suggestive epithets, nor did he particularly care. Tom's entire being was fixed on something else. Something that was waiting for him at home, right down the road. Something whose existence was impossible to even consider yet with each passing moment became more real to Tom than the objects flashing by in his periphery—a house, a tree, a mailbox, a cemetery.

If we make it back alive, Jake thought, *a return to the inn to find nothing but a brand-new chimney will go a long way in turning this foul mood around.*

"OK, ease up there, big guy," Jake urged. "Let's not create a *real* problem for ourselves by hitting some little kid's dog. Or some little kid, for that matter."

Tom took his foot off the gas immediately, and Jake took his first easy breath since they'd cleared Salem.

But even Jake held his breath as they came around the bend on Beacon Street. He thought he could see some movement beyond the trees on the property as he focused intently on the approaching inn. His eyes widened as Tom pulled up the meandering driveway and parked at the end of the line of three Marblehead police cruisers. He was careful not to block the path of the paramedic rescue vehicle stationed at the east end of the house, near the patio. Near the chimney.

"Oh my God," Marie uttered. Tom turned off the ignition. He sat in silence and tried to keep from screaming at the top of his lungs. He gently massaged his burning temples with his fingertips, a slow, circular motion, in an attempt to soothe his throbbing head. Faces in uniform turned their attention to the Ford Expedition that had just parked in front of their crime scene.

Jake turned around and looked accusingly at the pair of pale-blue eyes now peeking over the edge of the white plastic bag in the back of the car. *What's your story, then, matey?*

CHAPTER SIX

The Bristol Galley

May 1697

Israel held the knife in his fingertips and nimbly sliced off a small piece of potato. Pleased with its size, he placed it in his mouth between his gum and cheek. He slipped his knife back into the scabbard at his right side and looked around the small galley. The ship's cook, Diego Garcia, an old buccaneer from Hispaniola, always kept his galley wares cleaned and properly stowed away after meals, much the same way Israel had treated the tools in his carpenter shop so long ago. Although, he thought with some regret, it was a lot easier ridding the ship of rats when he left some scrap of food out in the open where they could be more easily killed. Israel had been known to pin a rat against the bulkhead with his knife from more than twenty feet away. But that was when he was smaller and could move much faster through the bowels of a ship. Time had changed all that; Israel was now one of the tallest of the crew, and the size of his hands and feet suggested that he hadn't stopped growing.

He turned to face the entering sunlight as the galley hatch burst open. "Isr'l, come quick, lad—there's more of them followin' us to starb'rd." Israel smiled. Ducking through the galley hatch, he followed James Barry out on the deck. The ship held a strong easterly wind in its sails. Israel leaned hard over the starboard rail as the *Bristol Galley* knifed swiftly through a rolling sea. A school of bottlenose dolphins swam alongside in rhythm with the undulating ship. This always put a broad grin on Israel's face, and old Jim was always looking for ways to keep the boy's spirits up. "Aye, Jim, there they be," Israel shouted with delight.

"How many do you see, Isr'l?" Jim asked.

Israel pointed as he counted. "One, two, three, four . . . five. No, I think I counted him afore." Israel kept moving his head in unison with the dolphins as they would disappear under the water and then reappear only moments later. "I don't know, Jim. They're moving in and out of the water so fast."

Jim joined Israel at the rail and peered over the side with him. "Well, now, Isr'l, don't you be worryin' about that. Important thing is that it's nice to see you have friends in the sea. Remember that, now, lad. You have nothin' to fear from the creatures of the sea. You need to be watchful of only one type of creature," Jim warned his protégé. "It walks on bowed legs over rollin' decks. And it can be pure evil. It's important to always have one good shipmate aboard with you, someone to look out for what's aft of you."

"Well, I got you, Jim. You're my friend, now, ain't you?" Israel asked. Jim was quick to ease the boy's fear. "Oh, aye, lad, aye. Don't you give no thought to that. Ol' Jim here will always be watchin' your back for you. And you for ol' Jim now, eh, lad?"

"Oh, aye, Jim, aye," Israel answered, deep concern creasing his brow.

Lifting his eyes beyond his friend to the quarterdeck, Israel spied the first mate of the *Bristol Galley*, Zebulon Drummond. Drummond had always made Israel uneasy and was now staring intently at the two. Israel lowered his voice, although Drummond was far enough away that he needn't have. "Jim, Drummond's eyeing us something terrible."

Jim seemed not to hear and gazed out over the ocean, a long, luxurious look, as if for the last time. "I know."

Israel squared around to face Drummond as he came striding toward them from the quarterdeck. Jim turned just as Drummond arrived. "There's work not being done here. 'Tis no time to run afoul, Barry."

Jim smiled at the first mate. "The boy here just has a touch of the sea, and his stomach won't let his legs stay below him."

Drummond looked hard at Israel. "Well, did you give him a cut of potato?" Drummond inquired.

"Ah, that we did, Zeb, that we did. And his stomach is comin' 'round right fine. He'll be up the riggin' just as soon as you please."

The young sailor made no attempt to appear ill but stood as straight as a mast with a mutinous glint in his eye. And although Drummond resented the smoke in Israel's gaze, he thought it best to ignore it. At least for the present. "Get aloft and secure those braces on the topsail yard, Hands," Drummond ordered.

"Aye-aye, sir," Israel said dryly, and he was instantly up the main mast rigging, his sun-soaked blond hair flying freely about his shoulders in the warm Caribbean breeze.

"Amazing recovery, eh, Barry?" Drummond snarled as he watched Israel fly up the rigging.

"Ain't that always the way of the young, Mr. Drummond?" Barry replied through a yellow-toothed smile.

Straddling the yardarm, Israel dug his fingers under the tight leather belt about his waist and retrieved a faded silk ribbon. Suspended fifty feet above the rolling deck of the thirty-six-gun ship, Israel secured his hair back in a tail with two free hands. He continued his trek, his long, sinewy arms pulling his body forward down the length of the yardarm, securing himself with crossed ankles that rested momentarily on the spar, then pushing forward again. The sun, shining bright and hot, glistened on his shirtless back, which was bronzed but not yet leathered by the sun and the salt air.

Israel looked down from his elevated station into the deep china blue of the Caribbean. One moment, he was directly above the deck of the *Bristol Galley*; the next, he was suspended over the sea as the ship rolled to port. He felt as if he had taken wing as he swung out over the water. At just the right moment, he waved to his shadow that was cast upon the sea. It appeared to Israel that it might be a ghostly sea creature just beneath the surface that beckoned him. Israel smiled as the sea ghost waved, bidding him welcome.

Jim and Drummond observed the boy from the quarterdeck, to which they had returned. "It is indeed a curiosity," Drummond commented to the second mate.

Jim watched the sails fill with wind as they completed their tack. "And what might that be, Mr. Drummond?"

"That one who so often plays as a lad would be as fine a sailor as these eyes have ever seen."

"Aye, Mr. Drummond, that he is, and a good lad, too, only in need of a firm and guiding hand."

"And whose hand might that be, Barry? Yours?"

"Ah, Mr. Drummond. You know that Isr'l and me serve good King William and this here ship."

"The king?" Drummond seemed puzzled. "Mr. Barry, this ship is a privateer, not a ship of the line. We've nothing to do with *the king* outside of possessing the letter of marque."

"Aye, ain't that the truth of it, Mr. Drummond," Barry returned with a smile and a nod. "So I'll take your suggestion and be that firm and guiding hand for the lad."

"Sail, port o' stern!" The cry came from Tobias, high aloft the mizzenmast rigging. Drummond and Barry turned on their heels and searched the horizon. The call brought Captain Jack Trenton bounding out on deck, where he joined Drummond and Barry at the stern timbers. Captain Trenton looked up to Tobias, who was peering through his glass. "Tobias, what colors does she fly?"

"I don't know, Captain," the Jamaican yelled in reply. "I can't see, but she's three masts and square rigged."

"Perhaps a fine prize, Cap'n, if we can catch her," Barry said enticingly.

"Perhaps a fine fight as well, Captain," Drummond warned Trenton as he eyed Barry, reminding him of his station. "She may be up to sixty guns, sir. If we engage, we may take on a fight we cannot win."

"Mr. Drummond," Captain Trenton replied, "I think it unlikely that we would find a fourth-rate ship of the line in the Windward Passage all alone."

Drummond was left mute. Barry rocked slowly back on his heels, an unrepressed look of satisfaction spread across his face. Captain Trenton thought for a moment longer. "We'll come alongside her. If she's twice our guns, we'll outrun her. If we match her muzzle for muzzle and she's heavy with cargo, we'll take her."

Drummond stood, seething.

"Mr. Barry!"

"Aye, Cap'n," Barry replied, stepping forward.

"Prepare the ship for action."

"Aye-aye, sir!" Barry turned to head amidships, and as he did, he locked eyes with Drummond. In that moment, it was understood that war had been declared. Not on the vessel running for the horizon, but between mates. He would need to watch Drummond. The first mate would look to find an accomplice, for the opportunity would likely come in the thick of the fight, and he might not be in a position to get to Barry himself.

Captain Trenton looked back over his shoulder at his first mate and spoke in a measured cadence. "Mr. Drummond, you'll be wise to remember that I have a 'no purchase, no pay' agreement with these men. If we do not capture a prize, they receive no pay. Look around you, Mr. Drummond. These men do not address disappointment in a civilized manner. Each one is a potential mutineer, and we are thirty days out of Hispaniola without so much as a sighting. Do you clearly understand the situation, *Mr.* Drummond?"

Drummond quietly cleared his throat and did not lift his gaze from the deck. "Yes, sir. Quite."

"Very well, Mr. Drummond. See to your duties."

"Aye, sir." Drummond turned with a perfunctory salute and strode off the quarterdeck in a slow-burning rage. Captain Trenton advanced to the ship's wheel.

"Helmsman, ease her to port."

"Aye, sir. Easing her to port, sir," the young but experienced seaman confirmed.

"Yes, gently, now—we don't want to concern our new friends and lose the wind at the same time."

"Aye, sir. Easing her to port, sir. *Gently*, sir." The helmsman's rolling eyes went unseen.

"There's a good lad."

Israel scurried the length of the top mainsail yardarm and scampered down the rigging. The deck was alive with movement. It reminded him of the times back home when he stepped on an anthill and watched the maddened ants run furiously about. An oaken chest was hauled out from behind the quarterdeck ladder. Two crewmen then cut the leather tie that served as the lock and began emptying the box of its luxurious cargo. They grabbed and tossed up into the air an array of brightly colored garments to the eager empty hands of their shipmates. Scarves of all colors, hats with bent plumes, expensive coats, silk breeches, and boots of every style sailed about the deck. Israel had cinched a bloodred sash around his waist and was donning a royal-blue waistcoat when Jim approached him. Israel looked up and inquired, "Aren't you going to prepare, Jim? It won't be long afore we're at them."

Jim looked up and noted that they indeed had made up distance on the ship. He rubbed a calloused hand across his stubbled chin. "Isr'l, watch out for Drummond. A difference of opinion has led me to believe he'll be a plottin' to see me to damnation afore this day is out. If it be so, it'll come from one who's loyal to him, more like as not. If you see him talkin' to anyone, all quiet and cozy like, you'll come and let me know, now, won't you, lad?"

"'Course I will, Jim. I never did lay no trust on that man; you know that to be true."

"There's a good lad." Barry smiled at his protégé. "Let's see, now, do you have all you need for a proper show? Remember what I been tellin' you for five years now? Appearances, appearances."

Israel broke out with a smile and a wink. "Oh, I've got them, Jim." Israel pulled two long scarlet scarves out from under his jacket. The two ceremoniously tied the scarves so that they completely covered their heads. With that done, Jim removed a small sack of soft, weathered cowhide and opened it. Israel looked on in awe as Jim slipped his thumb and index finger into the pouch. Solemnly, he removed the Devil's Kiss, a large silver ring, which he held up for Israel to behold.

The ring, which boasted a large black onyx cross in the middle of its round face, was anchored by four bright rubies set at the inside corners of the cross. Jim took in a lungful of air and then placed the ring on the middle finger of his right hand. As he did so, Israel could hear Jim release a long, easy breath. Barry then reached to his side and drew his heavy cutlass. In Israel's mind, there was no greater source of strength on earth than the hand that wore that ring and held a cutlass. Israel dared to ask Jim again, "It's true, ain't it, Jim—ol' Drummond can do you no harm when you have that ring on?"

"It be true, Isr'l," Jim told the boy as Israel became lost in the shine of the silver and the sharp flashes of light off the black and red gemstones. "This here ring can keep Satan's legions from doin' you harm as long as it be on your hand. And there's gospel to you." Jim hesitated. "Even still, lad, keep a sharp eye on Drummond. Quick with you, now, to your post."

"Alive with you, lads! Look fast and sharp! She's a Spanish merchant galley, and we match her gun for gun but for four!" Captain Trenton looked back into his scope, his excitement growing with every glance through the glass. The men were stooped low behind the bulwarks so that no Spanish glass would find them. Their bright clothing would instantly give them away. No merchant crew dressed like that. The Spaniards would know them for what they really were.

"Ah, she rides low in the water. She's heavy laden, men. We'll have her now," Trenton announced with a smile in his voice. Then the Spanish galley turned. Drummond was quick to notice it first. "There she goes, Captain. She's going to starboard. She's onto us, sure. She'll try to outrun us."

"Damn fools! We'll have her wind in our sails," Trenton observed. "Helmsman, stay dead astern of her! On my command, come hard to starboard!"

"Aye-aye, sir."

"Mr. Drummond," Captain Trenton said in a soft, confident voice. "Prepare for battle."

"Aye, sir." Drummond turned to the silent deck. "Prepare for battle! Prepare for boarding!"

A frenzied cry of fury came up from the crew, the likes of which the captain and first mate had never heard. No bulwarks could hide their intentions now. Every cutlass and dagger reflected the sun's brilliance into the eyes of their enemy. Every dry, crusty throat was rich and full with curses and laughter, the sign of a crew who comes to life only when there's killing to be done. A shipmate began to sing a familiar song, which made Israel smile. Israel joined in; singing always made his duties seem lighter, especially before a fight. He was lost in song and work until his eyes settled on the portside gun crew. Drummond, who had his back to Israel, was talking to someone. Isolated from the rest of the crew by several yards, Drummond looked nervously about, as if he might get caught telling secrets. Israel strained to see the other man, but Drummond perfectly blocked him from view. The intense conversation continued for another minute. Israel scanned the deck for Barry, but his efforts were fruitless. As he looked back, Drummond cleared away, revealing Doolin Pike, the chief gunner's mate, who was looking squarely at Israel.

Israel knew Pike to be a ruthless killer. In the two years that Israel had served with Pike, he had never heard the man utter a word outside of a command to his gun crew. He was as hardened a sailor as Israel had ever known. Pike leaned against the port rail. Prepared for battle, as always, wearing his high three-cornered hat and large purple greatcoat with deep cuffs and shiny brass buttons. With his arms folded across his chest, Pike rocked slowly back and forth against the rail. Two loaded pistols were tucked under his wide leather belt.

"We have her now, my good fellows!" Trenton cried. He shouted to the bosun, Robert Kent, "Up with her, lad! Up with our colors!" Kent hoisted the bloodred flag of the privateers up the staff. With the raising of the flag, the song being sung by only a few was now taken up by the many.

> *I fight, 'tis for vengeance! I love to see flow,*
> *At the stroke of my saber, the life of my foe.*
> *I strike for the memory of long-vanished years;*
> *I only shed blood where another sheds tears.*
> *I come, as the lightning comes red from above,*
> *O'er the race that I loathe, to the battle I love.*

And all the while, Doolin Pike stared deep into the eyes of Israel Hands.

The Spanish merchant attempted to come about to bring her guns to bear, but it was too late. The *Bristol Galley* had indeed put herself between the wind and the enemy ship. For as much of a dandy that Trenton was, the men had long ago recognized he was one helluva sailor. The crew had manned their stations and were ready for action.

"Hard to starboard!" Trenton shouted. "Give her a strong broadside, Pike! Keep above the waterline now!"

"Aye, Cap'n," Pike snarled back. The entire crew of the *Bristol Galley* held their breath. For one interminable moment, the Spanish ship floundered as her fore and mainsails began to luff and then the ship lay dead in the water. It was now just target practice for Pike and his gun crews. The helpless flapping of Spanish canvas was the only sound to hit the ear, save for that of carving water by the keel of the *Bristol Galley*. A large cloudbank passing by overhead put the pirate ship in a shroud of gray while the afternoon sun's rays broke through to illuminate her target. Pike was a precision gunner and waited patiently as he eyed his helpless prey. The *Bristol Galley* came alongside the Spanish ship and was in a prime position to slam her cannons into the hull of the lame vessel. Pike waited.

Israel, from his perch in the rigging of the mainsail, could hear the enemy captain shouting commands in Spanish. He didn't know what the Spaniard was saying, but he didn't sound happy. Some of the crew of the *Bristol Galley* began to shout at Pike to fire. They saw their chance to destroy their foe in a single, crushing blow fading with the sun and braced themselves for a broadside from the Spanish ship. And still, Pike waited. Israel looked to the quarterdeck and noticed that even Captain Trenton and Drummond shared an anxious look.

It soon became apparent why the Spanish had not fired. The Spanish captain needed to put his ship back into the wind. Sweeps appeared from the hatches along the hull. The Spaniards would attempt to row her into position. Within a few short minutes, the *Bristol Galley* could lose her advantage. The crew was getting hot, aiming their pistols and shouting threats and curses at the Spanish crew. Then Pike stirred and barked something indistinguishable to

Israel's ears but clear enough to his gun crews. Pike's hand went up as he looked up and down his line of cannoneers. And as the *Bristol Galley* began to roll to starboard and her muzzles came up on her port side, Pike roared the order. Eighteen portside cannons on two decks went off simultaneously.

Although blinded by the smoke from the cannon fire, the crew of the *Bristol Galley* knew immediately the destruction Pike had rendered. The shattering of the masts and the screams of the victims told the story that the eye could not yet witness. The long whine of tearing canvas sang of masts and yards falling to the deck and into the sea. The screams rising from the rigging and smoke-obscured deck of the Spanish galleon testified to the human suffering on board. The *Bristol Galley* pressed beyond the crippled ship and prepared to come about.

As they approached for their second pass, it was clear that no further cannonade would be necessary. The timing of Pike's salvo had been perfect. The Spanish ship had its entire deck obliterated from amidships to the fo'c'sle. The main mast and foremast were gone. Shattered timber and torn flesh littered the ship's remains as the screams of the wounded carried on the wind and echoed off the plump sails of the returning *Bristol Galley*.

The bowsprit hung limp in the sea while miles of rigging lay draped over the forecastle like a veil over the face of a dying lady. The Spanish captain stood bloodied and cursing on the quarterdeck. Although his ship lay lifeless on the water, it was clear that there was still fight left in the man. The crew of the *Bristol Galley* let out a raucous cheer for the fire in the man's spirit. They admired bravery above all else. And each sailor felt it a shame that they would have to kill him.

There would be no quarter shown to such a defiant foe. Pike prepared his starboard gun crews. "Make ready to send her to the bottom if she doesn't strike colors, you rovers," Pike growled in nearly unintelligible speech.

"We'll clear the quarterdeck of the bloody dog this time, Pike," declared gunner Ben Phillips. Through narrowed eyes, Pike gave Phillips a quick and knowing nod, which was as good as a broad grin and a hearty slap on the back, coming from Doolin Pike.

The *Bristol Galley* had come about and was bearing down hard on her prey. Pike knew they would be hull against hull in only moments and ordered his guns to ready. At that instant, Spanish cannons roared against Trenton's privateer. All but one missed the mark. A ball tore through the main yardarm, missing Israel by only a few feet. The heavy spar came crashing to the upper deck, killing one seaman instantly and slicing off the legs, ever so neatly, of another. Israel watched from above as the blood spit wildly from where his shipmate's knees used to be. *Another ship's cook is born,* Israel thought. The ship's surgeon hurried to tend to his first patient. There would be many more.

A mocking cheer rose up among the Spanish crew, while on the deck of the *Bristol Galley*, Pike raised his hand, ready to fire. The Spaniards could see clearly the gunners at the ready and took cover as best they could behind the bulwark stanchions of the weakened ship. From only thirty yards away, the starboard guns of the *Bristol Galley* ripped into the main deck, filling it with smoke and blinding the gunners. Seconds after the blasts, another terrible crash followed. The sharp snapping of timbers and the wrenching of planking announced the arrival of the *Bristol Galley*.

Hull against hull, the ships conjoined, and the screams of fury from the attacking pirates rose above the commands of Captain Trenton. "No quarter, lads, give no quarter!" It was a command that need not have been given. At this point, both Trenton and Drummond, who directed action from the quarterdeck, knew the battle was solely in the hands of their piratical crew. Trenton wisely reasoned it was best not to get between them and their passions and to simply proceed as if they were carrying out his orders.

Israel draped a three-foot length of stout rope over the mainstay and pulled each end to test for soundness. With his long knives secured under his belt and a brace of two pistols slung over his shoulder, he slid down the mainstay to the forecastle. In one bounding leap, Israel jumped from the fo'c'sle rail of the *Bristol Galley* to the quarterdeck of the Spanish merchant. At over six feet tall, Israel posed a daunting figure to the smaller Spaniards. Without either hurry or hesitation, Israel drew both pistols from their sleeves and leveled them at their targets. He fired them almost simultaneously, the first shot splattering the face of an officer with a raised sword in hand. The second shot, intended for the Spanish captain, fell lower than he'd aimed but dropped his victim nonetheless with a painful, and mortal, gut shot. Israel dropped both pistols, drew his knives, and, in rapid succession, dispatched two of the Spanish crew in as many throws. Both men fell to the deck instantly, dead before their heads bounced off the planks.

From the deck of the *Bristol Galley*, through the stampede of men boarding the Spanish merchant in front of him, Barry beheld his pupil and wondered: Who was really the student and who was the master? Israel fought devoid of fear, without consideration of even the possibility of personal harm or ultimate destruction. He had downed four men, including the captain, in less than a minute of being aboard the enemy ship.

When the boy looked back to the quarterdeck of the *Bristol Galley* for new orders, his eyes grew wide with fear. Drummond was moving from his post on the quarterdeck down the ladder to the main deck of the *Bristol Galley*, his eyes fixed on Jim. Israel looked forward to the fo'c'sle. Doolin Pike had likewise turned toward Jim. Israel screamed through the mass of embattled seamen fighting furiously on the slippery Spanish deck, trying to gain Jim's attention. His screams were in vain. Drummond approached Barry stealthily from behind, cutlass held firm and low at his side. Israel watched powerlessly as Pike brought one pistol up to aim. He knew that one shot was all the chief gunner would need. Pike *never* missed. Israel strained to raise his cry of warning above the cacophony of battle resounding from the deck. His efforts were futile. He ran to the rail of the ship in one last desperate attempt to warn Jim. Israel flailed his arms madly through the air to catch his eye. Jim saw Israel at the very last moment. The smile fell away from Jim's face as the fear he saw in Israel's countenance took root. Directly behind Jim, Drummond raised his cutlass as Pike clicked the hammer of his flintlock pistol back to full cock. Jim spun around and attempted to hit Drummond first. But he was too slow. Before he could strike, Pike fired from twenty paces, and the ball from his pistol ripped through the skull of the dead man who was still standing on his feet. A heartbeat later, the knees buckled, and the body hit the deck. Doolin Pike *never* missed.

Barry looked down at Drummond lying dead on the deck amid his own blood and brains. He looked over at Pike, who squinted and gave him a quick and knowing nod. Barry knew that that was as good as a broad smile and a hearty slap on the back, coming from Doolin Pike. A shaken Israel Hands looked on in grateful disbelief; the ring had true magic. Israel turned aside and rejoined the fight.

Tobias, armed with only the body of a slain Spaniard, held off an attacker by positioning the dead man between himself and the swinging cutlass of the enemy. Although the one was dead, the other had not the hardness of heart to pierce his dead countryman to get to the Jamaican pirate. Israel grinned at the queer sight. Tobias was peering over the corpse's right shoulder, dodging the cutlass and receiving the curses of the frustrated assailant, when he heard two muffled thumps. The Spaniard's eyes seemed to lose focus as a reactive hiccup brought bright-red blood up from his lungs. The cutlass dropped loud and heavy with a sharp clang. Tobias sidestepped the falling man as his face hit the gunwale hard before landing facedown on the deck. The Jamaican pirate discarded his dead shield and recognized the two knives sticking out of the man's back. He bent down and pulled them out by their carved-whale-tooth handles. Tobias straightened up and looked into the pale, sparkling eyes of Israel Hands. "You watch for long time afore you throw knives, Hands?" Tobias asked with a curious smile, wiping the blood from the knife blades before returning them to their owner.

"Not too long, Toby," the younger man replied with a mischievous grin. "Just long enough."

The battle amidships was all but over. Just some killing left to do. "No quarter, no quarter!" raged from the angry throats of the pitiless crew of the *Bristol Galley*. Israel shouted to bring all that was left of the enemy crew to the quarterdeck. Whereas Israel had no authority to give commands on the deck of the *Bristol Galley*, most of the crew deferred to the fearless youth amid action on enemy vessels. Threescore pirates brutishly conveyed the remaining twenty-six Spaniards to the quarterdeck and a swift death with one stroke of the knife of Israel Hands. Dozens more were already bringing booty up from the holds of the Spanish merchant and began stowing it away in the empty belly of the ravenous *Bristol Galley*.

Three Spaniards at a time were forced to kneel down, facing the pirate crew gathered to watch on the upper deck. One by one, Israel would step up behind them, lift their heads up by their chins, and ask them a ridiculous question. When they failed to answer correctly, if at all, he would slit their throats with one smooth, deep stroke of his knife. The sound of the forceful, wet air spewing in and out of bloody throats and the flailing kicks of half-dead men began to take their toll on even the most callous of the witnesses. Some men began throwing the bodies of dying Spaniards into the sea, where they thrashed about as life flowed from their blanched bodies and turned the foaming sea the color of a coral reef, just so they wouldn't have to watch them die on the quarterdeck.

In a short time, the blood had covered the quarterdeck and flowed in scarlet rivulets onto the main deck of the ship. Men looked down at their feet and observed the blood pooling at their bootheels. Many of the Spaniards awaiting execution passed out in anticipation of experiencing the cold horror playing out before them and were dragged unconscious to their doom. Israel, now completely bathed in blood, began to lose his audience. They lived for the heat and passion of battle that earned them the spoils for which they gladly killed. But this was different. This long, slow, orchestrated bloodletting was the work of . . . a butcher.

As Israel harvested his death crop, Jeremiah Briggs, the *Bristol Galley* quartermaster, tallied the goods being brought aboard. Barry, who himself had to turn away from the pirate justice being meted out on the quarterdeck, cast his troubled eyes downward to the sea and warned his shipmates of a new threat. "Mind you, lads, there be sharks below us. Now that Isr'l's given 'em a taste o' Spain, they'll be wanting more." Some of the crew peered over the rail to spy the activity beneath them. A deep-coral sea broiled with every dead or dying sailor pitched over the edge. A shiver of eight- to ten-foot tiger sharks darted in and out of view in the small sea between the tethered ships. A low, angry rumble seethed from the churning red foam of the feeding frenzy.

"What kind of sharks be they, Jim?" asked a nervous shipmate, about to cross over the boarding plank, lugging a keg of rum on each shoulder.

"The kind that'll bite off your rope end if you fall in the water!" Jim laughed.

The pirate repositioned the kegs to improve his grip. He looked down at the long, all-too-narrow boarding plank and considered the distance with a hard swallow. He set one timid foot down on the plank as playful shipmates shook the end that waited over the deck of the *Bristol Galley*. "You'll be shaking on the end of me cutlass, Barker, if you don't lay your hands off that plank."

Barker, Barry, and a few other members of the crew who were watching laughed until their cheeks hurt before returning to their business.

"What's the tally so far, Briggs?" asked Barry, who had, by the recent and sudden demise of Drummond, assumed his duties as the first mate of the *Bristol Galley*.

"Well," Briggs said, "we got fifty barrels of fresh water and stores of salt pork and beef, thirty barrels each so far, but Darby Sacks says the men just found at least fifteen more barrels of beef. I count one hundred barrels of sugar, two hundred bales of indigo, and fifty sacks of silver plate, and counting the two kegs Naismith is hauling," he added with a nod toward the man crossing the plank, "we have one hundred and twenty kegs of Jamaican rum."

"A fair haul," Barry said, nodding his approval. Suddenly, their attention turned to the sea as they heard the shrill screams of a man being torn apart by the razor-sharp teeth of a fourteen-foot tiger shark. Naismith was no longer walking the plank. Briggs made an adjustment in the ledger. "One hundred and *eighteen* kegs o' rum."

As the sun dragged its trailing light below the western horizon, Israel watched as the burning Spanish ship slipped into her undersea berth beneath a darkening Caribbean sky. Ten barrels of fresh water had been allocated to cleaning the remnants of battle off the deck and the bloody crew. Barry approached Israel as the youth stood before a water barrel. Israel immersed his arms above his elbows and slowly washed away the stain of so many dead men.

Barry announced his presence by resting a gentle hand on Israel's back.

"Hello, Jim," Israel said with an easy smile. "Do you think the dolphins will swim with us tomorrow?"

The innocence caught Jim off guard. "Ah, well, now, we'll just have to wait and see, won't we, Isr'l?"

"Aye," Israel said in sad acceptance, "I expect we'll just have to wait and see." Israel looked down at his hands as he continued to wash, trying to remove some of the more stubborn blood from around his fingernails. Jim Barry looked out over a blackening sea as the last strains of sunlight fused with the glow of a full and rising moon.

"We surely had ourselves a day, now, Isr'l, wouldn't you say?"

"Aye, Jim, we truly did. And Jim," Israel said with growing excitement, "did you see how the ring saved you from harm? Did you see, Jim?"

"Aye, lad, aye." Jim glanced down at the ring, still on his finger, and wiped away a drop of dried blood from its onyx cross as he searched for the right words. "Isr'l, you carried a heavy burden on your shoulders today. You've fine, strong shoulders, lad—that be true—but not made to carry the weight you bore today. Do you understand me, laddy?" Israel stared blankly at Barry, his head tilted slightly to the right. Jim continued, "The men on the quarterdeck, Isr'l, you didn't have to do the bloody job."

Israel looked confused. "No quarter, Jim. I heard the call of no quarter."

"Aye, lad, you heard right. I just wish you left it for the others to do."

"Oh, that's all right, Jim," Israel said, trying to put his friend at ease. "I paid it no bother. I want to do my part, Jim. You know that be true. I'll not refuse a chore that needs doing." Israel turned his attention back to the cleansing task before him. He worked at the blood under his fingernails with the point of his knife as the first mate leaned heavily on the rail and studied the smooth face of Israel Hands. He had never seen a man kill with such ferocity and yet so completely without passion. Israel, Barry knew, killed cold. His thoughts faded into the darkening sky. A sad, caring smile came over the face of the aging pirate that Israel couldn't understand.

The two men stood in solitary silence together, listening to a friendly sea lick the scarred hull of the resting ship. From below deck, the sound of rum-soaked men swapping sea stories danced up into the cool night air. Jim cared little about the tales being told below as he and Israel shared the midnight watch on the quarterdeck. They were mostly lies, anyway. Israel looked at Barry.

"I hope the dolphins swim tomorrow."

Lieutenant Drew

Saturday, June 19, 1999

Lieutenant Drew Kenealy was leaning over the dead feet of Vince LaCava when Tom came quickstepping around the corner of the house. The lieutenant paid him no mind as another plainclothes officer stopped Tom in his tracks with the open palm of a stubby-fingered hand on the end of a butterball arm. He allowed Tom to proceed only up to the yellow-tape barrier of the investigation scene. From his position, Tom could see only the long legs and big feet of Vince LaCava stretched out from behind the chimney.

"Are you Tom Stone, proprietor of Stonecroft Inn?" The question, and the way the plump little man posed it, reeked of bad melodrama. Tom pegged this guy to be the Barney Fife of the department. Barney with a thyroid problem.

Looking beyond his inquisitor, Tom watched as the examining officer continued his diligent inspection of the area around Vince's corpse. *Well, I guess that would be Sheriff Taylor, then, wouldn't it.* Tom's eyes darted about the scene in anxious disbelief. He turned around to speak to Jake, only to discover he wasn't behind him. Tom felt a soft, fleshy hand clutching at his elbow. Instinctively, he jerked his arm free of the physical trespass and was tempted to read the grabby little man the riot act but managed to hold his tongue and not compound the troubles that obviously lay before him.

"I don't like to be touched," Tom bristled.

"Understood," replied the officer in feigned empathy and offered Tom an open, guiding hand toward the driveway. "Mr. Stone—I believe you are Tom Stone?" the detective repeated, having never received a response to his first query. Tom nodded absently, his attention still placed on the organized commotion on the patio.

"Mr. Stone, I'm Detective Ingersoll, and I need to ask you a few questions," he stated, squaring off to face Tom eye to eye. But he didn't lift his head up when he spoke to Tom; rather, he raised two tiny, steel-blue eyes from beneath a furrowed brow to continue his questioning.

"Mr. Stone, had you employed Mr. Vince LaCava for masonry services?"

"Uh, yeah," Tom replied obtusely, still struggling to digest the fact that there was a dead man on his patio, a *good* man, and at the same time trying to make sense of the peculiar little man in front of him.

"And Mr. Stone, was Mr. LaCava indeed providing those services with your permission, on your property, at the time of his death?"

"Yes. Well, I guess," Tom said. "I mean, he was working when we left earlier."

"And what time was that, Mr. Stone?"

"Around noon, I think."

"You think," the detective repeated quietly as he recorded the statement in his notebook. "I see," he concluded.

Tom decided then and there that he didn't like the man. *And what's that noise?*

Detective Nathaniel "Nate" Ingersoll could not have been more than five foot six—five foot seven, tops—and was somewhere between 230 and 240 on the hoof, a perfect bowling ball. When the man wasn't speaking, a whistling sound came through his nose. When he was speaking, he wheezed with the pipes of a severe asthmatic. Tom figured that he was about one minute away from breaking out his metered-dose inhaler, or his "puffer," as the detective would no doubt refer to it, for some quick relief. A fashion maven in his own inimitable way, Ingersoll favored earth tones and dressed in the very best Kmart had to offer. Unfortunately, anything below the beltline often went unnoticed, and a pair of sole-worn wingtips were now entering their second summer of a brown-shoe-polish drought.

"Mr. Stone, where were you this afternoon?" the detective asked as he thrust a searching hand into his inside jacket pocket.

"Rockport. We had lunch and did some shopping."

Detective Ingersoll pulled out the inhaler from his pocket, shook it, and, holding it in a pudgy fist, put it to his mouth and self-administered two quick puffs. He held his breath for a few seconds, then slowly released a chestful of moist, garlic-scented air. He slipped the inhaler back into his jacket pocket.

"Mr. Stone, to your knowledge, was there anyone else expected here today? Maybe someone who might be bringing supplies to Mr. LaCava?"

"Not that I know of." He was trying to follow where the questions were going. Tom sensed something had shifted. "Are you saying you think he was killed?"

The muscles beneath the detective's sagging jowls tensed with Tom's question.

"Mr. Stone, I can answer no questions concerning this investigation. We are in the information-gathering stage. We have no answers at this time. We'll attempt to handle this case through local law enforcement agencies," Ingersoll droned as if he were repeating the same lines for the fiftieth time that day. "Any compromise in the integrity of this case may be sufficient cause to kick this up to the state, or even federal, level. Please, Mr. Stone, let's stick to the questions." Tom heard Barney Fife loud and clear and was growing a bit tired of the supercilious cop.

Tom watched as the detective continued to make entries in the small notebook. Holding a stumpy little pencil in stumpy little fingers, Ingersoll would have been a comical sight under different circumstances as he wrote with his mouth agape and a slightly protruding tongue while an odd, high-pitched hum resonated from his pug nose. Tom studied derisively the cartoonlike character scribbling before him, but his attention was soon drawn to the northern end of the house toward Doliber's Cove. Two female officers were speaking to Marie at the far end of the house, outside the sitting room. She sat on a stack of unopened bags of cedar mulch with her face cradled in her hands. With the backs of the officers facing Tom, he couldn't hear what Marie was being asked or what she was being told.

As Tom turned back, Jake entered his line of sight from behind the house. He was talking to the other investigator, the one who seemed to know what he was doing. But from a distance of fifty feet and with the breeze carrying the sound away from him, he couldn't hear what was being discussed with Jake any more than he could with Marie. *Well, of course. Divide and conquer,* Tom realized. *So are we suspects?* He could see that Jake was much more animated than he and Marie had been, but then again, when wasn't he? Jake kept pointing to something in the direction of Vince's body, which Tom couldn't see from his position.

Detective Ingersoll stopped his scribbling to scratch the fleshy scalp beneath his short, curly red hair. After a brief review of his notes, he shot a quick glance up at Tom. "Wait here, please, Mr. Stone," he said, and Tom watched the detective walk up to the patio, toward Jake and the other investigator.

Out of the corner of his eye, Jake could see a rotund figure approaching them. But his full attention was on Lieutenant Kenealy, who shared his concerns openly and presented his questions in the same way. The arrival of his associate pulled Lieutenant Kenealy—or as he had introduced himself, Lieutenant Drew—away from Jake and into a private conversation with Detective Ingersoll. Jake observed the duo and tried to evaluate the relationship. Lieutenant Drew was tall and lean, an inch, maybe two, north of six feet. He was direct in his speech and manner, but there was a smooth easiness about him. He possessed an unwavering air of professionalism that had put Jake at ease in the question and answer session that had just been interrupted. The poster child for male-pattern baldness, Lieutenant Drew had a ruddy complexion born not of drink but of genetics and exposure to the sun. He stood at the complete opposite end of the spectrum from the corpulent subordinate he was conferring with.

As Jake watched the two of them, he couldn't help but think that Lieutenant Drew was hard-pressed to remain patient with his associate as he thumbed clumsily through small pages of handwritten notes. After Ingersoll had read a portion of what he had recorded, it seemed that Lieutenant Drew would ask a question, prompting

Ingersoll to start scrolling through his notes again. This would cause Lieutenant Drew to straighten up and take a slow, deep breath, which would in turn make Detective Ingersoll all the more nervous, and all the more clumsy, as he fumbled through his notepad.

When Lieutenant Drew had heard enough, he issued a soft order and walked over to the grayish-white corpse. Jake watched as Detective Ingersoll ambled halfway back to Tom before summoning him with a beckoning hand. The paramedics who had been standing by, helpless in this unfortunate situation, jumped from their unit, walked around to the back of the rescue vehicle, and extracted a pop-up gurney. On the patio, one of the men had begun to unzip a bag of heavy black plastic when he finally noticed the size of the dead man. He looked at the bag, then at his partner, and shook his head. Lieutenant Drew motioned for the men to remove the remains with a pointing finger.

"Sir, we're gonna need some help with him," the driver said to the lieutenant.

Having furtively followed in Lieutenant Drew's wake, Jake stood silently at the edge of the patio, watching the small party try to get the big man off the stone-cold deck. Lieutenant Drew asked Ingersoll to get Sergeant Ehrlich, who was inside the inn. Moments later, a big man with sergeant's stripes came from around the corner. Not far behind him was Marie, accompanied by the two female officers. Jake moved quickly to meet her before she saw the body, but he wasn't quick enough. The gasp, followed by a groan, confirmed he had lost the race.

Lieutenant Drew lifted a protective hand up in front of Marie and turned her around before Jake could reach her. "Let's talk inside, folks. I think we'll all be more comfortable away from this." Tom was there at his side as Jake turned with Marie to go back into the house. The two men exchanged hollow stares as they shuffled along the expanse of the back porch. They proceeded into the gathering room from the back door as the body of Vince LaCava, feet protruding out from under the sheet that covered him because the body bag was too small, was hoisted ponderously into the back of the paramedic vehicle for the long ride home.

"Mr. Goddard?" Tom said, surprised to see his gathering room inhabited by the contractor and Detective Ingersoll. Ingersoll had exchanged responsibilities with Ehrlich when Lieutenant Drew needed some extra muscle to lift the dead mason. Tom smirked. *It was a cinch that the Pillsbury Doughboy wouldn't be much help.*

"Hello theya, Mista Stone. I'm awful sorry about awl this he-ah trouble," the man said in a shaky voice.

"Mr. Goddard, what happened here?" Tom pleaded.

"Again, Mr. Stone," Ingersoll said with a condescending smile, "it would be best if you didn't—"

"Thanks, Nate, I'll take it from here," Lieutenant Drew interrupted, to the amusement of all in the room, except for Ingersoll. It was a small spanking, but a spanking nonetheless. And it was clear by the way the man marched out of the house that he wasn't happy about it. Tom looked over at the troubled figure of Mr. Goddard, sitting motionless in the corner, who didn't seem to hear anyone get spanked at all.

Lieutenant Drew waited for Ingersoll's impressive shadow to clear the gathering room's threshold before he spoke. When he did speak, it was with a voice of calm deliberation. "Let me begin by introducing myself. My name is Drew Kenealy. I'm a lieutenant with the Marblehead Police Department. I'm the safety and communications officer for the department, and I'm the ranking officer here at this investigation. I am not, however, a detective. The young man who just left, Sergeant Nate Ingersoll, is the detective for this investigation. His approach may come off as a bit coarse, and he's a relative newcomer to the detective ranks, but he is a top-notch investigator and has my complete confidence."

Tom sighed in relief, happy to now be dealing with a competent authority.

"My role here is to control the scene, assist in the gathering of information, and serve as the media liaison. We want to make sure we inform the public of what is happening without compromising an investigation," the lieutenant concluded.

"How about if someone tells *us* what's happening?" Tom pleaded. "We came home and there's a dead guy in my yard."

"May he rest in peace," Marie whispered.

Lieutenant Drew nodded in appreciation of everyone's distress.

"Mr. Goddard was the one who found Mr. LaCava and rang us down at the station." The police officer stood beside the contractor, who sat staring at the floor. "Folks, let me tell you what I think," Lieutenant Drew continued. "I believe that we will find that Mr. LaCava died of natural causes."

"Natural causes?" Jake questioned. "The guy looked to be in his midthirties. How could he have died of natural causes?"

"He was thirty-seven," the lieutenant stated. "And look, we don't know his family medical history or what medical problems he was aware of himself. But again, that's what I think. We'll have to wait for the report to be sure."

"So, then, what's all the stir about if you truly believe it was a natural death?" Marie asked.

"The 'stir,' Mrs. Brean, is that there was a very odd finding at the death scene. When we arrived, we saw no sign of any struggle or violence. Well, maybe I misspoke. What we did find is this." Lieutenant Drew pulled out a smoking pipe sealed within a plastic zip-top bag. "In Mr. LaCava's mouth."

"Jake's pipe?" Marie asked.

"Is this your pipe, Mr. Brean?"

"Yeah," Jake answered in slack-jawed disbelief. "I mean, it sure looks like it."

"Geez, you mean to say that Vince went into the house and grabbed Jake's pipe and was smoking it?" Tom asked incredulously.

"Nah, Mista Stone," Mr. Goddard interjected. "Vince nevah wouldah done a thing like that."

"I don't think he did, Mr. Goddard," the lieutenant agreed. "I think this pipe may have been forced into Mr. LaCava's mouth after he was dead"—he paused—"*through* his teeth." Everyone in the room shifted uncomfortably in their seats. "Or it may be that he had it in his mouth at the time he had a heart attack and bit down on the pipe, breaking the teeth."

"Damn." Tom winced at the thought.

"That's gotta hurt," Jake said, putting a protective hand up against his own mouth.

"Not if you're already dead," Lieutenant Drew pointed out.

"Hey, wait a minute. If that was shoved in his mouth after he was dead, then someone was here at the time he died," Jake suggested. "Right?"

"Or shortly thereafter."

"That's one sick son of a . . ."

"I agree, Mr. Stone. If that's what happened. And *that's* what the stir is all about. We might have someone who is not averse to committing some very unsavory acts. I don't know—maybe he thinks it's funny. At any rate, it could be classified as only a misdemeanor, regardless of the vulgarity of the offense. So since Mr. Goddard found him as he was," the lieutenant said, turning to each man as he mentioned them by name, "and Mr. Brean, since it was your pipe found in the mouth of the deceased, and it being your property, Mr. Stone, I thought an explanation might help to ease the strain, if only a bit."

"I suppose, in a way, it helps to know he wasn't murdered, but it doesn't seem like much of a step up from that," Marie said, trying to glean the best from a horrible notion.

"I understand your concern, but as strange as it seems to you, where I used to work, this really wouldn't even make honorable mention at the end of the day."

"Where did you used to work?"

"Detroit. Twelve years on the force."

"Detroit?" Jake asked. "Tell me, is it as beautiful as they say it is?"

"I think it's on its way to being beautiful again. I met some wonderful people there," the lieutenant reflected. "Anyway, I'm originally from here," he went on to explain, "but I received a full academic scholarship from U of D Mercy, and being someone who doesn't like to turn down free money, I took it. As it turned out, it's where I met my wife."

"Oh, that's sweet," Marie sighed, a sucker for a romantic story. "What does your wife do, Lieutenant?"

Lieutenant Kenealy smiled warmly but remained mute and walked toward the door. He stopped at the threshold.

"By the way, in your interviews, you all stated that you haven't seen anyone on the property in the last couple of days, correct? I mean, outside of the folks like Mr. Goddard who have come on arranged business."

Innocent shoulder shrugs and head wags bounced around the room.

"Well, keep your eyes open, and if you do see anything that strikes you as being out of the ordinary, give me a call. My number's on my card there on the table."

With the exception of Mr. Goddard, no one seemed able to meet the gaze of the officer as he turned the knob of the front door.

"Try to have a good evening, folks. Thanks for your help."

"Oh, Lieutenant. There is one more thing."

"What's that, Mr. Brean?"

"When you're done with the investigation, you can keep the pipe."

* * **

Drew Kenealy finished with the preliminary case report and placed the hard copy in the "pending" file in the top bin of the four-drawer Steelcase file cabinet. He slid the drawer shut and depressed the lock button in the upper-right-hand corner of the tan metal case. He felt a little out of place, working at the station on Atlantic Avenue. His daily post was down at the Old Town House in Market Square. But there was a nice desk of simulated oak with his nameplate on it, fixed securely with four #10 wood screws and a few dabs of wood glue, and whenever a report of this nature was needed, this was the place to be. A twenty-first-century police department in a seventeenth-century town. He looked around the empty room, searching for something else to do. There was no one waiting for him, so it was a growling stomach that reminded him there was more to life than police work. A hot meatball grinder from Rinaldo's, for instance.

"Time to go home," he said out loud to himself. *Home? Well, it was time to leave, anyway.* He yawned and stretched muscles that had spent too many hours sleeping while Drew sat in front of a computer, filling out forms. He rubbed his noisy belly in apology for his neglect and fished his keys out of the unused ceramic ashtray that served as a holding tank for keys, paper clips, and other small-ticket items. His finger traced the rim of the smooth, cool pottery. It was painted the most godawful color. He had never really been able to pinpoint it. Sort of a swirling blue, green, gold, and—what the hell else was in there? Maybe a rust undertone shining through here and there. *God, it's ugly.*

He hadn't smoked in years, he thought vaguely as he studied the ashtray, and a thought came back to plague him again like a nosy mother-in-law. Vince LaCava didn't smoke either. And yet, apparently today, he wanted a smoke so badly he shattered his own dead teeth to get the pipe in his mouth. Drew shook his head. There was one bad man out there somewhere. He hadn't lied to the people at Stonecroft Inn. He had seen much worse in his years on the force. But he had to admit to himself, this one would make the list just out of sheer creepiness. Drew wondered how Tom Stone and the Breans would fare tonight. Not very well, he guessed.

Drew's eyes fell on the picture of Karen he kept on his desk. He was hungry and tired but managed a weary smile. He *still* smiled when he looked at the picture. He shook his head in wonder that after all these years . . . *Well, what're ya gonna do?* As he stood up to leave, his attention flipped back to Stonecroft Inn and Tom Stone. They had something in common, he and Tom Stone. They were both the husbands of dead wives. Drew spun the keys around his index finger, headed toward the illuminated Exit sign, switched off the office light, and shut the door behind him.

He turned the key in the ignition, and the white police-issued Toyota van jumped to life. Rolling slowly out of the Marblehead PD parking lot, he popped a disc in the CD player—a small perk for having to drive around in a white van with "Safety Officer Drew" stenciled on the side. The music played as he rolled down Pleasant Street to Rinaldo's.

* * *

Paris Quicci tapped his fingers impatiently on the red-and-white checkered cloth that covered the table in the far corner of Rinaldo's. The banker wondered if there was some sort of law that required all Italian restaurants to have the same damn checkered tablecloths with a Chianti bottle as a candleholder for the centerpiece. His curiosity vanished as he looked across the table at his dinner guest.

"Put down your damn notepad and talk to me."

"I just want to make sure I get the wording right, Paris, that's all."

"You were there, man, you talked to them yourself. I don't need you to read me some report. Just tell me what you can. What did they say happened?"

"No signs of any struggle, no notable wounds that we could detect, save for the broken teeth, as I mentioned earlier," Detective Ingersoll clarified. "We'll have to wait for the autopsy, but we're thinking accidental death or, more likely, death by natural causes."

"That's it?" Quicci asked incredulously. "A death at old 'Spooky Tavern' a couple of weeks before it opens, and it's declared a death 'by causes unknown'? Could that Stone character get any luckier?" Quicci asked rhetorically. "Talk about a bold marketing strategy."

"I think I see what you mean, Paris," Ingersoll said, shifting in his seat. "I mean, in a way, but a relatively young man died today. A good man. I knew him."

"Pfff." Quicci waved him off. "What are you gonna have, Nate?"

They turned their eyes to the menu. "Everything is so good here. It's hard to decide, isn't it?"

Quicci studied his portly guest and shook his head in disgust. A gesture of which Ingersoll remained mercifully unaware. "Get whatever you want, my friend," Quicci offered smoothly. "It's on me."

Nate looked up and smiled at the generous statement. He took a deep breath and summoned the courage to take the discussion in a different direction.

"Say, Paris, have you heard anything about my loan being approved? It's been three weeks now."

"The board meets next Wednesday, Nate—I told you that. Don't worry," Quicci said dismissively, his eyes never leaving his menu. "I'm watching out for you. You know that, right?"

"Oh, absotively," Ingersoll quipped with counterfeit good humor. "I'm just anxious to get those home-improvement plans underway. You know me, Paris—gotta have something going all the time," Ingersoll said in an awkward voice that fell far short of its intended pleasantry.

Quicci chuckled to himself at the absurd statement. "Well, one thing's for sure. You aren't gonna get any work out of that LaCava fellow." Quicci laughed at his own joke, and he laughed well. It was several minutes before he could effectively wipe the tears from his eyes. He regained his composure and spread the red linen napkin on his lap.

"I'll have the veal," Quicci said decidedly. He closed his menu.

* * *

Drew pulled into the only remaining parking space in the lot beneath the balcony of Rinaldo's. He recognized the black Lexus sport coupe and the '93 Cavalier parked next to it.

"This can't be good." He stepped from his van and gave the Cavalier a quick visual examination. "You're gonna have to wash this every week, Nate, if you want to reduce the effects of the salt air. I keep telling you, but you don't seem to hear me." Drew looked around to make sure no one had heard him talking to himself. "Wouldn't look good for a senior law enforcement officer of Marblehead to be seen having a conversation with himself in a parking lot," he said even louder to the open air. He was having fun now, all by himself among the vacant cars, and did an impression of one of his favorite book characters: "M-O-O-N, that spells *conversation*, laws, yes."

The restaurant was busy, with a twenty-five-minute wait. Lieutenant Drew gave a friendly nod to a couple of familiar faces sitting with their families, enjoying their meals.

"Evenin', Drew. Eatin' in or takin' out?"

"Hi, Angela," Drew said, tossing a small dessert mint in his mouth. "Taking out."

"What can I get for ya?"

"You know, I think I'll have a meatball grinder."

"Okeydoke. That'll be about ten minutes. You want a beer while ya wait?"

Drew shook his head. "We don't drink and drive, Angela," he said as he playfully wagged a finger. She wrote up his order as his eyes carried across the room. "I see some friends in the corner—I think I'll wait over there."

Angela smiled and hustled into the kitchen. Drew approached the table with mixed feelings of curiosity and irritation.

"Well, howdy, Sheriff," the banker joked mockingly.

"We're in New England, Paris," Drew said, dryly. "That's in the Northeast, not the Southwest."

"Ah, shucks, Marshal. I'm just a funnin' ya."

"You men order yet?" Drew asked, ignoring Quicci's stab at humor.

"Just our drinks," Quicci answered, pointing at something over the lieutenant's shoulder.

"Behind you, sir," the waitress said to Drew's back. He stepped aside as she served.

"Ask, and you shall receive," Quicci said as he beamed at the attractive waitress. His smile vanished instantly as he brought his eyes back to Drew. "Care to join us, Lieutenant?"

"No. I just placed a to-go order, but thanks for the invite. I just didn't want to leave without saying hello."

"Tough day at the office, I hear," Quicci commented.

"No. Pretty routine, really."

Quicci turned cold. "Kenealy, you still don't get it, do you? This isn't Detroit. It's Marblehead. And a man being killed in this town will never be considered 'routine' by me or by any other upstanding citizen of this community. I strongly suggest you serve the proprietor of that establishment with an order of seizure until a thorough investigation can be completed. Why, that could take months. I, for one, do not intend to sit on my hands and do nothing while there are actions being taken, by strangers, that run contrary to the common good of the community."

Quicci had gained an audience, which was precisely what he wanted. The curious, mystified group of eavesdroppers developed a fast appetite for more than just their linguine in clam sauce. Drew struggled to manage the rage rising into his throat. He could feel the blood rushing to his head and suspected that his face was similar in shade to the candle burning in the Chianti bottle. The lieutenant's stern glance struck Nate Ingersoll before he leaned in closer to square off with the other man at the table. Drew lowered his voice, shielding as much of the conversation as possible from inquisitive ears.

"Mr. Quicci, I strongly suggest you stand clear of an ongoing investigation before you find yourself faced with an obstruction charge." Drew turned and glowered at Ingersoll. "And you—I will see you in the morning. Perhaps we can spend some time reviewing suspension cases from the last twenty-five years. I'm sure we'll find that a good many of them had to do with leaking information to the press." He looked back at Quicci. "Or worse." There was a gentle firmness in the lieutenant's voice that unnerved the banker. For every man, there's an invisible line in the sand that another man dare not cross, even stumble across, without paying dearly for the trespass. Paris Quicci had just tripped.

Quicci's eyes darted left and right, which he used as a balancing pole in a cerebral high-wire act. He looked across to Ingersoll, who sat with a bowed head, his nose still stinging from the rolled-up newspaper in his master's hand. He searched for the clever retort that he felt was expected. All eyes fell upon him now, and he couldn't afford to be bested by a bald cop who still went to Supercuts. Curious ears waited.

"Of course, Lieutenant, you are correct. I was merely commenting on the information that I thought was already verified and of public knowledge. If I'm not in full possession of the facts, perhaps I should, in the future, consider the source. As you know, I would never interfere with an investigation. As a matter of fact, I would consider it a personal favor if you would feel free to call upon me if there is anything I could do in the way of assisting your efforts."

Nate Ingersoll looked on in perfect perplexity; his eyes wide, mouth open, and nose whistling, he wondered who might help him take the knife out of his back. Quicci flashed an innocent smile and brought his wineglass up to his face. With a swirl of the wine, a dreamy ecstasy bathed his features as the silky bouquet tripped over his olfactory sense receptors. He sipped smoothly, savoring the taste, and slowly brought his glass to rest on the linen cloth. "Mmm." He turned the bottle that sat before him and read the label. He looked up at Drew. "It was a *very* good year. Are you sure you won't join us?" Drew straightened up and stepped back from the table. It was tiring listening to the man, and the day had been long enough. "Have a good night, gentlemen." Ingersoll managed to raise a fleshy hand in a modest wave. The banker was able to spare a slight nod, almost as an afterthought.

Angela saw the lieutenant coming and met him at the register with his sandwich. He pulled small bills and some loose change out of his front pants pocket and counted out five dollars and thirty-seven cents. "Try to have a nice evening, Drew," the waitress said, flashing a warm smile. Drew tendered a self-deprecating smirk, now certain that the regrettable conversation was heard by all, and tightened the rolled end of the brown paper bag. He turned to leave and stood face-to-face with Sal Cummings, a shop owner down on Washington Street. "You have a good weekend, now, Drew."

"Thanks, Sal, you too."

"Lieutenant, you have a wonderful evening, sir," said Ted MacLemore, home on leave from the US Coast Guard.

"Thanks, Teddy. How are things in the Department of Transportation?"

"Just fine, sir."

"Attaboy."

"Hey, have a good one there, Drew."

"Thanks, Tank," he said, looking up at the three-hundred-pounder. "You go easy tonight, huh, no trouble?"

"I'll have two Diet Cokes and then have 'em throw me out," Tank said with a broad grin. It was an ongoing joke. Tank Zyrowski was an aging biker whose appearance was in stark contrast to his personality. He was heavily tattooed and worked on boat engines at the marina, but he was also a teetotaler who grew roses in the privacy of his backyard. Anyone who knew him could tell you that he didn't do drugs or drink alcohol, but only a few, including Drew Kenealy, could tell you about the roses. Tank appreciated Drew's discretion. Drew appreciated that Tank wouldn't tolerate any unsavory elements down at the marina. It was like having a guard dog that you didn't have to chain up. Not that any chain would be able to hold Tank.

"Looks like you got a wait ahead of you, Tank."

"Angela said about twenty minutes."

"Gettin' busy," Drew agreed.

"Hey," Tank said with a shrug. "Rinaldo's is a good place."

"You're right there, Big Z." Drew smiled as he walked out the door.

Rinaldo's was a *really* good place.

* * *

He hung his ring of keys on the key rack next to the doorjamb. Walking into the small kitchen, he set the grinder down on the retro 1950s Formica table and pulled a can of Diet Pepsi from the Frigidaire. Drew grabbed a napkin from the holder on the center of the red cracked-ice tabletop and sat down to feast on Rinaldo's fine cuisine. He wasn't sure if it was because he was so hungry or if it was just another attempt to be rid of the long day, but the sandwich, and the Pepsi, went down in record time. He sat back and let the last of the meal hit the floor of his stomach before allowing the extra air to escape with a roaring belch. Belching was one of the few privileges of living the life of a lonely man. Besides, Drew thought, in some lands, it would have been an insult to the cook if he hadn't done so.

Although his day had been long and had officially come to a close, Drew remained restless and paced about the living space of his small bungalow, unable to clear his mind. He stepped outside through the sliding glass door of his living room to get a breath of clean summer air. What a difference from the storm that had ripped through the town last night. The calling card of the severe weather was still strewn about his yard. He turned to face the eastern horizon and saw the familiar glow of the Marblehead Harbor lights. *The little town must be jumping tonight.* It was a happy time for the residents. Preparations for the Fourth of July weekend always carried a promise of fun times to come. The night sky was much darker just north of town, and he couldn't help but notice that it was the sky that hung above Stonecroft Inn. That northern sky spoke of darker promises and gloomier times ahead.

Drew was struck by a sudden need to call the folks at the inn. Something was amiss. He had seen it in the eyes of the owner and his friend. And yet with all the experience he had as a cop, he still couldn't put his finger on what it was. What he had come across that day did not make any sense at all. *How could someone come out of nowhere, commit this one bizarre act, and then leave? It's in a small nook, in an out-of-the-way place. And yet, somebody shows up out of the blue and does a chisel job on Vince LaCava's teeth?*

A question popped into his head that made him wince. *Why didn't I think to ask this earlier?* He was angry with himself for the oversight, especially considering the town he lived in. He put himself back on the clock, ducked into the house, and grabbed the cordless phone out of its cradle. He walked back outside while he punched in the number. He looked to the sky over Stonecroft as he listened to it ring, somehow feeling more connected.

"C'mon, c'mon, pick up." He swatted a mosquito on the back of his neck that, from a look at his hand, had already left him a pint shy. "Oh, hello, Mr. Stone? Lieutenant Drew, Marblehead police. How are things going?"

After hearing Tom's answer, he continued, "Good, I'm glad to hear that. Listen, I've got a question that I don't believe I asked you today. Have you been monitoring the boat traffic off your property?"

". . . Really? Anything closer than that? Anybody try to tie up to your dock?"

". . . OK, well, just keep an eye on it."

". . . No, not really. If they did, it would make for a difficult means of escape. It's a relatively slow mode of travel, and you remain exposed at all times. Hell, at low tide, you could walk across to Brown's Island—not a safe place for most boat traffic. It's just that your location makes for an unlikely stop for a vagrant."

". . . Right."

". . . Well, we already had Mr. LaCava's and Mr. Goddard's prints. And we have yours from when you applied for your license to operate the inn. We did the field prints on the Breans today, so we'll have to compare those five sets with the ones we dusted."

". . . Yes, I do. Because unless Mr. LaCava was smoking Mr. Brean's pipe while doing masonry work on a high ladder, someone else got it from inside the house. And because no valuables were taken, it seems unlikely that we're dealing with a professional thief who would have the presence of mind to wipe off his own prints."

. . . Well, I hope to God we do. Because if it turns out that there are no other prints, we'll have to go with what we have. And you and the Breans were away all day, with receipts and witnesses verifying your whereabouts, and Mr. LaCava is dead. And that leaves—"

. . . No, I don't believe so either."

. . . Yes, Mr. Goddard's a very good man."

. . . It would ruin him in this town."

. . . Neither do I. Listen, can you think of anyone else who might have been there?"

. . . Mr. Stone?"

. . . Mr. Stone, are you still there?"

. . . Oh, I thought I lost you for a minute."

. . . Tomorrow night? Nothing."

. . . Yeah, sure, that sounds good. Thank you."

. . . OK. Great. Can I bring something?"

. . . All right. I'll see you at six o'clock sharp. Thanks again, Mr. Stone."

. . . OK. Tom it is."

When Drew hung up, he realized he still had no answers, and it seemed none were likely to be forthcoming. His attack-from-the-sea theory didn't seem to hold water. Nothing was adding up, and Drew hated it when good math went bad. The offense was so minimal in its action yet so profound in its obscenity that it gnawed at him like the mosquito that was still stuck to the back of his neck. He couldn't get Stonecroft Inn out of his mind. Now he had an invitation. It had not been unlike a number of other murder scenes, where he had the sense that the killer was still there, in the next room or around the next corner. It wasn't Tom Stone or the Breans—he knew that for sure. Nor did he suspect Mr. Goddard of having committed that foul act any more than he did the pope. Although, Drew thought, he couldn't say for sure where the pope was earlier in the day either.

That was enough for one day, he decided. He was hot and sticky, and his neck was bleeding. Drew walked into the bathroom and turned on the shower. He looked at himself in the mirror. *Not too bad. I still got the build, if not the hair.* He smiled into the looking glass. *Good teeth too.* Drew hopped into the shower and soon had rid himself of the day's road dust. He tossed on a Boston Red Sox T-shirt and some plaid gabardine shorts. Comfort, not style, was king in the inner sanctum of Drew Kenealy.

Walking through the house, he opened all the windows to allow the stale air to refresh itself. His mood lightened as a slight breeze broke through the stillness around him. He cracked open the Frigidaire, grabbed the wine bottle by its long neck, and pulled it out. Reaching up to the shelf above the sink, Drew pulled down a tall juice glass and poured generously from the bottle. The white zinfandel shimmered pink in the crystal glass. *White* zinfandel? He wondered if Paris Quicci would consider it a culinary faux pas that he was drinking white wine when he'd had a meatball grinder for dinner. *What the hell—it's pink, anyway.* He spied the small white sticker on the side of the bottle neck. *Oh yes,* Drew determined, *Quicci would most certainly consider it a faux pas, not because of the color but because it cost three dollars and twenty-nine cents a bottle.*

Drew started humming to himself and walked over to the stereo to indulge in the pleasure of his most guarded secret. Tank had his roses. Drew had Sinatra. It wasn't that he was ashamed of Ol' Blue Eyes. How could he be? It was just something of himself that he kept private, a hand he played very close to the vest.

He sat back with his feet up on his Barcalounger and sipped his pink wine while Frank sang to lovers everywhere. He hoisted his drink high in the air, condensation beading stubbornly on the plain glass, and released his index finger to point to the sky, joining Frank in song about flying to the moon.

A warm buzz hummed throughout his body as the zinfandel took root. It would be a relaxing night, Drew decided—a few glasses of wine and an endless collection of Frank's best. Drew downed the last drop in the glass and was heading for his first refill and, although he disagreed with the Chairman of the Board about the effects of champagne, sang along just the same.

After his second glass, Drew danced with his imaginary lover, left hand extended up just below shoulder height, the other softly cradling her warm and delicate hand in his. Then a gentle, guiding hand placed seductively at the small of her back, leading her gracefully across the living room floor to the music of the master. Drew smiled as he tripped the light fantastic with the grace of Astaire. To the strains of one of his favorites, Drew and his partner moved slowly in their romantic embrace as Frank sang about lovers in the night. Drew grew sad as the band struck the final notes and he watched his dance partner return to her seat in the black void of reality; he shuffled off to the kitchen for yet another glass.

Standing at the counter next to the Frigidaire, he matched Frank heartache for heartache as he cleaned up after a sloppy pour. Depressing the foot pedal to flip up the lid of the polished-aluminum waste can, Drew dropped the saturated paper towels in the bin and sniffed his hand. His fingertips ripe with the smell of cheap wine, he gave them a quick rinse at the kitchen faucet and wiped them absentmindedly on his shirt. With rapidly diminishing hand-eye coordination, Drew almost spilled his final glass as well when he and Frank finished an emotional duet. It was a song about life and how sweet it can be at any age. As sweet as wine from the first to the very last drop. The song always made Drew a little misty, serving as a reminder of the all-too-fleeting moment that is life.

Walking a crooked line to the living room, Drew stopped at the small fireplace, picked up the picture sitting on the mantel, and carried it back with him to the couch. He looked at the photo, which had been framed twenty years ago. How young they looked on their wedding day. Drew brushed the dust off the glass to see his bride more clearly. It was time for Frank's solo. But the crooner sang a song of love and loneliness that struck too close to home. A song that promised to find him one day. When he was alone. When he was down. And tonight, it had kept its promise.

Drew had just enough time to remember all the wonderful days, and nights, he had spent with the woman in the picture before his eyes welled up with tears and were of no further use for seeing. So he cried with his eyes, and saw with his heart, all the things he used to have that were gone forever.

CHAPTER EIGHT

R. A. Putnam

Sunday, June 20, 1999

"What kind of art gallery is called the Cat and the Cauldron?" Tom asked as he and Jake made their way down Pickering Wharf in Salem. The fast-rising heat of the morning foretold a barnburner of a day ahead.

"Brace yourself, slick. I don't think the place we're going is an art gallery at all. I'll bet it's a—" Jake stopped short when he saw the name on the door of the two-story brick building. "Ah, here we are now."

"Wait a minute," Tom said with a restraining hand on Jake's elbow. "Finish your sentence. What kind of place do you think this is?" Jake smiled and opened the door.

A friendly face peered around a glass cabinet with the tinkling of the overhanging doorbell. "Hi, welcome to the Cat and the Cauldron. I'm Stacy." A young girl, maybe twenty, dressed in crisp white jeans and a sky-blue cotton blouse, stepped up to greet them. Her tight blonde curls bounced with every step she took. The welcome was warm, and the air was cool. A very pleasant welcome, indeed. "Is there anything special you're looking for?"

"Hi," Tom said, looking about at items that were totally foreign to him. "I hope we're in the right place. I'm looking for Mr. R. A. Putnam. I was told he worked here."

"Mr. Putnam?" she asked. "Excuse me for just a minute. I think I know someone who can help you." Stacy wore a curious grin as she disappeared behind the purple curtain that led to a back room. With her departure, the two looked around the store, pricing items they had never seen before.

"Hey, Tom," Jake queried, "how much did *your* 'ritual dagger' cost you? It was under fifty bucks, wasn't it?" The question drew Tom over to the display case to view the object for himself.

"Wow, that's cool," Tom said, peering into the glass cabinet. "So what do you think they use this for, like, animal sacrifices?"

"Yeah, probably," Jake replied as he shared in the ogling of the dagger. "Maybe even human sacrifices too. Although I doubt they'd ever have an interest in dulling their blade on your scurvy ass."

Amid the adolescent giggling, they didn't notice her enter the room.

"No dagger is allowed to shed the blood of a living creature. Not man. Not animal."

The new voice startled them, and both men straightened up as if they'd just been found out by the stern school headmaster.

"Huh?" Tom muttered.

Jake eyed him. "Good one, Tom."

"There are two rules in modern-day witchcraft—commandments, if you wish. The first is 'Do no harm to any living thing.' The second is 'Anything you do, good or bad, will return to you threefold.' Quite an incentive for clean living, wouldn't you say?"

It was hard for Tom to focus on what she was saying. With jet-black hair that cascaded over her shoulders and a soft gentleness in her deep-brown eyes, Tom didn't know whether to look or listen. It seemed, at least for the moment, that he was incapable of doing both at the same time.

"Yeah, uh, hi. We're here to see R. A. Putnam? I'm Tom Stone, this is, um . . . uh . . ."

Jake saw Tom struggling to remember his name. He shook his head but couldn't completely fault his friend under the circumstances. "Jake Brean," he said to assist the mumbling Mr. Stone.

"Hello. Nice to meet you both. I'm Rebecca Putnam."

"Huh?"

"Good one, Jake," Tom whispered, happy to use Jake's own line against him.

"What can I do for you?"

"Well, we were up in Rockport yesterday," Tom explained, "and we bought a painting from Maggie's of Chatham. Do you know the place I'm talking about?"

"Sure, they carry a number of my works there," she said as a smiling young couple entered the store and began to look around, with Stacy coming up front to greet them. "But if there's a problem with it, you probably need to speak to Maggie about it. They were all in perfect shape when I delivered them."

"Oh, no. There's no problem with the painting," Jake assured her. "It's just that we'd like to talk to you about it. Maybe get a little background on it."

She studied the men with a gleam of curiosity in her eye. "Where do you live?"

"I just bought a place on Marblehead, at the far end of town. It looks out onto Doliber's Cove and Brown's Island. I'm going to open it up as a bed-and-breakfast."

"I know the place," Rebecca said, then stared at Tom in silent deliberation long enough to make him uncomfortable. "Let's sit down," she finally suggested. "Why don't you come this way. We can talk with a little more privacy."

They followed her to the back of the large store, watching her hourglass figure glide beneath the full-length purple chiffon dress. She brought them through a heavily beaded doorway and into a room of pink and red with trace elements of black. She took a seat on one side of a small table, and Tom and Jake sat down across from her. The table was clear, save for the white tablecloth with pink flowers, and left the impression that what might normally be displayed there lay hidden away, just out of sight. Rebecca asked the first question.

"You bought *The First Mate*, didn't you?"

"How did you know?"

She studied the two men across from her and fixed on Tom. She looked so deeply into his eyes that he felt as though she was doing a retinal scan. She said nothing, but reached out and grabbed his left hand, and with her index finger, she traced along the creases in his palm. Tom shot a wide-eyed plea for help over at Jake, who, transfixed by the woman, didn't notice.

Rebecca then turned to Jake and looked deeply into his eyes as well. Without prompting, Jake thrust his left hand, palm up, toward her for inspection. The trace of a smile curled the corners of her mouth. She took a quick glance at his palm, gave it two quick, gentle pats, and sat back in her chair. Having drawn a favorable conclusion about her two guests, she took a deep breath and explained, "Years ago, I was on Brown's Island, just across from the property you now own. That's where I saw him."

"Whoa. Wait. What d'ya mean?" Jake asked. "You mean to say you actually saw this guy?"

"Let me give you a little more background," she said, wanting to keep things in their proper order. "First of all, as you probably know, I'm a practicing witch." Jake nodded his head, accepting what he already knew, but Rebecca caught wind of Tom's skepticism in the way his body stiffened as he sat back in his chair. "I'm what's called a 'solitary,'" she clarified. "That is, I don't belong to a coven. I am a practitioner of the craft of the Cabot tradition. The tradition started by Laurie Cabot."

"The official witch of Salem," Jake informed his silent partner, who offered only a blank stare in return.

Rebecca smiled thinly at the reference noted by the outsider, a common connection made by those who sought to link their two worlds.

"Most witches are solitaries; it's really just a matter of choice and practicality. We practice daily devotions, very similar to the daily prayers of Christians, Jews, and others. We pray to the Goddess to bring good to others as well as to ourselves." She studied the two men as she spoke, discerning whether it was worthwhile to spend time explaining to them the ways of her world. She looked deep into them, behind their eyes, and saw their struggle. Feeling she was in the company of good intentions, she decided to continue.

"You might hear a witch talk about 'drawing down the moon.' We draw power from the moon. The dagger you were looking at out front in the store, for example, would be used in a ceremony under a full moon, where pure fresh water would be poured into a chalice, and the full moon would be reflected on its liquid surface. Then, the blade of the dagger would be introduced into the chalice to 'split' the water, creating ripples and magnifying the reflection of the moon's light. We become closer to the source of all life in the light of the full moon. *That* is what the dagger is used for." She made the point clear.

"It was an occasion such as this that I was on Brown's Island. It was a beautiful night. So clear. So many stars to behold. The moon was bright and full. I had been sailing with a close friend that evening, and we dropped anchor just off the shore. I decided I would perform my devotions to the Goddess there, my body serving as the dagger, splitting the water in the chalice that was Doliber's Cove."

Jake glanced over at Tom, expecting to see the look you might get from a straight guy who just realized he walked into a gay bar. Instead, Tom had moved forward in his chair, elbows resting on his knees, and was hanging on every word spilling from the lips of this heavenly witch.

"Well, the night had been beautiful," Rebecca said, remembering. "And I swam to the shore of Brown's Island. I had just finished my devotions when I entered what we call alpha, or a trance state. In front of me, from the mouth of Doliber's Cove, sailed a ship from the early days. From the darkest days of the witch, the days of persecution," she clarified. "The ship ran in front of me, and the sailor on the deck stood there and stared at me as he passed. There was a hate in his eyes that I didn't understand. Then, I watched as the ship glided by."

Tom's eyes widened. "I'll bet that shook you up."

"Not at first. I watched with a sort of detached interest, as if there was a protective veil between us and he couldn't touch me. But then, after the ship sailed by, its wake rolled up onto the shore of the island and broke at my feet."

"You mean to say it was real?" Jake asked incredulously. Rebecca shrugged, unable to either confirm or deny.

"Where did the ship go then?" Tom asked, the alarm poorly concealed in his voice.

"It sailed toward your house and faded into the night."

Tom and Jake locked eyes.

Rebecca read faces as easily as she read palms. "You've seen him, haven't you?"

"What? No," Tom objected. "Are you serious?"

She said nothing. She waited, allowing Tom Stone's conscience and need to reveal themselves. Tom shifted uncomfortably in his chair.

"We don't really know what we saw," he soon confessed. "It seemed more like an impression than anything else. A few nights ago, during the storm, there was a flash of lightning. And for an instant, there was someone else in the room with us, but no one really got a good look at him. But somehow, I know it was him." Tom looked to Jake for support.

"It sounds stupid, but, yeah, it was him," Jake said. "That's how we all recognized him."

"All? There was someone else there too?"

"Yes, my wife was also there. You see, Tom and I met years ago when we were both respiratory therapists in the navy. We've been friends ever since, so my wife and I wanted to be here and help him get his new business off the ground."

"I'm not married," Tom interjected with a regrettable air of desperation. Jake winced in pain for his friend. Rebecca looked at

Tom for a moment, unsure how to field the remark. She chose the high road and offered an interested nod, suggesting that she might want to come back to that another time, but now was not that time.

"Where is your wife today? If you don't mind my asking?"

"No, not at all. She's back at the inn, doing some gardening, planting some flowers. You know."

"Ah, I see." She smiled. "Witches make her nervous," she said in good-natured amusement. Jake looked over at Tom, whose face was still a deep red.

"Yeah, well, apparently she's not alone."

Tom shot Jake a friendly warning glare.

"Tom, how long have you lived in the house?"

"Well, I'd been staying next door at Bishop's for the past few weeks until the contractors were finished with the major work on the suites upstairs, but I moved into the house a few days ago to start work on the small finishing jobs." Tom felt a welcome coolness flow over his face as the blood slowly drained from his cheeks.

"And when was the first time you noticed any disturbance?"

Tom glanced up at the ceiling, piecing the days together. "Well, I'd have to say it was the window breaking, and that was"—he looked at Jake—"what, three days ago?"

"Four," Jake corrected.

"That's right, four days ago."

"Was something thrown through the window?"

"No, that's the weird part," Tom said excitedly. "It just splintered into a bunch of pieces, but it didn't break apart."

Rebecca nodded as she started piecing the facts together. She stood and excused herself. The men looked on admiringly as she passed through the beaded door. She was gone only long enough for

Jake to giggle freely over Tom's stab at romance. "Damn, Stone, you're one smooth-talkin' sonuvabitch." Tom's shoulders were still heaving in self-deprecating laughter when she returned.

"Ah, good," she said, smiling. "Laughter is the spirit singing." She sat back down and pointed to the chart she held in her hand.

"Here's a chart of the phases of the moon. The last new moon was on the thirteenth of this month. That was last Sunday, and you moved in the following day. After a new moon, the moon starts waxing, becoming more visible, seeming to grow from the right side to the left, then fading, or waning, until there is no moon visible at all, or as it's called, the new moon."

"That's kind of strange, don't you think?" Jake suggested. "Shouldn't that be called the 'old' moon instead of the 'new' moon?"

"Your focus is on the end, or death, of the moon. Think of it as the beginning, the period of rebirth. Then you can see it as the 'new' moon."

Jake shrugged. *Whatever.*

"My concern, based on what I experienced myself of this being, is that he will increase his presence with the growing phases of the moon. When I saw him, the moon was full. He was vibrant, strong, and filled with hate."

"And apparently driving his boat over to your place, slick," Jake added needlessly, glancing at his friend.

"So what happens on the full moon?" There was no humor in Tom's voice. "Is he going to show up all pissed off again?"

"I don't know," she replied. "And what do you mean, again?"

Tom reviewed the appearance of the visitor of two nights previous, as well as the sad occurrence involving the death of Vince LaCava. Neither of the men was surprised that she had already heard of the latter incident; in these small towns, news traveled faster than a witch on a broomstick. To Tom, Rebecca seemed fascinated by the apparition he had seen. To Jake, she seemed frightened.

She took a moment when Tom had finished his story and lit a stick of incense. The waving stream of smoke rolled up into the air, touching all in the room with a gentle and vaguely familiar aroma. Rebecca didn't say what the name of it was, and neither Tom nor Jake cared enough to ask.

"Tom, all I can tell you is what I received when his existence was made known to me in the power of the full moon. He was filled with hate and sailed under the black flag. That's all I know because that's all I was shown. I painted it and then sold it immediately to rid my mind of the stench of his memory. Perhaps I should have burned it," she added thoughtfully.

"What do you mean when you say he sailed under the black flag?" Jake inquired.

"I mean he was a pirate. The Jolly Roger, or whatever they call those things, flew above him on the ship."

A glimmer of hope sparked the fire in Tom's heart.

"Well, if you know he was a pirate, do you know his name? Or what he did?"

"No, I'm sorry," Rebecca said, shaking her head. "I've told you all I know. I called it *The First Mate* because he seemed too mean to be a captain. I'm not sure if that makes any sense at all." She smiled sheepishly, further endearing herself to the already-bewitched Tom Stone.

"I know what you mean. He seems to be continuing to move up in rank. Like he still has something to prove," Tom said.

"Exactly," Rebecca agreed.

"Well, listen," Jake said, suddenly anxious to leave, "thanks for all your help. Can I get a business card from you? We'll keep you posted."

Tom saw that there was little else to learn from the comely witch, not that they had gleaned much that could help them, anyway, outside of hearing what her own experience had been. But if nothing else, Tom thought, it was nice of her to have shared her time with them. Rebecca stood up and tugged lightly on her dress, smoothing out the wrinkles and revealing beauty in a form no fabric could disguise. Tom hung back a bit, allowing Jake to grab a business card, say his goodbyes, and leave.

"Let me give you my phone number in case you can think of anything else." Tom scribbled the number on a small scrap of paper. He felt a warm glow emanate from her soft brown eyes as he handed her the paper, and he felt as clumsy as he did in the fourth grade when he had passed his first note to a girl. He didn't want to let go of the moment, but the moment left. "I appreciate your time," was all he could say.

"Not at all," Rebecca answered, then lowered her voice. "You should probably go straight home. I'm sure your friend's wife is fine, but I think it would be wise for no one to be left alone in the house anymore, especially through the waxing of the moon."

The thought spun through Tom's mind, a foreign notion at first. Then it clicked.

"Damn."

Tom had to jog to catch up with Jake, who was moving at a quick pace to where the car was parked on Derby Street. He knew from the purpose in Jake's step that he need not remind him that Marie might be in some danger. Jake was unlocking the car by the time Tom caught up with him, and the Bonneville was already moving when the passenger door was closed.

"Do you think she was for real?" Tom asked in an attempt to arrest the rising tension.

"Well," Jake started, trying to sound as relaxed as possible, "she certainly seems to have a flair for the dramatic. But she said some things that really hit home, didn't she?"

Tom stared out at the road ahead of them and considered all she had said.

"Yeah, she did."

"But do you know the part that scared me?"

Tom just looked at Jake and waited for him to answer his own question.

"When she said the wake of the ship broke on the shore at her feet. Ghosts don't do that sort of thing. If she was telling the truth, and I can't see why she would make it up, that ship was really there."

"Yeah, then he sailed it right into my house."

"Where Marie is now," her husband added as the tension began to unfurl. "Alone."

The traffic was light on the hot summer day, and the car rolled down Lafayette Street toward Marblehead with a foot rarely touching its brake pedal. It would be the next couple of miles through the narrow, crowded streets of old Marblehead that would slow them down. But they'd be there soon. *Nothing to worry about,* Jake told himself.

* * *

Marie dabbed the moisture from her brow with the back of her brown jersey gardening glove. She looked at the ground she had tended for the better part of the day with a critical eye. The deep-pink rambling roses at the corners of the house bookended half a

150

dozen floribundas and hybrid tea roses of red, yellow, and peach. Liking what she saw with the roses in the garden at the front of the house, she wondered about adding some more at the base of the stone wall that separated the grounds from Doliber's Cove. *Maybe some miniature roses would look good there,* she thought. *Put some color at the base of the wall but not detract from the look of the solid, handsome structure itself.*

Marie moved along the gravel walkway at the edge of the garden, considering her options, when she stopped to free a pebble from her light canvas sneaker. Looking back at the wavy gravel path, she was reminded of the smooth, uniform stones she saw stacked up at the end of the driveway. She slipped her shoe back on and walked to the end of the drive, gravel crunching underfoot. Just inside the stone wall that edged the road, Marie saw the stack of flat, gray slate. Inspired, she picked up the two-foot-by-two-foot stone and carried it ponderously back to the path in front of the house. The stones were much heavier than they appeared at first glance, and Marie wondered if she ought to wait for four strong arms to return home.

Impatience casting the deciding vote, she forged ahead and centered the stone in the path, smoothing the gravel out as evenly as possible with her hand. She stepped back to eye her new creation; she liked it but thought the use of a rake might be the best way to level out the entire path.

Returning from the small toolshed with rake in hand, Marie did some quick figuring. She had counted an even dozen stones. So with each stone being about two feet by two feet, and with fifty feet of path, she could space them two feet apart. *Should be perfect.* Marie loved the simplicity of the math. Uncommon these days. The smile on her face disappeared in a haze of bewilderment as she came around to see four slate stones sitting in a smooth gravel path. Sudden movement caught her eye, and her head snapped up to the roadside wall to see a young boy carrying another stone toward her. The boy paid her no attention. He approached the path and, without stepping on the gravel itself, lowered the stone to the center of the walkway. He stood up, swiped the long blond hair away from his eyes, and looked at what he had done. Then he turned and walked back toward the road.

Marie watched the boy as he walked away, then studied the path in front of her. The distance and placement of the stones appeared to be perfect. The gravel path had been leveled and lay as flat as the water of Doliber's Cove. She walked along the edge, amazed that this boy could smooth out the entire path so quickly and with no tool to help. Marie turned around as she heard him walking across the driveway. As he set the sixth stone down, Marie noticed that he wore no shoes. The dirt that clung to his feet suggested he had not bathed in a very long time. From what she could tell from the glimpses she caught of his face, the boy was young, probably between ten and twelve years old. But tall for his age—and apparently very shy.

"Thank you," Marie said, trying to break the ice. The boy looked up at Marie, a spark of surprise reflected in his striking blue eyes, as if he had not expected the woman to speak to him. He returned a coy smile and quickened his pace back to the diminishing pile of rock. Marie noticed his clothes as he retreated to grab another stone. So baggy, so dirty. So old. But the sun shone brightly on the towheaded boy, and his smile broadened as he returned and saw Marie smiling back at him. *He looks like he might be hungry,* Marie thought. She reached into the front pockets of her shorts, hoping to find a few dollars she might be able to pay him. Empty.

"Are you hungry? When we're done here, would you like to come inside and have something to eat?" The boy set the seventh stone down. He looked at the house. He then turned his gaze back to Marie and gave a slow, deliberate nod. *Ah, he is hungry,* she thought, *poor thing.* She smiled, and the boy returned for the eighth stone. He carried it back firmly against his breast. Marie's heart went out to the boy, as it was apparent his arms were getting tired. But he seemed intent on pleasing Marie and never slowed his pace. The thought came to her that the boy could just be lonely, and she felt a pang of sadness in her heart. Lugging heavy stones in the hot sun to make her happy seemed to be this young boy's plea for love and attention.

The smile on Marie's face broadened as the boy carried the eleventh stone on his head. Barely touching it with his hands, he enjoyed a boy's moment, performing a balancing act as he walked across the yard. Marie surveyed the path in front of him, making sure it was clear. She didn't want her little helper to take a tumble and get hurt. The gravel at the end of the path, right in front of one of the rambling rosebushes, looked a little lumpy. After the boy set down number eleven and went to get the last stone, Marie walked to the end of the path and knelt down to smooth the uneven ground.

With the wet heat of the day pouring over her, Marie again wiped the beads of perspiration from her forehead. She shook her head when she thought of how the boy had been able to carry all those heavy stones without so much as even getting a little red in the face. In fact, it occurred to Marie, he seemed completely unaffected by the heat. *Oh, to be that young again.*

With her back to the road, Marie did not see the boy pick up the last piece of slate. He lifted the stone high above his head, the smile gone from his face, and with a measured tread, walked toward the gravel path where Marie worked, preparing the ground for the last stone. The spark in the pale-blue eyes faded as he approached the path and his intended mark. The grass, thick and warm below his cold bare feet, ensured the stealth of his movements and allowed him to arrive unnoticed, until he stood directly behind her. He stared down at Marie, who remained on one knee over the gravel path. He looked up at the slab above his head and repositioned his hands before he let loose the stone.

The sound of a honking horn startled Marie, and she turned with a jump. The rock hit the center of the path with a loud thump, spraying her ankles benignly with gravel. Marie smiled at her husband as he pulled in the driveway, her hand still on her chest from the start he gave her with the horn. "Here's my husband and Mr. Stone," Marie said as she turned to the boy. Her eyes darted to and fro, traversing the yard. The boy was gone.

"Hi, hon, how ya doin'?" Jake asked from the window in a casual tone, cloaking his evaporating anxiety. Tom appeared nonchalant at his side, although breathing much easier himself. Jake turned off the ignition and moved from the comfort of the air-conditioned car.

"Hey, Marie, those colors are really something," Tom said, coming around the front of the car to better see the fruits of Marie's labor.

"Hi, guys." She looked behind her at the Technicolor display. "Yeah, thanks. I think we've got a good color mix going," Marie said, somewhat subdued, still confused as to the whereabouts of her little helper. "I'll put in some more ground cover, along with a few perennials here and there, but you don't want to crowd them. They'll continue to grow out over the next few years," she said with her hands on her hips, still surveying her handiwork.

Jake walked over to his wife and kissed her with the firm tenderness of a happy man. "You look great," he said to the pretty gardener. Marie smiled but was a little mystified as to where the compliment and the big kiss came from. "Thanks, but I'm kind of a mess," she replied, now looking at Jake with an air of suspicion. But he just smiled back at her.

"Go clean up," he said. "We've got a lot to tell you."

"OK." Marie took off her gloves and headed into the house with Jake close on her heels, leaving Tom to gaze in amazement at his colorful new front yard.

"So how was your day?" Jake asked, joyfully immersed in the banality of the conversation.

"Oh, it was fine," Marie answered. "I met the nicest little boy."

CHAPTER NINE
The Blood Quest

June 1697

Clear blue water and white-sand beaches were not what made the Bahamas a favorite retreat for the Brethren of the Coast. "Drinkin' and whorin', that's all there is to do here, lads," Robert Kent said to Tobias and Israel as the islands came into view. Even Doolin Pike, who ambled by as Kent was speaking, grunted his assent, causing all three to stop and reflect on the historic moment.

Israel turned toward Kent but couldn't bring himself to look him in the eye. "What, uh, I mean to ask what kind of, uh, well, are there different kinds of . . . ?" Israel's words trailed off into the warm salt air.

"What kind of what?" Kent asked. "Whores? By God, man, come out and say it."

Israel stood staring at the deck, shifting his weight from foot to foot, and wondered if this would be a good time to kill himself.

Tobias did all he could to stifle a laugh, and Israel's bronzed face turned a smoky purple.

Kent wasn't about to let Israel off the hook. "You tellin' me, man, that you never had no whore ever take to tuggin' on your lanyard?"

Israel's eyes grew wide with imagination. A strange, unfamiliar mixture of horror and intrigue lay hold to his mind. Israel looked up. *How did the island get so close?*

Israel came back around with a heavy slap on the back from the strong Jamaican. "Israel, you can have any color girl you want. You want white? You can have it. You want mulatto? You can have that too. You want negro? Yes, you can have this also." Israel considered the possibilities. They seemed limitless. His mind wandered, taking him through warm days, and even warmer nights, with women as varied as the colors of the garments in their oaken battle chest. He saw himself lying on a soft bed of woven palm leaves. The whores of the island would bring him barbecue meat, the way Diego Garcia made it. They would serve him strong drinks in real silver cups. Then they would come to him at night and give him all he ever wanted.

Robert Kent broke into Israel's daydream with alarm. "By God, man, stow your cutlass till you be ready for battle! You be too long at sea for the young rover that you be."

Tobias instinctively jumped back as he, too, noticed Israel's excitement. The two shared a riotous laugh at Israel's expense. Feeling the blood leave his loins and rush back up into his face, Israel went to the rail to conceal his condition. As embarrassed as he was, he looked beyond the moment, toward the island in the closing distance. He instinctively sniffed the air. Yes, Israel fancied, the possibilities were limitless.

Jack Trenton peered through his spyglass as he stood on the fo'c'sle, observing the activities of Nassau's harbor. The *Bristol Galley* had dropped anchor, and Trenton would let her keel swing with the tide before lowering the longboat. Jim Barry stood just aft of Trenton, close enough to hear a groan of concern escape the captain's throat.

"Problem, sir?" Barry inquired.

Trenton dropped the glass from his eye and considered the view in true distance. He took a deep breath of warm Bahamian air and released it before answering. He handed Jim Barry the glass without turning. "Do you recognize that sloop, Mr. Barry?" The first mate searched the harbor through the lens and locked onto a familiar sight.

"It's the *Sangre Busca*," Barry said, now appreciating the captain's anxiety. "Jose Blanco's vessel."

"Aye, she's ten guns, with another two on swivel fore and aft. I wouldn't mind finding her out in the open where we could send her to the bottom, but on land . . ." Trenton shook his head.

Robert Kent came up the fo'c'sle ladder and joined the two. "Ready to lower away the longboat, sir." Kent stood facing the backs of his two superiors as they continued to ignore him. He waited with growing curiosity and tried to determine what was so fascinating out in the harbor as to render the captain and first mate both deaf and dumb. Kent turned around and saw a dozen shipmates motioning for him to secure the order to lower away. *Drinkin' an' whorin', that's what they be thinkin'.* He hesitated to break in on what was obviously a point of interest to the captain and the first mate. For the life of him, he couldn't see what was of such wonder in the sleepy harbor. "Ahem," Kent ventured out once more. "Ready for your order to lower away the longboats, Captain." Although the captain remained lost in his thoughts, Barry turned around and told a story with raised eyebrows. The dawn of understanding spread across Kent's face. "Who?"

"Blanco," Barry said solemnly. Kent's eyes narrowed with indignation.

"By God, man, what's that bloody cutthroat doin' here?" Kent peered out into the harbor with naked eyes. He turned around quickly and scanned the deck for the cook.

"Does Garcia know?"

"No one outside this small circle knows at this time, Kent," Captain Trenton replied and turned to both men in consultation. "I believe it would be best to determine what Captain Blanco's intentions are before we become too enthralled with the many amusements of New Providence, don't you agree, Mr. Barry?"

"Aye, Captain. There'll be no rum on the lips of the *Bristol Galley* till we've put Beelzebub astern of us."

"Cap'n," Kent spewed excitedly, "let's weigh anchor and drop in on her now. A devil of a broadside and we put her on the bottom. They're sure to make for land in the longboats, an' then we'll have 'em all."

The captain raised a steadying hand. As much as he admired Kent's plan, he knew it to be suicide. "As soon as we fire a single round from our guns, we become the enemy of all here. They are, unfortunately, protected, as are we," Trenton said. He knew he was right, but it gnawed at him just the same. "However," he added, "if they take action against us, we could not but defend ourselves." Trenton turned away and became silent, allowing his words to take root in the minds of his subordinates.

"I'll lead the party, sir."

"Very well, Mr. Barry. Pick your men."

Trenton and the rest of the crew leaned over the rail and watched silently as the longboat was lowered away. Only Diego Garcia was not on deck, having received permission from Captain Trenton to remain in his galley. He sat alone in almost perfect darkness, shards of light peeking in from around the port lids. The cook shook uncontrollably from stem to stern in a cold sweat. He was the only member of the crew drinking rum, also by permission of the captain, but it wasn't helping. He clutched his cup with a trembling hand and drew it to his lips. Garcia whispered a silent prayer, then drank deeply; dropped his head to the table, cradled in the crook of his arm; and cried for the fear, anger, and hatred that consumed him. Then he said another prayer.

Aboard the longboat, Israel Hands made slow, deliberate strokes with his knife on the whetstone he held between his knees. Only occasionally did he lay a dispassionate glance upon the shore. Tobias, sitting beside him at the bow, seldom took his eyes off the palm trees and lush foliage that capped the white-sand beaches. Doolin Pike and Ben Phillips sat at the ready, with loaded pistols and muskets, behind Hands and Tobias. The six men at the oars pulled the craft swift and sure through the clear coastal water of New Providence. One of the men at the oars, Will Barber, found the breath to ask the question between exertions.

"Mr. Barry, sir"—*stroke*—"this Jose Blanco"—*stroke*—"what did he do"—*stroke*—"that we hate him"—*stroke*—"so much?"

Barry's eyes locked on the young man. "You keep your hands strong on the oar there, lad, and I'll tell you." The boy pulled hard, to the satisfaction of the captain of the longboat. "Aye, there be a good shipmate. You see, lad, our good and loyal cook, Garcia, be an ol' salt. Oh, you see him hop about on one good leg and one good branch of seasoned pine. But you don't see him the way the old crew do." The boy looked curiously at Barry but kept to his oar without a word. "He can serve up a galley of smoked meat that will keep you smilin' while you be reefin' the sheets up on the topgallant yard, and you know that to be true," Jim testified in praise of their cook. The busy oarsman nodded in quick agreement.

"But I tell you, lad, *there* be a true buccaneer. Sailed with Morgan, he did. Made the raid on Portobello and Maracaibo. And was with him when he sacked Panama." The boy's eyes widened as Barry continued, gaining the ears of other young oarsmen who yearned for adventure and to hear the story of their kindly, one-legged cook.

"You see, after sailin' with Morgan back to Port Royal, Garcia stowed away his shares and made for home. Being the proud owner of a small piece of land outside of Santo Domingo, he went back to Hispaniola to settle down and make a life raisin' cattle. And he was doin' jus' fine over the span o' years, raisin' cattle and a crew o' little ones." Barry shifted his weight. "Then, one fine mornin', a few years back now, he gets himself a visit from the captain and crew of a pretty new sloop called the *Sangre Busca*. Being an ol' buccaneer himself, he sees them for who they be. So he offers them all the smoked ham and beef they can eat and carry, and they seem merry enough. Now, you see, ol' Diego, being of friendly disposition, asks them to sit and rest afore shovin' off. There be a pleasin' day with plenty of wine bein' drunk when they hear a scream from inside the house. Diego goes runnin' in to see one of the buccaneers tearin' away at his daughter's dress, and Diego curses him to damnation. He turns to reach for his pistol on the table, and he sees there be a dozen muzzles pointin' at him."

Jim Barry paused, looked about to get his bearings, and caught the eye of Robert Kent, whose hand controlled the rudder. Kent met his gaze briefly and then raised his attention back to the approaching shoreline. The rigger, Darby Sacks, now manning an oar, looked down into the six feet of water that slid away beneath the longboat. He saw the shadow of the boat walking the bottom of the crystal sea, keeping perfect pace with her floating sister. Viewed from the ship, Darby knew, it would appear as if they floated on liquid air. His attention returned to his oar as Barry continued with the story.

"Well, it wasn't till the next day that we happened by. Trenton had dropped anchor in a wee cove at the base of the hill. We was friendly like with Garcia, and we be comin' to buy some smoked beef and pork. Comin' up the hill from water's edge, we was caught off our guard when a musket ball sent one of our shipmates to his knees, chokin' on his own blood. You see, we be comin' up as Blanco and his devil's horde be comin' down. And they being of the mind that we be friends of Garcia's, they start shootin'. And me bein' out front with a long-barreled musket, I give 'em ball for ball and take the leader in the arm."

"An arm that Blanco's surgeon had to take off," Kent added matter-of-factly, his eyes fixed on the shore.

The young oarsman pulled even harder at the oar.

"Aye," Barry acknowledged with a nod and a pause. "Well, they scurried as quick as a wink down the hill, and we be in no condition to be chasin' after them. When the *Sangre Busca* weighed anchor and unfurled sail, Blanco put a ball through the shrouds of the *Bristol Galley*. Trenton wouldn't give chase with so many of his crew ashore, so Blanco got away, and we ain't seen him since."

Barry paused and looked unseeing into the faces before him, his mind retrieving memories long discarded, memories that had been selected for oblivion at the very instant of their birth. "Ah, laddy, the sight we beheld when we reached Garcia . . . ," Barry confessed, shaking his head as he recalled the scene. "Pike be there," he said, tossing his head or pointing a thumb at each man as he remembered. "An' Kent, Sacks, Toby, Ben Phillips, an' Isr'l too. They all seen the devil's work." Barry shifted at his station as he began to ready himself for the landing.

"Well, Blanco and his crew tortured and raped Garcia's wife and daughter, to be sure," he continued. "They'd tied him up and made him watch. Whenever he closed his eyes, as not to see, they'd cut off a piece of his foot and toss it to some of Diego's own pigs. As ye can tell," Barry added, "ol' Diego closed his eyes some." The young oarsman winced at the thought and was grateful Jim's eyes were not on him but scanning the beach as he spoke. "Well, now, he was mostly dead when we found him. We brung him down the hill with us. The ship's surgeon made a fresh cut to his leg and slapped hot iron to it. That brung him around, I can tell you that. Anyway, lad, there's who we be lookin' for. We be goin' to pay respects to an ol' friend."

The boat landed on the beach with a jolt.

Israel and Tobias were the first out of the small craft and dragged the longboat up to the edge of dry land. Ben Phillips and Doolin Pike followed next and, armed with muskets, swept the area for any movement in the brush and trees. Once the boat was secured, Kent passed out the weapons. Barry had ordered only small arms to be carried by the party, in an effort to move fast and strike quickly. The men would carry only pistols, knives, and cutlasses. The muskets would stay behind with three men who would guard the boat and make ready for a speedy return to the ship. Barry had ordered Pike to remain with two less experienced men. Amid a barrage of threats and curses from the ill-humored Pike, Barry swiftly rescinded his order. Pike grumbled something incomprehensible to a confused shipmate ordered to stay with the boat in his stead, then shoved a musket into his hands.

Barry pulled Israel aside to speak with him out of earshot of the others. "Isr'l, I'm askin' you to take the lead on the trail. I don't know if they spotted the *Bristol Galley* or not. It's long, hard work for us if they did. We be needin' to look sharp through the cover of this here brush." Israel nodded in agreement as he studied the formidable jungle.

"Now, Isr'l, if we was to row directly into the harbor, we'd be seen for sure. Mind you, we be more than a mile away from town, and if we can come in from the back of town afore they spy this here lot, then we be the ones to be doin' the cuttin'. You folla?"

Israel nodded. "And if they did see us," Israel concluded, "they'll likely be waiting for us before trail's end."

"Aye, that's why I want you to put this on." Jim dug deep under his belt and pulled out the silver ring.

"Jim, the Devil's Kiss is yours!"

"It be your ring now, Isr'l. I want you to have it. You'll be alone in the front now. You'll need it plenty if Blanco's curse be waitin' for us."

Israel put the Devil's Kiss on the middle finger of his right hand. The honor overwhelmed him. He swallowed hard before he spoke. "I'll wear it just like you wear it, Jim. On this here finger."

"Aye, lad, no harm can befall you now." Jim offered up a sad smile to Israel, who, in turn, felt a sudden shudder of loss that he couldn't explain.

Barry turned to his charges. "Ready, lads? Isr'l's to take the point. Fall in line behind him—there be no waggin' of tongues. Keep a sharp eye and an even sharper ear." He turned to face the trail ahead, then smiled. "Go on, now, Isr'l."

Robert Kent and Darby Sacks shared a look when they spotted the ring on the finger of Israel Hands. The two immediately fell in line behind Israel and were followed in turn by Ben Phillips, Jim Barry, and Doolin Pike. Tobias covered the rear with two other battle-hardened pirates, including Pablo Sanchez, who had once sailed with, and utterly despised, Jose Blanco.

The pirate band crept swiftly through the tropical landscape, feet padding softly on the cool, palm-shaded sand. The only sound to be heard was the rustle of leaves moving against bronzed, lethal arms and the low, constant growl of Doolin Pike.

Meanwhile, in the dim light of one of the dozens of dismal shanties masquerading as taverns in Nassau sat a one-armed madman. Next to him, passed out from the heat and the rum, was his surgeon, the only Anglo on the crew of the *Sangre Busca*, Llewelyn Williamson. Beneath the table and between his knees was a mulatto whore named Angelique. Blanco paid no mind to either as the thin-planked door creaked open on rusty hinges. The captain shielded his eyes from the piercing burst of sunlight and strained to make out the identity of the man who carved the silhouette in front of him.

"*¿Capitan?*" inquired a nervous voice whose eyes hadn't had time to adjust to the darkness. Blanco recognized the voice of one of his men, Eduardo Ruiz.

"*Sí. ¿Qué es eso?*"

"*Capitan*, outside the harbor, it is the *Bristol Galley*." Ruiz took an uneasy step backward as he spoke to his captain, unsure of what his response would be but keenly aware of what it *might* be.

Blanco kicked the whore away from him and delivered a menacing blow to his surgeon, knocking the already unconscious man to the ground.

"Ruiz," Blanco asked pointedly, "are you sure?"

"*Sí, Capitan*, we saw a new ship arrive. It did not come into the harbor, so we look hard at it. It is the *Bristol Galley*. We see *Capitan* Trenton on deck and see they send a boat to shore down the beach. *Capitan*"—Ruiz hesitated—"we think we see James Barry in the boat that come ashore." Blanco smiled as he looked down at the arm that wasn't there.

"Go find the men," Blanco said, wild-eyed. "Bring them here. Drunk or sober, I want them all."

"*Sí, Capitan.*" Ruiz turned on his heel and was gone.

Blanco walked over to the hulk lying on the dirt floor and, in a maddened fury, kicked the man mercilessly in the ribs. The captain left his surgeon gasping for breath, agonizing in pain, and choking on blood and sand. Abandoning the shanty for the sobering sunlight, he tossed a gold doubloon in the dirt for the whore.

For the men on the trail, it was taking much longer than Barry had anticipated, and the hot, sticky tropical air was weighing heavily on their chests. Israel, Kent, and Sacks had gone to their cutlasses early to clear the jungle from the path. The men wiped the dripping sweat from their faces with their sleeves, only to receive it back from the saturated linen. After a trek of only half a mile, the party stopped in a small clearing to catch their breath.

A large parrot in its berth overhead noisily complained of their presence among the palms before flying away in protest. Israel strained to hear anything else that might be alive in the brush but could hear only his heart pounding in his ears from the jungle heat. The men needed a few minutes' rest and sat to quench their thirst. As the water bag was being passed around, Israel noticed that the path beyond the clearing was a little wider and much less obstructed by overgrowth. He brought it to the attention of Kent and Sacks with a nod of his head. Small, grateful smiles curled the lips of the men with the promise of an easier path ahead.

After ten minutes of being in constant motion, the water bag had given its all and lay empty at the feet of Pablo Sanchez. Tired but refreshed, the men sat with their own thoughts, trying to muster the strength to stand and continue. Then something caused the men to stir. Israel looked up at Barry as he tried to make out a sound. He knew Pike had heard it as well from the cautious grunt he hoisted from his throat. A low, rhythmic thumping. It fell soft on the ear, yet was fast and heavy. *Like heavy footfalls on soft ground. Like men running,* Israel thought.

Barry was the first to his feet and, just as quickly, the first to fall. The sudden blast from a long-barreled musket caught them off guard. Israel turned to meet the attackers, only to receive a blow to the forehead from the butt of a musket. He fell against the trunk of a large palm and rolled quickly to his left as a musket ball slammed into the tree inches from his head. He grabbed for his pistols, then realized he had laid the sling aside when he sat to rest. The small patch of ground they occupied quickly filled with fighting men and musket smoke. He knew some of his shipmates had been wounded from the directions of the screams.

Israel stayed low and crept toward the fight through the dirt, holding a knife in his teeth. He saw a pair of busy, unfamiliar feet. He grabbed both dirty ankles and pulled hard and fast. The Spaniard hit the ground with a dull thud, losing his weapon in the fall. Israel had rammed his knife through the downed man's throat before he could cry out. The only thing the men standing and struggling above them could have heard was a short gurgling sound.

The acrid smoke, still thick among them, stung the nostrils and throats of every breathing man. *"¡Vaya con el diablo!"* cut the rancid air as two well-shod feet flew past Israel's face. An angry laugh from a Spaniard, who Israel suspected had been Blanco, was followed by an answering pistol shot, which Israel was almost certain had been Pike. The smoke was slow to clear, as there was no wind through the dense brush. Recognizing the danger in remaining too long in the smoke-filled area, the remnants of the Spanish crew scampered away.

In time, the scene revealed itself. Four men from the *Bristol Galley* lay dead. Among them, Ben Phillips, Pablo Sanchez, and a man whose name Israel didn't know. Israel crawled slowly toward the last body. James Barry had fallen against a tree when he received a musket ball in the shoulder. Blanco had finished him with a through-and-through of Spanish steel that had pegged him against the base of the palm. Israel saw the Devil's Kiss on his own hand as he reached out and touched the shoulder of his dear friend. Israel was without a scratch; Jim Barry was without his life. He studied the death tableau. Hands that had seized up in pain at the moment of death now lay limp at his sides. His mouth agape, forever echoing a silent scream, cursing his killers. Wide, accusing eyes staring sightlessly at a vanished foe. Israel sat heavily in the sand, anguish crashing over him like breakers on a rocky shore. He had lost another father—and his only friend. Staring at the ground, Israel found himself alone in inexorable sorrow. Speechless, sightless, mindless.

* * *

The *Bristol Galley* made haste to pursue the dogs of the *Sangre Busca* and send Blanco back to the hell from whence he came. The survivors of the fight had laid their shipmates in shallow, hurried graves and returned to the ship to avenge their murders. The crew went to work in a maddened frenzy, each man determined to rid the sea of the nefarious beast. Rum was rationed out by littles—the men were already lathered, and there was work to be done in the heavy seas ahead. The *Sangre Busca* would attempt to make the Windward Passage before the *Bristol Galley* could be on her stern timbers. With the favoring winds of the strait, the *Sangre Busca* would be thrown like a lance deeper into the safety of the Caribbean Sea and beyond the vengeful reach of the larger, slower *Bristol Galley*.

Kent was assisting the surgeon in the wardroom as he removed a musket ball from Tobias's thick thigh muscle when Darby Sacks came through the hatch. Pike, who had been sitting at a nearby table, observing the surgeon's handiwork, glanced up and saw the gray, smoldering sky beyond Sacks.

"Dr. Bedford, you might want to patch up Toby pretty quick," Darby warned. "The squall's about on top of us, and she'll be steady for you no more."

Kent snapped his head up to Sacks. "Darby, have you seen Israel?"

"Aye, Mr. Kent," he answered somberly. "I seen him. He be dancing in the shrouds."

Pike, who had been silent and watchful, could but shake his head at the maniacal actions of a man forsaken. Kent left the patient and walked to the hatch, opened it, and searched the rigging of the mainmast. The sky had opened up, and the rain came down in driving sheets. The heaving seas covered the deck with white water as the pitching ship braced itself for oblivion. When he spied Israel Hands aloft, Kent closed the hatch against the storm and let the madman be.

Forks of lightning pointed bony, white-hot fingers accusingly at the mortal who dared approach. Israel struggled to hang on to the wet, slippery ropework as he grappled his way up the topmast rigging.

His blanched, pointed face pierced the fiery sky as gray clouds boiled black. The tears streaming down his face mingled with the water the sky was returning to the sea. His malefic screams decried the crashing of the thunder that roared angrily back at him. Israel climbed even higher through the topgallant rigging. He clung to the skeleton of the ship and rode the storm like a demon riding the night skies. Israel raged at the heavens and cursed almighty God.

Dead Wives

Sunday, June 20, 1999

Marie had grown sullen after Jake and Tom had divulged the details of their morning interview with the beautiful witch, or as Marie quickly came to think of her, *Elvira*. Although not one to harbor animosity, she was having trouble accepting their decision to seek the counsel of someone involved with the occult. Marie hadn't met Rebecca Putnam, but she had the distinct feeling she wouldn't like her very much, and she was seldom wrong about these things.

She realized there was an upside to all this as she thinly sliced the cucumber and tomatoes for the salad. Her husband was being extremely attentive to her every need. Maintaining a certain coolness toward him would ensure his complete subjugation for the next twenty-four to thirty-six hours, at which time she would need to, at least seem to, respond to his affection and soften her position—if only in Lilliputian increments. If she played it right and doled out the affection sparingly, she could maintain emotional control for another day and a half. The gamble, of course, was whether she could dampen any further desire for consulting the witch before he became resentful of her lack of attention. If she pushed too far, he would become the offended party and regain the emotional high ground. It was an age-old strategy for a healthy marriage. The give and take. The thrust and parry.

"Hey, hon," Jake said, coming up behind her. "I found a neat little custom jewelry place on Darling Street." He pulled a velvet box from behind his back. "I picked up this set of earrings for you. I thought they looked nice." He opened the small black box and revealed the handmade silver-and-jade set. She set the knife down, resting its blade on the cutting board, and took the box from Jake. *They really are lovely,* she thought. But there was danger here, and Marie saw it coming in perfect 20/20.

"Did you put them on the credit card?"

Jake was already sorry; he just wasn't sure why. "Well, yeah."

"Then I'm gonna have to pay it off next month. You really need to check with me before you do things like this. We're operating on a pretty tight budget." Spurned, Jake trudged up the ladder and retreated to the sanctuary of the bedroom. She looked at the earrings and smiled. *That was so sweet of him.*

Marie heard the creaking of the front door. Heavy footfalls on the atrium floor announced the entrance of someone who otherwise offered no introduction or greeting. Marie set the earrings down and looked out into the gathering room, expecting to hear Tom's familiar voice. It never came. There was a soft shuffling sound; then, nothing. Marie drew a quick breath to call out but instead paused. She leaned in, craning her neck, and listened with narrowed eyes. The door creaked again. It was a long, slow creak, an agony meted out against an invisible driving force that had come against it, closing the door against its will. A strained rusty howl that screamed out to Marie, to anyone who would listen: *Run! Something's coming, and I can't stop it! For God's sake, run!*

The door closed shut with a click. Footsteps on wooden planks. Heavy, but with a softness that suggested an attempt at stealth. The first two were singular, searching. The footfalls then took on a boastful certainty and struck out a confident cadence, marking a steady beat toward the kitchen. It was as if they could see through walls and knew exactly where they wanted to go.

Marie stared out into the gathering room from behind the dubious safety of the kitchen island. Her jaw clamped shut with fear. She couldn't move. She couldn't scream. Her feet were anchors. With herculean effort, Marie forced her fingers to close around the handle of the carving knife that lay on the cutting board in front of her. She pointed the tip in the direction of the oncoming footsteps. A face appeared from around the corner. It was not her husband, and it was not Tom.

"Hi, there," he said. "I saw Tom out front, and he asked me to bring these in to you."

Marie put the kitchen knife down on the butcher block and took a deep breath. *Oh, dear Jesus, this place is making me crazy.*

Lieutenant Drew handed her a bag. It was said in town that Drew Kenealy had a friendly, disarming way about him that immediately put people at ease. Marie hoped that when her heart started beating again, she would find that to be true.

"Oh, hello, Lieutenant. Well, what do we have here?" Marie asked as she opened the large brown paper bag to find several impressive specimens of zucchini and summer squash. "Thank you very much. Did you grow these yourself?"

"Yes. Well," the lieutenant conceded, "that is to say that the people who owned the house before me had a great vegetable garden going. All I do is try to remember to water it. Ten years later, these are the only things that have survived." He stared at the bag and gave a slight shrug. Marie wasn't sure if she saw shades of pride or embarrassment on his face.

"That was very nice of you," she said, as any good neighbor would. "They really do look great."

Drew smiled and plunged his hands into the pockets of a pair of faded blue Dockers. "Well, I'll let you finish what you were doing." He turned to go, then paused, an odd grin wrinkling his mouth. "I certainly hope that you weren't holding that knife to use on me," he joked. Marie forced a small laugh.

"Don't worry—only vegetables need fear me for the moment," she replied, tapping the knife handle gently as it rested on the butcher block.

The sound of feet descending the squeaky stairs behind him turned Drew around. "Hey, Lieutenant Drew," Jake said pleasantly. "How're things?"

"Things are good," Drew replied, extending his hand in greeting. "But they'd be a lot better if you'd all just call me Drew."

"All right, Drew," Jake said, finishing off the handshake. "And we're Jake and Marie."

"Great. I'm always glad to get that out of the way."

"What?" Marie asked. "Does everybody in Marblehead just call you Drew?"

"It's pretty informal," he said, nodding. "All the kids call me Officer Drew, or Lieutenant Drew, but yeah, the adults call me Drew. Most of us on the force are from this town. Standing on ceremony doesn't go over well with people you went to high school with."

Tom worked open the front door with a pair of preoccupied hands, spilling a score of large potatoes across the floor as he closed the squeaky door behind him with his foot. Drew and Jake rushed to assist, herding all the potatoes they could find on the floor. As they were gathered, Drew noticed the admirable size of the spuds.

"Hey, Tom, did you grow these here?" he asked, truly impressed.

"Nah, the bag tore open when I pulled them out of the car, so I had to carry them in my arms. It wasn't easy," Tom insisted. "I dropped quite a few along the way."

Behind Tom, Jake wagged his head at the sad commentary. "Attaboy, Hansel."

The three men transported the potatoes, without further incident, into the kitchen, where Marie was preparing a pork roast. "Oh, good. Thanks, guys. Just set them on the counter. I'll get to them as soon as I'm done with the roast."

"I'll take care of them, babe," Jake offered. "You just finish up there so you can join us outside." And without waiting for a response, he began washing the dusty vegetables. Marie kissed his cheek.

Tom grabbed a couple of Bud Lights out of the refrigerator and held them up for Drew's approval. "Absolutely," Drew answered as he grabbed the cold gift by its long neck and followed Tom out to the back patio. Drew paid a respectful glance toward the side of the house where, only the day before, Vince LaCava had met his death. He noticed that Tom kept "eyes front." *Well, can't say that I blame him.*

Tom led Drew to the seawall, where the top of the gangway slanted down to the floating dock that lay motionless on the glassy water between Little Harbor and Doliber's Cove. They didn't descend but stood on the higher ground to better appreciate the panorama.

Drew remembered when, as a kid, he and his friends used to try to skip rocks from the nearby shore to Brown's Island, directly across from him now—they'd never made it. He smiled at the boyhood memory. Ever since he'd returned to Marblehead after twelve years in Detroit, Drew never took for granted the beauty that was his New England hometown, nor the lifesaving miracle of memories.

"Tough way to start a new business venture, huh?" Tom asked, kick-starting the conversation and fishing for some new information.

"Yeah, Tom, it is," Drew responded without shifting his eyes from the water. "I wish I could put you at ease, but there's nothing I can tell you that you don't already know. I'm here as sort of an 'unofficial' welcome wagon."

"I know. And listen, I appreciate you coming by like this. Let's see," Tom began. "So far, I know a dead mason; a general contractor who's probably in some well-lit corner of his house right now, sucking his thumb in the fetal position because he's so afraid he'll be accused of murder; a well-meaning, if not an all-too-closed-mouthed, cop; and an extremely attractive witch. If someone would have told me a year ago that this would be my little circle of friendlies, I'd have told them they were nuts."

Drew laughed freely at Tom's eclectic list of new acquaintances.

"Are you guys gonna walk down to the dock or just hang out up here?" Jake called out from the house. They turned and squinted to see the Breans stepping out onto the patio, Jake closing the back door behind him.

"We'll go down to the dock if you don't think you'll get seasick, Jake," Tom teased.

"No promises, my friend, but lead the way." The four bounced twenty feet down the narrow gangway to the floating dock below.

"Absolutely amazing," Marie said, still impressed with the view as she sipped her wine. The early heat of the day was graciously receding with the dawning of evening. It reminded her. "By the way, dinner will be ready in about forty-five minutes. I hope everyone is hungry. Since we're having pork roast, I picked out a nice chardonnay. Does that meet with everyone's approval?"

"Yeah, perfect," replied Tom, not knowing what else to say. Jake snickered.

"Like you fuckin' know what chardonnay is," he whispered to Tom.

"That would have been my choice, Marie," Drew answered politely while making a mental note of a wine he could have with pork.

"So, Drew, let me ask you something," Jake said. He took another swig of O'Doul's; stepped toward the edge of the dock; and looked into the clear, shallow water below him. "Do you guys see any increase in crime due to all the 'witch business' going on in Salem?" The question pulled Marie by the ear and brought her from the bottom of the gangway to the center of the floating dock.

Drew shook his head. "No, not at all. We don't have any problems associated with witches or witchcraft. We see where crime comes from. It's a stairstep effect, really. Boston's crime problems become Lynn's crime problems. From Lynn's crime, it becomes Salem's crime, and from Salem, it comes here."

"So witchcraft isn't part of the crime problem here?" Marie asked, the frayed edges of confusion and disappointment showing.

"Absolutely not. It's not an issue here—or in Salem, for that matter. We see the same thing that every other community sees. Drugs, alcohol, vandalism—especially in the summer—and the occasional bar fight. As a matter of fact, most of the really spooky-looking 'witch stores' in Salem aren't run by witches at all. They're owned and operated by retailers. Most of the shops that are run by real witches are light and airy inside." Jake looked at Marie, who seemed a little disappointed by Drew's answer.

"Yeah," Tom said, "that's what we ran in to today."

"Ah, that's right. You'd mentioned a witch on your list of new friends," Drew said with a smile.

"Sounded more to me like they met a Barbie doll with a broom," Marie quipped, unable to hide the trace elements of jealousy in her voice. It wasn't lost on Jake, who smiled to himself.

"At a store called the Cat and the Cauldron, over on Pickering Wharf," Jake reported to Drew dispassionately.

"Do you know the place?" Tom asked, searching for some local insight from an honest man.

Drew nodded. "Sure do. But I've never had cause to go there. And in my line of work," he said with a smile, "that's a good thing."

As the sun began its descent in the sky behind them, they watched a school of tiny fish dart through the water beneath their feet. Whether they swam in pursuit of food or in pursuit of safety, the people on the pontoon dock above them couldn't know. But they were certainly going somewhere in a big hurry. Tom looked out over the calm waters of the inlet and wondered what unseen threat could be responsible for the scattering of the fish. His mind stuck on the thought of how many dangers nature holds, and the folly of those who ignore the signs, seen or unseen, of those dangers.

A beautiful mahogany powerboat motored slowly into view from the mouth of Little Harbor. At fifty yards offshore, the boat split the middle of the inlet as it moved toward Doliber's Cove. An attractive, bronzed couple tossed a friendly salute to the four on the dock as they glided by at a respectful 5 mph.

"Man, that is one gorgeous craft," Tom said. "Any idea what kind it is?"

"It's a 1924 Forslund," Drew answered indifferently. "Twenty-four feet, one-hundred-and-seventy-five-horsepower Volvo Penta motor. It'll do twenty-two knots in fair seas."

Tom shot Drew an impressed glance. "You sure know your boats, don't you?"

"I know *that* boat," Drew answered. "It's owned by a guy named Paris Quicci; he's the vice president of a local bank. That's him out there waving to us." He squinted to make out the identity of the female on board. "I don't know who his companion is, not that it matters. There's a new one on his arm every few weeks."

"I'm not feelin' the love, Drew," Jake said, eyeing the boatman with growing interest. "You don't like this guy very much, do you?"

Drew shrugged it off. "No, it's not like that. We just don't share much in common. He's a guy who knows what he wants and goes after it. Nothing wrong with that, I suppose."

"Does he usually get what he goes after?" Tom asked.

"I don't know. Sort of looks like it, though, doesn't it?"

Tom's eyes followed the boat on its path as the seagulls squawked noisily above the couple aboard, begging for a handout. The small wake from the passing craft made its way to the dock, and the four landlubbers enjoyed the gentle bobbing. Tom looked back at Jake with the easy movement below their feet.

"Are you getting seasick, Jake?"

"Still ain't got my sea legs," Jake joked. "Get me ashore, Cap'n."

Marie shifted her chardonnay to her other hand and looked at her watch. "Well, let's all go ashore. We can start with the salad. The roast should be just about ready when we are."

They turned to face the sinking sun and trekked single file up the gangway, the white, skidproof strips dulling the sun's reflection off the aluminum ramp. Once ashore, Tom cast a final glance back at the handsome craft that now motored noiselessly from the mouth of the cove and back out to sea. *Yeah,* Tom surmised, in response to his own question, *that guy gets everything he goes after.*

In the comparative darkness of the gathering room, the three men took a moment to let their eyes adjust to the absence of light before they moved to the table as Marie entered the kitchen to get the salad.

"Marie, do you need help with anything?" Jake called out.

"No thanks, I'm good."

With salad bowl and serving tongs in hand, Marie returned to a remarkably curious scene. Tom, Jake, and Drew stood as statues, staring at the far corner of the table.

"What?" she asked, scanning the far side of the room but perceiving nothing out of the ordinary. "What is it?"

"That" was all Jake said as he pointed to the far end of the table, at a potato sliced wafer thin and fanned out like a deck of cards.

"What is it?" Marie asked. "It looks like a sliced potato." The finding struck her as both odd and incidental.

"It *is* a sliced potato," Jake said.

"Well, what's the big deal?"

"Did you slice it and leave it there?" Jake asked with raised eyebrows.

"No," she said, quickly catching up with the others. "Didn't you?"

Jake and Tom looked directly at her, both shaking their heads.

"Does this mean something to you guys?" Drew asked Tom and Jake.

"Yeah," Jake said. "It does. Or at least, I think it does." He looked at Tom.

"It's an old sailor remedy for seasickness," Tom explained. "You put a slice of potato between your cheek and gum and just suck on the juice."

"Does that really work?"

"I don't know—never tried it. I never got seasick. I think the theory is that the juice makes your mouth produce a lot of saliva, which keeps you swallowing a lot, thereby helping you to keep from throwing up. That's the scuttlebutt, anyway. What I *do* know is that a lot of Bosons' mates, hull techs, and deck seamen swear by it to this very day."

"So why's it here now?" Drew questioned. "Who's seasick?"

"I am," Jake conceded.

"What?"

"When the wake caused the dock to rock, Tom joked about me being seasick," Jake said. "Anyway, that's my guess."

Drew didn't like being played for a fool, and he was beginning to sense that maybe he was wrong about these people. "So you're saying that someone heard Tom from the dock and cut up this potato for you as a seasickness remedy?"

Jake shrugged, unable to offer a more credible defense. Drew looked around the room and up the ladder before asking his next question.

"You think there's somebody in the house right now?"

"No one you'll be able to find," Jake answered, still staring at the potato. Marie sat down heavily on the chair behind her.

"What, you mean, like a ghost?" Drew asked with a dubious smile.

"Exactly," Tom answered.

Drew stared mutely at his hosts. *These people are nuts.*

* * *

It took a great meal, several glasses of chardonnay, and most of the evening to convince Drew that the people around the table weren't crazy. On the contrary, he thought, they seemed much more rational than he would be after such inexplicable experiences. It wasn't until almost ten o'clock that Marie asked Jake for help with the dinner dishes.

"Carol died on our anniversary," Tom revealed as he peeled the label off his bottle of Bud Light. He smiled as he worked his fingernail under the corner. "When we first started dating, she used to tell me that peeling off the label was a sign of sexual frustration. I thought she was teasing me, but I'll be damned—for the first full month after we were married, I never once peeled the label off the bottle." Drew smiled as his host laughed, but he also saw the sadness and pain that lived beneath the laughter. A Band-Aid masking a mortal wound.

"She wanted two things: to live until our twelfth anniversary and to see this bed-and-breakfast become a reality, but"—he shrugged—"cancer isn't known for its patience and consideration, is it?" Tom quickly wiped his eyes. He cleared his throat. "Aw, hell," he said, "it took her faster than most, and you know what? She was thankful for that. She called it a blessing. Glioblastoma. A fatal, aggressive form of cancer—a blessing? Can you believe that?"

"Well, I suppose it can be looked at that way, from a certain perspective," Drew said. He was on very shaky ground and knew it.

"Strictly in the sense that the length of suffering is less, I mean," he said, shifting his weight as he spoke.

Tom smiled. "Don't worry, Drew, I know what you mean. I just don't have much to say about what some people call 'blessings.' A blessing to me would be when the cancer goes away, not when it kills you. I remember wanting to strangle a couple of people at her funeral. These old church ladies would come up to me and tell me it was God's will." Tom shook his head in disgust. "I told them that if their god wants to 'bless' the people who believe in him with a slow, painful death, he could go right ahead, but I could make a better god, and I certainly didn't need him. Man, you should've seen the look on their faces." He took a long, hard pull on his beer, trying to wash down the anger and resentment. "You show me a god who wants to save people, then, *maybe*, I'll believe."

Drew nodded silently, knowing all too well the desperate anguish of a man who watched, helplessly, as the life of the woman he loved slipped away. It was a pain that still afflicted his own soul. As he considered Tom's story, Drew found himself spinning the glass of wine by the stem of the goblet, and he wondered if *that* was a sign of sexual frustration. He stopped immediately and looked at the room around him. "So this bed-and-breakfast you've got here, it was really a dream of your wife's, wasn't it?"

"Yeah, it was. I just wanted to see if I could make a go of it. She did so much work in preparation for this. It was the money from her family's endowment that allowed us to buy the place. I had reservations about moving forward with it after she died, but I felt I owed it to her. Owed it . . . to us." Tom displayed an embarrassed smile.

"Hey, listen, I used to look for Karen in crowds," Drew confided, "for almost three years after she was killed. So don't feel strange about wanting to hang on to the memories and the things that make you feel close to her."

"Isn't it unhealthy? Psychologically, I mean?"

"Do you still talk to her?"

"Sometimes," Tom said cautiously. "Usually when I'm upset or I've had a rough day."

"Does she talk back to you?"

Tom was mortified. "No."

"Then don't worry about it. You'll let go when you're ready."

Tom smiled at the logic, but his amusement was cut short when a previous statement caught up to him. "Drew, did you say your wife was killed?"

Drew nodded and spun the glass of wine in his hand. "It'll be ten years ago this Christmas. We were driving home from a party when a drunk teenager crossed the line, coming at us, doing about eighty. We both swerved at the last minute and almost cleared, but with two cars closing at a hundred and twenty-five miles per hour"—Drew shook his head—"even a sideswipe is suicide. Or murder. Anyway, he clipped the left rear of my car and sent us into a spin, and the passenger-side door—Karen's door—slammed into an oak tree on the side of the road. I was holding her when she died. She didn't seem to be in any pain, and I suppose that was"—he looked up at Tom and smiled at the irony—"a blessing. I guess I passed out from my own injuries shortly after that."

From inside the kitchen, Jake caught bits and pieces of the conversation going on in the gathering room. Standing just inside the kitchen entrance and drying the same plate for about five minutes, Jake had been listening, in fascinated disbelief, to the discussion going on in the next room.

"What are you doing?" Marie asked impatiently, waiting for her husband to get back to work.

"You wouldn't believe what they're talking about in there," Jake whispered excitedly. "They're talking about how their wives died, for crying out loud."

"You shouldn't be eavesdropping," Marie scolded in a returned whisper. Her vexation turned to intrigue as she considered the monumental emotional stride that Tom Stone had just taken. *And in an open discussion with an almost total stranger, no less.* She picked up a soggy dish towel and a clean, wet plate and stood next to her husband, wiping the dish mindlessly as they listened in on the discussion they'd waited nine months for their friend to have. They had hoped he would have had the conversation with them, but they realized now how far away they were from truly understanding what Tom had experienced. Jake looked at his wife, who stared down at the floor while trying to pick up the words drifting toward the kitchen. Realizing how lucky he was, he prayed he would never know the pain that Tom and Drew knew too well. They could hear Drew speaking fairly easily.

"Apparently, I had quite a bit of internal bleeding. I woke up in the hospital about a week later. I'd missed the services for Karen; they had the funeral in the dead of winter. You know," he added with a look of mild bewilderment on his face, "I thought they just held the casket in storage until the ground thaws in the spring. They don't, though; that's just a myth now. A holdover truism from the days before the backhoe." Drew emptied his wineglass and placed a refusing hand over the goblet when Tom offered a refill.

"Anyway," Drew continued, "I heard that most of the people who came to town for the funeral stopped by to see me in the hospital, but I was still out of it. It was so strange to wake up, feeling as if it were only a moment later, and find out how drastically my life had changed."

"You haven't connected with anyone since then?" Tom asked, coaxing the conversation in a different direction. "I mean, relationship-wise?"

"No, nothing serious. It was a few years before I was even ready to socialize. Even then, anytime I went out with a woman, it was only as friends. I haven't been able to find what I had with Karen. But I keep looking," Drew said, smiling broadly. "What about you? You ready to jump back in the game?"

Inside the kitchen, the two spies leaned toward the open doorway, trying to improve the acoustics by repositioning themselves. Tom gave a heavy sigh before saying in a loud voice, "You two are more than welcome to join us out here."

"What?" Jake shouted from his perch in the kitchen. "We're not listening." He winced at how ridiculous he sounded, even as the words left his mouth. He looked at Marie, whose eyes were spitting daggers.

"Well, then," Tom retorted, "you need to sew your shadow back on, Peter Pan, because it's standing against the wall in this room." Tom and Drew chuckled at the commotion as the shadows saw themselves for the first time, betrayed by the bright kitchen light behind them.

A few moments later, Jake stepped into the gathering room and cracked open a Diet Pepsi. His bearing was one of complete innocence.

"So, guys, what's new?"

Tom smirked at him and turned back to Drew. "What was the question?"

"He asked you if you were ready to jump back in the game," Jake interjected, taking a swig of his soft drink.

"I thought you weren't listening?"

Jake shrugged. "Lucky guess."

The expression on Tom's face seemed to darken as he considered the question. "You know, just recently, I've been wondering if it might be time for me to consider the possibility. I've got no plans to start looking, but I think I may be open to the idea of maybe socializing if I met an interesting woman. I guess I'm more curious than anything else. I have no idea what to expect or what it would be like. I mean, I haven't been with a woman other than Carol in over twelve years." He looked over his shoulder to make sure Marie was out of earshot. "I think I'd be scared shitless."

"Oh, believe me, you will be," Drew confirmed. "I remember the first time I went out with a woman, just a lunch date, no less; my palms were sweating, my mouth went dry. I tell you, I could barely talk to her I was so nervous. *That* was a tough date. But then I realized that the answer was to get out more often before I completely withdrew into my shell. It helped me a lot, I think."

Marie stirred her tea as she entered the room.

"So where'd you take her for lunch, Drew?" Jake asked.

"She worked locally, so we just went over to Driftwood's for chowder and sandwiches."

"Driftwood's? Isn't that where most of the police officers have lunch?" Marie asked, trying to make the connection in her mind.

"Yeah. Well, a lot of them do, anyway, but I wouldn't say most of them."

"You're a natural-born romantic, Drew," Jake said with a deadpan stare. "Anyone ever tell you that?"

"All the time." He glanced at his watch. "Wow."

Jake looked at Ol' Sentry: 10:45 p.m. "Is it past your bedtime, Drew?"

"I have an early wake-up tomorrow. Marie, that was a fantastic meal," Drew said, rising from his chair. "Thanks for a great evening, folks."

Tom stretched noisily as he rose from the chair he had occupied for hours. Jake and Marie fell in step behind Tom as he walked Drew to the door.

"Listen, don't be a stranger," Tom insisted. "Stop by anytime; there's always someone here."

"Even if we're not," Jake added flatly. Marie poked him in the ribs but looked over her shoulder at the empty room just the same. Drew smiled and shook his head as he turned to step outside.

"There's a joker in every crowd," he said as he waved goodbye and headed up the gravel driveway toward his house, which lay a little more than a mile down the road. Tom and the Breans returned the wave and closed the creaky door on the night. Marie headed upstairs for bed.

Jake looked at Tom. "Who the fuck said I was joking?"

Drew was halfway up the drive when an odd sensation came over him. He stopped in the middle of the wide gravel path to listen. He could hear the creaking of large timbers all around him. The earth beneath his feet seemed to give way as he swayed to and fro on solid ground. *How much wine did I have?* Heavy footfalls on hardwood approached him from behind at an increasingly rapid rate. He heard the distinct and shrill scraping of metal against metal, like a sword being pulled from its scabbard. A foul stench swept over him like a wave crashing on the shore. Drew spun around defensively to stand against the impending attack. He stood alone. The cool sea breeze blew soft in his face.

CHAPTER ELEVEN
Paris Quicci

Monday, June 21, 1999

It was exactly 1:15 p.m. by Paris Quicci's watch, and his timepiece was never wrong. His previous watch went south on him once, and the good folks at Rolex would never forget the firestorm that ensued. Truth be told, he preferred it that way. The benefits that stemmed from another's mistake or misfortune were so much more rewarding. He allowed himself a self-satisfied smile. As usual, he was right on time. He even surprised himself sometimes. *How can one person be so good all the time?* He never failed—he was out the door every week by one fifteen. Hal Somerbrook might be home by one thirty. Two o'clock at the latest. But he was never home from working the early shift at the Mystic Generating Station in Everett, some sixteen miles away, before one thirty.

The high, thick hedges in the front yard of the wood-shingled bungalow blocked any and all questioning eyes from observing both

Paris Quicci and his car passing the better part of the noon hour every Monday at Chez Somerbrook. Quicci scanned the grounds from the safety of the half-opened door before he took one step out onto the front porch. Deanna Somerbrook, long and lean in the leg, narrow in the waist and mind, grabbed him by the wrist and turned him around before he could complete his second step. She pulled him into her and wrapped her arms around his neck. As she opened her mouth to him, he let his hands slip down to caress her round and firm ass. Like a ripe melon, he thought, and he wanted to thump it again.

Remembering the time, he pulled back and gave a tug on Deanna's thong. "Next week, I want you to greet me at the door wearing nothing but this." Her chestnut hair bounced deliciously over her shoulders as she pressed her swimmer's breasts against him. She wrinkled her small, straight nose at the thought. A wicked smile appeared on her face. "I'll greet you any way you want, anytime you want. You just let me know how you want it." She grabbed him by the belt buckle and jostled him as she talked. "Hell, I'll do it with that lazy loser of mine sleeping right there on the couch if you'd like."

"Easy, sweetheart," he cautioned as he deftly loosened her grip from his belt buckle, brought her hands up to his lips, and kissed her fingertips. "We got a great thing going here. Don't blow it." He looked at her with hard, dark eyes. "Do you understand me?" Deanna dropped her eyes and nodded gingerly. He studied her for a lingering moment before moving to his car.

Quicci slipped easily into the driver's seat and checked his appearance in the rearview mirror. Sliding a manicured hand over the crown of his head, he lightly pressed into place the few hairs that dared to stray. He brought his black Lexus coupe to a gentle purr and crept out to the mouth of the driveway, crawling past the hedgerow, wary of any unseen traffic that might be coming. He sat low in his seat. It was no time to spot familiar faces. Or more to the point, it was no time for familiar faces to spot him. He glanced up into the rearview once more, this time to toss a kiss into the reflection of Deanna as she closed the door behind him.

The drive back to work was as smooth and quiet as it was every week, with only the melodic lines of Beethoven's Piano Sonata no. 8 in C Minor playing softly in his ear. The black coupe rolled leisurely over the gentle rise and fall of the paved landscape, melting into the curves like a soft whisper on warm skin. Quicci moved through the town, hypnotized by the smell of leather and the strains of a master massaging his instrument. The spell might have carried him into his office, had he not spotted Nate Ingersoll's rusting Chevy Cavalier in the bank parking lot. *This had better be official business,* the bank executive thought, knowing full well it wouldn't be. Somehow, with Nate Ingersoll, it was always personal. He pulled into the reserved parking spot and inspected himself one last time before leaving the car.

Charlie Braddock was rolling his cart of cleaning supplies back out to his van when he spotted Quicci.

"Good afternoon, Mr. Quicci."

"Hi there, Charlie. How are you? And how's that fine young man of yours?"

"Just fine, sir. Thanks for asking."

"Hey, now, listen," Quicci said in his most solicitous voice. "You gotta make sure we sit down sometime soon and work out a tuition plan for that lad. He'll be off to college before you know it, and we don't want you holding the proverbial bag when it's time to pay up, do we?"

"I appreciate that, Mr. Quicci; I really do," Charlie said with an uncomfortable smile melting from his face. "But I'm not sure I can afford—"

"Charlie," Quicci interrupted, "hold it right there. That's what I'm here for. To help you find your way through that financial fog. We're not going to let that boy of yours down, are we, Charlie?" he said with a wink and his most patronizing smile.

"No. No, sir, we won't let him down," Charlie responded, feeling obligated to play a supporting role in his employer's motivational skit. He watched, a bit bewildered, as the bank vice president strode away from the scene of the hit-and-run encounter. As if an afterthought, Quicci stopped in his tracks and turned back to Charlie.

"Are you through cleaning my office, Charlie?"

"All set, Mr. Quicci."

"You're a good man, Charlie," Quicci said, taking a few steps toward the bank before looking back at Charlie. "And there's damn few of us left."

The hard heels of his shoes clapped sharply on the high-gloss tiled floor of First National Bank. Looking straight down the end of the wide corridor to his office door, Quicci passed the row of chairs in the waiting area outside his office, one of which was occupied by a nervous Nate Ingersoll, who stood up as the banker marched by as if on martial review. Nate was about to speak when a commanding hand silenced him. He was next directed to the office door by a pointing finger of the same hand. The milquetoast fell in step behind the man with the purse string tied to that finger, and the two disappeared behind the office door—oak veneered and steel reinforced.

The vice president took his place behind the desk in a high-backed chair of burgundy leather. A small pile of business lay stacked neatly in the center of the desk. Quicci took the long, sharp knife that served as his letter opener and began to free the contents from their envelopes. Ingersoll sat across from him, nervously fingering the coffee-stained manila envelope that rested on his lap. The strain of the moment pressed hard on the detective's respiratory system as he retrieved his albuterol inhaler from the inside pocket of his seersucker sport coat. Quicci glanced up as he continued to review his correspondence, distracted by the wheezing produced by the detective's cramping airways. "You know, maybe if you lost some weight, you'd be able to breathe. Did you ever think about that?"

Nate depressed the canister of relief with two quick squeezes of his thumb and forefinger. The lifesaving mist entered grateful lungs; his airways began to dilate, and the spasms eased. As his respirations slowed, he dabbed the sweat from his forehead and the back of his neck with a wrinkled handkerchief.

"I'm trying, Paris. God knows I'm trying. I've lost three pounds already." He forced a smile to mask the pain. The origin of which, whether from his ailing lungs or from the insult by his friend, was unclear even to Nate.

"Three pounds? In how long?" Quicci asked, doubting the claim. Nate shrugged and shook his head, buying himself enough time to choose his words carefully. His answer had to be right on the money. Reason being that whatever he said was likely to come back at him, much like a major-league pitcher who throws a perfect fastball, only to see it come right back at him even faster off the lumber of an angry batting champion.

"Well, I weigh myself every week, so I lost it just last week. I may have dropped even more than that by now," Nate replied. *Didn't give Paris much to hit with that pitch.* With a wadded handkerchief,

Nate wiped away the dampness that had seeped into being beneath his eyes.

Paris used his knife to free another letter and began to read. Detective Ingersoll looked down at the large envelope resting on his lap and stroked a nervous thumb over a dog-eared corner of the gummed flap. His eyes were pulled up from the object on his lap when the man across from him began to speak.

"One week, huh?" Paris said, tossing his junk mail and unwanted communiqués in the small receptacle next to his desk. He leaned forward and rested both elbows on the protective glass that covered his desktop.

"You know, you could lose three pounds in sweat alone from one light workout. But you don't want to work out, do you? You want to sit there and just keep getting fatter. I swear to Christ, Nate, you're too damned lazy to even move your bowels. Someday, you're going to be sitting down to inhale another fat burger, and you're going to clutch your chest as your left arm goes numb, turn purple, and hit the ground, dead."

The strength expended to endure the aspersions of the man behind the desk left Nate emotionally exhausted.

"Paris, I've got the documents," he said flatly.

"And that's another thing," his faultfinder quipped. "I thought I told you not to come in here to talk about your loan without an appointment. Do you know how this looks? If the police want to talk about their own financial business, they can stop in anytime? I told you that I was handling it personally. That should be enough for you. Now, if you don't mind, I'm going to—"

"No, no, Paris, that's not it. I'm not talking about my loan." Nate looked around the private office, as if someone else might be listening. It was a little too cloak-and-dagger for Quicci's taste, but Nate continued, true to the genre. "I've got *the* documents. The ones you wanted."

The warm, healing waters of total consciousness bathed the features of Paris Quicci. His countenance changed. The chameleon now stood before a bright and sunny background. He radiated from inner joy and sought a way to express his pleasure.

"Nathaniel, oh, but you are good. That's what we're all about, you and me," Quicci asserted. "I watch out for your best interests, and you watch out for mine. True friends, that's what we are." Quicci bounced an index finger back and forth between the detective and himself.

Nate wanted so much to believe Quicci's dictum. He would have given his life for it, right then and there, if only it were true. He slid the thin envelope across the glass desktop, past the framed pictures of the bank vice president and his 1924 mahogany Forslund, until it came to rest in front of the banker. Quicci leaned back in his chair, folded his hands cross-fingered in front of his chest, and placed his elbows on the padded armrests.

"Oh, no, no, no, my friend. Not here. Why don't you pick that up and tuck it away someplace nice and safe," Quicci said, refusing the package. Nate wore a bewildered look, which wasn't an altogether unfamiliar expression. "I tell you what, Nate. Why don't you come on by tonight? We'll have dinner at my place. Then we can talk about what you have there."

Nate shrugged and reached across the desk to pick up the envelope. The banker, having never touched the documents, watched as the envelope left his desktop and was folded and stashed away in the inside pocket of the detective's ample jacket.

"In the meantime, I'm going to make a few phone calls to some of the decision-making fence-sitters I'm working with," Quicci said with a reassuring wink. "I'll see if I can't help them make up their minds on the little issue of your loan. How's that sound?"

Ingersoll beamed. "That sounds great, Paris. What time? Maybe about eight?"

"Oh, no, my friend," Quicci countered. "We've got a lot to talk about. What do you say about seven?"

"Great, seven it is. Should I bring anything?"

"Just your appetite, Nate." He paused. "And that envelope there."

"I won't forget *this*, Paris—don't worry," Nate said, patting the garment that housed the manila envelope. "Unfortunately, I always have my appetite with me; it's a damn curse is what it is."

"Hey, now, don't go getting down on yourself," Quicci said, his tone serious and reproachful. "Look, I ride you about your weight because I care about you. That's what friends do. But you've got to keep your head up, you understand? Huh? Capisce?"

"You bet," the fat man said, tight jawed, blinking back self-deprecating tears. Quicci came around the corner of his desk and placed a friendly hand on the back of the detective's bargain-basement sport coat as he stood to leave, guiding him toward the exit. Quicci opened the door, and with a short, convivial nod, he patted Nate on the back. "See you at seven."

Quicci started to close it before the big man had cleared the frame. The banker then locked the door and returned to his desk in some haste, opening the large drawer on the lower right side. He slid it open and fingered to the tab marked "Personal." He flipped through half a dozen files before he extracted the one he was looking for: "Ingersoll, Nathaniel." A large red stamp in bold letters marked it: denied. Grabbing a new, unblemished folder, he wrote the detective's name on the unmarked tab, placed the file contents into the new folder, and tossed the old folder into the trash bin. Quicci looked at the folder. The beige cardboard discard with the big, bright, bold red letters seemed to talk to him. "Yeah, you're right," he responded to the cardboard. "I'll need you later." He reached into the bin, retrieved the folder, and returned it to its original drawer. Then, the vice president of First National Bank took pen to paper and started a wine list. He was having a friend over for dinner.

* * *

The doorbell rang at precisely seven o'clock. Quicci looked at his watch. "Damn, that man's never late for a free meal." He stood up from the leather reading chair in his home office and set his book down on the table next to him. He leaned back in a graceful arch to relieve the tension in his lower back and stepped over to the portable copy machine in the far corner of the office. He pressed the white plastic rocker switch, and the small IBM came to life with a faint but steady hum. "That's it, baby. Wake up. *It's showtime.*"

A second chime of the doorbell prepped Quicci's mind for a challenging evening with a tiresome bore. "I'm coming, Lumpy," he said to the impatient man standing on the friendly side of the front door. "Keep your shirt on." His mind quickly kicked into a mental slideshow of Nate Ingersoll, shirtless. Quicci shuddered, doing what he could to cleanse the vulgar image from his mind. "Let me emphasize, *please* keep your shirt on," he implored, with a de facto strain of sincerity. He stopped briefly before he left the room to straighten one of the many framed financial and civic awards that crowded the walnut-paneled walls.

He padded leisurely across the Mediterranean-tile floor and reached for the crystal doorknob to bid his guest welcome. Quicci opened the door and immediately glanced down at Nate's left hand. *Good.* The nervous man held the manila envelope in his moist, spongy paw. Unbeknownst to the detective, it served as his passkey to gain admittance to the home of his friend.

Quicci spied something different about the envelope slapping arrhythmically against the wide trouser leg. *A new stain,* he noted. *Looks like Nate may have treated himself to an ice cream cone this afternoon. Mint chocolate chip by the shade of it.* He pulled his head up to meet Ingersoll's expectant gaze and managed a belated welcome. "What are you standing out there for? Give me a courtesy knock and then come on in and announce yourself, buddy," Quicci ordered with fraternal congeniality, secure in the knowledge that this would be the first and last time Nate Ingersoll saw the outside of his front door, let alone the inside. "That's the way we do it here at Casa de Quicci." The broad smile on his face served as a much-needed welcome mat for his anxious visitor.

It had never been easy for Nate Ingersoll to develop meaningful and lasting friendships. That is to say, he hadn't a friend in the world, and he didn't quite know what to make of the uneven acquaintance of Paris Quicci. Never before had he, to the best of his recollection, even been on speaking terms with an individual of Quicci's caliber. Intelligent, arrestingly handsome, and financially independent at age thirty-three, Quicci exuded a self-confident charm that drew people to him. He was everything Nate Ingersoll was not. And, for the life of him, Nate couldn't figure out what a man of Quicci's standing could possibly glean from a friendship with a sloppy cop who had been passed on from Boston to Concord, then to Lynn, and then to Marblehead in the course of seven years. The only reason he'd made it to Marblehead was because the extra training he'd pursued in the Boston PD made him eligible for an open detective position on the force. But he still didn't feel at home here. He wanted to be Marshal Dillon, but he felt more like Festus. Most of the guys on the force were representative of cutting-edge law enforcement. Young, smart, physically fit; hell, half a dozen of them patrolled the town on mountain bikes. Now *that's* Marshal Dillon.

Quicci welcomed the caller into his home the same way he had escorted him out of his office—a guiding hand on the wide back of the human bowling ball. He glanced back over his shoulder and scowled at the aging Chevy Cavalier leaking oil onto the glossy blacktop driveway. As maggots gnaw voraciously on the rotten carcass of a dead animal, Quicci could have sworn he could actually see the rust devouring the metal car in front of his very eyes. *No matter,* Quicci thought, *I'll toss some cat litter down on the spots after he leaves.* Tonight there were bigger grouper to fry.

"Go right on through to the living room there, Nate," Quicci said, leading his guest from behind.

The foyer opened to an area so expansive Nate felt as if he had been sucked out of some small portal into a shining void of light and chrome. The wide marble corridor on which he crept bordered a three-step drop into a living space so vast that the awestruck visitor felt himself stiffen and lean slightly backward, fighting the sensation that he was falling. Large skylights in the peaked twenty-five-foot ceiling threw shafts of light down sharply against a snow-white Berber carpet.

"Wow, this is some place you got here, Paris," he said as he wiped his brow with his handkerchief.

"You like?" the proud owner asked, pleased with himself and all that he had.

"What's not to like?" Nate said in a voice that shied away from the truth. As bright and spacious as it was, the room was cold and unfriendly, a flowing work of ultramodern art, glass, and bent chrome. Gray stone sculptures of odd shapes in precarious positions stood unhappily on stands of polished black marble. The room was expensive, he had no doubts about that, but it was without heart and devoid of human warmth.

"What're you drinking, my friend?" Quicci asked as he brushed by Nate on his way to the crescent-shaped wet bar, which was centered in the middle of the far wall. Nate stood back and tried to take in the bizarre scene. The bar, with tubular chrome framing and thick glass tops and surfaces, served as the centerpiece of the entire room. All elements of the decor drew the eye to that one spot. It was like the altar of a church. A cold, unearthly altar that stood on proud display before the congregation of metal, glass, and stone. In the pulpit of that church stood the preacher. The pale light of the dying sun shone through the skylights above and, lacking the sanctity of stained glass, cast an unholy glow on the face of the preacher. Nate now waited for the sermon, wondering what would be the message of the preacher in the crystal and chromium pulpit. He took an elevated seat up at the communion rail of the church of "Me." And for the first time since he'd known Paris Quicci, Nate Ingersoll was scared.

"I'm having single-malt scotch, neat," Quicci said as he poured. "You're having, wait, let me guess." He sized Nate up like a carny guessing a ticket holder's weight at a county fair. "You're a beer man, I'd wager. Am I right?"

"Right on the money," Nate said, happy to grab hold of anything that might help steady his nerves.

"Hot damn! Never miss," Paris said. He shrugged. "It's a gift. I can always tell what a man's drink is. Or a woman's, for that matter. It's like the clothes they wear—it's a reflection of both who they are and who they want to become." Nate self-consciously pressed a flattening hand over his slightly wrinkled powder-blue oxford shirt. Quicci didn't notice, or at least, he didn't let on if he did.

"Not only that, my friend," he continued, "but I can also tell the style *and* color of a woman's panties." He paused and looked dead into the eyes of the beer drinker. "And even better than that, I can always prove it too." Quicci gave a sly wink as Nate set down his king of beers, the aluminum can clinking thinly on the thick glass surface. Lacking any firsthand experience to draw from, Nate stared dumbly at the red, white, and blue can in front of him and imagined, just for a moment, that he had a life.

The conversation lagged as one sipped while the other drew deeply from their chosen libations. Quicci, the detective noted, eyed the documents resting beside him. Nate tapped the large envelope he had placed on the barstool next to him with nervous fingers. "Paris, I've got to tell you," he started. "I'm really uncomfortable about this. I know your intentions are good, but I—"

"I can't tell you how relieved I am to hear you say that!" the banker interjected, cutting him off.

"What? What do you mean, Paris?"

"Look," Quicci explained, "you and I are on the same page as far as this thing goes. I know that. And I never question your faithfulness as a friend. It's one of the few real friendships I cherish." Quicci almost choked on his words as he looked at Nate, sitting there and staring back at him, head slightly tilted, like a fat, confused cocker spaniel. *A cocker spaniel whose face sweats.* He forced the image out of his mind. "But you know, I just think that there's a better way of going about it, don't you?"

"Oh, gosh, yes, Paris," Nate said, relieved almost to the point of tears. "I can't tell you how much better I feel. You know what?" he said as he slid off his barstool. "I'm gonna get this out of our sight right now." Nate turned to leave, the envelope in his hand.

"Hey, where ya going?" The alarm in Quicci's voice caught Nate off guard. He looked back, unsure of the reason for his friend's perplexity.

"Well, I was just going to take this back out to my car, so we can both relax a little."

"Nah, don't worry about that now. Sit down; have another beer. I haven't even told you what we're having for dinner."

"This'll just take a minute. I'll be right back." Nate was approaching the three steps mounting to the foyer when Quicci came around the bar, his dark eyes seeing red. But he pulled up as a thought came to him.

"Hang on there, big fella. I want to talk to you about your loan." The words stopped Ingersoll in his tracks, and he spun on his heel over the white carpet. *The master whistles, and the fat cocker spaniel comes running.*

"Is it approved, Paris?" Nate asked, hope swelling in his chest. Quicci smiled. "Oh, Jesus God, thank you, Paris." He pulled up his stool and crowded the chrome frame in front of him.

"Well, it wasn't easy," said the miracle worker. "You know you've got shit for credit, don't you?"

"I always pay my bills, Paris. I'm never late."

"I know, but you never *buy* anything on credit. Hell, you paid cash for that rust bucket you got out there staining my driveway."

"Well, I did buy some furniture on layaway," Nate said sheepishly.

"Yeah, I saw that. One piece of furniture. What the hell is a 'rattan room divider,' by the way?"

"Well, it's a big thing that—"

"Never mind. Look, I took major heat over this one. But I told you I wasn't going to let you down, didn't I?"

"You sure did, Paris. I can't thank you enough," Nate said, his head shaking somewhere between gratitude and disbelief.

"Just one more hurdle to clear, and that will be that."

The joy fell from the face of the detective in the blink of an eye. "So it's not finalized yet? I'm not approved?"

"Don't worry. You're approved by the board. I just need the bank president's signature to finalize it, and he's out of town. That's all."

"When will Mr. Forlini be back?" Nate asked, allowing himself to believe once more.

"Oh, well, he's due back at the end of the week, so we should have this finalized in a week or two."

"Two weeks? Just for a signature?"

"He's a busy man," Quicci said with raised eyebrows. "But I'll fast-track it for you. You should be approved by the middle of next week."

"Thanks, Paris. I do appreciate everything you're doing for me." He shook his head. "Why do these things take so long, anyway?"

The question allowed Quicci to reveal some of the daunting challenges a banker faces when seeking loan approval for a client— from traversing mountains of bureaucratic red tape to surviving the leech- and piranha-infested waters in the swamps of corporate politics, before reaching the top of Mount Debt and securing the loan. All this, only to be compelled to face off in an eternal wrestling match with the two-headed serpent of financial management: risk and reward. Although Nate appeared fascinated, most everything Quicci said was lost on the listener. Quicci wasn't disappointed at his guest's confusion. On the contrary, that was exactly the way the story was supposed to end.

Nate averaged a beer every fifteen minutes, and after three-quarters of an hour, he asked for directions to the little detective's room. When the bathroom door snapped shut, Quicci snatched the envelope from the barstool and headed down the hall to his office. When Nate returned, Quicci was behind the bar, buying another round. Nate smiled as he descended into the sunken room. "Whew, like I always say, Paris, you don't buy beer—you just rent it."

Quicci laughed heartily at the wit of his guest.

They dined on smoked salmon, asparagus spears, and wild rice catered by Cicero's. The host had laughed in the face of convention with his selection of a fine pinot noir instead of a traditional white wine. It was a splendid meal, made even more elegant by the hallmark Cicero presentation. As time passed lightly, Nate Ingersoll couldn't remember what on earth had caused him such alarm earlier in the evening. He was having the time of his life. They laughed well into the night, the way good friends do.

Neddy

December 1708

The musket ball was deeper than either Ned or the surgeon had first believed. The surgeon had been poking and prodding Ned's shoulder for the better part of a bottle in an attempt to remove the heavy lead shot. A brief inebriated argument ensued surrounding the possibility of leaving the ball in the man's shoulder. The surgeon finally convinced Ned that leaving it in would poison his blood and ultimately provide for a most unpleasant death. Both decided it was a good time to take another drink.

Readying himself for another go, Ned bit down hard on the leather strap that was his belt before it rendered service as a mouth bit, sweat beading up on his shaved head. With shaking hands, the surgeon advanced a searching probe deep into Ned's shoulder, doing his best to follow the path of the projectile. Although it was still morning, the rising heat outside was turning the surgical theater into an oven. The small, stuffy room doubling as the surgeon's operating arena was nothing more than a rickety shed stuck to the ass-end of a Port Royal whorehouse.

The dark, fleshy shaft welled up with blood as the doctor sent the metal probe down for another look. The sudden stoppage and the dull thud of the probe on the lead ball were felt in the unsteady hands of the surgeon rather than heard through his hairy ears. "Aye, there it be!" shouted Ned, recognizing the discovery by the sharp, shooting pain it produced. "Now, get it out quick and proper afore I be the one to start cuttin'."

The surgeon held the probe in place so as not to lose the ball and reached for the long tweezers. Ned winced as the pointed tip of the instrument stabbed tender edges of screaming flesh.

The heat and tension of the room squeezed pills of sweat from deep pores on the brow, nose, and cheeks of the physician. Saline beads dripped into fleshy ravines to form tiny rivulets that pooled in the pockmarked landscape before spilling over and converging with others that sought the same ocean of freedom. The confluence drained, unimpeded, to the lowest point along its ruddy course and came to gather and grow at the tip of the man's nose. The drop continued to build, its size and weight defying physical laws that neither man present really understood. He strongly wished to rid his face of the tickling nuisance but, without a free hand, struggled for more creative ways of dealing with it, and he dared not turn his face to his shoulder for fear of losing contact with the ball—and soon after, his life.

Ned caught sight of the hanging droplet and was temporarily distracted from his present concern and struck a deal with himself then and there. If the droplet fell on or near his throbbing shoulder, the doctor would die a painful and bloody death. If, however, the doctor was able to wipe the droplet away and get the ball out, the doctor would live—well, at least for now.

The surgical tweezers followed the path of the long, thin probe down the bloody tunnel and made contact with the curved surface of the ball. As the probe was slowly removed from the wound, Ned noticed that the drop of sweat had swelled even larger and was now dangling precariously from its perch. The physician would surely wipe it now, Ned thought. But a low growl escaping from the doctor's throat alerted Ned to the new problem. As the metal extractor played roughly with the ball, a fresh flow of blood once again filled the raw, throbbing wound and spilled over a heavily muscled shoulder onto the supporting wood-planked table. Ned slowly moved his right hand to the knife at his side. As he fingered the smooth wooden grip of its handle, the surgeon turned his head slightly to his right, away from Ned. Ned slid the knife out of its sheath and held it firmly, below the edge of the table and out of sight from the quaking physician. In a single breath, the surgeon jutted out his chin, dropped his lower lip, and blew. The huge drop of sweat became many tiny droplets and rained inoffensively to the floor of the shed. Ned relaxed his grip on his knife as the doctor improved his hold on the instrument and, in one decisive move, extracted the ball from his left shoulder and reached for his cauterizing iron.

Israel Hands burst through the door as the healer slapped a white-hot iron to the wound to stop the bleeding. Ned screamed in burning torment and dropped his knife to the stone floor, causing a delightful tinkling to ring out against the backdrop of foul curses. "Ah, Neddy, there you be! Looking as bright as the sunny morning. Up with you, lad!" Israel laughed drunkenly, supported by the busty whore under his left arm. The patient was still recovering from the shock induced by the searing of his flesh with hot metal to pay much attention to his boisterous friend. Ned lay despondent and moaning as Israel hovered over his shipmate and gazed empathetically at the scene. "Wake up, sleepy lad, wake up. Time to greet the new day," he sang in lullaby fashion as Ned slipped in and out of consciousness. Israel grew bored. He peered closely at the smoldering wound from inches away and then rolled his eyes back up to the face of his sleeping friend. Holding the bottle of rum in his right hand, he swung it pendulously by the neck in front of the patient's closed eyes. "Wake up," he chimed quietly. Israel uncorked the bottle with his teeth, spit the stopper to the floor, and poured rum freely onto the wound. Ned's eyes shot open with a start, and he instinctively delivered a backhand to the offender that sent him flying against the wall, breaking several wooden slats and giving Israel a concussion. The physician looked on in horror. He had gained yet another unruly patient, this one as big as the first and just as troublesome.

When Israel came to, Ned was still lying on the table, and the physician was gone, no doubt pleased to have escaped with his life. Ned seemed to be feeling better; the sweat had dried from his brow, and he wore the wicked smile that made Israel wonder if he knew something that Israel didn't. Israel scanned the room. "Where's the whore?"

"Left with the surgeon. After I paid him."

Israel nodded. "How are ye feeling, Ned?" he asked as he regained his sea legs.

"Once I have Cooky to tend me a day or two, I'll be fit and proper as you please."

"Well, let's get you set up so as you can defend yourself from pirates if they's to come for you."

Ned laughed freely and felt his recovery begin. "Have you seen Cooky about, Isr'l?"

"No, but I'll be quick about finding him, Ned. Don't be concerning yourself about that. I'll be back with Cooky and some food."

"Don't forget the rum," Ned reminded him, then smirked at the absurdity of his statement as he moved stiffly to a heavy wooden chair in a corner that faced the door. With his head throbbing, Israel bent over and picked up Ned's knife from the tile floor. He walked it over to Ned, who was still breathing heavily after the slight exertion from the short walk. "You keep an eye on the door, Neddy. I'll announce myself afore I come in." Ned nodded in understanding, and Israel left his friend alone to rest and heal.

A familiar bark brought Ned out of a fitful sleep. He was warm with a coming fever when the door opened. Peering through bleary eyes, Ned discerned the approach of a familiar shape. It hopped across the floor, slobbering noisily along the way. Cooky was at Ned's face just as fast as his three legs could get him there. The happy tongue-lashing that Cooky doled out brought a satisfied laugh from the patient. After saturating his master, he turned his attention to a fresh scent. Cooky smelled the injury and began at once to lick at the sore and weeping wound. Israel shut the door behind him and handed Ned a sack of pork ribs, matching Cooky nurture for nurture. Satisfied that they were back on course, Israel found a spot on the floor next to Ned's chair and sat down to share the evening meal.

"Thought I was about to lose another shipmate today," Israel said. Ned stopped chewing for a moment to consider the statement.

"You almost did, not that the doctor didn't do all he could to make sure of it."

Israel gave a quick snort, spit out the cork from a bottle of Madeira, took a deep pull, and passed it up to Ned. Over the course of the three years they'd sailed together, the two had become inseparable. In that time, they had fused together as brothers. Kindred spirits, Israel had heard say. Israel didn't know what a kindred spirit was, but he thought they were probably right. What he did know was that this was the tastiest pork he had eaten in a long time. "How's the meat setting with you, Neddy?"

"Ah, better than salvation itself, Isr'l," Ned replied, thoroughly satisfied with his meal.

"I stopped by and spoke to White Charlie today," Israel said, licking the grease from his fingers before wiping them on his breeches. "He said he figured I'd be by to see him. Can't say as to whether he was scared to see me—man's so white as to already be a ghost." The notion caused Ned to smile as he tossed another pork bone to Cooky, payment for tending to his shoulder. "Said he knows the jack tar who put the ball in you. Seen him afore in his tavern." Israel took another swig from the bottle and handed it back to Ned. "Says his name is Samuelson, sails on a Dutch sloop called the *Ellen Elizabeth* that flies the Union Jack. Says every time he comes in, it's always with the same lot, four altogether, the ones we seen. So then I went down to put glass on the vessel. She still ain't taken on provisions. She rides high."

Ned stopped drinking and set the bottle down on the flat arm of the wooden chair. "All right, Isr'l. We wait for a fit and proper time, and then we'll get them. We'll need Jack, Fancy William, and Doolin Pike. That should do right proper, don't you think?"

"Aye, Neddy, just as fit and proper as you please," Israel said with a grin. "I'll tell the lads tomorrow. I don't want to tell them after they been spilling rum."

After a prolonged silence, Israel looked over at Ned and Cooky. Both dog and master were fast asleep. Israel stood and stretched. He would take the midnight watch.

Israel awoke with the sun and the sound of Cooky lapping up the bloody fluid that seeped from Ned's shoulder. The temperature was rising fast, and the little shed was nothing more than a stifling wood-slat box. Israel shook Ned to wake him up. To his surprise, Ned woke easily and in a clear calm that betrayed his angry wound. "Best get you up and moving about. Do you have your sea legs, Neddy?"

"Well, let's just see," Ned answered as he started to ease forward out of the chair that he had slept in. "Away with you, Cooky," the master commanded as he waved off his three-legged friend. Cooky backed off with a whimper but quickly nonetheless. Israel took an old rag that was abandoned by the gratefully alive physician and converted it into a sling. Although Ned was still in quite a bit of pain, there was no fever to be detected, and the only impediment he noticed was the limited use of his left arm.

When Israel scraped open the shed door, the white light hit Ned's eyes hard. Two days in a dark room had left him ill prepared for the blazing Jamaican morning. But the air that filled his lungs seemed to be the very breath of life itself. The fresh morning breeze coming in from the sea boasted a bounty of cocoa and cinnamon being brought up from the hulls of the ships. Several large vessels had come to port in the past two days, and their goods were still being brought ashore. Ned and Israel walked slowly down the narrow streets of Port Royal to the harbor and the docks below. The town was teeming with people. Sailors, merchants, and, of course, whores filled the bars, shops, and alleyways.

The local constabulary fell back and hid in the shadows. They served no purpose other than being target practice with so many pirates about. The loot being brought to shore from the decks and hulls of pirate ships was the lifeblood of the Port Royal economy. The magnificent homes scattered across the lush hillsides and the shops of the wealthy merchants were built on pirate gold. Whether they called themselves privateers, pirates, or buccaneers and whether they looted in the king's name or their own mattered not at all; they were thieving, raping, murdering sea rovers, and Port Royal was their lair.

Ned and Israel worked their way down to the docks, past the banana bearers and the drunks who littered the streets, and found themselves a table outside White Charlie's. Although Ned was keen to speak to White Charlie, he knew it wouldn't be possible until the sun went down. Instead, he would use this time to search the crowd for old shipmates and a vessel that might catch his eye. Israel and Ned would soon be out of money and in serious need of a new ship in search of a prize. White Charlie's was an excellent location for them to pass the time. Israel's favorite whore, Anna, brought two large wooden cups and a bottle of rum to fill them with. She was paid with a thirty-shilling note and a friendly swat on her stern.

Israel cinched down the scarf that covered his shaved pate from the scorching sun. Although completely free from the lice that had infested his scalp on the last voyage, Israel decided to keep it shaved through the hot months ahead. Ned shared Israel's comfort theory and kept a tightly shorn crop. As did the rest of their shipmates. All but Doolin Pike, whom the lice never infested. Israel didn't know why; he just figured the lice were simply too frightened of Pike to bother him.

They sat below an awning of palm fronds that was supported by a light framework of New England white pine. Israel studied the familiar wood and wondered if it might have come from home. "I think I would like to go home someday, Ned," Israel said dreamily to his companion, who had been monitoring the activities on the wharf.

"What's that, Isr'l?"

"Home, Ned. I think I should like to see home again."

Ned looked sharply at Israel, as if offended by the statement. "You *are* home, Israel Hands. You best not be forgettin' that."

"What say you, Ned? Port Royal be my home?"

"Not Port Royal, Isr'l. The sea. The sea and the rollin' deck below our feet. There be home for the likes of you and me," Ned said as his mood lightened considerably. "Life for us, Isr'l, is found in a bottle of rum and between the legs of a whore. And if we live right, it ends quick and proper as you please at the point of a better man's cutlass."

"Well, then, Neddy," Israel said with a smile, "it appears we'll be living forever."

Ned tossed his head back in a full-throated laugh. A sharp, stabbing pain in his shoulder banished any remaining humor from his mind. He pointed to the largest ship in the bay. "You see that there galleon, Isr'l?"

Israel turned and saw a magnificent ship at anchor that shimmered like gold under the morning sun. His eyes widened as he nodded in appreciation of the vessel. "Oh yes," Israel replied. He picked up the bottle of rum in front of him and refilled their cups.

"Someday, Isr'l, I'll be master of a vessel like that, and I'll answer to no one but the devil. You mind me, now. If we can find a fast sail and a cap'n who be worth his salt, we could take a prize such as that," Ned said wishfully.

"Well, I think you be dreaming, Ned. But I like the way you dream, and if you ever come to master your own skiff, I'll sail with you."

Israel called for food, which was brought out almost before the words had sputtered from his lips. The meat was cold but quite tasty. Ned tossed a chunk of beef out Cooky's way, but the three-legged canine was no match for the swarm of hungry seagulls that noisily patrolled the skies of Port Royal.

The two sat in fine humor for a few hours, draining several tumblers of rum. At about the same time Israel felt the need for Anna's affection, Ned spied a familiar face—Willie, an old shipmate, waddling up from the docks. Israel observed the old sailor with a disinterested eye, then grabbed a bottle and ushered his whore to the back room.

Ned hailed to Willie and, holding a bottle up in welcome, insisted on his company. He offered his old shipmate Israel's abandoned cup and filled it to the brim. It was clear to Willie that Ned was looking for a billet. The aging sea dog gave Ned a toothless smile and drank greedily from the cup. Willie brought the cup down hard as he choked down the heavy rum.

"Ah, Neddy, it's good to be ashore again, I can tell you that," Willie confessed, catching his breath. "Two months searching the passage and not a sighting. The crew was about to mutiny if we didn't make for port. The cap'n's a good enough sailor but too much a gentleman, thinking a letter of marque puts him there with Cap'n Morgan!"

"Ah!" Ned said in exasperation. "Ain't it always the case? And so often to be sure. What's always missin', if you got the right crew, is a cap'n who can lead them to a prize! Why, me and my mates be searchin' for just that. I tell you, Willie, there ain't a privateer cap'n to be found in these waters who be nothin' but a dandy." Ned looked around for watchful ears. "Do you know a ship with a cap'n got salt water in his veins who be lookin' for a crew?"

"Well, I tells you, Neddy, I hear of a sloop just lost some of her crew when they faced into a grapeshot wind from a Spanish galleon. I hear tell that the cap'n be the cut of a sailor, kind you might want to weigh anchor with."

"Well, now, see here, Willie. It be several days afore this here wing of mine be fit and proper as you please. Do you know when he might be settin' sail?"

Willie raised his head in search of a familiar sight down at the docks. "There you be, Neddy. Spy down the end of the wharf there, now—you see?" Willie asked as he pointed with a spindly finger to a black-hulled sloop at the end of the wharf.

Ned responded with an affirmative groan from the back of his throat. "What's her name?"

"She's the *Sea Mist*, Neddy. And a fine, swift lass she is," Willie said in smiling admiration of the sloop.

Israel came back to the table, adjusting the razor-sharp cutlass at his side. He stared coldly at the old sailor who occupied his chair. Ned looked on as the young pirate menacingly eyed the old. "Ah, Isr'l, you be lookin' at an ol' shipmate of mine." Israel's gaze did not leave the man sitting in his chair, nor did it soften. "Willie, this here be the amiable Israel Hands," Ned said in jest. He leaned closer toward Willie and spoke in a confidential tone. "As my friend here is of a particularly surly nature, it may be best if you empty the chair you be sittin' in," Ned prompted Willie with an easy laugh.

There was something in the eyes of Israel Hands, a blackness that swam just below the pale blue that filled the old man with fear. Willie lifted his old bones from the chair with all the speed that was still his to exert. "Well, Neddy," Willie said, excusing himself, "I best shove off and see to my duties." He turned to Israel, tried to say something, but could only muster a hard swallow and curt nod. Israel held his lifeless gaze on his mark until the old man was out of sight. Ned observed the silent encounter with great humor.

"Isr'l, you can send a man to Davy Jones with that look in your eye! Shackle me to an old sea whore if it not be true!"

Ned and Israel were still beneath the awning of White Charlie's tavern as night fell. They showed no sign of the rum they had consumed, although they had been drinking all day. The night spewed seamen from every ship in the harbor into the streets of Port Royal. It also brought out White Charlie.

From a darkened corner of the bar, Charlie approached the two warily and spoke in a voice that mingled fear with anger. "I don't want any trouble from you. What's done is done. Ain't no changing that. I told you who they were, Israel, and I don't think they'll be coming back. They's sure to know you'll be looking for them." Charlie glanced nervously about. "Where are the others?"

"They'll be here soon," Israel replied coolly.

White Charlie took a deep breath. "Come inside." Ned and Israel followed Charlie into the bar, where a fire had been started in the fireplace in answer to the cool ocean breezes that knocked at night's door.

Charlie took a seat at a table by the fire. He sat with his back to the door, as he knew his guests would refuse the position. Ned and Israel sat directly across from Charlie with their backs to the fire. Charlie squinted against the light of the flame to see the pirates silhouetted as two black ghosts in front of him. Ned noticed that it was a significant discomfort to his host and thought more of him for enduring the hardship. Israel saw the same in the albino, but he didn't care. He marveled instead at the fact that Charlie looked more like *White* Charlie in the bright light of the fire. His hair was the color of

Bahamian sand, and his skin, even whiter, was that of a pearl, with shades of pink and blue beneath the shiny white. Charlie's pink eyes pleaded with Israel for calm and understanding.

"You know, Israel, that I told you the truth of the men who shot Ned. You know the name of the man on the trigger and what vessel he sails on." Finding no yield in Israel Hands, Charlie turned to Ned. "You have every right to exact recompense, Ned. There's no denying that. All I ask is that you not go to killing in my place. If they come here, which I doubt . . ." Charlie's words faded as he found himself without advice to offer.

Ned nodded gently to the nervous man and said in a reassuring voice, "'Tis all right, Charlie. We'll take the fight to them. We'll cause no mischief in your fine establishment." The albino heaved a great sigh of relief. Ned's attention shifted to the open door beyond Charlie. "Now, if you don't mind, could you please furnish the table with five clean tumblers and several bottles of rum? Our shipmates have arrived." White Charlie stood and turned to see Fancy William, Jack Quinlan, and Doolin Pike breach the doorway.

Pike took the seat next to Israel while Jack sat beside Ned. Fancy William took White Charlie's empty chair, which was very much to William's liking, as the firelight reflected playfully off his ruffled silk shirt. Israel noted that all three were armed with only pistols or knives, no cutlasses. The men were prepared for drinking, not battle. The newcomers saw the displeasure in Israel's eyes and dared not to begin a conversation but, rather, decided to brace themselves for a broadside.

"This is how you prepare to meet with fire the men who put lead in the body of your shipmate?" Israel scolded the three. "You come here with but three pistols and knives between you, and you think you'll be ready to commit justice? Are you the same men I fought alongside these past years? Ah! You're a fitting crew to man a jolly boat in a pond!" Israel said with ill humor.

White Charlie returned with the rum, a small bunch of ripe bananas, and a bowl of lemons and set them on the table, then left without a word. Once free of the outsider's ears, Jack was eager to explain. "Israel, that's what we wanted to talk to you about. They would be expecting us to greet them with the cutlass tonight. William walked down to the dock and spoke with the cap'n of the *Ellen Elizabeth*, and he said it be a fortnight before they be ready to sail. You said near the same to me yourself, Israel, that we have the time we need. I say we wait a few days and let them think we sailed. Then we strike when they don't expect it." Uneasy eyes darted back and forth, hoping to gain Israel's acceptance.

Doolin Pike submitted a low, thoughtful grunt in agreement with Jack. Israel and Ned looked at each other. Ned fought the desire for immediate retribution and nodded in alliance with the others, leaving Israel to stand alone. Although disappointed with the postponement of action, Israel shrugged in resignation, grabbed a bottle of rum, and filled every man's glass. They sat quietly, fingering their cups and gazing into the brown liquid as the light danced off its shimmering surface. With heads bowed in contemplation, each man developed ideas of how to engage the enemy.

From behind the bar, White Charlie observed his patrons, who appeared to be gathered in prayer. All wore scarves of faded color on their shaved heads, save Doolin Pike, whose thinning gray hair touched his shoulders in greasy spikes beneath his cocked hat. Then, one by one, the heads bobbed up, some with smiles on their faces. White Charlie turned away, wanting no knowledge of what evil their prayers had produced.

Pike leaned across the table and speared a lemon on the end of his knife. The others followed suit. They bit heartily into the fruit and savored its powerful healing properties, enduring the painfully sour taste. Fancy William followed his lemon with a ripe banana, stripping away its peel with great deliberation. All shared their ideas as to the best and most efficient way to dispatch their foes. Ned was given the privilege of having the final say, being the offended party. All were pleased with the plan, except for Fancy William, who always preferred fighting on the deck of a ship to fighting on land, especially sand.

"Now, who here be lookin' for a berth?" Ned started, getting everyone's attention but Israel's, as he continued to watch the door for any unwelcome familiar faces. "I seen an ol' shipmate of mine today as I sat just outside that door enjoyin' the Lord's fine day. I hailed him over as he come up the lane, and we gets to talkin' as ol' shipmates will do. Old Willie was always the reliable sort, so I asked him if he could name a worthy vessel for me and a few good shipmates. He tells me there be a sloop called the *Sea Mist* that's got a cap'n worth raisin' the red flag."

"A privateer?" Fancy William asked as he brushed unwanted lint off new petticoat trousers.

"Aye, and a fine strong sloop beneath our feet," Ned answered cheerfully, detecting the disappointment in William's voice.

"We'd do well to find a good crew, take over the ship, feed the cap'n to the sharks, and raise our own flag," Jack advocated, much to Israel's delight.

Pike groaned his approval of the plan as well.

"As long as we sail under the protection of the law, there be no law for us," Ned reminded them.

"And some fat gentleman in Charlestown, Boston, or London gets half of all the booty we spill our blood for?" Israel rebutted.

Pike groaned in concordance with Israel.

"Let's find out who sails that Spanish galleon," Israel continued. His eyes narrowed. "I'll wager he's a dandy. There must be hundreds of men who would sail with us. We fit her with forty guns and with the right crew and cap'n, we could lay waste to all our enemies."

"And who be our enemy, Isr'l?" Ned asked with growing suspicion. "France?"

"Aye, France. And Spain. And any other flag that comes against us," Israel concluded.

Pike, again, grunted in agreement. Ned looked past Israel to Doolin Pike. "Well, you seem to be in fine voice tonight, Pike."

Pike responded with a gruff, throaty bark, and the table erupted with laughter.

The outburst caught the attention of a young sailor who had been drinking alone at the end of the bar. The sailor studied the group from across the room and seemed to recognize one of them. Israel caught sight of him through the laughter and watched with increasing wariness as the man hurriedly finished his drink and made for the door. Israel stood abruptly as soon as he left and, without a word, went after him. The others, although knowing instinctively what Israel was up to, hadn't seen the man and watched in confidence as their shipmate took up the pursuit. A discordant grumble from Pike spoke voluminously of his desire to join in the hunt. Fancy William considered Pike with empathetic eyes and patted the aging pirate gently on the wrist.

A quarter-hour later, the four men were joined in quiet conversation when Israel returned to the tavern. There seemed to be nothing remarkable about his return, except for the small dark spots that speckled his broad canvas pants. Everyone waited for Israel to empty his glass of rum, then Ned asked, "Who was he?"

Israel met eye for eye at the table. "He was a risk," Israel replied.

"Well, did he say what his name was?" Fancy William inquired.

"I didn't ask," Israel answered as he poured another glass of rum.

"Was he from the *Ellen Elizabeth*?" Jack asked hopefully.

"I don't know." Israel shrugged with an air of nonchalance, maddening the others.

"You didn't ask," Ned said reproachfully.

"That's right," Israel responded, facing the challenge.

Pike croaked his disappointment at the lack of information obtained.

Ned emptied his cup in a single gulp, spilling rum over the rim and down his cheeks onto his chest, thick with black hair. He slammed the cup down on the table and wiped the wet from his mouth with the back of his sleeve. The performance received a wry smile from Israel while the others sipped their liquor quietly and waited for the waters to calm.

"Well, since Isr'l here took care of our friend just as proper as you please, we best be believin' he come off the *Ellen Elizabeth*. It be sure death to all at this table if we be believin' otherwise." Ned's comments drew nods from the others.

"Then we better strike fast. They'll be lookin' for us sure, once they find their dead shipmate," Jack said, looking at Israel and hoping that Hands would swear that no body would be found. But Israel provided no such assurance, and four nervous heads began to search the dim, smoky room for any other curious eyes.

"Well, lads," Ned announced, "we best weigh anchor and find a nice quiet spot out of range of an angry crew."

Without another word, all five rose from their chairs and made their way through the bar. White Charlie was quick to clear the table in support of their exit, which earned a hostile parting growl from Pike. All but Israel had left when he spied a sailor with his face nestled snugly between the breasts of his favorite whore. Anna flashed a wicked smile at Israel when she noticed him watching. Israel felt the rising burn of white-hot anger in the face of the insult. Ned came back through the door in search of his missing shipmate. "Isr'l," he whispered, grabbing his friend by the arm. "Come on with you, lad." And the two men disappeared into the night.

* * *

A small crowd gathered at the water's edge the next morning. One of the local merchants recognized the body as being one of the crew of the *Ellen Elizabeth*. A nervous constable sent a young boy to the *Ellen Elizabeth* with an order for the captain to send a party to claim and dispose of the body. The constable then walked off hotly in the opposite direction of the boy. A retreating Jamaican tide had rolled impassively away, leaving the lifeless, pruned body stranded on the white-sand beach. A few lingering onlookers remained once all those with better ways to use their time had left. The two-legged vultures scanned up and down the beach. Once secure in the safety of their isolation from condemning eyes, they rifled through the clothes and took anything that remained on the corpse. By the time the dead man's shipmates arrived, there was but a naked body for them to remove.

Rez Samuelson ran as fast as he could when he heard the news. He knew instinctively that his brother had been found. Woodson and Thomas were at his side as he came upon the body. A groan of pure mortal grief escaped his gullet as he beheld the stripped, murdered body of his young brother. He bent down to inspect the corpse. There was but one wound. And that was a clean, deep slash that ran across his throat from ear to ear. It was the kind that came from being attacked from behind. It was not a simple robbery by a drunken sailor gone wrong. It was the cold, deliberate murder of a boy at the hands of a strong man out only to kill. Rez knelt in the sand with Eric's head lying limp in his lap and covered the cruel slash with a bright silk sash that came from around the waist of Jim Thomas.

He closed his brother's glassy eyes and marveled at how young the boy looked, especially in death. Eric was only fifteen and much too gentle a boy for a life at sea. How many times had he tried to tell him? But Rez was all the family that Eric had, and so there was little choice for the boy to make after all. Jim Thomas clenched his teeth to hold back his emotions as he watched his friend cry over the dead body of a boy who had brought so much joy to the *Ellen Elizabeth*. Josiah Woodson avoided the scene altogether and gazed blindly up at the empty streets of Port Royal as the sun kissed the sleeping town awake. The illuminating yellows, pinks, and reds of the buildings and roofs shimmered blearily on the watery canvas of his eyes.

By midday, Ned was down at the end of the wharf, where the *Sea Mist* lay at anchor. Nearby, Israel sat shirtless under the hot sun and whittled mindlessly at a piece of driftwood he'd plucked from the sand. Watching the activities of the town at a distance, he was able to monitor the approach of any sailor who seemed a bit off course. Occasionally, he turned to observe the conversation going on between Ned and the captain of the black sloop. From Israel's vantage point, Ned seemed to be getting along famously with the man, which came as no surprise to Israel, for he knew Ned to be able to charm the devil himself.

Israel turned as he felt Ned drawing near. Ned smiled. "We sail on the morning tide, my friend. On the good sloop *Sea Mist*, with seventy fine, strong shipmates." Ned slapped Israel on the back, and the sharp sting brought him to his feet. Ned was walking the heavy planks of the wharf, heading for town, when Israel called to him.

"Neddy." Ned turned and waited as Israel walked slowly to him. "What about the cap'n?"

"I think he be a good man, Isr'l," Ned replied, understanding Israel's meaning.

"What about being your own master, Neddy?"

"In time, Isr'l." Ned smiled at his anxious friend. "Isr'l, you can't be killin' everyone." Ned looked down at the piece of wood in Israel's hand. "What have you got there, now?"

"Oh, I just been shaving away on this driftwood while I been waiting for you, Neddy." Ned took the wood in his hands and smoothed his fingers over the carved features.

"Ah, 'tis a fine hand you have with your knife there, Isr'l," Ned said admiringly. Then something struck him as familiar, and he recognized the face. "I'll be damned if this here not be your whore!"

"Aye, Neddy, it's my Anna. This here is my memorial to her," Israel said somberly.

Ned laughed. "Isr'l, you don't make a memorial to them that's still livin'!"

"I know," Israel said.

* * *

Rez Samuelson, Jim Thomas, and Josiah Woodson scoured the taverns and whorehouses for the murderer of young Eric Samuelson. Their inquiries were only of the most general nature; they had no clues as to the description or identity of the miscreant. Through an emotional fog, they searched and questioned anyone who would give them the time and had the patience to listen or care, all the while not knowing that they themselves became a larger target for those who would do them harm. Leaving their names and that of the ship on which they were billeted, they pleaded for any information to be forwarded to them before they set sail. They didn't know any of the people to whom they submitted their plea. They therefore wouldn't have recognized their enemy if he had been standing there, talking to them.

"It's them, Ned. It's the ones who put the ball in you," Jack reported.

"You sure about that, Jack?" Ned asked.

"Aye, spoke to them myself, and Fancy William was with me," Jack answered and then turned to Israel. "You said the man's name was Samuelson, Israel, true?"

"Aye, Jack. That's the name White Charlie gave me." Jack turned back to Ned and nodded confirmation.

Ned sat back in easy repose and was clearly enjoying the moment when Fancy William spoke. "They have a longboat down the beach, Ned. And there are plenty of dunes between here and the boat."

"Just like we planned it last night, Ned—get them on their way back to the ship," Israel offered.

"Aye." Ned nodded. "But we'll need to put a watch on that boat. William, take two brace of pistols and two muskets. If they put a watch on the boat, you let the lead fly when you hear us returnin' the pleasantries to them that extended theirs to me," Ned said pointedly to William as he lightly patted his injured left shoulder.

Doolin Pike took a sling of pistols from around his neck and turned them over to William with a grumble for luck.

Ned looked at his small band of men. "Remember, lads, we sail on the *Sea Mist* afore another Port Royal sunrise, so if you still be here when the sun come up, well, laddies, chances are you be nothin' but food for the crabs, anyway, so I'll see you again in hell." Ned offered an evil smile. "Now, let's drink."

* * *

Rez Samuelson tried to relax with his two loyal friends and take some small refreshment in a tavern they had visited on several earlier occasions. They told their story here as well, and with few exceptions, were received with compassion and understanding. The owner of the tavern specifically was beside himself when he learned of the story. The poor man, who had been the victim of a horrid skin disease, seemed personally affected by the tale. So much so that he fled into the darkness of the night without consideration of his business.

* * *

Fancy William could see from his hidden position on the backside of a kelp-strewn dune that the smoking lamp was lit aboard a brig anchored just offshore. The company that remained on the ship had gathered around the flame to light their pipes. He could only guess at what sort of lies were being told on her decks at that moment.

William smiled as he recalled some of the wild sea yarns he had himself spun before the mast. He looked up and down the beach for the presence of a watch for the longboat that rested on the shore a mere twenty yards in front of him. It was unusual, in a place like Port Royal, to leave a small boat unattended on a beach, especially at night. Yet there she sat with no one to see to her safety. William sighed in boredom and glanced up at the moon to see the time. He tugged at the ruffled sleeve of his shirt, ensuring the edges appeared evenly from beneath the greatcoat of which he was so fond. He didn't see the man behind him level the pistol at his head. The last thing Fancy William heard was the pistol going to full cock.

* * *

228

Josiah Woodson moved among the dunes with a swiftness that left both Rez Samuelson and Jim Thomas in the distance. A storm that hit Port Royal the previous week had washed mounds of seaweed high on the shore, where it remained, fermenting among the small hills and valleys. It was as difficult to maneuver around the muck as it was to run through the sand itself. Josiah stopped on the crest of a dune for his slower, winded companions and, truth be known, to catch his breath himself. Rez was the last to reach the others and was now doubled over, his hands resting on his knees, waiting for nature to return breath to him, when something snapped in the bushes beyond the sand. The moon, full and bright, and the stiff ocean breeze moving through the brush made many suggestions as to the possible source of the sound. The brush was a myriad of shapes and movement, none to be recognized or trusted. Guardedly, they began to move as one over the dunes, back to their waiting boat. Keeping a wary eye on the tree line to their right, they stumbled over clumps of seaweed and mountains of sand. A muffled pop of small-arms fire heightened their sense of danger as they quickened their pace toward their longboat, the direction from which they heard the shot. With their hearts pounding in their ears, the fear around them began to close in.

Doolin Pike stood between two dunes in a valley of sand, and as the moonlight revealed a man cresting the summit of one, he let loose with both pistols. The report from the guns hit Rez Samuelson's ear a moment after both balls had ripped through the chest of Josiah Woodson. Woodson staggered forward a few steps and searched with blind hands for the cutlass at his side. The blood that flooded his lungs erupted in a red gush as he fell dead, facedown in the seaweed. The crabs that had sought solitude in the kelp scurried from beneath its mass for a more secure sanctuary.

Jim Thomas was looking up from the bottom of the dune and heard the shots. He watched as Woodson fell from the top of the dune and out of sight, then turned to see the rush of a silhouette from out of the brush. He had only the time to notice the glistening metal tip of the spear before it ran him through. The force of Jack's blow took the feet out from under Thomas, and in one fluid movement, he was pinned helplessly to the ground. Jack looked up at the crest of the dune to his left and locked onto the fearful eyes of Rez Samuelson. Sliding the cutlass from its scabbard, Jack marched defiantly up the dune toward Rez. The Dutchman bolted toward the beach, away from the deception of the sandy dunes, only to be met by a formidable black hulk as it raised its cutlass high in the air. With his face hidden from the light of the moon, his killer brought his blade down with the lightning swiftness of merciful death and separated the head of Rez Samuelson from his body, reuniting the brothers for eternity.

Jack and Doolin Pike found Ned kneeling over the headless body, wiping the blood from his cutlass on the dead man's clothes. Ned seemed less than pleased as he continued to look over at the head he had just removed. "What's wrong, Neddy?" Jack asked.

"This here feller," Ned said, pointing with the tip of his cutlass, "he not be the one that put the lead in me shoulder."

Jack stared at the face on the disembodied head that reflected the lifeless glow of the moon. "That's the man, Ned. Samuelson. Told me his name himself. William was there too."

Jack looked around for William, whose absence, along with Israel's, was beginning to register concern. Ned rose as he stared down the beach at a shadowy figure moving closer on the wet sand. Jack strained to make out the identity of the approaching silhouette. "That's not William," Jack said.

"No," Ned confirmed, "it be Isr'l."

"Where's William?" a curious Jack shouted even before Israel had reached them.

Israel remained silent until he joined his shipmates and stood staring at the head that lay at Ned's feet. "Who's that?" Israel asked.

"That's Samuelson," Ned said with noted displeasure. "But he not be the one that shot me."

"But that's the name White Charlie gave me," Israel said curiously as he scratched his itchy scalp. Ned and Israel stared, expressionless, at the head until Jack interrupted their thoughts.

"Israel, where's William?"

"Nah, he's done for," Israel said without shifting his gaze from the head on the beach. "But I done for the one who got William." And that was all.

Jack shot a questioning glance at Pike, but the old salt merely turned his gaze out to the sea in acceptance of their loss.

Ned was cross with Israel for the good kill that had gone bad. Whether the confusion was Israel's or White Charlie's, it didn't matter now. He had killed the wrong man, and Ned had always prided himself on killing only those who, in his eyes, needed killing. He was always comfortable leaving random slaughter to his close friend, Israel Hands. And Ned knew that at this point, it would be useless to try to explain the difference to his henchman; he had long ago realized that it made no difference to him.

Ned forced himself out of the black mood that enveloped him. "Step lively, then, lads. We'll be fillin' canvas afore the sun shines on the likes of this poor unfortunate. Let's wash up and present ourselves as fit and proper as you please to our new cap'n. What say you, Israel?" Ned said, in fine humor.

Israel beamed in the radiant moonlight. "Aye, Neddy, we've had a fine time, but it's to sea we should be going." Israel looked to Pike, who gave an agreeing nod. Jack, who remained sullen over the loss of Fancy William, murmured something barely audible in favor of leaving, which made it unanimous.

The meeting was disturbed by a deep, low groan coming from just up the beach, between two large sand dunes. It was the moan of a man, mortally wounded and pinned to the earth by an eight-foot spear. The four men listened to the laments of the dying man for several minutes until Ned shook his head and broke the silence. "Ah, shipmates, he's still too far from dead."

"I'll go. I was the one who left the task undone," Jack said in disgust.

"Now don't you go worryin' 'bout that, Jack. You stay here with Pike and myself." Then Ned turned to Israel. "Israel, if you please."

Israel ambled unhurriedly toward the dunes and the task at hand. Ned addressed the other two. "We best be off now, lads. The sea be callin' her children home." They looked down and watched the rising tide as it slapped at the head lying on the shore and, with each wave, caressed it longingly back to the sea.

Ned looked up. "All right, shipmates, to quarters."

As they made their way up the beach toward the town, they heard the tormented screams of a man torn between pain and terror. Only Jack broke his stride and turned in horrific wonderment of what was happening beyond the dunes.

"Come on, Jack," Ned said soberly. "Isr'l will be along directly."

* * *

The morning breeze suggested that another hot Caribbean day was about to unfold. Captain Jonas Stingley stood at the rail beside his

232

quartermaster as the last of the provisions and crew came aboard. All hands were ordered to stow their gear below and report immediately to their stations. There was a very favorable wind, and Captain Stingley was not about to lose it. Life pulsed again through the arteries of the four new crewmen of the *Sea Mist* as they went to work immediately. The memories of their stay in Port Royal fell away from them like old skin. Their backs toiling in the hot sun brought purpose and reason into their existence, and all things were made new again.

With the sails unfurled and the *Sea Mist* slicing her way toward her next prize, the four new men were given orders to report to the purser. None seemed to be inconvenienced but for Doolin Pike, who had still not completed his assessment of the sloop's gun capabilities. Nonetheless, all reported as ordered and lined up single file to register with the purser as official members of the crew. Jack stood at the head of the short line.

"Name!" the obnoxious little man seated behind a small table demanded of Jack.

"Jack. My name's Jack Quinlan."

"Jack? You mean, 'John'?" barked the purser.

"Aye," Jack answered coldly, not appreciating the deportment of the ill-tempered man. "It's John."

"Well, dammit, man, say so! I don't want to know any name but the one to put on the death list of this here voyage," the purser said with an evil grin. "Next man, state your name!" he demanded without looking up, his attention remaining fixed on the parchment in front of him as he waited for the reply. All he received in response was an angry, menacing growl. He looked up into the face of Doolin Pike and read the endless list of sea crimes in the deep creases of the man's face.

"What was that?" the purser begged, the fire in his voice clearly extinguished.

"Said his name's Doolin Pike," Israel answered angrily as he stepped up from behind Pike. "And my name's Israel Hands." The purser was beginning to gain a feel for the new members of the ship's crew and thought it wise to extend some simple civilities to them. He looked beyond Israel as he and Pike returned to their duties.

"And you, sir, what be your name?" the purser asked, feigning sincere interest.

"Ned. They call me Ned," he said simply, knowing the game was on.

"Ah, if you please, sir," the man implored. "Your Christian name. It's for the ship's log."

Ned smiled and nodded. "Teach. Edward Teach."

CHAPTER THIRTEEN

The Dream

Monday, June 21, 1999

It was all Tom could do to get up the stairs. He and Jake had been on their feet all day, digging postholes for the fence that would frame the parking area, a nautical-themed design with dock pilings, which were really just cut-down sections of old utility poles, serving as the fence posts and mooring lines as the rails. It was a worthy task with its own rewards—improving the aesthetic presentation of the inn, working outside in great weather with a good friend, and breaking a bit of a sweat in the process. Should have been fun. It wasn't.

By the time all the pilings had been set into place, Jake estimated they'd excavated about two and a half tons of granite from the thirteen holes they'd produced. Tom estimated that Jake was prone to gross exaggeration but conceded the day had given birth to *a lot* of rocks. Even though Tom had the foresight to rent a gas-powered posthole auger to save them considerable lower-back strain, each time they'd struck rock, the power tool was abandoned, and the shovels were taken up.

Tom and Jake were still pouring cement to anchor the creosote-coated posts when the sun went down, and they were forced to complete the post-leveling process by porch light. It was 9:00 p.m., according to Ol' Sentry, when they came in for the night. The long day drove Tom's physical energy reserves to an all-time low. He was tired, he was hungry, and he craved a shower. But more than anything else, his back and feet howled for relief, and so he sought comfort in the soft embrace of the armchair and footrest.

Too weary to make such decisions on his own, Jake followed Tom mindlessly into the sitting room and plopped down on the couch in front of the TV. Both were staring at the television screen when Marie entered the room, carrying a tray of sandwiches and soft drinks.

"I made some roast beef sandwiches for you guys. Are you ready to eat? You must be starving."

"Just go ahead and set 'em down, hon. We'll eat in a little while," Jake replied, his words coming slowly, his voice listless. "We just want to relax until our feet stop throbbing. Then we'll eat."

"OK," Marie said, setting the tray down on the coffee table upon which Jake rested his aching dogs, still encased in a pair of sweaty, dirt-caked socks. Marie grimaced. "No wonder you don't feel like eating. Who could eat with those smelly things in their face? Get 'em off the table, Jacob, and maybe your appetite will return."

"OK. Thanks, hon," Jake said, not hearing a word Marie said. Marie leaned over and kissed her husband's grimy brow.

"This is too much excitement for me. I'm going to bed."

It was five minutes before either Jake or Tom realized that Marie had gone to bed and that the TV wasn't on. Not that they were missing much, they soon realized. Tom stood with a groan and switched it on, but because the cable wasn't scheduled to be hooked up until the following morning, they were forced to watch whatever signal could be sucked in by a cheap set of Kmart rabbit ears.

One station was coming in fairly well. It was in Spanish. The Stone-Brean brain trust sat mesmerized by a nighttime Latin American talk show. The hostess was pretty enough, with bulges in places that most American men would willingly forgive but American television never could. She was speaking to a man who was dressed in black western wear, with silver studs down the outer seams of his pants and the cuffs of his shirt, topped off by a big black Stetson. Jake mustered the energy and predicted that the man had something to do with palomino horses. Tom just stared. After several minutes of what must have been rather engaging conversation, the audience broke out in laughter and thunderous applause.

"I don't know what they're talkin' about," Tom mumbled, "but whatever the guy in the black hat did, it must've been a success."

"*Sí.*" Jake nodded, already half-asleep. "*Muy grande* success."

"Man, I can't handle this anymore," Tom complained. "I'm going to take a shower and go to bed."

"All right. I'll put the sandwiches in the fridge," Jake said. He groaned as he stood and stretched. "Then I'm gonna be right behind you."

Tom trudged up the main staircase, his legs on autopilot, and found his bedroom door without the assistance of the hallway light. He tossed his clothing off into the darkest corner of the room. Closing the bathroom door behind him, Tom stepped gratefully into a cool shower and stood under the ablutionary spray, letting the sweat, dust, and thoughts of the day wash down the drain in a swirl of dirty water.

Feeling close to human once more, Tom opened his bedroom window and felt the night, still warm and wet, coming in from the sea. He reached up and tugged at the short length of beaded chain and turned on the ceiling fan. He sat down heavily on the side of his bed and stared up at the revolving blades. He felt the smooth, flowing coolness on his damp skin. Tom fell back in bed and became hypnotized by the dark-brown vanes that whirled above him. He was exhausted.

The events of the day kept spinning around in his head. He couldn't stop wondering how many pounds of granite he'd pulled out of his yard, glacial till from the last ice age. What a crazy day. *Sí. Muy* crazy. The warm sea air coming in through the window, bathing over him, was the last sensation he felt before sleep began to overtake him. That and a pair of grateful feet, tingling in delight.

As he drifted off, Tom heard the sound of a bell far off in the distance. A ship's bell. Ding-ding, ding-ding, ding-ding. Six bells. He turned to see whose hand held the bell's lanyard. A young sailor with eyes as blue as the morning sky above and long blond hair that reflected health and hope dropped his hand from the bell rope. He flipped the helmsman's sandglass that started counting the next thirty-minute mark.

Tom smiled at his shipmate as the youth tossed him a quick salute and scampered up the rigging with the speed and surefooted confidence of a man with years before the mast. Tom gazed up into the crystal-blue sky of morning as the ship rolled unhurriedly over the gently undulating swells of a friendly sea. The melodic, low-pitched timbre of the ocean as it peeled off from the bow brought Tom to the ship's side for a better view. His hands clasped the thick rail of the galleon, and he leaned over the edge to watch as her stem turned blue water to white foam. The sun lay warm and comforting on his back. A drop of briny sea reached up and touched his lips. The salt on his lips and the rolling deck below his feet seemed reassuringly familiar and yet, at the same time, strangely foreign.

Tom looked up at the bleached-white canvas that was filled with sky and felt as if he were flying. The ship's crew moved about the deck as with a single purpose and lifted no needless voice in the execution of their duties. The riggers aloft seemed to dance with nimble, graceful ease as they climbed in the shrouds and scurried across the spars at dizzying heights. Tom had never felt so free in his entire life. Yet he wasn't sure where he was. And he wasn't sure what his duties were.

"Well, it be high time I be about ship's business," Tom heard himself say. "Afore one o' them swabs takes me for a grommet." *What? Where the hell did that come from?*

A fuzzy, dim confusion clouded his mind. There had to be some purpose for him being on board. What was it? Why was he here? He peered up into the rigging; the spry young seaman with blond hair was looking down on Tom. The lad seemed bright and chipper enough.

"Ahoy, there," Tom said with an uneasy smile, sounding a lot like some bad pirate movie. "Can you tell me, what am I to do?"

He was looking up into the white sheets, the brown masts, and the brilliant blue sky. The pleasant young seaman with the striking blue eyes stared at Tom without saying a word. Beyond the sailor, Tom could see the dark clouds rolling in, wispy and gray at first, as if smoke from Jake's pipe. He gazed out at the sea that was now shifting and beginning to churn, waking from her slumber. She was disturbed. Shifting his focus to the rigging, he saw that the young sailor was coming down. But as he descended, the sailor changed. He was broader in the shoulders, and solid muscle rippled beneath once-blousy shirtsleeves. His long blond hair was now a weather-worn brown. But the eyes were the same. Sort of. They still reflected the same pale-blue hue. But even they had changed. If not in color then in character. *Was it more a difference in quality, or was it tone? Or intention?* Tom blinked and looked again. Then he saw it. A bolt of cold, deadly fear shot through Tom. The change was the presence of evil itself. This *was* the same man. This was the boy who rang the bell and climbed up the rigging. And this was the old man who sat in his gathering room and stared malevolently at him while thunderously pounding his dead, fleshy hands in warning.

The world around Tom had turned violent. The ship scaled mountainous white-capped peaks and fell into the abyssal troughs of a raging sea. Even still, Tom didn't know if he was more frightened of the rising storm or of the angry menace that had just stepped from the rigging to gain a foothold on the gunwale. The pitch of the deck had become treacherous, and Tom began to appreciate the imminent threat of being washed over the side. He saw that the sea had turned a deep red. As scarlet foam crashed over and onto the ship, Tom realized that it wasn't water, but blood, that splashed across his boots and pooled and coagulated at the scuttles. The sky was a boiling cauldron of smoke and ash.

Hot soot fell from black heavens, burning holes in the canvas sails that had been torn into strips of useless fabric by the ferocious wind that buffeted the sea. Tom shielded his eyes from the burning rain and tried to see through the smoldering ashes falling from an unseen fire in the sky. Its remnants burned into Tom's flesh as they came down like manna from hell. The mainsail was completely ablaze and threatening to pass on its fate to the foresail when Tom's attention returned to the maddened sailor striding across the blood-soaked deck.

Tom immediately lost his fear of the sea, the wind, and the fire from the sky. His nemesis advanced toward him, pace quickening with every step. The sailor pulled a cutlass from his belt and displayed his blade in swiping figure eights in front of Tom. It whistled as its edge cut the air. Tom gazed down at his empty hands and wondered which god—that he didn't believe in—might help him now. Or might that same god choose to stay his hand now in order to turn his back on Tom later, when Tom showed up dead at his divine doorstep? It really didn't matter, Tom decided. *Dead is dead.*

He brought his eyes back up to witness the transformation of his foe from man to monster. The pale-blue eyes had turned black and were leveled at Tom with a savage glare. His hair had gone dark as well and flew wildly about his head, a thrashing, unholy halo. The man's lip began to curl, and then he spoke.

"You wonder what you are to do? Is that what ye'd have me answer for you?"

Tom's revulsion at the sound of the demon's voice was equally matched by the stench of its breath. In fact, they were one and the same. The voice—a low-pitched shriek that struck with such a savage, piercing reverberation that Tom had to clench and cover everything he could. He clamped his mouth shut; the sound was like a slow, grinding dentist's drill boring into silver fillings in search of a healthy, raw nerve. He closed his fists to protect his fingernails, as the voice seemed to be pliers, peeling back the nails, ripping them from their beds. With tightened fists, he covered his ears, protecting his vulnerable eardrums from the sensation that they were being stabbed by long, dull needles.

The voice sputtered from its throat and seeped out from around the choking, gulping, and swallowing of dead blood. Its breath was a stream of hot, fetid vapor that spewed and deposited droplets of putrefied flesh and caked at the corners of its mouth.

Tom forced himself to concentrate on what was being said, knowing that thinking clearly might be his best, and only, means of escape—and survival.

"Yes," Tom answered. "I . . . I'm just not sure of where I am or of what I'm to do." He tried to keep his voice steady and not sound frightened, but he heard the words roll out of his mouth in choppy waves. The demon moved in closer and brought the point of his cutlass up so that it was level with Tom's eyes. Tom clenched empty fists and tried to prepare to die.

"Well, you come to speak to the right man, shipmate." The sailor wore an evil grin and moved even closer to Tom, a foul black mist falling inches from Tom's face. "Aye, I'd be the one to tell you what you'll do." With widening eyes and a knowing nod of his head, the sailor answered Tom's question. "You'll give me back what's mine, shipmate. Aye, there's the truth of it. You'll give me back what's mine."

Tom's mind burned with curiosity. "What do I have that's yours? Please, tell me," he implored.

The sailor's eyes flashed with unbridled rage as he brought his cutlass high above his head and, with one swift stroke, sent it crashing down. Tom fell back and simultaneously lifted the heavy-bladed sword in his hand to block the attack. The force of the sailor's blow was evenly matched by the strength of the blade in Tom's possession. The bewildered assailant recoiled as if yanked backward by an invisible hand. Tom saw the surprise in the eyes of his enemy and knew it mirrored his own. *Where did this sword come from?* It didn't matter to Tom. Not then, anyway. It mattered only that he had it, and it kept the evil at bay. But there was something on the sword that looked familiar. On the handle of the sword was a crest or a coat of arms—something like that. Tom didn't know what it was any more than where the sword came from.

Tom held it out defiantly at the enemy who paced menacingly back and forth across the deck, searching for an opening, looking for a weakness. All around them, burning ashes continued to fall. Droplets of fire streaming tails of black smoke singed the deck of the doomed ship. His eyes darting about, Tom searched for a way out of this nightmare. "What is it?" Tom asked his stalking foe, terror rising in his voice. "What's burning in the sky?"

The sailor tossed his head back and laughed with hellish delight. He gazed at Tom with the eyes of eternal rage.

"What is it that burns?" the sailor asked. He turned his head upward to the sky once again and inhaled deeply through flared nostrils. "Can you not smell it? Can you not taste it?" He opened his mouth and caught a glowing ember on his tongue. He closed his mouth and eyes to savor the flavor. "Mmm." He looked back at Tom. "You *know* what burns, shipmate." The sailor smiled thinly, bright-red blood rimming his lips.

"Sins."

* * *

Tom woke with a start, his chest heaving. He quickly scanned the room and saw he was alone. His breathing began to slow. He raised an unsteady hand to his brow and wiped away large droplets of anxiety. Tom stared at his wet fingertips and wondered when all this was going to end. And *how* it was going to end. Nightmares and visions; nothing seemed to be making much sense lately. A feeling of doom wrapped around him like a cold, wet blanket, enveloping him, holding him down, suffocating him.

These macabre attacks on his subconscious were beginning to take a physical toll. His dreams had been invaded, and Tom saw a savage dawn on the horizon, when what attacked him in his sleep would turn to his waking hours to do battle. *What is it that I have that belongs to him?* A memory flash of the cutlass coming down on him triggered Tom's mind, and he instinctively reached for the sword at his right side, only to grab a fistful of linen sheets, and then he remembered. *Where had the sword come from? Had it been there the entire time?* The reassuring thoughts of the sword allayed his fear of the demonic sailor and brought with them a sense of relief and hope. Within a few minutes, the exhausted innkeeper tripped into periods of brief and fitful sleep. But it was enough.

He was up with the morning sun and sought resurrection in another cool, refreshing shower. The shampoo stung the back of his neck as he lathered his thick, coarse head of hair. What had once been pure black had now turned to salt and pepper and, much to his chagrin, seemed to be saltier with every waking day. He winced as the shower stream struck the nape of his neck, stirring up the hornet's nest that was already stinging him. He patted the area tenderly as he toweled off and felt with educated fingers the large welt that had arisen just above his left shoulder on the back of his neck. *Damn spider bite, I'll bet.* He opened the mirrored cabinet door and saw that he was painfully deficient in the area of skin-care products.

Tom tossed on his summer uniform of shorts and a T-shirt and headed downstairs to search the contents of the first-aid kit he had placed in the cabinet beneath the kitchen sink. He was surprised by the smell of coffee wafting up to greet him as he came down the ladder. He was even more surprised to see Jake sitting at the gathering room table, sipping the morning brew and reading the *Marblehead Reporter*. Tom consulted Ol' Sentry, standing at attention next to him. He looked back at Jake.

"It's not even seven o'clock. What are you doing up so early?"

"I don't know," Jake said. "I just didn't sleep very well. I think I actually may have been overtired. You ever have one of those nights?"

"Oh yeah," Tom replied, touching the painful welt. "I just *had* one of those nights. I think I got bit by a spider or something. I've got this burning sensation on the back of my neck. I think I have some bacitracin or hydrocortisone cream in the first-aid kit."

Jake squinted with morning eyes to view the blemish as Tom moved into the kitchen. From across the room, Jake could see an angry wound.

"Jeez, Tom, that looks pretty bad. Come here for a second." Jake stood and took a closer look. "Holy . . ." The fear in Jake's voice was undeniable.

"What? Is it bad?"

"Yeah, I'd sure as hell say it is."

"Well, how bad is it? What's it look like?" Tom's eyes darted back and forth, trying to envision the back of his stinging neck.

"It looks like that."

Tom turned around. Jake pointed to the far wall, to the painting that now hung above the smaller, disused fireplace. The first mate stared back at the gawking landlubbers.

Tom was clearly lost. "What? It looks like the painting?"

"The ring," Jake said. "The mark on your neck looks like a burn. And . . ." He hesitated and shrugged. "It's a red circle, with a black cross in the middle of it."

Tom moved with trepidation toward the painting, as if he were in imminent danger of the first mate breaking free of his two-dimensional prison and the wooden frame that entrapped him. The sailor's right hand rested easily on the hilt of a sinister-looking knife sheathed beneath a wide leather belt. Wrapped around the middle finger of that most dangerous hand was a large silver ring, its face a pool of bloodred stone beset by thin strips of black onyx in the shape of a cross.

Slowly, he turned his back on the painting and on the image living within that oil-on-canvas world. A dubious look wrinkled Tom's face. He stared at Jake. *The practical joker is at it again,* he thought, but he knew from the look on Jake's face that it was no joke. He held his gaze on Jake, not knowing what else to do with his eyes, and slowly walked back to the kitchen, still refusing to believe what he knew was true. "I'm going to get something to put on it."

"Yeah, good idea," Jake said. *Like that's gonna fuckin' help.*

As Tom rifled through the first-aid kit, bits and pieces of his dream came back to him in a montage of sounds and images. The churning, bloody sea that splashed over the deck; the maniacal sailor who sought his death; the fire raging in the sky. It was just a dream, he told himself. Yet still, the burning ash that had fallen from the sky had left its mark. The thing had marked him. *"You'll give me back what's mine, shipmate."*

Then it clicked. "That's it! It's the ring," Tom shouted, coming around the kitchen's half wall and back into the gathering room. "That's what he wants," Tom said, pointing an accusing finger at the painting. "And that's what was on the nob of the sword handle. And when I held that sword in my hand, he couldn't hurt me. He didn't even dare come near me."

Jake, who had gone back to reading his newspaper, was startled by the outburst. "What the fuck are you talking about, Tom?"

Tom didn't answer but sat down heavily on a chair next to Jake and gazed across the table to study the painting. His face was set like stone as he sized up his enemy.

"We've got to do something, Jake. This son of a bitch wants to kill me."

"I know, buddy. I think I know where to start."

Jake went to the refrigerator and slipped a business card out from under a small magnet that looked like Super Mario and boasted great pizza and speedy delivery. Then he picked up the phone.

CHAPTER FOURTEEN

Rebecca's Visit

Tuesday, June 22, 1999

"Thanks for coming," Tom said, stepping back and allowing his guest to enter.

"Thanks for calling," Rebecca replied as she walked inside. "My, this room is magnificent." She turned back to Tom. "May I take a moment?"

"Sure." Tom shrugged, uncertain of her meaning.

Rebecca walked freely through the gathering room, arms at her sides, elbows slightly bent, palms up, and nose tipped in the air, as if trying to catch an elusive scent. "There's significant history here," she said, her eyes widened in excitement. "In this room." The smile fell from her face as she shot a wary glance at the door through which she had just passed and then behind her at the staircase. "Although not all history is good history, I'm afraid."

She closed her eyes and began to breathe deeply and evenly. Jake came squeaking down the ladder to see the new arrival. Tom held a cautioning finger up to his friend, then pressed it to his lips for silence. Jake stood at the base of the stairs and watched, a cynical smile rippling across his lips as Rebecca seemed to slip into a trance. As her breathing slowed and deepened, an odd sensation came over Tom. A calm befell him, a feeling of well-being in body, mind, and spirit that brought about a heightened sense of awareness. It was as if a knotted iron band that had been wrapped around his spinal column had begun to uncoil. All things around him started to slow in their cadence. The swinging pendulum, encased within the wood-and-glass body cavity of Ol' Sentry, seemed to lag in its path, its momentum slowing until it came to almost a complete stop, its motion nearly imperceptible. Tom could feel his heartbeat slow with the decelerating rhythm of the clock. A calm, serene spirit came to rest upon the room, and Tom felt at peace and perfect ease.

Jake stepped nervously away from the ladder and took his first quiet paces into the midst of the insensible duo. He watched Tom as his eyelids began to fall, looking as if he were back in school, listening to a mind-numbing afternoon lecture after a turkey sandwich lunch. He waited to see if Tom's head would start to fall forward. It stayed erect, but Tom looked as if he'd fallen fast asleep standing up. Jake stepped in between the two silent figures and bounced a look back and forth between them. He held up a hand and waved it slowly in front of Rebecca's closed lids.

"Hey, there." He paused. "Hellooo?" No response. "Yoo-hoo, witchy-poo?" Rebecca smiled as she opened her eyes and looked at Jake. He turned again to Tom, who came back to life in a series of blinks. "Have a nice nap?"

"Wow," Tom said, sluffing off the alien, yet pleasant, sensation.

"That was kind of freaky," Jake stated. He turned to Rebecca. "What the hell did you do?"

"I entered my alpha state," Rebecca explained. "I'm sorry—I should have told you what I was doing, but I needed to gain some additional knowledge of this room before we talked."

"First of all," Jake started, "I don't have a clue as to what you just said, and secondly, I was asking about what happened to Tom when you went into your alpha phi epsilon state, or whatever it is you did."

Rebecca's eyes widened. "Tom?" She looked at him with an air of hopeful wonder. "What happened, Tom? Did you experience something?"

"Well, when you went into your trance," Tom began, "I started feeling very relaxed. Not really tired, just . . . good. Really, really, good." Tom flashed a self-conscious smile.

"That's good, Tom." Rebecca beamed. "That's wonderful. It shows that you're truly seeking guidance and are open to the help and protection of the Goddess. What you felt was her protective love. It brought you warmth and comfort. I have to tell you, I had no idea you could be so open. That's truly wonderful." She reached a gentle hand out and softly touched Tom's forearm. It was but the reassuring touch of a friend. To Tom, it meant a little more. On the outside of the ethereal aura looking in, Jake slowly shook his head.

Marie was in the sitting room, resolutely ignoring the pagan visitor and watching the nightly news on the recently connected cable TV. Jake wandered toward the front door and peered around the gathering room wall and beyond the atrium to ascertain if his wife might be within earshot. He seriously doubted she would share in the joy that Tom was making wonderful progress in becoming a full-fledged, card-carrying member of Wicca. *That's all we need—add Hurricane Marie to the ghost and the witch, and we'll have one helluva party!*

"Yeah? Well, did he also tell you he's working on about two hours of sleep?" Jake asked, breaking the spell that Tom was under.

Rebecca moved to the table. "Why don't we sit down? Let's talk about your dream."

Tom pulled out the chair at the head of the table for Rebecca. He wondered if she would be able to sense who else may have sat in that chair. She looked at her painting, hanging above the small fireplace. "From what you told me of your dream over the phone, I'm surprised you have it in the house," Rebecca said, referencing her artwork.

Tom considered the painting for a few beats. "I guess at first, I thought of the old adage 'keep your friends close and your enemies closer.' But really, I was looking for some key to the riddle. A solution that might make this thing go away. I don't know if the answer is somewhere in that painting or in the dream I had, but I'm not getting rid of anything just yet that may provide me with some clue. What I do know is that this guy, this . . . sailor or pirate, is pissed off and thinks I have something of his, and he wants it back. Plain and simple."

"And we're pretty sure we know what it is that he wants," Jake interjected.

"What's that?" Rebecca asked, intrigued.

"That ring," Tom said flatly, tossing his head at the painting.

"What makes you so sure?" she asked, gazing at the ringed hand of the first mate.

"Show her the back of your fuckin' neck," Jake ordered.

Tom shifted in his chair and turned his face away from Rebecca. He dipped his head and revealed the mark on the back of his neck.

"Oh my." Rebecca winced at the sight. She extended a curious finger and gently circled the outer edge of the mark. "Let me know if I hurt you at all. I just want to make sure that I'm actually seeing what I think I'm seeing." She gingerly traced the black cross in a field of red, a demonic eye glaring back at her. "The blackness—it's a burn, like you've been branded. The surrounding area is a blood blister, but the shaping is perfect." She shook her head in wonder. "This is extraordinary." She looked to the picture again. "You're saying this is a result of your dream? That you received this burn *in the dream*?" Rebecca asked, her eyes shifting from Tom's neck to the canvas.

"Yeah. Hot ash, fire; it was falling all around me."

"OK, let's come back to that. I want to talk about what happened a few minutes ago, when I entered my alpha state." She looked at Jake, expecting a smart-ass comment, but none came. "Different religions may call it by a different name—a higher consciousness, a meditative state, or an altered state. A trance, if you will. Call it what you want, but it's in this state that I'm able to communicate in other ways."

"Like talking to the dead?" Jake asked without challenge.

"Clairvoyance is a form of communication that may be used in alpha, yes. As is precognition. Or telekinesis. We believe that all knowledge of the universe is within all of us. And we can tap into that endless resource of knowledge when we are in alpha. Tom, I believe you entered your alpha today for the first time," she said with a smile.

Jake looked at her with doubting eyes and pointed at Tom. "You're telling me that this guy knows everything there is to know in the world?" Jake laughed at the notion.

Rebecca shared the chuckle. "We all have the *capability* to access that knowledge. We need to learn how to tap into that resource.

When I first came in, I sought to find out if we were in any immediate danger of attack. As I discovered we were not, I turned my thoughts to Tom and asked the Goddess and all living things to bless him and keep him safe. Tom, whether he knows it or not, was tuned in, and you saw how he was blessed."

"Look," Jake said. "I'm not exactly sure what I saw, but if you can do that, why don't you just adios this ghoul's ass outta here, and we can all get on with our lives? We're planning on opening a business here in another week. And if this thing isn't gone by then, my friend here might be," Jake said, giving Tom a light clap on his shoulder. Rebecca saw and felt the fear.

"After you called me this morning and told me about the dream, I opened my book of shadows—that's a journal that every witch keeps—and I went back to when I painted that picture. Then I remembered. I never saw the ring when I encountered him that night as he drifted by me on the bay. I had a dream that night as well. The image kept floating in front of my eyes, but not in any context. I didn't know what it was. A ring? A medallion? I wasn't sure. I was sure it was an amulet, but in what form?" She shrugged. "I didn't know. I painted it as a ring because it made the most sense to me at the time."

"It's a ring," Tom said, secure in his knowledge.

"And what the hell is an amulet, anyway?" Jake asked in growing perplexity. "I thought it was one of those necklaces that teenage girls put their boyfriends' picture in."

"That's a locket," Tom said with a haughty air.

"How do you know?" Jake asked. "Oh, that's right, you just popped your alpha cherry a little while ago, didn't you, princess?"

"An amulet is a protective charm, worn by a person to ward off evil spirits," Rebecca said, ignoring Jake's crude comment and getting the conversation back on track. "They're sometimes called a talisman. I think that might be what he's looking for. He could be afraid of going beyond without it. That's if he realizes he's passed from this world at all."

"Well, he hasn't passed from this world completely enough for me," Tom said.

"I don't know," Jake said, unsold. "Amulets and talismans? Sounds like a lot of hocus-pocus, if you want my opinion."

"Jake, you and Tom both have medical backgrounds, right?" Rebecca started.

"Tom's a physician assistant," Jake replied, "but I'm a history teacher."

"Yes, I know, but you were a respiratory therapist when you were in the navy, and I'm guessing you've seen your share of drug study results."

"Yeah." Jake shrugged. "So?"

"So correct me if I'm wrong, but don't they always have a group that takes a fake remedy? A placebo?"

"Yeah, they do," Jake said, smiling, not knowing where she was going with this but suspecting it might be worthwhile.

"Well, what percentage of the study group that has taken the placebo shows a physiological response similar to those who had actually been given the real drug?"

"Sometimes between thirty and forty percent," Tom chirped.

"You see my point? It doesn't matter what you or I think. It only matters what his belief system tells him is true," she argued, pointing at the picture. "If he believes it has the power to save him, then it does."

Jake sat silently, circumspect, his eyes on Rebecca. He knew she was right. It wasn't what *he* believed that mattered; it was what their menacing visitor believed that fueled this spreading wildfire. He conceded the point. *But where to from here?* "OK, we think we know what this thing *wants*, but we still don't know what this thing *is*. Is it some kind of demon? An evil spirit? I mean, the thing attacked Tom in his dream, for crying out loud."

"No. It's not an evil spirit," Rebecca assured them. "Not in the sense that it's a demonic spirit. It was, at one time, a flesh-and-blood human being. But it possesses and displays an energy that is clearly beyond the textbook definition of a ghost. Most ghosts present themselves as reappearing phantoms. Like a loop of film playing over and over again. Other ghosts that are part of a haunting may actually gain knowledge from their interaction with the living. They might learn a family's schedule and where they may be in the house at a certain time. Often, they use that information to find one individual alone, away from everyone else. However, the worst scenario is when a phantom first appears by a display of power, or force. Then, in a short time, it exhibits an escalation of that force. It becomes aggressive, violent, and sometimes deadly. It's like an avalanche, really. It begins as a slow slide of white powder, almost attractive in its smoothness. Then, by the time you realize the true danger, you're running helplessly from a roaring, rushing mountain of snow and ice. That's what I believe you have here. And this house has sustained it for about three hundred years." She looked again around the room. "Like I said earlier, not all history is good history. There was evil here before our sailor died; I can tell you that."

It was suddenly as if the energy in the room had been sucked up the chimney flue. The three sat in sullen silence, disheartened by the prognosis. It sounded to Tom like another terminal case. But if Witch Doctor Putnam was correct, then Tom would at least meet with a quick death, and after all, wouldn't that be a blessing?

Tom forced himself to break the oppressive silence. "Well, I suppose it could be worse," he offered, but he stopped there, unable to reach beyond the optimistic disclaimer.

"That reminds me, Rebecca," Jake said, not moving from his slouched posture in the chair. "You haven't met my wife yet, have you?"

"It just got worse," Tom mumbled into his chest as his chin came to rest on his sternum.

"No, I haven't, but I'd very much like to," she said as she looked to the open passageway and the sitting room beyond. The sound of the television, only occasionally, found its way from its secluded hideaway in the maple armoire to the other side of the house. "Although she's not real keen on modern-day witchcraft, if I remember correctly."

"Oh, I think you'll find that she's not real keen on *any-day* witchcraft," Jake warned. "C'mon, she's watching the evening news," he said to Rebecca as he rose from his slouch. "She ought to be in a really good mood now." Jake shot a cautionary look at Tom. *Brace yourself, slick.*

It wasn't just the opinion of her husband; most people who knew Marie Brean would tell you she was the most caring, loving, and delightful person they knew. And it would be the truth. She was open to, and respectful of, all faiths and beliefs. Except one. When it came to the occult, Marie Brean became God's little wolverine. Those times when she would become feisty, Jake would refer to her as such, all in good fun. After all, the last thing he wanted to do was piss off a wolverine.

Marie had made her feelings known to all; there was no room at the inn for the likes of witches, warlocks, or devil worshippers. She didn't have to say anything; she simply didn't extend her hand in welcome when company had come a callin'. As a matter of fact, she didn't even get up from her chair in the sitting room when the knock sounded. Jake knew that the news was not that entertaining, especially on a slow news day. Now he was about to stick his hand into the wolverine's den.

"Marie, I'd like you to meet our guest." Jake's voice was even, if not slightly pointed. "This is Rebecca. I told you she'd be coming by. She knows a thing or two about what we're dealing with, and I thought you might want to join us."

Marie leaned her head back in the chair and rolled it over her right shoulder, observing the witch with an almost casual eye. "Hi," Marie said flatly. Then to Jake, "No thanks, I'm good in here."

"Hello," Rebecca returned, a hopeful lilt in her voice. "Maybe when the news is over, you could join us for a few minutes. I'm just trying to help put some of the pieces of this puzzle together. Another rational mind would be very beneficial."

"Look, I don't want to seem rude," Marie said as her spine stiffened in the chair, "but I really have a hard time with the fact that you're a witch. The guys have told me how nice you've been, and I think that's great. And they told me about your code, or your laws, or whatever you call them, and I think that's great as well. And I know that you're not a Satanist or you wouldn't have made it through the front door. But you can't stand there and tell me that many practitioners of witchcraft aren't practicing black magic. Which, in the end, certainly serves Satan. And that's too close for me."

"People who practice what we call bad magic are not a part of our tradition and not representative of the craft," Rebecca explained. "We're dedicated to helping and healing those around us; that's what we're about," Rebecca responded gently, although without much hope of moving the irascible wolverine.

"It was nice meeting you," Marie said dismissively, then turned back to the story about the boiling cauldron of hate in the Middle East.

"Nice meeting you too," Rebecca said with an unhappy smile. She turned and left the room. As she did, she gave Jake a sad little shrug as if to say, *Well, we tried,* and went back to the table where Tom sat alone, unwilling to witness the inevitable war of the worlds for himself. Jake stood inside the sitting room walls, staring at his wife. She felt his eyes and turned to meet his gaze.

"What?" she asked, the killing frost carrying over to her husband.

"Oh, nothing. I'm just wondering, who's the *real* witch?" It was harsh, probably undeserved, Jake thought, but it was the smugness with which his wife treated their guest that bothered him, not her opinion. It was more than enough said, and Jake returned to the table to join the others. It had been a bad idea. He should have just left well enough alone.

Rebecca had laid out a chart with the phases of the moon when Jake bellied up to the table once again.

"That's the chart you had at the store the other day, isn't it?"

"Yes, it is. I want to plot the disturbances, including your dream, Tom, against the phases of the moon. If I'm right . . ." She trailed off, completely immersed in her chart. The two men leaned in and, with narrowed eyes, tried in vain to telepathically extract the final whispers of thought from Rebecca's mind before she fell silent.

"Tom, what was the first occurrence, and what was the date of that occurrence?"

"Well, let's see. It was the window shattering, and that happened in the morning. It was the day before Jake and Marie arrived, so it was . . ." He looked at Jake.

"The sixteenth," Jake said, a newfound interest in the lunar approach to understanding the supernatural taking hold.

"And your first day living in the house?"

"That was Monday, the fourteenth. Now, I was here during the day, *every* day, for the last month, but it wasn't until the fourteenth that I moved in because the bedroom renovations weren't complete."

"And nothing happened on the fourteenth?"

"Well, nothing to speak of, but that was the night I started having weird dreams."

"OK, and you all had a shared vision before you saw me, correct?"

"Yeah," Jake said. "It was just a split second—you know, sort of leaves you wondering if you really saw anything at all."

"But it was from that experience that you all recognized the phantom as being the same man in the painting?"

Both men nodded.

"It was after that that I saw him," Tom added. "He was seething at me; there's no other way to put it. He was sitting right where you're sitting now."

Rebecca didn't flinch at the statement but continued on. "OK, and then your dream last night, Tom, where there was actual physical contact made. Give me a minute here."

Jake and Tom fidgeted like expectant fathers, tapping their feet, twiddling their fingers, and shifting in their seats. It was several minutes before Rebecca sat back in her chair.

"Well?" Jake finally asked.

"Well, I've got some good news and some bad news. Which do you want first?"

"The bad news," Tom said without pause.

"The bad news is, this thing is going to kill you. Or at least try to."

"I'd say that's bad news," Jake concurred.

"OK," Tom said, his voice cracking like lake ice in spring. "So what's the good news?"

"I think I can tell you when it will be, and you can either fight it or make darn sure you're no longer in the house."

"I've put everything I have into this house," Tom said, rejecting the notion of leaving. "I open for business in ten days. I'm not going anywhere. So tell me, how do I fight this thing?" The front Tom put up was admirable, but he sorely wished he owned the courage of his words.

"Well, his powers are on the rise, and they'll peak at the full moon, which is less than a week away. My guess is that there will be at least one more attack before then. I believe that simply from what he's shown us already, multiple visits, increasing in intensity. So you'll have to be careful. While the moon is waxing as it is now, my powers are strongest to assist you. In other words, my spells to help you with your health and strength are rising with the moon. Unfortunately, they're at their weakest in fighting an adversarial spirit at this time. That will come as the moon is waning, but by then it would be . . ."

"Too late," Tom finished. Rebecca nodded.

"We need to focus on what we can do to protect you," she said, then shifted her eyes to Jake. "All of you, and we need to find out all we can about the history of this house. Maybe it'll provide us with some critical piece of information—I don't know."

"Now that's *my* little red wagon," Jake insisted. "I'm in. When do you want to get started?"

"Hey, wait a minute," Tom objected, not wanting to be left out of a cozy study session with Rebecca. "I already researched the history of the house. I told you all about it, Jake."

"We're not talking about the *Reader's Digest* version, slick. We're talking about what *really* happened here. Believe me, no docent named Elsie at the historical society is going to be able to tell you that. You've got to find the old guy whose front lawn is overgrown with weeds, whose house smells like moldy paper, and who now bends over dusty old manuscripts, reading with a magnifying glass. There's somebody like that in every town. It's the guy nobody knows, and if they do know him, they think he's a nutjob. But he's got the goods. He's in possession of the real pearls of knowledge."

Rebecca smiled. "I know that guy."

"When do we see him?" Jake asked, eager to get underway.

"I'll call him tomorrow. Usually, he requires a bit of advance notice before he sees people. So I'll press him to see us the day after tomorrow."

"Why's he need advance notice? So he can clean the place up?"

"No, so he can locate the information that they're looking for." She smiled. "It's funny—he takes very good care of his yard, but other than that, his place is exactly as you described it. How he can find anything in that mess is beyond me."

"OK, Thursday morning, then," Jake said, confirming their date.

"I'd certainly like to be there to see what he's got," Tom was quick to add.

"I need you to stay with Marie," Jake said. "Could you do that? I don't want her to be alone here."

"What about this?" Tom proposed. "If all four of us go we could stop for breakfast and . . . ?" He looked at Rebecca and quickly realized the absurdity of the foursome ever being together. The last thing he wanted, besides being killed by a malevolent spirit, was for a religious war to break out. Tom conceded. "Yeah, no problem, we've got a lot left to do here, anyway."

Rebecca reached into her bag that lay at the floor near her feet and pulled out two books. "Let me give you these, Tom. They'll provide some background information and describe how we live and worship and practice our craft. They're not intended to convert you, just to answer questions that I'm sure you all still have. Anyway, take a look. It may help."

Tom glanced at the books and quickly placed one on top of the other.

"What're they called?" Jake asked, his prying eyes on the book titles that Tom endeavored to conceal.

"The Power of the Witch," Tom said with a defensive air.

"No, what's the other one, the one on the bottom?"

"Never mind—she gave them to me. Get your own copies."

"Well, it appears you boys need some time to work things out," Rebecca teased. "I'll call and confirm with you tomorrow night, Jake."

"Sounds good," Jake replied, his eyes still probing for the second title.

"I think I'll say goodbye to your wife before I go. It couldn't hurt."

"Wanna bet?" Jake said.

"Good luck," Tom added.

Tom watched admiringly as Rebecca glided gracefully toward the sitting room. Just as she cleared the archway, Marie let out an uncharacteristic shout. "Bull! That's bull!" She was yelling at the TV and the field reporter broadcasting from outside the abortion clinic, the black smoke still pouring out of the shattered windows of the bombed facility. Rebecca caught only the tail end of the report: "A dedicated pro-lifer said this would not be the end of the attacks. The police here are following up on every piece of evidence they have to find the bomber, but unfortunately, there's not much to go on at this point. Back to you in the studio."

Marie clicked off the television. "Ugh," she growled in disgust.

"I just wanted to say goodbye," Rebecca said, treading softly on sensitive ground. "A horrible tragedy," she added, extending the olive branch yet again. Marie looked over her shoulder, still fuming from the news report, and as if they had been in the middle of a conversation, took up the issue and carried it forward with Rebecca.

"Well, what really gets me angry is when someone does this and says they're pro-life. *I'm* pro-life. I mean, come on! They're obviously not pro-life if they're willing to destroy life. And the media never point out the contradiction; they seem perfectly satisfied to lay the blame on the entire pro-life movement. Those poor people who were in the clinic. My God." Marie shook her head in impotent protest. "The ones who did this are nothing more than murderers looking for an excuse to commit their crimes. How can the world associate those people with the pro-life movement?" she asked rhetorically. "The mere fact that they're blowing up buildings in an attempt to kill doctors who perform abortions proves that they're *not* pro-life. And people never fail to put us in league with these monsters."

"I know just how you feel," Rebecca confessed.

The simple statement of truth stopped Marie cold. It had not been delivered as an accusation but as a shared experience. A common hurt, realized and expressed through six soft-spoken words from behind a meek and compassionate smile. Marie stared dumbly at Rebecca for what seemed to be a long time, although it was only seconds. They had stepped away from the precipice. The cavernous void that had stood between them began to crumble, filling into itself with the very earth that had separated them. What was left was a valley, deep and wide but now passable, if either cared to make the journey.

"Well, I was just leaving. Bye, now." The witch smiled and disappeared behind the archway.

Jake and Tom were standing expectantly in the gathering room, ready to break for the door if the fur began to fly, when Rebecca returned. "That sounded like it went fairly well," Jake said with an even mix of hope and surprise.

"Well, she's got bigger things on her mind right now," Rebecca replied, excusing her hostess as she slung her bag over her shoulder. Tom walked slowly to the door, with Jake and Rebecca trailing after him.

"You're gonna call tomorrow night, right?" Jake asked.

"Yes, probably early evening. Will you be home?"

"We'll be home," Tom interjected. "You know, you don't have to call. You can stop by if you'd prefer. And maybe we could get something to eat. Or something." Tom wished he could retract the words before they even left his mouth. But it was too late. And there it was.

"Thanks, Tom. That's very nice of you, but I really am incredibly busy right now."

"Oh, well, then, perhaps some other time," Tom sputtered, his tongue thick with embarrassment.

Rebecca smiled. "Perhaps."

Jake read the message loud and clear. *She said don't bet on it, slick. And you're damn lucky she gave you a net to land on.* Jake knew Tom had to be hurting with that one. He could almost feel the telephone pole of rejection hitting Tom squarely between the thighs. Jake winced in pain for his friend.

"All right, Rebecca, until tomorrow," Jake said as she turned to leave.

Another voice, soft and distant, caused the three to turn around.

"Good night, Rebecca," Marie said, standing between the two rooms. "Take care."

Rebecca, as pleased as she was surprised, smiled and held up a hand in farewell. "Blessings."

CHAPTER FIFTEEN
The Parting

August–October 1718

"How many is this?" Israel asked, resting his hands and chin on the end of the long-barreled musket.

"Fourteen, by my count," Elijah answered.

A small gathering of ship's company stood on a low hill at a socially acceptable distance by order of their captain. They watched from afar as a fiddle player struck out a lively tune and was joined eight beats later by a grinning, toothless sailor on a squeezebox. Several of the banished group began to bob their heads to the music. They tipped a clay jug and passed it around and watched the gay celebration down below with varying degrees of contempt and amusement.

Ned Teach and his new bride danced lightly among the crowd of well-wishers. Dressed in a soft-green silk coat, with pale-yellow ribbons tied in his long black beard, the captain of the *Queen Anne's*

Revenge, that good ship that was so recently, and so needlessly, run aground by its master, mixed effortlessly with the royal ministers and the landed gentry.

Israel felt the low rumble of displeasure from the men flanking him as much as heard it, and he knew their situation was not likely to improve for some time. Despite this, Israel tried not to smile as the quiet growls of his shipmates turned his thoughts back to Doolin Pike, a true and honest pirate now seven years with Davy Jones. Israel took a deep, doleful breath, dispelling the memory, and turned to take in the haze-gray view of Pamlico Sound. He wondered what had gone so wrong.

It was not long ago that the crew of the *Queen Anne's Revenge* scoured the Caribbean for bounty and blood. The crew was known and feared by all, due largely, Israel conceded, to the appearance and demeanor of their captain. Even those Brethren of the Coast who cruised into their sea lane yielded to them. Stede Bonnet, that fat, useless pig who had dared to sail under the black flag, soiled his breeches at the sight of the *Queen Anne's Revenge.* And Drew Herriot turned over sloop and service to Captain Teach and his pirate crew as if it were an honor. They were the best, Israel held, to ever sail the Spanish Main. And here they were, with no promise of return to the sea, watching Neddy strut about in a circle of women, planters, and politicians.

He sometimes blamed himself for pressing Neddy to become more than what he was. As he had learned from James Barry, so Israel had passed on to Neddy: "Appearances, appearances." Ned learned fast and found identity and comfort behind a cultivated, wild-eyed look and a long black beard. After two years under Captain Hornigold, he and Ned became the most fearsome duo to sail on the same deck. Even Hornigold breathed a sigh of relief when he and

Neddy sailed away on the *Queen Anne's Revenge*. They were more than shipmates; they were brothers against the world and would damn all who dared come against them. But something was happening. Israel felt he had lost his friend on some unnamed voyage, and a stranger now stood in the high boots of his once and only brother.

The truth of the matter was that the name *Blackbeard* gave wing to fear when heard or spoken; God forbid you actually saw the man. Israel knew this and felt the unquenchable fire of jealousy and resentment burning within. For when it came to bloodletting, it was Israel's hands that turned red and Israel's soul that turned black. The captain, all the while, stood on the quarterdeck and stared menacingly at his foe. Now the man of action watched the man of appearances dance the allemande.

"Do you truly believe the folk care for him that much?" Elijah asked no one in particular.

"No," Israel said after brief contemplation. "I think it be more fear than affection." Five heads nodded agreement. They watched the townsfolk come to life whenever Teach's smiling eyes met theirs.

Jacobus Hughes wiped the moisture from his brow with the back of his sleeve and squinted into the sticky, white Carolina sky. The warm sea breeze coming in from the sound salted the sweet scent of magnolias that filled the air. He cocked his head and studied the captain's new bride. "Tell me again. What's her name?" Jacobus asked.

"Mary," answered Henry Somerset. Jacobus swiveled his head and glared at his shipmate. "I know that, Henry. What's her last name?"

"Teach," Liam O'Brien stated in a thick Irish brogue, which sounded like *Taytch*. A collective chuckle broke out among the group. Only King Richard, an ex-slave whose knowledge of English did not allow him to follow the path of such subtle humor, remained silent, but he smiled when he saw Israel laugh. Jacobus shook his head and mumbled something to himself.

Henry turned to Israel. "What do we do now?"

"What do you mean?"

"Captain Teach turned gentleman on us, Israel. You know that. Look down there and tell me who you see. Not one of his crew. Aye, we be sent away like the house dog when the reverend come to supper. That fat one down there be Governor Eden," Henry said, pointing. "He be the one who spoke the words over the ceremony. Ol' Teach, Israel, he be more than marrying that pretty girl," he added scornfully. "He be courting the life of a land gentleman."

Israel detected a trace of blood in Henry's voice. "That be Captain Teach to you," Israel warned.

"No disrespect meant, Israel, you know that. But you were our cap'n on the *Adventure*." The statement put wind in the sails of the others as well, and they each stepped closer to their leader as their circle of trust tightened.

Elijah reminded Israel, "You were the master on the sea then, not Cap'n Teach on the *Queen Anne's Revenge*, and you know that be true, Israel."

Israel nodded slowly. "Aye, we steered a proper course now, didn't we, lads?" Israel admitted.

"And Teach took her from you after he run the *Queen* aground, didn't he, Israel?" Elijah demanded as the heat of the day seemed to add another angry voice to the conversation. "And for what? Why'd he do it?" Elijah commanded. "To steal from his shipmates, that be why. To separate them from him and the treasure. He tells Bonnet to go ashore and seek a pardon from the gov'ner, and when he returns, he finds his hold empty. Meanwhile, Teach sets a course for open water. Most of the crew object to the way he treated Bonnet, and many a man speaks up and tells him so." Looks of hard agreement are exchanged through narrowed eyes as Elijah rips the scab off the memory. "So when we spy an island that be no more than a sandbar, Teach maroons twenty-five men. Teach says that the rest of the crew now has a larger share. But I start to wonder if, next time, Teach might fancy a sandbar for me."

Israel turned away from the hornet's nest.

"That's not our way," Jacobus reminded the first mate. "You know that, and damnation, Teach knows it too. But he stole from shipmates who earned their share."

"Let's go back to the ship and vote it," Liam O'Brien rightly requested.

"No. Ned Teach will be cap'n as long as he's alive," Israel said without conviction. "Or until he says different."

"Would that be so?" Elijah challenged. "Tell us, Israel, how much gold do you have left in your belt? Enough to buy a fine house like our cap'n there?" The challenge went unanswered.

They looked down the gentle slope of the grassy knoll to the celebration in the yard of their captain's new estate and wondered what the world had in store for them. When the breeze was right, for it swirled in a clockwise circle within the hollow, they could hear the pleasant scratching of the fiddler's bow. The seafarers watched as genteel ladies in silk dresses curtsied to the bowing gentry in rhythm with the tune. Captain Teach mixed comfortably among his new family and friends. He had allowed only King Richard to sally forth to the party and bring liquor and meat back to his men who celebrated from afar. A loneliness settled in Israel's heart that he had not known since the death of James Barry.

At a safe distance, Governor Charles Eden was enjoying a lustful gaze at the new Mary Teach. A sweet, young, fair-haired innocent, he had long fancied her and had not, until recently, discarded the possibility of a discreet relationship with her himself. A deep, sinister voice from over his shoulder woke him from his carnal daydream.

"Aye, would you care to have a look under that skirt now, Gov'ner?"

Eden jumped at the voice and turned in shock and horror to see the laughing, steely eyes of Blackbeard inches away from his.

"Captain Teach, I . . . I . . . you startled me, sir." Eden attempted to gather himself. "I'm sure you have me at a disadvantage. I do not know what you mean, my friend," he said, his upper lip twitching into a nervous smile.

Teach stood straight up and roared with cannon-shot laughter, then bent down again to stand eye to eye with the man who tugged nervously at his shirtsleeves with soft, unblemished hands.

"You know my meaning well, now, don't you, Gov'ner? I mean, would you like to bed my new bride?"

Eden's eyes widened in horrified disbelief. The man in front of him must be mad. On the other hand, he had heard rumors of just this sort of perversion perpetrated by Blackbeard. But now the question was being directed at him. A negative answer might be received as an insult, which could result in his immediate death. An affirmative answer, however, if the question was posed only in jest, could also result in his immediate death. The only thing he knew to be certain at that moment was that he faced a grave decision.

The governor nervously twiddled the hem of his waistcoat, transferring the pork grease unthinkingly from trembling fingers to the fine beige silk. He pulled back slightly as Teach leaned in close, as if to study the lines on the face of the small man from different angles. Eden strained to find an answer as beads of sweat popped from the pores of his fleshy scalp. He peered into the cold, flinty eyes of the cutthroat and involuntarily released a high-pitched whimper through an embarrassed smile. It was all the answer he could muster.

Teach sprang to life once again with a booming laugh and a heavy hand laid to the governor's back, knocking him off balance. "Aye, they be the thoughts to make a man go mad, now, ain't they, Gov'ner?" Teach said with a wicked grin.

Eden had regained his composure enough to mask a sigh of relief before responding. "Ah, my friend, she's a delicate flower who is now safe in the strongest arms in the colony."

Teach stared benignly at Eden, his thoughts having seemingly drifted away. "So now, you think my arms be the strongest in this here colony?" Teach said when his thoughts returned.

Eden nodded, although he sensed he might have uttered some unintentional aspersion.

Teach put his hands on the governor's shoulders and gently turned the man to face the half-dozen men on top of the rise in the near distance. He pulled Eden close to him. "Do you see those six rogues who be standin' on the hill and lookin' down on all here, just as proper as you please?" Eden looked, shrugged, and nodded. "Well, now, Gov'ner, do you see the tall one there, the one near the middle?" Eden nodded once more, beginning to feel somewhat like a marionette. "Well, that be Isr'l Hands." Teach looked at his old friend with admiring eyes as he spoke. "Me and Isr'l been shipmates longer than ol' Teach can remember. Why, I seen him gut a man with a cutlass in one hand while he held him up off the deck with the other." Teach went mute, held captive for a moment by the brutal memory. "He be the strongest man I know."

The governor turned to his host. "You mean to say that he has strength to rival your own?" he asked.

Now it was Teach who nodded. "Aye, that be the truth. And he be the bloodiest sea rover ever to sail with the likes of ol' Ned Teach," he said in a voice so small that Eden thought he might have been talking to himself. Teach leaned in closer, as if to share a confidence. "Only he still don't know who he be," he said with a wink. "Not yet."

A pained look of confusion crossed Eden's face. "Why, whatever do you mean? Who could that man possibly be but the very man you have just described?"

"Gov'ner, that man be from the devil's own loins."

Eden stared at the expressionless face of Captain Teach and recognized the clear sobriety in his eyes.

"That there be our little secret, eh, Gov'ner?" Teach added with a faint smile.

"Of course, Captain Teach, of course," Eden said quickly, delighted to enter, on an intimate level, the secret world of Blackbeard the pirate.

"Besides," Teach said with a debauched grin, "what do I need strong arms for when my new bride will be dancin' on ol' Teach's yardarm!" The two men returned to the crowd of guests, howling in laughter.

On the hill, six brooding pirates grew more melancholy as the day wore on and the heat and liquor gained a foothold. They'd had their fill of food and drink and moneyed society and decided to taste all the delights the big town had to offer. Even though Teach and his crew were free from harassment from the law under the recent pardon from London, they remained fully armed whenever they walked the streets of Bath Town. For it seemed to them that their liberty was a far more certain and valuable commodity when they were the ones to protect it.

They staggered off the hill without a parting glance to their host and his fine new house and his fine new friends. They crossed the sheep-shorn grass of the governor's mansion, which sat on the land adjoining the captain's. Rebelling against the slightest hint of authority, the pirates slung drunken curses at the house slaves who stood in the governor's doorway and stared at the fierce-looking men from behind the half-opened door. King Richard was the angriest of all, challenging the house slaves to come and join—or stay, only to live and die in abject servitude. Israel finally called him off, and King Richard, the Lionheart, as he was often called, fell in immediately. He was particularly fond of Israel, for it was Israel who had sliced off a piece of potato and told him to place it inside his cheek when his stomach was wrenched by rough seas. It was through Israel's tutelage and by learning the tortuous skills of seamanship that King Richard had truly found freedom.

It was the same with most of the crew. They'd learned to trust Israel. In the heat of battle, he was first to board an enemy vessel and search out its captain. He feared nothing and no man. He was a ruthless killer and a preeminent sailor. Yet as a shipmate, he was slow to anger and exceedingly patient with the new hands who tried their best. His loyalty to and long-standing friendship with Teach were legendary. But recently, the tension between the two had all the crew at loose ends. Both men could be seen to stiffen at the shoulders as one approached the other to discuss some shipboard matter. Some of the men felt that Teach treated Israel no better than a dog and that Israel's once-fierce loyalty was on the wane. Outwardly, Israel scoffed at the notion of friction between the two, but now the tension threaded through the fabric of the crew, and the men began, secretly, to choose sides.

Darkness settled on the town. A yellow, waning moon peeked over the eastern horizon as the last rays of sunlight faded in the west. Bath Town was bustling as the six drunken shipmates tripped down the dusty streets of the seaport. The town found new life whenever certain ships dropped anchor and their pirate crews came ashore with exotic chattel to sell and tales of derring-do to share with the eager ears of the fascinated and gullible landlubbers. It was the best time for colonials to purchase goods from foreign lands at prices they could afford. And when it was Blackbeard the pirate who lay at anchor off the North Carolina shore, the town burst at the seams with activity.

As they stumbled through the night, sounds of mischievous freebooters releasing pent-up energy struck the air as the raucous drama was played out, often tragically, that followed every successful raid. For when the morning came, they would find themselves working off a debt to a tavern owner or entering years of servitude to a gentleman whose property was destroyed, bound to toil until the debt was paid. Many a worthy sailor had lost a good billet in recompense of an ill-gotten debt.

"Ah, the lads are in fine voice tonight!" Elijah said, trying to coax a smile from Israel.

"Aye," Israel agreed. "There'll be the devil to pay in the morning." A sharp cry erupted from behind some nearby building and was followed quickly by the hollow report of a pistol. All heads turned toward the sound.

"Well, that settles that, now, doesn't it?" Henry Somerset quipped.

"How about the Red Dragon, Israel?" Jacobus prompted, bringing all heads back to the issue at hand. "Why don't we go there?"

"You lads go on. I'll be about directly," Israel said, looking out over Pamlico Sound and into a deep-gray emptiness. His shipmates stared in silence as Israel walked slowly away from them. There was nothing they could do but watch.

"Let's go to the Red Dragon, Elijah," said Jacobus. "You like the place, don't you?"

Israel walked along the streets of Bath with his musket laid across his shoulders and his hands draped over the stock and barrel. He had fallen deep within himself once more, with no concern as to time or place.

"I know you, Israel Hands," said a harsh voice from behind. Israel turned quickly, bringing his musket to the ready when he saw an old woman standing in the doorway of a small wattle-and-daub abode. "I know you sail with Blackbeard. I see you," she said, studying him through narrowed eyes. "I see the blackness in your soul. Black as pitch. Black as sin!" she cried with macabre excitement. "The very shadow you drag behind you is but a bloodstain."

"I've no humor to spare on you, witch," Israel said testily.

"So I be a witch?" the old woman cackled. "And would you know how to treat a witch, Israel Hands?" She leered at Israel with a knowing eye. Israel's thoughts took him back to his boyhood in Salem. He fixed a suspicious eye on the woman. "Aye, aye, you would, now, wouldn't you?" she said, pointing a crooked, accusing finger at him. "I know you, Israel Hands."

Israel felt his blood run cold as he stared at the curious shrew. She unnerved him. "What would you have of me, old hag?" Israel feigned an impatient nonchalance but leaned heavily on his musket to steady himself. He didn't know what forces he faced but was confident that the woman was a witch. Her apparent knowledge of his past professed a mystical insight, a gift from another realm. And this old woman was no angel.

The woman looked up and down the street at the shuttered windows and barred doors of the shops and houses of her neighbors. In the absence of spying eyes, she beckoned Israel to enter the house. The aged clay mortar clung weakly to the timbers and crumbled at Israel's touch when he pressed his hand against the outer wall and peered cautiously into the dark room.

"Come in, Mr. Hands. We won't hurt you." There was someone else in the room with them. Israel reached across his body and firmly gripped the knife beneath his belt. A rustling sound in the near corner put him on alert. He drew his blade, ready for the fight. Very near to it, another sound, hard and heavy, was followed by orange sparks spitting into the darkness. A fire quickly flickered and snapped to life as the woman threw another piece of dry pine into the pit. Israel took a deep breath and straightened from his crouched position. A lazy calico cat that had been enjoying her nap screeched, more in anger than in pain, when falling sparks found their way to her skin through her patchy coat.

"Oh," the old woman said. "I'm sorry, Cat." Israel's eyes followed the cat as it streaked past him and out the door to the comparative safety of the streets of Bath Town.

"Your cat?" Israel asked, slipping his knife beneath his belt.

The woman thought for a moment. "Aye. I suppose she is."

"What be her name?"

"Cat."

Israel nodded politely. "Good name."

Israel surveyed the one-room dwelling now bathed in soft-yellow firelight. Two chairs faced each other across a small table that sat in the middle of the room. A small cot lay near the fireplace, and a large hutch stood guard in the opposite corner of the room. And that was all.

The woman shuffled to the table, puffing slightly from the exertion of restoring the fire. She motioned breathlessly for Israel to sit down at the table with her. "Careful now," she said in breathy warning. "The back of that chair be broken. Don't put no weight agin it." She looked across at Israel and smiled, showing several missing teeth. Her entire countenance began to irritate Israel.

"You said you know me, woman. You know my name, to be sure. But what do you know of me?"

"I know the hate and fear and anger. You wear it like you wear that ring. It don't ever come off."

Israel instinctively reached for the ring. He turned it on his finger. He had almost forgotten it was there. It had become a part of his hand.

The old woman fixed her gaze on Israel long enough to add to his growing irritation. "You were picked by God at birth and ought to have lived a life far from the one you are living. But you turned your back on all that's good, and you chose to live for the Dark Master."

Israel wanted to draw his knife and end the wretched woman's life. *You know me not, old hag,* Israel thought and wanted to say, but curiosity got the better of him. "Go on, witch, but be careful. There may be a noose around your neck before the sun rises."

A jack-o'-lantern smile crossed her lips, and she reached for Israel's hand. He offered resistance at first, but she drew his hand firmly toward her, the shallow smile still carved on her face. She turned his palm toward the firelight and studied its lines. Her smile faded. She pulled her hands away and wiped them unthinkingly on the dirty apron that protected her ratty woolen dress from further destruction.

"What?" Israel asked with genuine concern as he read the horror and disgust on the face that moments ago framed a friendly, if unsightly, smile. "What is it that you see? What is this magic that you possess?" Israel demanded, standing abruptly from his chair and knocking it over. "A curse on you, woman, if you don't tell me what you know! Do you see me dead?"

The woman trembled in fear of the menace standing before her, although Israel suspected it was not so much fear for her own safety but of what she read in his hand.

Her breathing calmed. "Do I see you dead?" She managed a very uneasy smile. "Do I see you dead?"

"Well?" Israel pressed.

"No, Mr. Hands, I see no death in you."

A bewildered smile dawned on his face. "What say you, then, that I shall live forever?" The thought almost made him laugh.

She smiled back at him. There was an edge of cruelty in her smile. "Yes. If you like," she said.

"Augh!" Israel grunted. "You be no witch, old woman—just mad. And I'll take my leave of you now." He walked to the door and picked up the musket he had lain against the wall. He turned back only when she called out.

"A word of warning, Mr. Hands. That ring may protect you in this world, for it was surely kissed by the devil, but it cannot save you from the next. Hold fast to that ring, Israel Hands, for when it's off your hand, the Devil's Kiss can protect you no more."

Certain of her insanity, Israel responded with a smirk and a shake of his head. He dug beneath the red sash around his waist and withdrew a single gold coin from a small leather pouch. He tossed the doubloon onto the table in front of the old woman, where it spun for a few seconds until it settled with a hard snap. She was still staring at the coin when he walked away.

* * *

It had been more than two months since Israel had encountered the mad old hag, but her words continued to haunt him. He had been having trouble sleeping. Sometimes, as he began to drift off, he would feel a pressure on his chest, as if a heavy object was lain upon him, making it hard to breathe. And sometimes he thought he could feel the old hag moving over him and whispering in his ear, bidding him to come join her.

"Well, Israel, have you decided what you're going to do?"

Israel turned to track the voice. Elijah Munroe was climbing up the ladder behind him.

"No," Israel replied. He turned back to carving the piece of driftwood over the rail of the sloop. "I expect Ned will be back directly, and we'll see if we can sell the sugar and cocoa here." Elijah joined him at the rail. "You're not thinking about leaving until the shares are paid, are you, Elijah?"

Elijah sighed as he considered the possibility. "Well, I don't rightly know, Israel. It ain't like it used to be. Since we left Carolina, we been to Philadelphia and Bermuda." Elijah flushed with anger every time he spoke of the ill-fated trip. "Philadelphia! What in damnation were we doing in Philadelphia?"

Israel smiled, knowing Elijah was bound to answer his own question. "I'll tell you what we were doing. We were advancing the name and interests of 'Blackbeard, the pirate,' that's what we were doing. Nothing more than that." Elijah shook his head in disgust. "And then, when they started chasing after us?" Elijah tried not to smile. "And how we started running? My Lord, Israel, do you remember how we laughed that night?"

Israel couldn't help but chuckle as he recalled being part of a drunken pirate band that ran through the streets of Philadelphia, being chased by city folks with sticks and clubs. "Remember the Lionheart that night? How wide his eyes were?" Israel asked, then added quickly, "He thought if they caught him, they were going to make him a slave again."

Elijah smiled, shaking his head. "No, I don't remember King Richard's eyes, but I do remember he was the first one back to the ship."

The two enjoyed a laugh along with the memory. Laughter had become a rare commodity aboard the *Adventure*.

"Philadelphia be damned, Elijah. We took a prize off Bermuda, didn't we?"

Elijah waved a dismissive hand at Israel. "A French merchantman who all but abandoned ship before we could lay upon her? Israel, there was no gold, no silver. No rum! Not much by way of a prize in my eyes. Just sugar and cocoa. Oh, but we could have made a fine chocolate cake!"

Israel smiled, although he found the tinny whine in Elijah's complaints somewhat irritating. "I need to know what Ned plans to do," Israel explained. "If the vice-admiralty court rules that we committed an act of piracy, we lose our pardon, and it's off to sea again, my lad. Then we'll see the old Ned Teach I remember sailing with, pursuing every sail unfurled."

Elijah regretted that he could not share in the hope he heard in Israel's voice. "Well, we'll know soon enough," he said, pointing. "Look."

Israel followed Elijah's direction and saw a small sail that was bringing their captain back to the sloop.

"How fare you, Ned?" Israel shouted across the water. His words brought most of the crew to the rail.

"We fared just as fit and proper as you please!" Teach exclaimed with arms outstretched to receive the cheers from the ship's company. "You'll all be rich just as soon as we divide such a bounty!" More cheers erupted.

"Did you hear that, Israel?" Elijah said mockingly. "We'll all be rich from the bounty we have to sell." He paused. "He must be planning to maroon some more of us."

Israel wanted to smile but suspected Teach had something in mind very much along those lines. "I don't know about that," Israel said after weighing several possibilities, each one as disturbing as the next. "It seems more likely that he'll not be putting to sea anytime soon. He'll want to sit and get fat on his land with his new friends while we float out here, collecting barnacles on our hull."

Israel walked over to talk to the captain as he climbed aboard. The crew stepped aside and made a hole for the first mate. "How much of *our* money did they demand in order to rule that it be a case of salvage?" He could see Teach was offended that he received no greeting before Israel questioned him so abruptly.

"The prize is ours, Isr'l, all fit and proper," Teach declared before answering the question. He brought his chest to full swell, as if he had negotiated a criminally beneficial outcome on behalf of his crew. "Eighty hogsheads of sugar. Twenty to Chief Justice Knight and sixty to Gov'ner Eden." There was no spark in his eyes to match the liveliness in his voice.

"Knight and Eden," Israel said in disgust. "Now there be two of the filthiest scoundrels to ever draw breath. Sometimes it's hard to tell who the real pirates are."

"A small price to pay for safe harbor, Isr'l," Teach replied.

It was true. Israel forced a nod. "Then I'll call for all hands," Israel said as he turned to exercise the duties of the first mate.

"Belay that, Isr'l," Teach said to his old friend. He turned to another. "Mr. Roberts, all hands on deck, if you please."

Israel went numb at Teach's order. Mr. Roberts, who fancied himself a seafaring man, had joined the crew not long ago. Not every man had the disposition to remain for long in the cold shadow of Blackbeard. Mr. Roberts, however, did. Stealing away in the dark corners of the ship when not on duty, Roberts claimed an anonymity not easily attained on a vessel like the *Adventure*. Biding his time, like a cockroach waiting for the last flicker of light to be extinguished before venturing out in the open, Roberts made use of every opportunity to ingratiate himself to Teach while maintaining a safe distance from the wrath and cutlass of Israel Hands. Now, he crawled out from the shadows as he was called upon to carry out the duties of the first mate. The order was an affront to Israel in a brazen and spiteful move by his old and dear friend.

Teach went below to allow the men to assemble on deck. Elijah Munroe, Henry Somerset, King Richard, Jacobus Hughes, and Liam O'Brien gathered around Israel as Teach retreated belowdecks. "How can you stand by that Judas, Israel? And don't talk to us about him being cap'n, neither," Elijah warned.

"I'll talk about no such thing," Israel replied in a controlled fury. "We chart our separate courses tonight. After the shares are divided, so are we."

Henry wanted more than a midnight parting. "Aye, Israel, we ought to put an end to a dog that begs and barks for the gentlemen of the land then turns to bite his own kind."

"No, Henry. Ned Teach is still seaworthy. He just don't want to be."

"All hands on deck!" Mr. Roberts cried out in an irritatingly high-pitched voice. "All hands on deck!" Most of the crew looked at one another in confusion at the grating new sound that scratched at their ears. Mr. Roberts, who was indeed a dandy—and the sort who less than a year ago, Teach himself would have run through simply because he was an offense to manhood—fought back a trembling fear as his order went unheeded. Although a lubber, he was not stupid, and his mind was quick. "All hands on deck. Captain's orders. All hands on deck. Captain's orders."

Two groups gathered before the quarterdeck, and when the grumbling of the group in the back and the excited chatter of the group in the front had quieted, Mr. Roberts opened the hatch to the cabin below, and Blackbeard climbed topside to address the crew. Israel looked on in disgust at the show being played out in front of him. Teach had come out attired as if he might be going into battle. Dressed in a black velvet greatcoat, he wore purple silk knee breeches and stood heavy-booted. Bright-red ribbons had been tied at the end of his beard, and a high tricorn hat sat atop his pate. The effect it had on the inexperienced men on board was predictable. They stood in awe of the greatest sea robber who ever sailed the Spanish Main. The effect it had on Israel and his sun-weathered shipmates was quite the opposite.

"Lads, the vice-admiralty court has seen fit to award us this here prize, with all salvage rights due us." Leaning forward just a bit, as if telling the entire crew a secret, he added, "And your cap'n graciously accepted the decision of that fair court." An animated cheer rose from the lickspittles who had positioned themselves directly in front of their captain. It didn't escape Teach's eye that his dissenters lay back against the port rail and hung low in the mainsail rigging. Israel leaned against the mainmast, listening carefully for the sound of treachery.

"Now, lads, the ruling is that this here French merchantman belongs directly to him that owns the vessel that found it. That bein' the case, and the *Adventure* bein' my sloop, well, the court says that this here merchantman belongs to me." Teach shook his head in feigned objection to the ruling. "Well, now, lads, that don't seem all fit and proper, no, sir—not to ol' Teach, it don't. So I give a lot of thought as to how I can make it fair for all hands. Since I be sellin' this here merchantman and splittin' the small price she'll bring with the vice-admiralty court, I hereby forfeit my share of the booty to you lads, to be divided up equally just as fit and proper as you please." Teach stood before them, beaming, the benevolent master, taking care of his helpless wolf pups.

There it be, Israel thought. *The dagger to the heart of the crew by the hand of their captain.* As a captain's share was but double that of any crewman, Teach's offer was far from generous. The price he would receive for the sale of the French ship would bring him considerably more than the sum of the entire haul. The men directly in front of Teach murmured to one another while still trying to determine just how well they fared on the deal. Many among that group were delighted but said nothing, as they had yet to even weigh anchor since joining ship's company. Those men nearest Israel swore oaths to one another, but not so loud as to allow Teach to hear them. There would be a time for that. Darkness had fallen on the autumn sky, and Israel could no longer see well enough to read the face of his old friend.

"*Captain* Teach," Israel barked, clearing the deck for battle with his mocking tone. Blackbeard's face went rigid as he clenched his jaw.

"What is it, *Mr.* Hands?"

"Beggin' the captain's pardon, sir, but why don't we split shares *after* we sell the ship and include the money from the sale with that which we got from the cargo?" Only those men loyal to Israel were defiant enough to voice their support of the plan with which he had so boldly challenged the captain. Standing head and shoulders above the rest, Israel and Neddy had unbroken eye contact over the slumping shoulders and bowing heads of the smaller men between them. But it was a challenge Blackbeard had prepared for, and he smiled.

"Ah, Isr'l, you have a right fine mind for what's fair, now, don't you, lad? And it's a fine idea that we must surely discuss in far greater depth." Teach turned to his new first mate. "Mr. Roberts?"

"Aye, Captain?"

"Mr. Roberts, fetch us a few bottles of rum and join me and Isr'l in my cabin, so we can give his plan the time and consideration it deserves."

Israel knew Teach well. He smiled and slowly shook his head as he looked at his once and longtime friend.

"Don't do it, Israel," Elijah pleaded as he pulled Israel close to him while the others of their tight band gathered around the two. "You don't follow a wounded animal into its cave."

"He won't kill me if he knows you'll do the same to him," Israel predicted. "Keep a weather eye; don't let any of these wharf rats scurry up behind you."

Teach went down into his hole. Israel followed but kept a few sword lengths between them. Teach was already seated at the table and facing his cabin door when Israel entered. Roberts stood crouched over to the right and rear of Teach. As with all shipboard overheads, there wasn't more than about five and a half feet of clearance in the cramped quarters, causing all to move about in the position of a perpetual bow. Roberts was hanging a small lantern from the center beam, and a tallow candle burned on the table in front of Teach. Beyond the dim yellow illumination offered by the two small flames, the cabin was dark, save for the flinty shimmer that sparkled off Teach's large silver goblet as he held it up for Roberts to fill with rum.

"Sit down, Isr'l, sit down," Teach said in a convivial tone. "It's been too long since we been able to set and tip the jug and toast those long gone, now, hasn't it?"

"I suppose so, Neddy," Israel replied, reminding the man seated across from him of his true identity. The slight was not lost on Blackbeard.

"Ah, now there's my ol' shipmate. 'Tis music to ol' Teach's ears, to hear his old friend, Isr'l Hands, call him Neddy. And the very sweetest music at that!" Teach turned to Roberts. "Now you be rememberin' what I say here, Mr. Roberts, and count yourself a lucky man to find a friend like I got here in Isr'l."

"Aye, sir," Roberts replied in a lifeless monotone.

Israel glared at Roberts with utter disdain and resisted an almost overpowering urge to unsheathe his knife and drive it to the hilt beneath Roberts's rib cage. But he had more on his mind now than playful amusement. That would come later. Now, he needed to clear things up with Ned.

"Isr'l," Teach said in a calm voice, more concerned than angry, "you put me in a bad way in front of the crew. That was neither fit nor proper. And you know that to be true."

"The men deserve more from you, Neddy. They deserve to be dealt with fairly; they deserve to be told the truth." Israel strained to maintain his emotions as he felt the anger coming to a full boil in his chest. "And I'm not talkin' about them swabbers you got topside hoping to get even a sniff of your farts. I'm talking about men who sailed with Hornigold, Woodes Rogers, and Long Ben Avery. You be cheating them out of what's theirs. And you ain't never done that before, Ned. Never."

"Don't tell me what's mine and what's theirs, Isr'l. I'm the one that says what's due you."

"That ain't our way, Ned."

"I'll see you to damnation afore you tell me of 'our ways'!"

Israel sat back in his chair, took a deep breath, and let it escape his lungs very slowly before he spoke. "You lost it, Neddy."

"Lost what?" Teach said, a bit confused by the sudden calmness of Israel's voice. "I've lost nothing."

"The love of the fight."

"There be more fight in me now than you care to know about, Isr'l."

They sat, staring at each other. A mantel clock, sitting snugly on the small desk secured to the aft bulkhead, tapped out loudly against the deafening silence. It was odd how the clock seemed to keep the pulse of the ship in the calm—a strong and steady heartbeat while in safe and quiet harbors—yet became a worthless ornament that ceased to beat when at sea. And it was only at sea while chasing a prize that the ship was truly alive. *Another useless trinket to adorn the cabin of the famous Blackbeard.*

But the clock was ticking now and didn't miss a beat in the midst of the rising storm within the cabin. Mr. Roberts sat nearby, waiting. Israel smiled weakly in bitter remembrance.

"Do you know what the worst day of my life was, Neddy?"

Teach emptied his cup of rum in one long draw and slammed it down hard on the table. Uncorking a new bottle, he filled his cup again. He looked at Israel with steely eyes and slowly shook his head. Israel continued, the strain of regret clear in his voice.

"The worst day of my life was the day I first heard the name *Blackbeard*. It was the same day that my friend Neddy was lost at sea. You didn't know my friend Neddy, did you, Captain Blackbeard? Now *there* was the greatest pirate who has ever lived." Israel choked back the memory and swallowed hard.

"You don't have the numbers, Israel," Teach said, refusing the sentiment.

"What numbers would you mean, Neddy?"

"The numbers you need to take over as cap'n. Well more than half the men will side with me. You know that."

"Which of them topside would you be callin' men? The lubbers you brought on board just to drink with you and be counted? Why, Neddy, you can't even call them swabbers."

Up on deck, the crew was a swarm of restless inactivity. Two distinct groups milled about smartly, staying busy doing nothing. More than a dozen men were hoping Israel would soon be on deck, declaring himself captain of the *Adventure*. Then they would draw up a course of action for the next run. These were men who had spent their lives before the mast. Many had been privateers; a few were old buccaneers from Hispaniola, perhaps the last of their breed; and one or two were corsairs who had strayed far from their Mediterranean port. They had all become disenchanted with Captain Teach's posturing and his apparent lack of piratical interest.

The rest of the crew, numbering about twenty-five men, consisted largely of landsmen and inexperienced seamen. Many had signed on so that they could one day tell their grandchildren that they had sailed with the legendary Blackbeard. The two factions understood one another, and Teach's supporters gave those loyal to Israel Hands a wide berth. Bottles of rum were passed continuously from shipmate to shipmate. Anxious glances were thrown at the main hatch, all anticipating the emergence of their champion.

But there was no sound coming up the hatchway. Elijah and Liam wanted to go below and drag Mr. Roberts topside by the thumbs, slice him into bits, and throw the pieces overboard, just to see if they would float. Enough blood in the water might bring the sharks around for a visit, and that would lighten the mood on the sloop splendidly.

Teach sat shaking his head as he stared at Israel with an expression that straddled the maniacal border between sorrow and fury. Israel glanced over at Roberts, who sat at the small desk beneath the glowing lantern, listening to the conversation with an air of nonchalance. Teach followed Israel's gaze toward Roberts.

"Mr. Roberts, would you mind goin' topside and fetch us another bottle?"

"Aye, sir." Roberts's eyes met Israel's for a brief second, then looked away as he stood to leave.

The cabin timbers creaked softly as a small tide swell gently rolled the *Adventure* from port to starboard. With the rolling of the ship, the pendulum on the clock stopped suddenly. Israel sniffed the air and sensed some misdeed was about to unfold. His hand went calmly to the pistol tucked under his belt, until his empty hand remembered he had deemed such a weapon to be unnecessary in the presence of his old friend. His eyes locked onto Roberts as the man stood stiffly and blew out the candle that burned in the lantern. The man seemed nervous and looked about the cabin as if he didn't know what to do next. For a moment, Israel thought he might actually be going to fetch more rum until he remembered that the bottle on the table was near full.

"Roberts," Israel started, "what need to blow out the candle when you'll soon be back with the rum?"

Israel read the panic on the man's face as Roberts stood in mute indecision, looking to Teach as if to save him. Teach coolly leaned over and blew out the candle that sat on the table, plunging the room into complete darkness. Israel felt Roberts brush by him and knew he was making for the hatch. Then, a distinct click came from across the table. It was the sound of a pistol being tripped back to full cock. It was followed immediately by a second click.

Israel spoke out from the darkness with a heart filled with fraternal sadness. "Ah, Neddy, you've come to this?" The only answer he received was the metallic snap of flint striking a poorly primed pan as the pistol misfired. For a fleeting moment, Israel saw the opportunity to escape and leaped from his chair to make for the hatch. But the second pistol didn't misfire, and the discharged ball hit Israel squarely in the left knee. The red-hot lead shredded flesh and shattered bone. He was howling in pain before he hit the deck.

The banshee squall from down below startled the crew and brought several men running to the cabin. King Richard was first down the ladder, followed closely by Henry Somerset and Elijah Munroe. They entered a small space that was pitch black and filled with the sulfuric taste of gunpowder. Henry called for a lantern, which was passed down to him. Its yellow glow against the deep-gray smoke that filled the cabin revealed a sight that would surely someday be played out in hell once more. Through the acrid haze, they could see Blackbeard sitting on a chair in front of them, scarlet ribbons in his beard, pistols in his hands, and a gleeful glint in his eyes. At his feet, writhing in pain, was Israel Hands, bleeding out profusely on the deck of the cabin.

"You be a boil on the arse of Ol' Scratch, Teach!" cried Liam O'Brien when he saw the terrible condition of his friend. Teach took no notice of the curse but remained silent and motionless in the midst of the choking cloud. They didn't bother asking Teach why he did it. The threat had been eliminated, maybe even killed. King Richard tore off his bleached cotton shirt and handed it to Elijah, who quickly applied a tourniquet to the shattered leg. Israel appeared pale and lifeless as he slipped mercifully into unconsciousness.

Elijah knew the only hope to save Israel was to get him to Bath Town and a doctor. But the only physician he knew in Bath Town was now a guest of Captain Teach on board the *Adventure*, and there was little chance that he would offer his services to a man whom his host wanted dead. Elijah would have to find someone else in town, someone who didn't live in fear of reprisal from Blackbeard. Those people, sadly, were very few.

When word of what had happened circulated among the crew, Israel's men assumed defensive positions on board to avoid the possibility of a sudden rush and took possession of the skiff, still tied to the side of the sloop. They secured the area around the hatch as the men hoisted Israel up the ladder by tying a rope around his chest and under his arms. Once topside, King Richard lifted the wounded Hands in his massive arms and carried him to the rail, where he was lowered down to the boat below in the same manner.

All Israel's men had drawn pistols and cutlasses, and no one dared attempt to stop them. Some of Israel's faithful wanted Teach dead for what he'd done. But not one of them was fool enough to go down into a black hole where a fully reloaded Blackbeard was waiting. He would have to be left alive, with an unskilled and unbloodied crew. What Blackbeard had won in numbers, he had lost in skill, experience, and cold-blooded ruthlessness.

As the fifteen men sailed away from the sloop into the night, the dark figure of Captain Teach rose from the cabin below and rejoined his crew on the main deck of the *Adventure*. He stood at the rail and watched the skiff as it drifted quietly over the waters of Pamlico Sound.

An aging corsair from Malta, sailing with the friends of Israel Hands, said something no one understood and pointed back at the sloop, slowly disappearing in the night. Through the thickening mist of the cool October night, they could make out the fading form of the pirate captain, saluting them with a waving hand, as if bidding them fair winds and following seas.

On the main deck of the *Adventure*, Blackbeard turned from the night that had swallowed up his old shipmates. He called for more rum to be brought out for all hands. It was a night to be remembered. A musician who had joined the crew broke out in song on the squeezebox. General gaiety prevailed on the *Adventure* as men swilled rum and peered into the dark world of the most famous pirate on the Spanish Main. In time, the hard liquor loosened their tongues enough to ask their captain why he shot his first mate. The sodden pirate smiled. "If I don't every now and then kill one of you, you might forget who I am."

The deck erupted with laughter, but every man jack on board swallowed hard from his jug when they heard his answer.

The night passed as a pirate's dream. Blackbeard, on the deck of his pirate ship, told tales of murder and mayhem on the high seas. Tales of treasures lost and treasures gained. Tales of myths and legends. Tales as tall as masts.

CHAPTER SIXTEEN

The Blessing

Wednesday, June 23, 1999

Father Novarus was not what Tom or Jake expected. Had either of them gone to church with Marie on Sunday, they might have saved themselves the shock. But because Tom had held fast to his belief of "atheism through apathy" and Jake had clung tightly to his mantra of "I don't have to go to church because I'm on vacation," neither was prepared when the door opened. Had it been the thirty-first of October instead of the twenty-third of June, they would have bet money that the first words they heard out of the man at the threshold, dressed in all black with a Roman collar, would have been "Trick or treat."

"Hi, I'm Father Al." The smiling young man extended a hand out for Tom to grab.

"Hi, Father, I'm Tom Stone." He eyed the priest with a look of amused skepticism. "Come on in."

"Thanks." The priest entered to see another man standing a few feet away. "Hi, I'm Father Al," he said, an echo from moments before.

"Jake Brean. Nice to meet you. Marie will be down in a minute." *Dear God in heaven, is he old enough to drive?*

At five foot five—if you measured him first thing in the morning—Al Novarus was a cherub-cheeked young man with a sparkling white smile straight out of a toothpaste commercial. He swept a handful of silky black hair off his forehead with thin, delicate fingers, revealing a pair of dark-brown eyes so large and round that they appeared to be in a perpetual state of surprise within an olive-shaded and hairless face. Father Albert Novarus was quite possibly the most diminutive man Tom or Jake had ever met.

"Can I get you something to drink, Father?" the host asked, closing the door behind him.

"Oh, ice water would be nice. Thanks."

Tom moved toward the kitchen but pulled up short. "Listen, I'll be honest with you. I don't mean to sound disrespectful, but I'm gonna have a hard time calling you Father."

"That's what my dad said when I was ordained," the young man laughed. "Call me Al."

"Just like the Paul Simon song," Jake said, more for his own amusement than as a historical reference. Al smiled as well.

"One ice water coming up, Al," Tom called out from the kitchen.

"You know, it's funny," the priest said to Jake. "But I find myself making house calls dressed in uniform, as I refer to it, so that people know I'm really a priest."

"Somehow, that doesn't come as a big surprise to me," Jake said, opening his hand to offer the priest a chair at the giant table.

Marie's footfall was light and swift as she descended the noisy ladder. She didn't want to leave the priest alone for too long with the heathens. "Father, thank you so much for coming," she said with sincere appreciation.

"Call him Al," Jake said glibly. Marie launched a reproachful glance at Jake that struck him right between the numbers.

Tom returned from the kitchen and handed the glass of ice water to the cleric.

"Thank you, Tom." Al took a small sip, just enough to wet his whistle, and watched the glass as he slowly set it down on the table. When he looked up, the priest appeared to have aged ten years. The boyish charm had gleaned a sharp edge; gone was the happy-go-lucky, wide-eyed innocent. Gone was the simple novitiate they had greeted at the door. The man of the cloth who sat at the table with them, carefully considering his next few words, was a tried and worthy warrior of God. He looked directly at Tom. There was a stern, hard quality in his gaze, but no judgment. "Tell me, Tom, what do you believe?"

Tom looked at Father Al with vacant eyes that suggested he hadn't heard the question. He had, in fact; he just wasn't prepared for the theological detour the conversation had just taken. The words spun through his mind like alphabet soup swirling around a child's lunchtime spoon. Tom waited for the letters to fall into place and form the words that might serve as an answer, but they simply fell away and vanished to the bottom of the soup bowl.

"I don't know what you mean."

"Sure you do," the priest countered. "Think about it. What do you believe?"

It came as a challenge and made Tom uneasy. As far as he was concerned, Al had been asked over to provide a routine blessing on the house. And Tom had consented to even that small task more as a favor to Marie than from any burning desire or *belief* on his part that any of this was going to do diddly-squat. He thought the priest was on board with the simple plan: come in, say hi, bless the house, and don't let the squeaky door hit you in the cassock on the way out. But it appeared to Tom that he and Al were not on the same page.

"You know, Al," Tom replied with a humorless smile, the defensive wall growing with every word falling from his mouth, "Marie said you were coming over to bless the house, and I suppose that's OK, but I don't really know what good it's going to do."

"What do you want it to do?"

"I don't know. Keep the ghouls and goblins away, I suppose." There was an edge to Tom's words; he sounded angry, and he didn't like the sound. He had no intention of being disrespectful, but the priest was going somewhere Tom didn't want to go. It didn't faze the priest. There was a faint curl to Al's lip.

"Do you think a blessing is going to keep the ghouls away, Tom? And it's my understanding, from talking to Marie, that that's exactly what you believe you have here. That or something very much like it."

Father Al stared at Tom, who stared at the table, hands clasped together, mind churning in search of a credible answer still beyond his reach. The priest's eyes never left Tom, cutting the Breans loose, leaving them free to float silently away from a conversation that was fast becoming a bit too contentious for their comfort.

"Well, I suppose a blessing couldn't hurt, right?"

"Right," Al confirmed. "It couldn't hurt. But what you really want it to do is help. And it all comes back to my first question to you. Tom, what do you believe?"

Tom was growing impatient with the little man's impertinence. This visit wasn't supposed to be about his beliefs, not even about an unwanted and uninvited guest in his house. Staring at the priest as he tried to formulate a response, he considered whether he might now be playing host to two unwanted guests. Tom didn't think this priest really wanted to know what Tom believed. It was more likely that the priest wanted Tom to believe what *he* believed. Well, Tom couldn't do that. "I'll tell you what I believe," he said, bitter resentment gushing from his words. "I believe that God killed my wife. And even if he didn't feed and water the cancer that grew inside her, then he sure as hell sat back and watched it grow. That's what I believe," Tom stated with finality.

"Yes, Marie told me of your wife. I'm sorry, Tom. It was tragic. I remembered her in the mass this morning."

Al moved forward in his chair, and Tom sensed an unhealed wound was about to be torn open once again. "I also understand the tendency to blame God for such tragedies. We seek explanations, try to comprehend the incomprehensible. We look for answers so that we might be able to accept the unacceptable. Without answers, it seems impossible for us to move forward. We need them to go on with our lives. But the answers don't come. And it will never make sense," the priest said, a lonely understanding in his words. "Tom, you looked up to heaven and cursed God when your wife died. You screamed at God in heaven for an answer, but heaven was silent. You looked for God everywhere. Everywhere except where He was. He was with you, Tom, there at your side all the time, holding you up and mourning with you the death of the one *He* loves so well."

Tom held his head up, too proud to look down as water crested the lower lids of his eyes and spilled down his cheeks. Al leaned forward and spoke in a hushed tone that only Tom could hear. "God will never force himself upon you, Tom, but He's praying that someday you'll ask Him back into your life." The priest grew silent and bowed his head. A minute later, Al looked up at Tom. "Tom, will you accept God's blessing on your house?"

Tom blinked his eyes clear and nodded.

"Then let's get to work."

There was no look of triumph on Father Al's face. He carried the weight and the scars of many hard-fought spiritual battles. Even under the best of circumstances, he knew the desired outcomes were never assured. Father Al stood, and the others around the table followed suit. He motioned for approval to place his small black bag on the table. "May I?"

"Sure," Tom replied, moving a pewter candleholder to clear the way. Father Al jerked a squat glass jar of holy water from the black bag and set it out on the wooden surface. A small Bible came out next, then another larger, leather-bound book. He set the bigger book directly in front of him and reached in and drew out the stole. He kissed the cross at the center of the long white sash and placed it over his head and around his neck. As he made the sign of the cross, Jake and Marie instinctively blessed themselves in kind. Tom's head jerked a bit as he watched the others, sensing there was something he should be doing, but he didn't quite know what. He decided to just keep his hands in his pockets and his mouth shut.

Tom listened intently as the priest began to walk throughout the house with the holy water in one hand and the Bible in the other.

In step behind the praying man, Tom could catch only bits and pieces of the prayers.

". . . and His Son, our Lord and Savior, Jesus Christ."

Tom watched as the holy water splattered the walls of the sitting room.

"... bind and command all the powers and forces of evil to depart, right now, away from us, our homes ..."

That's right, Tom thought as they walked back through the gathering room. *Get this room real good.*

They followed the priest up the stairs.

"... and by the power of the Holy Spirit ..."

And through the bedrooms.

"... and we thank you, Lord Jesus ..."

He continued to pray and sprinkle holy water in every room, on every window, and on every door. Father Al was still praying when they came back downstairs into the gathering room. Once in the room where they had begun, he turned to the three standing there and showered them with holy water.

"... and I seal you all in the protection of the precious blood of our Lord and Savior, Jesus Christ, which was shed for us on the cross. Amen."

"Amen," the Breans solemnly responded as they made the sign of the cross.

"Amen," Tom added, a little self-conscious but afraid not to answer.

Al sat back down, the smile returning to his face. The others joined him at the table. He had begun packing his small bag when Marie spoke.

"Father, Tom and Jake have struck up a friendship with the artist of that painting," she said, directing Al's attention with a tilt of her head. "She's a fascinating woman, actually, who also happens to be a practicing witch."

Marie paused, bracing herself for a thundering fire-and-brimstone sermon that didn't materialize. Father Al simply prompted her to continue. The absence of the anticipated pushback left her with the unsettled feeling that she was free-falling, and she almost lost the point she was trying to make. But Marie regrouped and forged ahead.

"Well, as she's given Tom a couple of books for him to read, I was wondering if maybe you might be able to offer some guidance to Tom." Marie trailed off at the end, but the priest saw her concern.

"Would you mind if I see the books, Tom?"

"Not at all. Hang on—they're in my room." Tom pushed away from the table and took two creaking steps at a time up the ladder. Jake and Marie exchanged wide-eyed looks. They hadn't seen Tom display that kind of energy since they'd arrived.

"You know," Al said as he studied the painting, "that woman has some talent. What's the name of the work?"

"*The First Mate*," Jake and Marie chimed in chorus.

"*The First Mate*, huh?" Al repeated. "Yes, that's a very nice painting, indeed."

"You want it?" Jake asked, deadpan.

The squeaking stairs told them that Tom was retuning as Al continued to eye the portrait.

"He likes it," Jake said, telegraphing a message to Tom with his eyes. Tom looked at the priest.

"You want it?"

Al laughed. "No, no." He saw the books in Tom's hand. "OK, let's see what you've got there. *The Power of the Witch* and *The Witch in Every Woman*. Oh, I've seen these before," the clergyman said as he leafed through one of the books. "This friend of yours, the artist, is she a Cabot witch?"

"Yeah, she is," Tom said, a little surprised at the extent of the priest's knowledge of his competition and the even tone in which he spoke of them.

"Well, it's a nature-based, pagan religion, which, if I remember correctly, has its origin in ancient Celtic traditions. Does my memory serve?"

"Spot on, Padre," Jake sang out. He turned to Tom. "*The Witch in Every Woman?*" Jake shook his head as he looked upon the crimson face of his old navy buddy.

Marie couldn't find the humor in her husband's teasing in light of the spiritual and moral magnitude of the issue at hand. It had simply played out as an unnecessary distraction in her mind. "Father, aren't you concerned about him reading these books?" There was a challenge in her tone.

Father Al shook his head with a smile that might have been misconstrued as patronizing.

"Marie, every Sunday, there are people filling up the pews in every Christian church in the country. And come the next Election Day, many of these same people will cast a vote saying God has no place in our schools or in our town halls. These are Christians, the so-called children of God, and you ask if I'm concerned about the pagans?"

Father Al turned to Tom. "Your path will lead you to a fork in the road, Tom. I have the feeling that you're going to come to that place soon. I'll pray that your path is a clear one. I suggest you pray as well." He studied Tom for another moment, then asked, "Do you own a Bible, Tom?"

"No. I don't," Tom said, hoping he had just sidestepped a homework assignment.

"Here." Al slid the book over in front of Tom. "Have mine." The curled edges of the black book were brushed to a light brown from years of diligent and lengthy study and reflection. "I have some passages highlighted that have been a great help to me. You may find that they help you on your own journey."

"Journey?" Tom asked, truly puzzled. "What journey?"

"Your own spiritual journey. It *is* a journey, Tom. Make no mistake about that. And it's a journey on which you'll have to travel alone. Peace is found on the journey when you walk the right path."

"How do I know which one is the right path?"

"Don't ask me," Father Al said with a wry smile. "It's your journey."

The priest stood from the table, bringing Jake and Marie to their feet. Tom remained seated, staring dumbfoundedly at the black book with gold lettering that he held in his hand. He scrolled through it quickly with his thumb. A lot of highlighted areas. *Why do people show you they care by giving you stuff to read? Don't any of these people go to the movies?*

"There's something you all should know," Al said before he turned for the door. "This presence that you've been dealing with, it's not demonic. You know that, don't you?"

"Yes," Jake replied. "We've been told that already."

"The artist?"

"Yes. And that's a good thing, isn't it? I mean, that this thing isn't demonic," Jake said.

"Absolutely. But because this entity is of human origin, it carries within it the very same evil it held fast to in life, and that presents another problem for you."

"What's that?" Tom asked, afraid to hear the priest's answer.

"It maintains its free will."

"Oh no," whispered Marie.

"Hold on a minute, what do you mean?" Tom asked, his concern stemming more from the dread in Marie's tone than from the priest's statement. "It maintains its free will—to do what?"

Father Al provided an apologetic shrug before answering. "Well, free to do whatever it is that it wants to do. At least, God won't stop it. He can't." Al stared at Tom and saw the struggle within. "You see, Tom, the problem with God is that He keeps His promise. He promised to let us live our lives as we choose. Make decisions on our own. Live the way we want to live. We want free will? Well, we've got it. We live and die by our decisions, on an individual as well as a societal basis. That can be a wonderful thing. It all depends on the decisions we make and the actions we take. We reap what we sow, Tom. And unfortunately, this thing can still choose its own path. Take the action it chooses to take."

Marie curled her face into the crook of Jake's shoulder. Tom was dumbstruck. He looked down at the Bible in his hand. "Then what good is this Bible if it won't have any effect on the ghost?" Tom asked when his ability to speak returned.

"The Bible isn't for the ghost, Tom. The Bible is for you."

"Isn't there anything else you can do to help?" Tom pleaded. "How can I fight this thing?"

Al slipped his fingers into his shirt pocket and produced a small prayer card, then handed it to Tom. "Recite this after you've spent some time with the Lord in scripture. This is a binding prayer, Tom. It will probably sound familiar. You'll recognize it as one of the prayers I recited during the blessing." Tom nodded in a noncommittal sort of way. *Yes, no, well, maybe—we'll see.*

Al smiled, picked up his bag, and thanked them all for their hospitality. Tom opened the door, but the priest didn't leave. He stopped at the threshold and turned to Tom.

"Everything we've done here today, everything you have—the blessing, the Bible, the prayer card—they mean nothing without the key that unlocks their power."

Tom's eyes widened. This was what he was looking for. The key to power. Power over this beast. "What's the key, Father?"

"The key, Tom, is faith. Your faith. So there's still one question yet to answer. What do you believe, Tom?"

The easy fix was gone. And it all came down to this. Tom wished with all his heart that he had a different answer. But the priest deserved the truth, and Tom realized that he did too. *What do I believe?*

"I don't know."

Research and Highballs

Thursday, June 24, 1999

At 4:35 p.m., Jake came bursting through the door with Rebecca striding to keep up. "Always good to pull in and see the old place still standing," Jake said, the air of triumph impossible to miss. "Wait till you hear what we found out."

Three startled heads spun around as if on a spindle. Jake did not expect to see the third but was happy he was there. "Drew, my man, *qué pasa?*"

"You seem like you're in a pretty good mood," Drew said with a broad grin.

"I am. I've got some great news. This thing? The ghost? It doesn't want to kill us. Well, not all of us, anyway. It only wants to kill Tom."

"Hey, that *is* great news," Tom quipped.

Rebecca followed up the rear, juggling books, charts, and several bags. Drew jumped up to help with the load.

"Oh yeah, you two haven't met," Jake realized as he observed the chivalrous lieutenant.

"Drew Kenealy, meet Rebecca Putnam. Rebecca, Drew's a lieutenant in the Marblehead Police Department."

"Hi, Drew. Thanks for the help."

"Hi, Rebecca. My pleasure."

"Drew, Rebecca's a witch." There it was, in all its unbridled splendor. Jake's tribute to the truth at the expense of decorum pained him not at all. And he paid no attention to his wife's admonishing glare.

"Rebecca's also an accomplished artist, Drew," Marie added in atonement for her husband's breach of deportment.

The compliment was not lost on the artist, or the witch, depending on which gospel you subscribed to. Rebecca was fairly glowing at the supportive statement as she set her lightened burden down on the large table.

"Oh, so you're the one who painted that?" Drew asked, nodding at the canvas, his hands busy juggling books with odd titles.

"Yes, but I'm surprised to see that it's still up there," Rebecca said, looking at Tom, unsure of how much to reveal in front of the police officer.

"Well," Tom said, "I thought that if he sees that we've hung up his picture, maybe he'll decide to accept the compliment and leave us alone."

"Don't count on it. This son of a bitch means business," Jake said, bringing the focus back to what they'd just discovered.

"Jake's right," Rebecca said. "We've got a lot to cover, but"—she paused, still not certain what a Marblehead police officer was doing there—"is this not a good time?"

"No, no, it's fine," Drew said. "This is a friendly visit. I'm a good cop," he joked, smiling at Rebecca as her cheeks began to pink up.

"I'm glad to hear it. And by the way," she countered, "I'm a good witch."

The connection was obvious to the others in the room, leaving the Breans with the funny feeling that something might have just happened between the cop and the witch. Tom experienced an altogether different sensation. It left him feeling a little out of place. Feeling out of place in his own home was becoming a state of being, and he didn't much like being in that state.

Marie thought it an appropriate time to play hostess. "Listen, why doesn't everyone sit down, and I'll grab the vegetable tray and put something together. I'm going to have a glass of wine. What can I get everyone else?"

"O'Doul's for me, hon," Jake said, already poring over his notes.

"I'll join you in a glass of chardonnay, Marie," Tom said in a pretentious, almost British manner. He drew the unwelcome attention of Mr. Brean but ignored the stare.

"Drew, what about you?"

"I'll have a beer, Marie, if it's not too much trouble."

She looked at Rebecca for her order. "You know," Rebecca said, considering Drew's choice, "a beer sounds good. I think that's what I'll have."

If there was a hole to dive into, Tom would have taken a flying full gainer right into the bottom of that pit.

"But let me help you with that, Marie," Rebecca said as she joined her in the kitchen.

Jake turned to the lieutenant when the ladies had cleared the room. "To what do we owe the pleasure of your company on your day off, Drew?" Jake asked the welcome guest.

"I came by to bring you some good news."

"Oh? What's that?"

"I got the autopsy report back on Vince LaCava." He paused for effect. Once sure he had attained the proper tension level, he cut the cord. "Acute myocardial infarction."

"Thank God," Jake said. "I'll bet Mr. Goddard is relieved."

"Beyond description."

"Does Marie know?"

"Of course—you think I'd keep it a secret until you got home?"

Jake dismissed the question in favor of another. "Hey, my pipe—what'd it say about the pipe?"

"What, you want it back now?"

"Fuck, no! I mean, what was it doing in his mouth? How did he break his teeth?"

"Pathology says that the article was responsible for the fracturing of the teeth and was probably the result of the jaws seizing due to the MI."

"Probably?"

Drew shrugged. "That's what Dr. Rosenbloom's report says."

"Do you know this Rosenbloom guy? Is he any good at what he does?"

"Yeah, I know Dick Rosenbloom. His disposition matches his name, but he's an excellent forensic pathologist. A scratch golfer too. Or so I hear."

Jake looked at Tom. "You see, when you're a doctor, you also have to play golf. So I guess, being a physician assistant, that would make you, what . . . a caddie?"

Drew laughed heartily at the friendly barb, and even Tom, to his chagrin, was forced to appreciate Jake's twisted logic. The only one in the room not laughing was framed on the wall behind Drew and stared menacingly at Tom Stone.

"Sounds like we missed something pretty funny," Rebecca said to Marie over her shoulder as she reentered the room. She carried three beers, one of them fake, and two glasses of wine on a tray in front of her with the skill and ease of an experienced barmaid.

"Well, I hope it wasn't at our expense," Marie followed.

The laughing subsided as the food was set before them. Three hungry men grabbed from the tray of veggies and dipped their bites in ranch dressing. After sampling a few carrot sticks and cauliflower blooms, Jake wiped his hands on the front of his pants and started tapping his finger on the open notebook.

"All right, listen to this," he said, settling in. "Rebecca takes me over to this guy's house. Nice guy, but a bit of a strange ranger, if you know what I mean." He looked around the table for communal nods saying *Yes, of course, we know what you mean, Jake. Please continue.*

Jake continued. "So this guy—"

"His name is Jasper Endicott, by the way," Rebecca interjected, giving "this guy" an identity.

"Yeah, this Jasper guy, he opens the door, and I look in and see absolute mountains of books and papers all over the joint. I mean to tell you it looked like a small city of paper skyscrapers. And this is *after* the guy . . . Jasper," he corrected himself, "did a twenty-four-hour cleanup job."

"More importantly, he had the information we were looking for," Rebecca was quick to point out.

"Boy, did he ever. Rebecca, let's start with what you have. I want to save my stuff for the grand finale." He turned to Tom. "This is gonna knock your socks off, slick." Tom, somehow, remained unmoved.

"I covered the period from the turn of the century, the twentieth century, that is, forward. The first thing I found"—she glanced up at the lieutenant—"and this might be of particular interest to you, Drew, was in an old police logbook from 1902." She reviewed the words she transcribed before continuing. "May 3; Albemarle, Constance. Arrested owner of the Stonecroft. Charge of fraud and thievery. Claim of false representation levied by Mr. Juniper Smith, citizen of Marblehead. Psychic medium unable to reach Elmira Smith, twelve years the late wife of Juniper Smith. Released, pending hearing."

"So she was a huckster," Drew said with a shrug.

"Well, maybe, but she did have a touch of Houdini in her. Eight days later, on the eleventh of May, Constance Albemarle disappeared. No one ever saw her again."

"So what?" Tom quipped. "She took it on the lamb, as Bogey would say."

"Perhaps. But on the night of May 11, 1902, there was a full moon."

"Well, that makes it sound a little spooky, but it doesn't really prove anything, does it?" Marie asked, making sure she was following the bouncing ball.

"No, it doesn't, but let me go on," Rebecca said as she turned the page in the spiral-bound notebook.

"There's a lot of 'buts' in this story," Jake said to the other men with a confirming nod and an amusing air of omniscience.

"In 1951," Rebecca continued, "the house, still called Stonecroft by the people of Marblehead, was uninhabited, given over to the weeds and wildflowers, apparently. On two occasions in the summer of that year, police found the remains of animals; the first one a dog, the second, a goat, killed in a ritualistic fashion on the large granite slab at the original entrance to the house." The four listeners turned as one to face the flat granite step that lay on the other side of the wall they were looking at. Rebecca did not pause. "The police attributed the killings to a cruel hoax played by some antisocial teenagers. No details beyond that were ever released."

"There's just one more item." She looked at Drew. "Were you aware that in 1975, the owner of the house committed suicide?"

Drew shook his head. "I know there hasn't been a murder in Marblehead since 1950, but there have been a number of suicides. I didn't know specifically that there had been one here. How did he kill himself?"

"Not he," Rebecca corrected Drew. "She. An old woman, ninety-four years old. Hanged herself in the upstairs bedroom."

"Ninety-four? Who kills themselves when they're ninety-four years old?" Drew shook his head, disquieted. "In all my years as a police officer, I've never heard of a ninety-four-year-old woman hanging herself."

"Let me guess," Tom said. "She hanged herself on the night of a full moon."

"No. She hanged herself the night *before* the moon was full."

"More afraid of him than of death itself," Marie whispered, contemplating the weathered face of the first mate. She marveled at how such malevolence could emanate from one who had once walked the earth and sailed the seas.

"Then the admiral must have bought the house shortly after that. I know he owned it for over twenty years," Tom stated. He glanced at Rebecca and explained, "I bought the house from the previous owner, Admiral Wharton. I served on his staff for my last four years in the navy, and we ended up retiring at the same time. He wanted to live in Florida and needed to sell this house. I'd told him that Carol and I wanted to run a little B&B in New England. It worked out great.

Anyway, with the generous inheritance that Carol had received, along with some creative financing, we got the house. Well, I got the house. Carol got cancer."

Rebecca nodded.

"Why didn't anything happen to Admiral Wharton?" Marie asked Tom, more to get his mind off Carol than to continue the morbid discussion. "Did he ever mention anything to you about strange occurrences?"

"Of course not. Do you think I'd have kept that information from you?" Tom's pain was still fresh. "Besides, I don't think he ever lived here. He leased it out while he went from one duty station to the next."

"And just look at all the fun he missed," Jake said lightly. "Let me tell you what I got. In July of 1863, the family who owned the house, named Fletcher, lost a son in the Battle of Gettysburg. The owner had three daughters, but that was his only son." Jake dragged an educated finger down his page of notes. "Let's see, oh yeah, going back another hundred years to prerevolutionary—"

"Hey, wait a second," Tom objected. "You're jumping around pretty quick—you just said the guy lost his son at Gettysburg."

"Yeah. And?"

"Well, is that all?"

"Is that all?" Jake looked at him, mortified. "Isn't that enough?"

"Tom, it's not just criminal or violent acts that generate enough negative energy to feed and sustain malevolent spirits," Rebecca explained. "Tragedy serves as a much more powerful attractor than any other single catalyst. Losses of the heart are magnets for earthbound spirits. It becomes the visceral lining of the house, that all else may grow from within it. Murder, suicide, betrayal, and paralyzing grief are the main components for a haunting. Especially a haunting of an angry, vengeful spirit."

"Murder?" Tom objected. "Nobody said anything about murder."

"Well, I was just about to when you interrupted me," Jake replied. "When the house was just built, around 1690, it was a small tavern with a couple of extra rooms upstairs for the weary traveler or the drunken sailor waiting for his ship to sail. Everything was fine until 1692, when the owner of the tavern, Seth Barlow, was murdered." Jake lifted his eyes from his notes and gazed at Tom.

"It was the very same summer that the Salem witches were executed," Rebecca added, as if she had just dragged out the old family album. "Although there didn't seem to be any direct connection between the executions and Barlow's murder. At least, not that we could see," she concluded, looking at Jake, who nodded his affirmation.

"Do they know who killed him? Did it say?" Tom asked.

Jake opened his palms to heaven. "Didn't say. Apparently, they never charged anyone with the crime. Maybe it was one of his guests. Maybe some drunken sailor off one of the hundreds of ships that sailed in and out of Little Harbor." Jake glanced up at the wall and poked a finger at the painting. "Maybe it was him."

Tom and Marie were both eyeing *The First Mate*. Drew was not. He was looking inquisitively around the room. Jake watched the cop. The policeman's pensive green eyes darted from corner to corner, never settling on any one spot for too long.

"What is it?" Jake asked.

"I was just wondering what it could have been about. Folks back then didn't kill just for fun, like they do nowadays. Maybe it was the unfortunate result of a drunken brawl. Heck, if it had been a busy night, perhaps it was a robbery gone awry. Maybe the robber knew the owner, so he felt he had to kill him. But if the murder was committed in this house, then it most likely would have happened in this room."

The statement brought their minds back to the twenty-five-by-thirty-foot stone and wood box that surrounded them. Somewhere, within a few feet from where they sat, a man had been murdered. Every shadow became a phantom; every dark spot on the floor, a bloodstain. And the face of the man hanging on the wall began to look guiltier than ever before. Not that he cared.

Something shifted and twitched at the edge of the mind of Rebecca Putnam. There was an undeniable shadow that hid from the light of memory and fled from the eye of discovery. She couldn't see it, but she knew it was there. "What was the owner's name again?"

Jake checked his notes. "Barlow. Seth Barlow."

Rebecca shook her head. "There's something very familiar about that name. I can't place it, but I know I've heard it before. I just can't remember where or when." The others at the table quietly sat, providing her the space to remember. She finally waved the thought away in frustration. "I don't know. I'll check in my book of shadows when I get home; maybe I made a note of it there."

"What's a book of shadows?" Drew asked.

"Oh, it's basically a journal that every witch keeps."

"Kind of like a diary, then?"

"Yes, but it's much more than that. Everything that happens in my life, I record in my book of shadows. As the years pass, it acts as a reference guide as you move through your magical life, allowing you to draw from your experiences. It will also assist you in your transformation in the passage of time and—"

"Transformation?" Drew interrupted.

"A witch's transformation in life," Rebecca continued. "From maiden to mother to crone."

"I see," Drew replied with an easy smile. But he didn't see at all. Nor did he care that he didn't. He could see Rebecca. And that was fine with him.

For the first time in a long while, Rebecca felt a wave of shyness come over her. A warm, prickly rush that brought a wondrous fear that made her want to giggle. She felt her face glow pink and her mind go blank. Recovery came, regretfully, with a quick, deep breath that was more a shudder of excitement. "Anyway, I'll check when I get home," she closed in almost a whisper.

Drew pulled his eyes away from the dark-haired beauty, as any further gazing would border on lechery. He hoped in vain that his attentions had gone unnoticed by the others. He wondered if lechery was a misdemeanor as he took a swig of beer. Drew stared for a moment into the amber lager. He'd write himself a ticket later.

Tom watched as Drew set his beer down. The thick glass mug knocked deep and loud when it came in contact with the dense oak table. Tom looked down into his now-empty crystal wineglass. *Fuck it.*

"I'm getting a beer," Tom announced, excusing himself from the table. "Can I get anyone else anything?" Amid a chorus of "no thank you," Tom retreated to the kitchen to grab a Bud Light and was already peeling off the label before his butt hit the chair again.

"You know, that would actually make sense," Jake said, scrolling through the timetable in his mind, "if our friend here is the one who killed the owner. Rebecca, wouldn't your buddy on the wall over there be a contemporary of the murder victim?"

Rebecca was skeptical. "Maybe, but I think he's an eighteenth-century pirate."

"Well, if he were an early-eighteenth-century pirate, he still could have killed Barlow, couldn't he?"

"He would've had to have been awfully young if he did," Drew pointed out. "Heck, he would've been a kid." The thought gave the men at the table a chuckle.

Rebecca looked at Marie, who had grown quite sullen. Rebecca didn't know deeply tanned women could turn so pale. Apparently, they could.

"He would have been maybe eleven or twelve," Marie said in a lifeless tone. The laughing stopped immediately as the words cut an icy swath through the room. Marie forced herself to peer at the painting once more.

"Yes, the eyes. I don't know why I didn't notice it then. I guess it was his age. But those same electric-blue eyes. It was him, and I didn't even know it." She turned to her husband, who sat slack-jawed, staring at her. "The day you came home from seeing Rebecca about the painting, he was working with me in the yard. Did you see him when you pulled in the driveway?"

Jake could only shake his head, and Tom could only mimic Jake.

"No, I didn't think so. I turned to say something to him when you arrived, and he was gone. Disappeared." She looked accusingly at the face on the wall. "It was him. He killed Barlow. And he was only about twelve years old when he did it."

"Damn." Jake then asked on behalf of all at the table, "Who the hell is this guy?"

CHAPTER EIGHTEEN

The Hag and the Harness

November 1718

Israel woke with a start. Soaked in his own sweat, he lay naked under the coarse wool blanket, his left leg throbbing in pain. "Here, drink this," a scratchy old voice told him. He followed orders without hesitation and downed the contents of the goblet. "Now lie back down and get some sleep. You ain't gonna get no better if you keep trying to walk on that," she scolded, shaking a bony-knuckled finger at the end of the cot.

The reference to what lay beneath the blanket made him curious enough to hoist himself out of the fog. He lifted the ragged cloth and gazed through bleary eyes at the two white sticks that extended down to the end of his wood-framed berth. The stick on the left seemed to have a large black knot in the middle of it. It was with only half a mind that he realized those sticks were his legs. His head fell back onto the sweat-soaked ball of cloth that served as his pillow, a shirt he'd never wear again. He drifted off once more into a sleepy delirium.

Israel didn't know how long he'd been asleep. It must have been at least a fortnight. This time, when he did wake, consciousness came without the searing pain that had previously been the very cause of his waking. His vision had improved as well—that is, if he had been marooned in a dark, dingy cave somewhere. His neck was a little stiff but not so much as to prohibit movement, and he was able to turn his head in relative comfort. He gave a start when his eyes beheld a thin, pale face, weathered by time and want. Stringy hair, long and gray, framed the yellow, peering eyes that looked at him as if waiting for an answer.

"Remember me, Israel Hands?" the face screeched at him. Israel recoiled reflexively. The face laughed. The cackle frightened Israel more than did the harsh, piercing voice, which unnerved him considerably.

"Huh, who are—"

"I be your witch, Mr. Hands," she said, mocking him playfully.

"You be the old woman in Bath Town," Israel said with a hint of a smile, pleased to feel his memory returning.

"Old *hag* is what you called me. But I let it pass. And it's in Bath Town that you be now. Been here these last three weeks."

"Three weeks?" Israel's surprise caused him to attempt to rise. The pain returned as his leg muscles went into spasm. He winced and fell back on the cot.

"You best rest some more, Mr. Hands. You ain't fit for nothin' yet. Tell you true, I'll be pleased as can be when you can get up and take a shit outside instead of on my floor."

Israel looked down in horror and disgust to see a hole torn out of the center of the cot.

"That's right—it's me been wipin' your arse these past three weeks and pickin' up every lump of shit you drop on the dirt below you. Did you think it might have been the angels in heaven that done it for you?"

The old woman looked at Israel as shame and embarrassment pumped the blood back into his face. "Ah, but don't be concernin' yourself with that, Mr. Hands. You got more problems than havin' a crusty arse. That ball went clean through your leg, but you still almost died of the poison. You're a fine, big, strong fella . . ." The woman's voice trailed off. "Least you were when they brought you here. But you're alive—that's what counts," she finished as she took a seat in the wobbly chair. She turned her clay pipe upside down and tapped the burned tobacco out onto the dirt floor.

"Where are they?" Israel asked. "The ones who brought me here to you?"

"Oh, them? They're gone. Only saw two of 'em after that first night. They couldn't find nobody to tend you. So they left you with me."

"Who were the two?" Israel asked, not that it mattered now, but he wanted to know.

"Well, let's see. The one who seemed to be in charge, I think his name was Elijah."

Israel smiled. He knew Elijah would have stayed true.

"The other one, he was a darky. Don't remember hearin' his name. But he stayed, Lord knows, long after he shoulda left. There was folks around here who was plannin' on takin' him away in chains to the auctioneer. He was a strong one, he was. Somebody coulda got rich off him," she said, packing her pipe with fresh tobacco. "But he run off before they could get 'im. He sure hated to leave you, though.

He just finally left about three days ago." The woman touched a piece of straw to the candle burning on the table and lit her pipe.

Israel was quiet for a time before he spoke. "His name is King Richard. His mammy named him after Richard, the Lionheart." He smiled, holding back the tears that welled in his eyes. "She named him rightly." He looked at the old woman and held the memory of the two men up to her as testimony that the life he had led had not been in vain. "They were my friends," was all he could say.

Israel dropped his head back down on the cot and turned to face the wall to hide the rising tide of emotion. The old woman rose from her perch and tossed another log on the fire. She swung the iron pot on its arm back over the heat. "Rest some more, Israel," the woman said in a voice as warm as the fire that blazed away in front of them. "The stew should be ready shortly."

Israel slept.

* * *

The early-morning sun shone brightly through the open door, permeating the protective cover of his eyelids. Peering against the radiant light with a squint so tight it hurt, Israel pulled himself up in the cot and swung his legs over the side. He looked down at the puny flesh of his legs, laid bare by the truth of brilliant sunlight. His thighs were shriveled ham hocks, and his calves were but thick bones with a pauper's share of dangling flesh off the back. His nails, like talons, curved long and yellow beyond the tips of his toes. His left knee remained a shattered joint in the early stages of healing. And while it was still discolored and swollen, the pain was fading, and it was no longer hot to the touch. The old woman had told him that after the first two days, it oozed white sap and stunk of rotten meat.

Israel sat quietly for a few minutes until the wind returned to his chest. Just sitting up had left him feeling as weak as a baby bird. He looked around the one-room dwelling and wondered where the old woman had gone. *Hopefully to get us something to eat,* he mused as he shifted his long shirt around to cover his loins. Israel looked for a musket or a stick of some sort. Something to help him stand so that he could walk to the door.

"Lookin' for this?" the scratchy, familiar voice asked. Israel shielded his eyes from the light and beheld a small, bent silhouette in the doorway, holding up a walking stick for his approval.

"Aye, that will do just fine," Israel said with the makings of a smile as he anticipated standing upright for the first time in almost a month.

"Here you go, laddy," she said, closing the door behind her. "Now, mind you, you be weak as a newborn calf, so don't try to do nothin' but stand."

Israel smiled. *Laddy.* It had been more than twenty years since he had heard someone call him that. He took the stick; the smooth, round end that served as the handle confessed to many years of loyal service to an old woman with a crippling illness. He looked at her with sincere appreciation for all she had done and promised her, "Just for now. I'll get my own stick today and smooth the end like this. Now, I mean to walk a bit. Just over there." The old woman waved off Israel's gentle words with a gnarled hand and took comfort in the one good chair.

He took two timid steps. The second sent a sharp, shooting pain up the inside of the wounded limb that tore through his groin and up to his shoulder. Despite the pain, Israel was encouraged, having expected far worse. His gait was slow but steady as he learned from the pain, quickly discovering the limitations of movement that were placed on him. He didn't like it, but it didn't stop him. He sucked air from between clenched teeth in quick sips. The dozen painful steps to the door left Israel tired and shaky—but happy. He placed his hand on the door latch and turned it. Leaning on the latch for a little additional support, Israel pulled the door open and looked out over the streets of Bath Town.

"All you wanted to do was open the door?" The old woman laughed. "All you had to do was ask—I'd have done it for you."

"No," he replied. "I wanted to see the morning. I had to look it in the eye."

Israel glanced down and beheld his new body in the unforgiving morning light. His legs, as thin as clay pipe stems, were whiter than Bahamian sand. The hair on his legs, once light and fine, now grew as black and coarse as dead tree stumps rising from a Carolina swamp. Nor was the hair that fell in front of his face as he remembered. The sun-ripened crop from his youth had yielded to a light brown in early manhood. Now, in his thirty-ninth or fortieth year, he supposed, it was thin and gray. He looked back at the smiling old hag seated at the table—her withered skin, crippled body, and stringy gray hair—and wondered exactly who she was.

By the time he made it back to his cot, Israel was exhausted. He fell more than sat, wincing in exquisite agony as he swung his leg up to join him. His chest heaved as he struggled to regain the breath lost through his exertions. The energy in his body had been gratefully spent, and the pain passed quickly. Without another word, Israel fell asleep.

* * *

They sat in silent companionship as the last of the evening gave way to night. The old woman had found Israel a fine, strong stick to fashion for his own, and he had put his knife to good use the entire afternoon. He'd carved into the long shaft the forms of people and events that had forged his life. For the first time in many moons, Israel passed a tranquil evening in perfect contentment. He sat at the end of the cot, near the fire, as he smoothed the rougher edges of his walking stick. He looked across the room at the old woman as she sat at the table, flipping cards from a deck. Every now and then, she would mumble something to herself and then flip another card. She was a curious old woman, Israel thought, and as homely as a mud fence, but she possessed a kind and generous heart. Israel smiled at his "old hag."

"Old woman," Israel said, smiling.

"Yes, Israel," she replied, returning the smile without looking up.

"What did you see that day?"

"What day would that be?" she asked, her eyes not leaving the cards. "The day they brung you here with your leg shot up?"

"No, the day you looked at my hand. The first day I saw you. What did you see in my hand?"

The old woman looked up at him with a hard eye. "It don't matter none, Israel. Don't be askin' me about things that don't matter none." Her irritable tone surprised Israel, but she quickly turned her attention back to her cards.

"Well, it matters to me," Israel said, thinking it might prove amusing to push the old woman on the question. "It's my hand. Why can't you just tell me what you saw?" He smiled and studied the old woman before answering his own question. "Because you didn't really see nothing at all, did you, you old witch?" He laughed as he teased her with a growing comfort.

She looked at him with a face set in stone, and Israel stopped laughing.

"Don't take off that ring, Israel."

Israel looked down at the ring loosely hugging his bony finger. "I never take it off—you know that. Look, here it is," he said, holding his fingers skyward to prevent the ring from falling into the dirt. But she continued as if he hadn't said a word.

"You wear a curse on your soul, Israel. The ring protects you in life, but nothing can protect you from the darkness. Not when you're dead. And it's the darkness that's claimed you for its own. It's you who done it, Israel. You chose it for yourself. You asked it to live inside you and fed it with every man you killed."

What was it that Israel saw in her eyes as she spoke? Anger? *No. Sorrow.*

She slowly shook her head. "And then you asked it to protect you from tasting death yourself. It's likely Teach's ball would've ripped through your heart if not for that ring. It's the Devil's Kiss you've called upon all these years to save you. Now, it won't let you go. Keep that ring, Israel. Because when it comes off, death won't be far behind." She looked at him with mournful eyes. "You be damned to walk in darkness, Israel. That's what I saw in your hand."

Israel turned away from the woman and stared into the fire, beyond the burning logs to the embers below, pulsating orange and yellow. Her words struck as an assault, and he battled the fear and anguish that lay siege to his mind. He wanted desperately to rebuke her testimony, but he knew she was right. He had always sensed the darkness within. Ever since he was a boy, it responded to his call. It was with him as quickly and as surely as a good friend in his time of need. The work they had done together had become legend. But somewhere along his path—and for the life of him, Israel couldn't give it time or place—it had stopped being a friend and had become his master. Through the eyes of the old woman, Israel finally saw the true nature and intent of his master.

He turned the ring upon his fisted hand and offered the old woman a heavy, haunting smile. "You know, old hag, it just might be that your eyesight is not what it once was." But he didn't have the strength to hold it there, and the smile fell quickly from his face. He could see in her eyes his own helplessness reflecting back at him.

She wished she could relieve him of his grief and remove the burden of his destiny. But it was beyond her, just as it is beyond any mother to remove the sins of her son. Her heart began to ache as if under a crushing weight. She had come to care more for this unfortunate than she had ever thought possible. Certainly more than she had intended or desired. She would pray for his redemption if she prayed to the god of forgiveness, but that was not her god. If the god of the trees, or of the water, or of the sky had the power of the Dark One, she might have been able to assist in his reclamation. But they did not. She, too, would soon return to the service of her god at the end of her life; her decaying body would provide nourishment for the flowers and trees that would draw her spirit upward and into life again. Israel had also served his god, and it was to the Dark One that he would return.

Israel sat on the cot with his head down, twisting his walking stick, the tip breaking into the dirt floor. Through closed eyes, he searched desperately for some evidence of the possibility of salvation. He tried to recall some gentle or gracious moment, something that would show him to be above the beasts of the fields and forests. Israel leaned heavily on his walking stick, digging deeper into the ground. His thoughts died away as the carvings caught his eye. He held the stick up to his face and reviewed the scenes of his life that had sprung from his own heart and hand.

He started at the bottom and turned the stick in his hands as he marched back in time. Teach, with his twisted black beard, was at the very bottom. *Where he deserves to be*. A scene of the *Adventure* was carved just above the pirate. A display of various flags that he had sailed under as either privateer or pirate. Crossed knives and cutlasses, Israel's weapons of choice. He rubbed a gentle thumb over each one as the memories returned in vivid detail. He smiled broadly when he came to the two crossed pistols, a salute to his old shipmate, Doolin Pike. And James Barry. Israel noticed that he'd captured the man's features but not the spirit in the man's eyes. But how could he capture what he could not see? Just below the handle, he studied the twenty nooses that represented those who had been executed as witches in Salem Village. But only nineteen had been hanged. One, Giles Corey, had been pressed to death. Israel reminded himself of the role he played in crushing the life out of the man.

He reviewed his life, etched out for all to see and condemn, on the knotty branch of a dead tree. An array of cutthroats, weapons, and crimes against man and God, all set nicely below a smooth, rounded handle. Israel turned the stick and looked at the handle. It wasn't round at all. A self-deprecating smile creased his face because he did not recall carving it. But there in his hand was an exquisitely sculpted skull. The deep-set nose and eye sockets were cloaked in shadow while the neatly crafted teeth displayed a pearly, sinister smile. Israel was then confronted with the truth, revealed to him by his own hand. There was his god, sitting in dominion over every stage of his life. His god was death, and he could never stray from his service to his god. An abysmal gloom enveloped Israel as his mind walked him to the precipice and peered into the bottomless emptiness of his eternity.

Israel spoke with a voice of immutable sorrow. "Old hag, where do I go from here?"

She slapped a card down hard on the table. "You go on!" she barked. "You don't lay down and die in my house. You have the ring; now fight for your life. Do what you need to do to stay alive. There be no cause to think you won't live another ten years." She looked down at the table and flipped another card. "Who knows, you might even find a way to cheat your dark prince out of what you owe him." She pushed her matted gray hair back over her shoulder and continued to turn her cards. Israel watched in silence as his bony fingers tapped nervously on the skull of his walking stick.

He turned his gaze back to the fire, the red-hot flame reflected sharply in his cold blue eyes. Israel scratched the crown of his head, his long fingernails raking through the thinning field of oily hair. It appeared he might have to change course once more, the need to survive serving as his sextant. He considered his current situation, and as content as he was, recuperating in the home of his aged nurse, he doubted he could make a life for himself here. Israel looked down at his mangled leg. His heart called out to return to the sea, but the thought of signing on as a ship's cook was more than his calling heart could bear.

Then a familiar sound caught his ear. He stood awkwardly and limped to the window in the wall near the door, the skull on his stick smooth and comfortable in his hand. He opened the thick wooden square that covered the window, and the cold air, carrying the song, slipped into the room. Israel smiled with closed eyes and tried to recall when he had first heard the old tune. It was in his early years at sea—that much he knew—and his smile broadened, showing the stain of decay on the edges of yellowed teeth. "Shut the window, Israel," the old woman demanded. "The air's got a sharp bite to it tonight."

"Quiet, old woman," Israel whispered soothingly. "Listen to the sweet sound that plays upon it." His old hag listened with a doubtful expression pressed on her face until she could take it no more.

"Ain't no sound out there at all. Even the crickets are dead till spring. Now close that window, lest you want the chest sickness upon us."

"What are you saying? You hear no music?"

"Only thing I hear is me talkin' to you and you not listening to me. Now shut the window, Israel."

Israel stuck his head out the window and continued to listen, the melody falling strong and clear on his ear, but he soon pulled his head back into the house, closed the wooden square over the hole, and latched it shut. He shook the cold off him—the old woman was right about that—and made his way slowly back to the cot. The heat from the fire felt good on his face, and the bones that forged his thin frame drank in the warmth. The old woman got up and tossed another log on the fire to replenish the heat stolen by the song on the night air. She looked at Israel as she shuffled back to the table. "I suppose you'll be seeking your fortune when the sun come up," the old woman said with a question in her voice.

"I suppose I will." He looked at his walking stick again with more forgiving eyes. "When I was a lad, I fashioned some very fine items, indeed, with but a knife in my hand." He considered a notion for a moment before speaking again. "I think I'll go to the docks tomorrow. There may be a need for my services."

The old woman smiled and flipped a card.

* * *

The morning broke cold and hard on Israel's aging bones. He leaned heavily on his walking stick as he limped down the narrow lanes of

Bath Town. Israel felt the heavy stares and whispering eyes of the townspeople as he made his way to the docks. It had been a long time since Israel had walked the streets of a town alone. The sensation was an odd one, unnerving, and yet he felt a sense of independence he had not known for years.

Gone were the hearty shipmates who strode defiantly at his side; gone also were the cutlass and pistols that he had held as close as any friend. He was armed only with the tools of his trade, as would be any craftsman plying his talents on the busy streets of the growing town. But he wasn't just any craftsman seeking a day's wage. He was now known to be an enemy of Blackbeard, who still held captive the minds and hearts of the townspeople. Where once the name Israel Hands would have commanded the respect of the local populace, it now prompted only contempt and disdain, and the man they once feared was now the object of their animosity.

He detected an odd pulse in the town. Israel noted that although most people appeared to be going about the business of the day, their attention waned from time to time and was redirected out to the waters of Pamlico Sound. The murmurs between neighbors and friends were shielded from his curious ears as he made his way down to the wharves. The nonsensical notion that the entire town shared a secret that was to be kept from him seemed as preposterous as it was factual. He did his best to pay them no mind as he walked past the taverns and the shops that led to the open expanse of the docks on the sound.

The people seemed so much bigger. Israel counted himself among the small, insignificant personages of the town, almost as a child. The sailors swaggering down the cobblestone streets seemed to look down on him as they passed him by, spewing curses at the crippled old man who stood between them and the taverns and the whores. Clothed in colorful garments of red and gold, fabrics of silk and velvet, and tall boots and high hats, their dress captured Israel's eye, and he felt a boy again. A boy alone, walking the streets of a seafaring town.

He spied a small group of age-old mariners standing at the water's edge, looking out to sea amid sporadic bouts of lively arguments. Because one of the men owned a fine wooden leg, Israel felt it was a circle that could be easily joined. He stepped up within earshot of the conversation before venturing too close to the group. He wanted to listen before joining the fight.

"They be eight pounders. I tell you, them's Blackbeard's guns." Israel looked at the men with a start as they continued their heated exchange.

The tallest one, with dark hair and deep-set eyes, looked down at the wooden-legged man. "I'll not argue the point of them bein' eight pounders, but there's many a ship that got that size gun, and you can't tell me for certain that it ain't some other sloop, or ketch, or schooner that be firing at Blackbeard." The tall, dark-haired man completed his sentence with all the air his lungs could spare and had the red face to prove it.

"So now you're tellin' me, Michael Donovan, that you think there be a man fool enough to come after Blackbeard in nothin' but a sloop—or a ketch or a schooner, for that matter—and swap him ball for ball?" asked the wooden-legged man.

The conversation came to an abrupt halt when one of the men thought he heard the report of another cannon and held his hand up for silence. They stood peering out over the water, some with their heads cocked to funnel the sound. Israel listened hard but could hear nothing. He ventured a statement in hopes of gaining entrance to the conversation.

"Teach might just be trying to wake up his crew." Five heads turned sharply toward the outsider.

"You mean Blackbeard?" barked the man farthest from Israel, who, until then, had not said a word. The man's bright-red hair suggested something of the fire that burned in the man's unpleasant disposition.

"*I* mean Teach. *You* mean Blackbeard," Israel growled, backing the man down. "And he'd fire at a seagull for practice if he was so inclined." Israel had captured the group's attention. "How long has he been firing?"

"Not long," said Michael Donovan. "Truth be told, we're not sure he's firing at all," he added, directing his words at the wooden-legged man. "That's what we're trying to figure out. Strange sounds are carrying across the water this morning. Sometimes sounds like gunfire, sometimes not."

The owner of the wooden leg shook his head in frustration. "Donovan, you be deaf in one ear and can't hear out t'other if you don't think we been hearin' cannon fire. I'm done with you," the little man finished with a wave of his hand, shooing away the conversation more than the person.

Israel smiled at the irascibility of the short man with the wooden leg. Supported by his walking stick, Israel limped over to join the group. As he approached their circle, the man with the bright-red hair turned pale and slack-jawed and, without another word, retreated from his comrades to gain the safety of the crowded streets.

The man with the wooden leg spoke first. "Did you carve that stick yourself?"

"Aye, that I did," Israel replied amiably.

The man smiled warmly and extended his hand. "Cherub McKeever."

"I'm Israel Hands," he said guardedly, still not certain which way the wind was blowing in his life.

McKeever looked at him with a cautious smile and nodded. "I know."

Israel looked up at the other men within the circle. With faces downturned, they were either afraid or unwilling to meet Israel's gaze, and like their predecessor, they quietly melted into the crowd like snow on a spring day. He looked back down at the curious little man. "Cherub? I don't think I've met a man by that name before."

"Nor are you likely to. My given name is Gwendolyn. Gwendolyn McKeever."

Israel couldn't mask the expression of horror that washed over his face.

"Aye, that's why I go by the name o' Cherub. Me friends give it to me." He considered his statement for a moment. "At least, I think they were me friends." He squinted up into the gull-filled sky and offered Israel a disarming smile.

"Do you think you might be willin' to give me poor stump here some attention with that knife of yours? 'Course, I'd be expectin' to pay you for your trouble." Both men studied the wooden column that served as the bottom half of McKeever's right leg. "Say, oh, five pounds for carvin' the pictures to my liking?"

Israel's eyes bounced up to meet McKeever's, his smile so broad it pushed water from his eyes. McKeever motioned Israel to follow him with a tilt of his head, and the two hobbled up the street, lost to all around them in one-legged conversation.

It was a gawky sort of thing, with leather straps and brass buckles that secured the wood to his leg and hip. A compressed piece of cloth, serving as a pad for the fleshy knee, sat firmly in a cup fashioned at the top of the wooden peg. When McKeever handed it to him, the smell reminded Israel of the bowels of a ship at the end of a lengthy voyage. But he quickly put the odor out of his mind as his knife began to dance on the wood. McKeever was fascinated by Israel's talent and intensity, evincing the skill of a craftsman and the passion of an artist.

Israel worked the wood in sublime harmony with McKeever's descriptions and stories. He captured not only the faces and the times but also the emotions of the subject and the nuances of the moments. When Israel had finished, it was McKeever who had to wipe the moisture from under his eyes.

"Well done, Israel." McKeever glowed as he scrutinized his new limb. "Aye, well done indeed." On the full length of the wooden leg was now the image of every whore Cherub McKeever ever had the pleasure to know.

"And you'll find it none the weaker," Israel promised. "You've fine, strong timber there."

McKeever could not lose the grin from his face. He pointed at them one at a time and called each by name, becoming giddier as he went along. Then he stopped and asked beneath a furrowed brow, "Israel, who's this?"

"Oh, that's my old whore, Anna. I hope you don't mind I put her there," Israel said.

"Nay, not at all, Israel. She looks fine there, don't you think?" he asked, holding it up to catch the light. Israel nodded rather sheepishly. There was a gleam in Israel's eye that McKeever was quick to spy.

"Ah, she was special, this one. You loved her." It gave Cherub McKeever pleasure to see the aging pirate blush. "Did you marry her?" he asked with innocent, teasing humor.

"No," Israel answered matter-of-factly. "I killed her."

* * *

The old woman cackled with glee when Israel ducked under the doorway that night with a jug of ale under his arm and a leg of mutton hanging in a sling around his neck. It did Israel's heart good to see the woman so happy with the gifts he bore. She had saved his life and cared for him when nobody else could or would. Now, food was scarce in the house, and he was gratified that he could provide such a meal for his old hag. He heard something boiling in the pot that hung over the fire. He set their food on the table and hobbled over to the cauldron and lifted the lid. The woman was boiling some kind of root for supper. "Not much of a meal," he said, setting the lid back down. He returned to the table with a smile. "Why don't we have the mutton instead?"

After the meal, Israel felt a warm glow in his belly that tells a man that life is good, at least for the present, and that the future could be as well. He watched the old woman as she dug at a chunk of lamb stuck between her teeth with a small splinter of wood. He took another swig of the thick, heavy ale. It was a meal in itself. It tasted good going down, and he wondered why he didn't drink it more often. *Well, maybe I will.* His thoughts had drifted to another place when he abruptly broke the silence. "I think it will be here that I'll make my home."

The old woman stared at him, afraid to speak, afraid to hope. Israel continued, "We both need help, old woman. Maybe together, we can keep from freezing and starving to death. Me, with this here leg, I'd be nothing but a ship's cook if I put to sea again. But I can make my way ashore with this here knife," he said as he gazed at the blade like a groom admires the form of his bride on their wedding night. "I can make a life here," he added, feeling hope, once again, fill the sails of his existence. "What say you, my old hag?"

The old woman's eyes brimmed with tears as a surging tide of emotion swelled within her. She had cared for Israel like a son from the moment the wounded pirate bloodied her cot. Alone for the past twenty-seven years after her own son and husband had died, the old woman now seized upon the hope of dying in the company of someone who cared for her—her new son. She gave way to the flood of tears that had been bottled up for almost three empty decades as her sobs cleansed and healed the pain of her wounded heart.

Israel wanted to provide some sort of comfort but felt helplessly unfit. He stood stiffly behind the old woman, supporting himself with his walking stick in one hand and awkwardly patting the woman on her back with the other. The woman's tears soon turned to laughter as it quickly became apparent that the art of bringing comfort to another human being was lost on Israel Hands.

"Oh, sit down and let me be, you clumsy old salt!" she shouted with unbridled elation. Israel shuffled back over to his bed, satisfied with the resolution of the situation. He was home, and he was determined to do good by himself and for *his* old hag.

His eyes searched the dim room, looking for a tool that wasn't there. So he gripped his walking stick with his hands spread about a foot apart and began to burrow into the dirt floor alongside one of the hearthstones. *An odd thing,* he marveled, *hearthstones on a dirt floor.* He scraped the dirt away from the edge of the stone until he was able to reach his fingers under the cold slab and hoist it from its earthen foundation. He set the large, heavy stone aside and took out his knife. He carefully dug a small hole in the hard-packed dirt. Into a small leather bag, Israel put the remainder of the money he'd earned, then placed the sack in the newly cleared space. He looked at the old woman to ensure she saw where he would bury their treasure.

She acknowledged his message with a single understanding nod of her head. Israel placed the stone back in its original position.

He lay down on the cot and pulled the blanket over his weary bones. The evening had turned cold, and his leg did not fare well on these nights. "Good night, old woman," Israel said as he closed his eyes.

"Good night, Israel," the woman replied tenderly. Then she smiled. "You know, Israel, all mankind hides their valuables under their hearthstones. You'll not fool anybody that's looking to steal from us." But Israel was already snoring loudly. The old woman shook her head. "And you fancy yourself a pirate."

* * *

"Israel Hands!" The bellowing voice wrenched him from a sound sleep. He bolted upright in bed, only to be knocked back down by the butt end of a musket. Israel felt the white-hot pain shoot through his face as his mouth quickly filled with blood. He leaned over the side of the cot and spewed blood and teeth. He pressed himself up with arms that twitched in pain and shock.

Israel looked through narrowed, bleary eyes at the five men who had invaded his new home. He saw that one, presumably the man who shouted, wore a British naval officer's uniform. Three of the others were bluejackets, men who'd enlisted in the British navy, so called for the short blue jackets they wore. They were not pleasant men. When not assigned to prisoner duty, they'd often serve as members of a press-gang. A fifth man among them seemed to be a civilian, or at least not of the same company as the others. One of the bluejackets had picked up his stick and was examining it when he laughed and showed it to his shipmates, who smiled and nodded.

"That's mine," Israel snarled through shattered teeth.

"Yours?" the sailor chided with a cockney accent. "So you want it back then? Right, 'ere you go." Gripping the stick at its base, the sailor swung it hard against the back of Israel's injured knee. Israel howled in agony and momentarily ignored the unremitting pain in his mouth. He jumped as best he could at the sailor with the stick but was again struck down by the hand of another.

The third bluejacket moved in to exact his pound of flesh from the ruined pirate. He'd drawn his cutlass before entering the house in anticipation of a fight and took great umbrage at finding the miscreant sleeping quietly by the warm embers of a dying fire. All was forgiven, however, when the rogue lurched at his shipmate, and the bluejacket saw it clear to bring the flat of his cutlass hard against the side of the pirate's face, taking with it the better part of his right ear.

A red plume of blood splattered the wall behind Israel as he dropped to the cot once more, unconscious. His ear, having been pitched across the room, lay in the dirt at the feet of a sobbing old woman. The bluejackets scurried to shackle the wrists and ankles of their prisoner while a struggle could be avoided.

A cold blast brought Israel out of a nightmarish slumber as a bucketful of near-freezing water shocked him back to consciousness. Israel choked on the water and blood that had forced its way down his throat. He coughed convulsively as his lungs gasped for air. One of the bluejackets tossed him an old rag that lay on the table.

"Tend to your ear," the man commanded.

Instinctively, Israel put a trembling hand up to his right ear, only to discover it missing. It was also then that he noticed the heavy metal chains that bound his wrists. He hung his head as a low moan, rife with pain and despair, emanated from somewhere deep within him.

Israel took the dirty cloth that lay in his lap, folded it lengthwise several times, and tied it around his head. The pressure applied to the wound brought instant relief. The sharp pain caused by the heavy blade converted to a dull, steady throb that Israel was sure would be with him for the foreseeable future, which might not be all that long after all. For the moment, the pain had subsided to the degree that would allow him to think and reason. He asked the first question; his following question was answered before it could be asked.

"Who are you?"

"Lieutenant Robert Maynard, of His Majesty's navy. Israel Hands, you are under arrest for piracy and robbery on the high seas. You stand accused of being in league with one Edward Teach, also known as Blackbeard."

"I'm no pirate, mister," Israel said through bloody lips. "Those days are done. I'm a carver of wood, nothing more." It was a poor defense, Israel knew. But he had neither the strength nor the presence of mind to make a more effective argument at the time.

Maynard didn't consider his statement for a moment. "Bring him."

Two of the bluejackets grabbed Israel by the arms and yanked him to his feet. His head felt as if it would split in two when they hoisted him off the cot. A blinding white flash ripped through his brain with every step he took. He was grateful, and a bit disturbed at the same time, that his mouth offered him the least discomfort of all. It had been fortunate, Israel thought with ghoulish humor, that many of his teeth had been loose already. He'd noticed recently that he was able to move some of them with his fingers without difficulty. Hard food had become tedious to chew, and his gums had been bleeding frequently. Israel considered it just another kiss from the devil and put it out of his mind.

As he was being dragged from his newfound home, he looked to the table where the old woman sat. Until this moment, he had been under relentless assault, and all his senses had been employed in the interest of self-preservation. Now, resigned to his fate, he beheld her helpless frame and wondered with a breaking heart what would happen to his old hag. She held her face in ancient hands, gnarled by time and strife. Consumed by grief at the loss of her second son, Israel's old hag sobbed inconsolably as he was torn from her life forever.

He was led down the empty streets of Bath Town in an uncommon display of martial majesty, yet oddly, they seemed to be parading him through the streets of an uninhabited town. With his crippled leg dangling precariously behind, Israel hopped on his good leg in order not to be dragged down to the docks. He eyed his captors as they strode down the lanes of the town and finally recognized the fifth man among them. Israel didn't know his name but remembered him as the fiery redheaded man he had seen the previous day in the company of Cherub McKeever. He stared at the informant, but this time, the man returned Israel's gaze with a look of haughty triumph. It was Israel's turn to look away. He had not the strength for a fight of any kind, regardless of how weak the foe.

The sun shined brightly on the town, nature's false promise to the people of Bath Town, for the cold had come to stay. The excessive demands made on his physical person led Israel to suck the cold air hard and deep into his straining lungs, causing them to spasm. The coughing fits rendered him deadweight, and the bluejackets dropped him to the ground until they ceased. Although Lieutenant Maynard marched in a manner that suggested he was in a hurry, he did not seem to be perturbed by the delays. Whenever Israel was lowered to the ground, the officer took the opportunity to readjust his uniform and the saber at his side. At these times, he would order his attendants to put themselves in good order as well.

The sailors had just hoisted Israel up off the cobblestone street when he began to hear a noise. He looked around again before the sailors mustered the strength to continue hauling an old cripple across town. There were very few people to be seen on the streets. Those who were in view seemed to be in a hurry to get where they were going. No one paid Israel and his party any mind whatsoever, but Israel was not upset with the lack of attention he received. He took advantage of the time his escorts spent resting to ask a question.

"Where might you be taking me?" he asked, trying, himself, to catch his breath. "What's to be my fate?"

"You are to be tried," Maynard said, blowing warm air into his cupped hands. "Then you are to be hanged," he concluded, devoid of emotion.

As they continued their march down to the docks, Israel looked keenly for an opportunity to break free. They came to the end of the small lane that fed into a wide street. They were now flowing in the same direction as the scampering townsfolk. The street soon opened up to the wharves, and there Israel and his military escorts came upon the backs of a crowd of people.

Israel was plagued by curiosity, but the sailors didn't seem to think the scene was at all out of the ordinary. The people parted slightly, with some encouragement from the pushy guards, to allow the naval party and their prisoner passage. The townsfolk began to hurl insults and curses at Israel. He was mortified at the treatment he received and wondered if this was to be the site of his trial and execution. What had he done to deserve such hatred from a people who, to his knowledge, he had never harmed?

All questions but one remained when they'd finally elbowed their way to the front of the crowd. The people of Bath Town cheered Lieutenant Maynard and his detail as returning heroes and screamed for Israel's immediate and bloody death. When the last of the throng had opened a path for the group, Israel saw the reason for the frenzied mob. Tied to the dock in front of him was the sloop the *Pearl*. It was the vessel that would take him to his journey's end. Israel swallowed hard when he saw his final destination was to be damnation. There would be no escape. From the end of the bowsprit of the *Pearl*, suspended by a rope harness, dangled the severed head of Blackbeard the pirate.

Dinner and a Phone Call

Friday, June 25, 1999

Lieutenant Drew sat at the computer in his basement office in the Old Town House building on Market Square. The words were coming hard to him today. In fact, they weren't coming at all. He knew why; it was a cinch that you weren't going to be able to write if you weren't able to think. His article on child car-seat safety was due to the editor of the *Marblehead Reporter* by 3:00 p.m. tomorrow, and he had penned not a word. He sat in fretful idleness and stared at a white screen, the black, quarter-inch vertical line blinking patiently, waiting for a few friendly words to keep it company, yet at the same time flashing a warning that time was running out.

Maybe car-seat safety isn't going to cut it this week, Drew thought, leaning back in his squeaky chair. He rocked slowly back and forth, playing with the sound and wishing to God he could think of anything other than Rebecca. He picked up the yellow Ticonderoga pencil and stared at the ceiling. He had known many a man to occupy his time by throwing pencils up at acoustical ceiling tiles. He had once walked into a room where there must've been a hundred or more pencils stuck in the ceiling. It was actually a fairly impressive sight, as Drew recalled. But the guy ended up on the unemployment line after that charade. *Who needs a cop who sits around doing nothing but staring at the ceiling all day,* he reminded himself.

Alice Kelmer walked in as the lieutenant sat studying the yellow pencil rolling between his thumb and index finger. Alice lived just across from the Old Town House and would stop by every now and then to see how Drew was doing. An integral part of the Marblehead women's auxiliary and rumor mill, Alice was what many referred to as "local flavor."

"Hello there, Drew," Alice said in a friendly, scratchy voice, always sounding a little too much like fingernails on a chalkboard to be termed pleasant. "I say, Drew, did you talk to that McElroy boy lately?"

"Which one, Alice? There's three of them."

"Stanley, the middle one. Oh, he's a pistol that one is, Drew. We'll have to keep an eye on him, believe you me." Drew could see the wind start to fill the sails of the USS *Alice Kelmer*, who spoke with the unlimited firepower of a battleship and was just as wide at the beam. "I saw him shooting that gun of his, splashing his paintballs all over the fence."

"Isn't that their fence, Alice?"

"Oh yes, it's their fence all right, Drew. But one bad shot, and there'll be paint splattered on the side of my house. Maybe on my roses. Did you ever try to get paint off a rose petal, Drew?"

The lieutenant just stared at Alice as she continued her diatribe while she studied the police memos pinned to the corkboard on the wall next to her. "Well, believe you me, there's nothing tougher in this world than getting red paint off my icebergs or my Betty Boops. And the Betty Boops are single roses, and you know how delicate those petals are, now, don't you, Drew?"

"Yes," Drew agreed, placating the woman. "They are delicate, and it would indeed be very difficult to get paint off them." *Although not as difficult as getting, oh, let's say, the most beautiful woman in the world out of your mind, even for a second, but a difficult task, nonetheless.*

"Well, I should say so. I think you ought to take a walk across the street and speak to that boy, Drew. I really do."

Alice handed Drew a letter, folded in thirds, and then rifled through her purse on a quest for her car keys. "Now, Drew, this letter has my itinerary as well as the address where I'll be staying. I'm going down to Florida to spend at least a week with my sister, Eleanor. You remember her, Drew; she's the one who has the big feet. Always has, ever since we were little girls. Mother always said that Eleanor took after Aunt Velma, who had big feet as well. Well, now she has the sugars, what they call diabetes, and her feet are just as big as all get-out."

"Your aunt Velma has diabetes?" Drew asked, trying like hell to stay with the story.

"Oh, for heaven's sake, no, Drew," Alice replied. "Aunt Velma's passed. She's been gone for well over twenty years now. Died of consumption down in Carolina. Mother always warned her she'd pass if she didn't get to a desert climate. It's the air, Drew, the warm, dry air that she needed. But Aunt Velma never did listen to Mother." Alice looked at Drew with doleful eyes and shook her head. "You know Aunt Velma."

Drew nodded his sympathies with wide eyes. He didn't have a clue.

"So now Eleanor has the sugars, and I've been telling her for years that she needs to start watching what she eats. Diet is so important when it comes to good health, don't you know, Drew?"

"Yes. Yes, I do," Drew said with an untroubled smile.

"Well, I've got to run. You take care of yourself now, Drew. You know how I worry about you. So young, and still no wife." She looked at him pitifully, shook her head, and clicked her tongue in lamentation over the solitary existence of her favorite police officer.

"You go on and have a nice visit with your sister, Alice. I don't want you worrying about me, your roses, or the McElroy boy."

Alice looked at him as if he'd gone mad. "Why on earth would I worry about the McElroy boy? Now, Drew, you just leave him be. He's a good boy, and the McElroys are wonderful neighbors. My goodness, Drew, you really have to learn to trust people more. I know that must be hard in your line of work, but do make an effort," Alice pleaded. "For me? Hmm?"

Drew simply nodded. He'd try. Dear woman.

"Believe you me, Drew, you need to find yourself a nice lady friend." She rendered a clumsy wink and left the office. He smiled as the screen door clapped shut behind her.

Drew sat for a minute, shaking his head and waiting for the giggles to pass, when the screen door clapped shut once more. "What'd you forget to tell me, Alice?" Drew asked without even looking up.

"That I was free for dinner tonight," a melodic voice replied. "But my name's not Alice. It's Rebecca." Drew's head snapped up as crisply as Old Glory in a high wind. The sound of Rebecca's voice caressed his ear as smoothly as satin on skin. It was the furthest thing from nails on a chalkboard that he could possibly fathom.

"So it is," Drew said, pleased that his voice sounded so calm yet afraid the wild excitement in his eyes betrayed his emotions. "It's a mistake that I can assure you will never happen again."

He looked at her and waited for his breath to return. The first word that came to him was *exquisite*. The second word that came to him was *delicious*. Her simple black dress hugged her curves without clinging to them, allowing the garment to do things its designer could have only dreamed about. Drew watched, enchanted, as she crossed the room toward him, her movement so smooth and refined it would have been a sin to call it walking. Rebecca stopped when she reached his desk and leaned on the edge, wearing a playful smile every bit as intriguing as her dress. Drew could only stare and hope he wasn't drooling. This Goddess thing was starting to make a whole lotta sense to him, as he was looking at one. And she was there to see him. *Or was she?*

"So who's Alice?" Rebecca asked her prisoner. "One of the many women in your life?"

At first, he wasn't sure he heard her correctly, what with his heart banging away in his ears like a hammer on an anvil. It was more like reading lips than hearing words at this point.

"What can I say? I'm in demand," Drew replied, pleased with how evenly the words came out. She smiled as if it were true.

"So what are you doing now?" Rebecca asked, looking around the quiet room.

"Oh, just trying to write a column for the *Reporter* on child safety seats," he said, too thrilled by her presence to be overly concerned about an unwritten article anymore. "It's not going so well."

"No? What've you got so far?"

Drew pointed to the monitor's empty screen. Rebecca came around the corner of the desk and leaned in to look. She was close enough that Drew could smell her light perfume. He couldn't place it, but would have called it *Heavenly* were it his to name. He wanted to fall into her. To lose himself in her and never return. He was completely bewitched.

"Oh," she said in a soft voice faintly rimmed with embarrassment. "It's not going well at all, is it?"

Drew snapped back to reality. "Oh, never mind that. I can write that anytime," he said, waving off any concern and quickly changing the subject. "So what brings you out this way? You going over to Stonecroft?"

"No. I was just wandering around, you know, doing nothing," she said, dropping hints like bread crumbs.

"You know," Drew said, "I can arrest you for loitering."

"Really?" She looked at him with a capricious smile. "Will you use the handcuffs?" They both laughed. The game was going well.

"Want to go to dinner?"

"Oh yeah."

Drew logged off the neglected computer and called in to head-quarters on his Nextel. *Just like on TV,* Rebecca thought.

"Hey, Greg, I'm leaving for the day. Locking up Precinct One." A response clicked over.

"Copy that, Drew. Have a good one."

He looked at Rebecca with raised eyebrows. "Ready?"

They crossed Washington Street and, turning a corner, proceeded at a leisurely pace down the gentle slope of State Street. They passed the wonderful old houses of bright reds and yellows and subdued browns and blues. Rebecca adored the simple beauty of the quaint town and wondered why she hadn't taken the time to appreciate it before now. They took a moment to peek into the windows of the antique shops and marine art stores where State Street dead-ended at Tucker's Wharf.

Drew looked off to his right, across Front Street to Driftwood's Restaurant. His favorite lunchtime haunt wasn't open for dinner, which shaved the choices down nicely for Drew, who still vacillated between several eateries. It was just as well that Driftwood's was closed because it was usually packed with all his friends—or as Drew referred to them, the usual suspects. *Those sharks would be all over Rebecca,* Drew told himself.

"Why don't we go . . ." He faded off, deep in thought.

"Someplace where you won't run into any of your friends?" she teased.

"Listen," he started apologetically, "I really don't date much. If those guys see me come in with someone as attractive as you, well, they'd be riding me for days."

"Hey, don't worry about it. I understand," she said in a soothing tone, shading slightly pink from the compliment. She looked around the wharf and saw the wood-shake building with blue-and-yellow awnings. "The Landing," she noted, turning to Drew. "Do you want to eat there?"

"Sure. Or we can go to the Barnacle. It's up the street just about another quarter mile."

Rebecca looked up the tight street, its old houses packed sardine close and crowding the sidewalk for space. The lazy curve of the road gave the appearance that some of the buildings spilled out onto the narrow lane. "I'd like to walk a bit more," she decided. "Do you mind?"

"No, not at all. The Barnacle it is."

They strolled side by side past Richard's Marine Service and Marblehead Trading Company. Rebecca pointed out the date markers and historic nameplates on some of the old houses that pushed up against the street. She marveled that so many seaside homes could have survived centuries of New England coastal weather. Drew marveled that he could have someone this wonderful walking beside him through the town he loved.

Drew looked up the lane and saw two elderly women standing on the sidewalk, engaged in animated conversation. *Clear the sidewalk, ladies,* he ordered in his mind. *Bald man and a dream coming through.* And as if by magic, they parted. Drew couldn't remember feeling this way, at least not in a long, long time. It was as if his heart was floating among the clouds. Drew looked up into the sky, where his heart was soaring, and said a silent prayer. *Dear God, please, whatever you do, don't take me now.* Rebecca looked at him with smiling green eyes as Drew began to hum one of her favorite songs.

* * *

Jake had decided to stay at the inn with Marie. In the last twenty-four hours, his wife had become leery of entering rooms that were not occupied by another living person, especially the gathering room. That suited Jake just fine. He'd much rather have her where he could see her. Jake stood his watch vigilantly, ready to protect her from any physical assault that might come against her, for the threat of attack from an unworldly foe was as real as it was unpredictable.

Through the silence of the house, Jake listened for Marie in the sitting room. Nothing. She must be jotting down a few notes. He looked down at his brown Docksiders and listened to the thick ticktock of Ol' Sentry. Jake tapped the toe of his shoe on the wooden floor in time with the clock behind him. He found himself walking the wide, worn floorboards of the gathering room as if he were standing watch out at sea, keeping a weather eye out for the enemy's sail. It was bizarre to find himself standing watch inside an old house for the appearance of a long-dead pirate. Jake shook his head. *They couldn't make this shit up.*

The phone ringing in the sitting room startled him from his musings. He no longer walked the deck of the USS *Never Dock*, the imaginary ship on which Jake stood his watch, but back on dry land and listening to his wife field yet another call. He glanced over his shoulder at the clock that ticked away: 5:25 p.m. How many calls had that been? "Fourteen by my count," Jake said out loud to himself. *Damn, when you coming home, Tom?* Jake wondered. *Not that it would make any difference.* He could hear the calm, reassuring tone of Marie's voice as she dealt masterfully with the caller. The outcome, however, was no different from the others.

Marie set the phone back in the cradle with far greater self-control than Jake could have managed. He stepped away from the archway, giving his wife a wide berth to enter the room. She looked at Jake and tried to speak, but the tears welling up in her eyes said it all.

"I know," Jake said. "I heard." Marie walked to his open arms and embedded her face once more in his already-tear-spotted T-shirt. "Tom ought to be home soon," Jake whispered.

It was after six o'clock before Jake heard the gravel crunching on the driveway. He watched from his seat at the table as the SUV pulled up to the far end of the drive and parked beneath the shade of the red maple. Jake tapped his restless fingers and stared at the door. He felt the gentle hand of his wife settle on his shoulder, a soft, reassuring squeeze providing him much-needed encouragement. The front door creaked open, and before it creaked shut, Tom knew that something was very wrong.

When the full weight of Jake's story had hit home, Tom's head hung low in subjugation to the cruel whims of fate. Jake watched helplessly as Tom sat in complete silence, shaking his head in an abject display of surrender. He brought his chin up from the table and searched the face of his friend for an explanation that Jake didn't have. The phone rang. Tom pushed the chair away from him with the back of his knees and stood defiantly.

"Tom, why don't you let Marie answer it," Jake suggested. "I don't think you're in the best state of mind to field these calls. You'll just end up making matters worse."

Tom considered the suggestion for a moment as the phone continued to ring, each tone assaulting the ear like a jackhammer and chipping away at his nerves, already stretched thin and rubbed raw. Finally, he nodded to Marie, who moved quickly into the sitting room to get the phone. He glared at Jake as he dropped heavily back into the chair. "Just how much worse do you think it can get?"

Marie was back in less than a minute, wearing the most bewildered look that Jake had ever seen. "Jake, Tim Buckley's on the phone." At first Jake thought she might be kidding, then quickly realized all jokes were out the window at this point.

"Isn't that your buddy in Connecticut?" Tom asked.

"Yeah," Jake said, moving to the phone. "And if you check your guest registration book, you'll see he's also scheduled to be staying here on Labor Day weekend."

Marie took a seat and shared the silence of the room with Tom while they waited for Jake to return. They didn't have to wait long. Jake was back in less than two minutes, wearing a mask of incredulity that was not unlike Marie's moments earlier.

"You're not gonna fuckin' believe this."

* * *

"How's your swordfish?" Rebecca asked.

"Fantastic. How're your clams?"

"Really good."

"You know what I like best about seafood?" Drew asked.

"What's that?"

"It all goes so well with beer."

"Here, here," Rebecca said, laughing as she raised her glass. The rims of their pilsner glasses came together as lightly as a kiss, with a gentle clink tolling the union. Rebecca and Drew took an easy swig of their Narragansetts.

They had managed to get the last open table out on the deck of the Barnacle and basked in the fading glow of the evening summer sun. Rebecca looked out over the active water of Marblehead Harbor. She watched as sailboats and powerboats engaged in a water ballet in the narrows of the harbor, all captains alert, careful to avoid the bobbing red markers of the lobster pots that spotted the mouth of the inlet. Rebecca's eyes followed the blue water across the harbor to the lighthouse on Marblehead Neck. "This is adorable. Such a busy little town, but it still seems so quaint."

Drew nodded. "It's a very special place."

"Tell me about it," she said. "I think I could fall in love with this place," she added, her playfulness yielding to a deeper emotion.

Drew regarded her with love's perfecting eye. The gold of evening light shining warmly on her alabaster skin, the light sea breeze caressing dark locks that lay soft on silky shoulders. He had to wonder: Was the woman across from him real, or was he looking at a dream? *If she's a dream, I won't wake up. If she's real, I won't let go,* Drew promised himself.

A few seconds later, he realized she was no dream. She'd have vanished in a puff of smoke when his pager vibrated him back to reality. "Who's calling me now?" he said out loud to himself. "I'm off duty." He stared at the number, which seemed vaguely familiar, but he was having trouble placing it. When the tumblers of his memory finally dropped into place, he looked up at Rebecca, who easily read the concern on his face.

"It's Tom Stone."

Drew excused himself to make the call. Rebecca requested that he do so from the table, anxious to hear the latest, but Drew looked through the open windows of the restaurant at the patrons who sat eating at the counter just inside, looking back at him, and decided he needed to make the call elsewhere. "I'll be back in a minute." It was just that when he returned.

"Well?" Rebecca asked.

"He didn't want to discuss it over the phone," Drew explained. "So I told him I'd walk over after dinner."

"*We'll* walk over after dinner," Rebecca corrected him.

It was what he hoped she would say. And although they enjoyed the rest of their meal in pleasant discourse, both were restless to hear the news from Stonecroft. Rebecca reached the finish line first, and Drew flagged down their waiter for the check before he had set his fork down on the plate.

"Let me get that," Rebecca insisted, reaching for her purse when the check appeared on the black plastic tray adorned with two peppermints.

"Nope, I've got it. Besides, I asked you to dinner, remember?"

"All right," she conceded. "But I'll pick up the tab next time."

"You drive a hard bargain, lady, but you've got yourself a deal." *Next time?* Drew thought. *Cool.*

"How far is Stonecroft Inn from here?" Rebecca asked as they left the restaurant and started up Franklin Street. "It can't be far."

"No, it's not far at all, just about a half mile as the crow flies," he replied. "Add a few more steps for each bend of the road."

She smiled at him. "Just a nice stretch of the legs."

They walked in silence, each collecting their thoughts and allowing themselves to speculate on what might lie ahead. The wind picked up as they passed Old Burial Hill.

* * *

The front door opened even before Drew could reach out a fist to knock on it. The doleful expression on Tom's face as he greeted them added more than a dash of foreboding to their already-seasoned imaginings. Jake and Marie were at the table in the gathering room. It had become the heart of the house, even though the sitting room was now comfortably furnished with all the trappings of luxury. In addition to the new cable TV, unseen behind the hand-carved doors of the armoire, there were two oversize leather reading chairs, a matching couch and love seat, and a large coffee table to complement the arrangement, surrounding a substantial natural fireplace that might add to their comfort in the cold, harsh nights still many moons from now.

And yet, the gathering room remained center stage. It was not that it served as the source of energy, for it was quite the opposite, especially today, Rebecca sensed. Rather, it seemed to draw energy into it and to send it on through some dark and sinister portal. Rebecca hadn't noticed it on her previous visit. Now she could almost smell the foul exhaust that passed through the entrails of evil to afflict the living. A plant will absorb carbon dioxide and return life-giving oxygen. Evil inverts. It rips from nature all that is good and life sustaining and returns in its place the filth that lines the womb of hopelessness and death. Rebecca was amazed the others could stand to be in the room, until she realized they did not feel the rise of evil around them as she did.

Marie and Jake were poring over a green, canvas-bound ledger and comparing the entries with scribbled notes from a scattering of loose, unbound pages. Jake leaned back in his chair when he saw Drew and Rebecca.

"What would you say if I told you that the crazy sonuvabitch in the painting behind me was the least of our problems right now?" Jake asked. Both Drew and Rebecca looked from Jake to the painting on the wall. Rebecca had the sudden urge to tear it down, toss it into the fireplace, and start a nice summer bonfire. And no matter what Jake was about to tell them, she knew he was wrong; the crazy son of a bitch in the painting *was* their biggest problem.

"What's happened?" Drew asked. Jake glanced up at Tom, who continued to pace the floor, arms folded across his chest, head down, mouth clamped shut.

"We started getting phone calls today," Jake explained. "Tom was in Boston, tying up some legal loose ends with his lawyer; Marie and I were here. We were planning to go down to the Flag Hanger Gift Shop and do some patriotic shopping for our Fourth of July opening. Hell, Drew, we were even going to stop by to see if you wanted to go to lunch. But you can't do that when the phone keeps ringing. You can't do that when every single guest who had booked a stay this summer calls to cancel their reservation."

Rebecca's eyes grew wide. "You've got to be kidding. Every one?"

Jake jerked a thumb at Tom, who paced at the far end of the room, detached from the conversation, adrift in a sea of lonely confusion. "Does *he* look like I'm kidding?"

"What were their reasons?" Rebecca asked.

"Well, you see, here's where it gets really interesting. They said they just had a change in plans, or their vacations were canceled due to too much work at the office, or some kind of bullshit story along those lines. Then"—Jake looked at his watch—"about an hour ago, I received a call from Tim Buckley. He's a good friend of mine who has a reservation to stay here over Labor Day weekend." Jake broke off and turned to Tom. "Which, by the way, he confirmed he *will* be here."

Tom surrendered a weak but grateful smile.

"Anyway, Tim had just received a call from someone who started asking him questions as to what he knew about the owner of Stonecroft. Things like 'Have you had any previous contact with Tom Stone?' and 'Did Mr. Stone exhibit any angry or threatening behavior, even over the phone?' Weird stuff like that. Then the guy said that the autopsy was 'inconclusive' and that they probably wouldn't be able to charge anyone with murder, but they're still trying to follow up on any possible leads before they close the case."

"Before *who* closes the case?" Drew asked, bristling with anger.

Jake offered a wry smile. "That's exactly what I asked Tim. He told me the guy who called him had introduced himself as Detective Nate Ingersoll, Marblehead PD."

Drew was speechless. He couldn't even blink his unseeing eyes. Jake watched in growing fascination as the police lieutenant gave the impression of a video that had been stilled by the pause button.

"No," Drew said, coming back to life. "He couldn't have done that."

"Well, apparently he did," Jake asserted.

Tom glared at Drew, a man nearing the end of his rope. "I'm done, you know. This will end it for me." Tom spoke with the empty pain of a man who had nothing left. "By the end of July, the bank will own my house."

The Warning

Friday, June 25, 1999

The day had exacted a devastating emotional toll, and the hour was late. Jake and Marie had long ago sought succor in the land of Nod. For Tom, however, sleep was something he could only dream about. A nervous energy pulsed through his body that kept him pacing restlessly around his room. Searching for something to free his mind from its endless wanderings, he stepped into the master bath and opened the mirrored medicine cabinet above the sink. A quick and pointless inventory of all the brand-name products for healthy teeth, skin, and hair was taken, then just as quickly forgotten as he closed the cabinet door. He stared, bleary eyed, into the reflective glass that cast back the image of what he had become. The dark crescents that rested beneath his empty gaze, set against a pasty canvas of clammy skin, bore testimony to the strain of recent days.

Tom grabbed the plastic tube and squeezed smooth white paste over the soft bristles of his toothbrush to dust the stale, tacky cobwebs from his mouth. The fresh taste of mint, however, served only as a stimulant, and in that sense, he bemoaned the pleasant sensation. He spit the white foam into the basin and leaned into the sink to rinse. He took a mouthful of water directly from the brass tap. The mirror looked at him as he swished the water forcefully around with his cheeks and saw his eyes widen in shock. He spat the contents into the sink with whale-spout force. He spat repeatedly to rid himself of the familiar yet disagreeable taste. His tongue darted about his lips and mouth as if searching for the source. The taste was overwhelming.

"Salt? What the . . ."

Tom cupped his hand and held it under the running faucet and sampled, once more, the brine pouring through his pipes. He grabbed the shower door handle and jerked it open. Twisting the single-lever spigot, Tom was immediately shrouded in a hot, salty mist. His mind reeled. *I don't have a well. I have city water. How can there be salt water in my line? How can this be unless it isn't . . .* Tom stuck a hand back into the seaborne mist and turned the shower off. He was drying his arm with a hand towel when he heard the music.

Tom walked the few short steps to the bathroom door and peeked out into his bedroom. A mixture of music and mayhem carried into his room from some distant point beyond. Just how distant Tom didn't know, but he had a pretty good idea. He stepped out from behind the protection of the thin tongue-and-groove pine-paneled door and crept across his floor to the bedroom door that opened to the hallway near the top of the ladder. The music was louder from his new station. Tom heard two different instruments. First, the distinctive sound of a violin, but with the lively and scratchy way it was being played, he guessed it would have been referred to as a fiddle. The other sounded like a squeezebox, the simple, ancient ancestor of the modern-day accordion. *They should have quit while they were ahead,* Tom mused with nervous humor.

He listened more closely. Voices. Voices that at first had been only fused and muted background noise but now gained definition; although he still couldn't pick out individual words, he could discern different speakers.

Tom rested a pensive finger on the light switch next to the door. Letting his hand fall, he turned off the light, plunging the room into darkness. He quietly turned the doorknob and opened the door just a crack, only enough to poke his head out and gain one good eyeful of the gold and fluttering light splashing against the ceiling at the top of the ladder. The voices wafted up the stairs like the ebb and flow of the tide. One moment he could clearly hear every word spoken, then the sound would roll away, replaced by a muffled rumble.

He stepped out into the hall, his heart pounding in his chest. He glanced over his left shoulder at Jake's bedroom door. He stepped slowly toward the door, backward, refusing to turn his back on what might come at him from down below. Tom reached out and rapped quietly on the door with less than a full arsenal of knuckles. He waited a moment and placed an ear to the door but perceived no movement on the other side. Tom knocked again, hard, using a tight fist to tap out his distress signal, yet yielding the same result. He reached down and turned the knob, which twisted easily in his hand. The door had not been locked but would not open. Tom put a shoulder to it and leaned into the door with the force of his entire weight. Still, it refused to open, and Tom realized any further attempts would prove just as futile.

Only Tom had been invited to the party, and as frightened as he was, he knew his attendance was required. After all, it was being thrown in his honor. Walking boldly if not briskly, Tom strode to the top of the ladder. It wouldn't be like the last time he'd met his uninvited guest. This time, the first mate had brought his friends.

Tom could hear the voices as clearly as if he were standing next to them. One voice called out to someone referred to as Pike, which was then followed by a gruff, inarticulate response from someone who sounded farther away than the others. Or maybe the man just didn't speak very loudly. Whatever the case, the curt response was met with howling laughter from what must have been a dozen rowdy men. *At least they're laughing,* Tom thought. *Now's as good a time as any.* It was when his foot settled on the first creaking step that the noise from below halted. That was when fear stormed up the ladder, gripped Tom by the balls, and squeezed.

He dropped one foot after the other, a tiny seed of courage taking root from the steady cadence struck out by his feet on the bare wooden steps. He could feel the angry glares from the men below even before he could see their faces, and as much as Tom had tried to prepare himself for what he might find, his knees weakened just the same when he reached the landing.

The room was gone. The place he found himself in was familiar nonetheless. He'd been there before. He gazed across the deck of the ship and stared back at the menacing faces that studied him, sizing him up. Maintaining his balance with one hand still on the rope railing, Tom looked back up the ladder at steps that faded into the upward darkness. A black sky erased all light above the hostile faces of the silent crew. The dim illumination of the scene was provided by two lanterns that swung eerily on unseen ropes above the heads of the pirate brood.

More than a dozen men stood in front of Tom, fifteen or so, he surmised without taking roll call. All appeared to Tom's mind as being spectral images—holograms, really. They were there, but they weren't real. Not in the sense that their leader, the first mate, who stood in their midst, was real. They all considered Tom as he stood in petrified fascination on watery knees. And although the crew seemed to lack the solidity of the first mate, Tom suspected they were more than ready, willing, and able to carry out the most detestable and deadly orders spewed from the mouth of their commander.

Tom leaned heavily on the taut rope rail as each man muttered his opinion, one to another, on what should be done with the innkeeper. They turned as one to the first mate, who stood with one booted foot resting on a short barrel, sharpening his knife on a wet leather strap. He took no notice of the crew around him but glowered at Tom, a hint of indecision in his eyes. A slow, pernicious grin cracked his lips.

Tom's heart thundered in his chest as the first mate leaned down and picked up the canvas sack that lay at his feet. With an easy swing, the pirate hurled the bundle across the deck. The bag crashed to the boards at Tom's feet with the heavy, awkward sound of clunking coconuts, its contents spilling out of the open-ended sack. Tom saw his own severed head leave the bag first, followed by Jake's and Drew's immediately after. All three wheeled several feet, clearing the way for the heads of Marie and Rebecca to roll free from the canvas mouth.

Reeling from the sight, Tom stumbled backward against the wall, his knees buckling beneath him. The first mate laughed as spiritedly as might the merriest of all souls and was joined in chorus by the loyal crew gathered around him. The mocking laughter rebounded and echoed within the walls of Tom's brain, taking on a warbling, tinny sound as he fell forward on his hands. A cold dampness formed at his temples, and Tom recognized the signs and symptoms of psychogenic shock. Familiar images began to swim before his eyes as the gathering room began to reappear. The complement of the ship's murderous crew faded in and out before evaporating in a wash of deep-blue light. All that was left of the nightmare was the first mate, who stood laughing in the middle of the room, and the severed heads, whose glazed eyes stared sightlessly at Tom. The heads had been cleaved cleanly with one neat and deadly stroke of a cutlass. *At least it was a quick death,* Tom thought. *I guess that's a blessing.* Then the room went black.

* * *

Marie woke with a start. *Had someone knocked?* She wiped her eyes with sleepy fingers in an attempt to remove the vision from her sight. A boy stood before her in the far corner of the room. It was her little friend from the garden. Despite her fear, Marie was overtaken by curiosity. With his head down and shoulders jostling, the boy appeared to be crying. It was the sound that alerted her. He wasn't crying; he was laughing. He lifted his head and peered at Marie with eyes so pale they were almost white. A fiendish grin was only partially obscured by the twitching fingertips that played before it.

She tried to turn and wake Jake, who slept undisturbed at her side, but she couldn't move. She was too frightened to even make a sound. The boy pulled two knives out from behind his back. They were old and worn, with smooth wooden handles. He slowly brought the blades together and slid them, one across the other, in a steady rhythm as he approached Marie. An evil, humorless grin held fast to his face.

Jake slumbered on in the dark depths of a dreamless sleep. Slowly, he began to rouse. As if with the rising of the sun, light shined softly through his closed lids. Jake opened his eyes to see that the sun was not at all on the rise. In fact, the fluorescent green numbers on the bedside clock next to him told him it was exactly midnight. He turned back to the center of his pillow and saw a gray light emanating from beyond the foot of his bed. He narrowed his eyes, trying to pull into focus the glowing image in front of him. It was as if someone were walking toward him in a thick fog, a dim light trying to pierce the cold, gray vapor.

He quickly looked over at Marie, making sure she was safe, and found her sleeping peacefully at his shoulder. The light grew in its intensity as it began to close in on itself. From the middle of the fog, a form developed. Diffused and ill-defined at first, within a few seconds, a few eternal seconds, Jake was able to make out the figure as it came toward him. It was an old woman. An old woman swimming in a sea of gray mist and slithering like a snake several feet above the bed. Her slate-gray hair matched the color of her mottled skin as she turned up her head to look at Jake.

There was no smile to be found in the black void of her open mouth. The smell of necrotic flesh assaulted Jake's senses with every heave of the old hag's chest. The glassy black orbs in her deep-set eye sockets held only emptiness. She hung above Jake as he lay paralyzed in bed, then slowly descended upon him. Her body settled on his frame as hard and heavy as a cold slab of granite. He couldn't breathe, and as she pressed her weight against him, she stole the last of the spent air that escaped from his lungs, her black mouth pulling savagely at his fading breath. He felt his lungs begin to burn. Searching for the life-sustaining air that she refused him, Jake's body convulsed beneath the crushing weight. Suddenly, his struggle subsided, and a calm surrender crept in as the gray mist enveloped him.

Marie fought against her fear and the grip of the hypnotic vision that held her captive. In a sudden burst of determined energy, she lunged for the lamp on the nightstand, and with a flip of the switch, she expelled the intruder from her sight in a blast of light. She grabbed Jake's shoulder and shook hard. He woke with a startled gasp and bolted upright in bed, wild-eyed and pulling for air like he'd been held underwater to the point of near drowning.

"The boy," Marie cried. "I saw him. He's here. He's in the house." They sat and panted side by side, searching the lighted room for any signs of their intruders. Jake didn't appear to have heard a word she said.

"That fuckin' bitch came at me," he finally said, still chasing his breath. "Thanks, babe. You just saved your old man's ass." She looked at him, puzzled. He didn't explain. Jake jumped out of bed and ripped open the bedroom door, almost tearing it loose from its hinges. He shouted for Tom as he ran out into the hallway.

"Here." A low, quiet voice ascended from below. Jake flicked on the light at the top of the ladder. For the second time in a week, Jake found Tom alone at the bottom of the stairs. Tom sat with his back against the wall, legs extended out in front of him. He looked blankly up at Jake with dark, hollow eyes and appeared to Jake to be more dead than alive.

CHAPTER TWENTY-ONE
Trial

March 1719

It was odd, Israel thought, to look back on the arduous, terrible voyage from Bath Town with rueful longing. But the truth was that the interminable journey in the bowels of the *Pearl* was but a summer voyage when considering his present situation. He remembered how he could always tell when they were approaching some new Virginia port on the James River. A cheer would rise up from the townspeople when they saw, with their own eyes, the horrific spectacle that hung from the bowsprit of the sloop. Their thirst for a bloody end to Ned Teach's life made him wonder if some of those who cheered ought to have been chained beside him, down in the *Pearl's* dark hold. But the freezing stench of shackled men stowed away belowdecks for weeks on end through December on into January now seemed a warm memory.

For now he was learning that existence in the recesses of the Williamsburg Public Jail extracted life from both body and soul.

371

Racked with pain, he yearned for merciful relief with every grain of sand that passed through the hourglass. Mottled flesh hung limply from his aching bones. Black and purple blotches appeared without physical insult on every part of his body. His fingers and toes showed a deep yellow below the nails that yielded to brown at their tips. He wished he had a dog that might lick away the white fluid that seeped from his eyes. Yet from the pit of despair that enveloped him, he managed a smile. He had reached up to scratch the only part of his body that didn't hurt, only for his fingers to remember that he no longer had a right ear.

The smell of the rotten earth was oppressive. The coming of spring had begun to warm the once-frozen ground and resurrected evidence of past human offenses. Although he had no intention of proving it, Israel was certain that if he were to start digging, he would uncover the bodies of those who had died there, buried in shallow graves below his thin bed of moldy straw.

It was the first time he had been in the royal colony of Virginia. He promised himself that if he were to make it out alive, he would never return. Israel took a deep breath and let it out slowly. He wondered: Did the ring, stowed securely beneath his belt, have enough power to save him from the gallows? There was the devil to pay if it didn't. They'd brought them here to die. The last remnants of the crew of the notorious Blackbeard would return to their captain when they'd finally danced at the end of a rope.

He knew little of the political fight that had gone on between the royal governor of Virginia and the proprietary governor of North Carolina. What he did know was that Governor Spotswood of Virginia wanted testimony that would lend support to his actions of arresting the pirates in North Carolina and extraditing them to Virginia.

Specifically, Spotswood needed witnesses to swear that those in custody continued pirating even after they had accepted crown pardons. Because this action was condoned by the governor of North Carolina without regard to the safety of the citizens of neighboring Virginia, Spotswood took it upon himself to see that the pirates were dealt with, one way or another. The preferable way, of course, was hanging them, and any man who faced the noose would do whatever he needed to do to avoid such an end. Spotswood would get the testimony he so desired. Although Israel doubted that any convicted pirate, no matter how compliant, would receive the clemency he wanted in return.

Israel sat in the dirt with his back against the wall. He rested his chin on his good knee that he'd pulled up tight against his chest and embraced with both arms. He sat without hope and contemplated his fate. His crippled leg lay extended in front of him with curled toes pointing to the cell door a few feet away. A rectangular shaft of cold sunlight shined harshly against the rusty iron latch set high in the heavy oaken door. Their plan to see him tried and hanged was assured. The question of how soon seemed closer to being answered when a face appeared behind the iron bars of the aged wooden door. Israel was certain they had come for him; he was the only one left of the four men originally dumped into the six-by-eight-foot cell.

"C'mon, Hands," the jailer commanded. "His Excellency would like a word."

Israel struggled slowly to his feet, the exertion taking a heavy toll on his weakened frame and watery lungs. "Well, we mustn't keep *His Excellency* waiting, now, mustn't we?" Israel grunted in reply.

Although it was likely a prelude to his hanging, the waiting had become unbearable, and Israel was relieved that something was happening. He had been allowed out of his cell only a few times since he'd arrived, and that was just to empty the piss pots of the other prisoners. On one occasion, he had slipped on ice and spilled their disgusting contents on the steps of the jail. Since then, he'd been stripped of the privilege of emptying them and was no longer allowed out of his confinement. That was more than a month ago, and Israel was eager to see life beyond the cold stone walls of his cell. Any life. Even if that life was dedicated to his personal destruction.

As near as he could figure, there were only a few of Teach's men still alive. Israel would hear of them being brought before the court and providing testimony against their former master. Some had come back to their cells and had spoken confidently of their favor with the vice-admiralty court, only to be dragged back for sentencing and execution later that same day. *Justice due and justice paid by the grommets and lubbers of that scurvy crew,* Israel thought.

But when he thought of how they'd hanged Henry Somerset and Liam O'Brien, his blood turned cold. The anger he'd known all his life took fresh root in the pit of his stomach and quickly spread throughout his entire being. Like a bound madman screaming for freedom, the hate pounded for escape, ready to lash out at anyone insane enough to release him. The treatment Henry and Liam received at the hands of the jailers left Israel yearning for his knife and a free hand. They were men who lived as they believed, not as others believed they should. They deserved to die at the end of a cutlass, not at the end of a rope. The other scoundrels could go to the devil, but Somerset and O'Brien, well, they'd earned better.

"You're putting shackles on these crippled old bones?" Israel asked in disbelief. "And where do you think I might be running off to?"

"Orders of the governor," the guard said. "We take no chances with any prisoner."

"Well, then it's certainly been a while since the governor has seen me run," Israel said to his own amusement. Another guard entered the cell, and the two men grabbed Israel by his upper arms and carried him brusquely out of the cell and up the stairs to the first floor of the jail.

"Prisoner Hands to the admiralty court," the guard said to a prissy little registrar sitting behind a Chippendale desk. The clerk looked upon Israel as a hated thing and entered his name in a thick ledger that lay on the desk in front of him. Satisfied with the simple entry, the clerk turned to the guards and dismissed them with a curt nod of his powder-wigged head.

Although the winter freeze had lifted, it was still raw and windy as they walked Israel across the street on a diagonal course to the courthouse in the capitol building. The tattered rags that clung to Israel's fleshless bones did nothing to protect him from the blowing wind, and he shuddered uncontrollably in the grasp of his husky escorts. The gooseflesh over his entire body tightened the wilting skin while jack-o'-lantern teeth chattered noisily behind blue lips. As the agents whisked him up the thirteen steps at the front of the capitol building and through its doors, Israel's feet barely touched the ground, which was the only good thing he could claim from his journey.

Once through the doors, Israel found immediate if only momentary comfort. The roaring fireplace in the large anteroom returned forgotten warmth to his quaking frame, and the highly polished wooden floor felt smooth and even below his bony feet. His two custodians remained silent at his side as they peered expectantly down the long corridor to their left. Israel stared into the blazing fire, lulled into complacency by the comfort it provided. He was able to admire the fine woodwork surrounding him for just a few short minutes before he was summoned to a room at the end of the hall.

Heavy double doors were opened, and Israel and his guards entered the court. Israel had readied himself for anything, but he was not prepared for the artistry that was on display in the elegant room. First was the hand-hewn judge's bench, which the skillful hands of a master carpenter had certainly toiled many a day to bring to life. Israel looked on with a regretful heart at the magnificent work of a genius, and he wondered: Might he, if he'd sailed a different course in life, have been able to attain this level of skill? He saw that the finely crafted accent pieces were carved from Virginia walnut, whereas the facade of the bench was maple and depicted a scene from an age long past. Israel didn't know who they were, but they wore long robes and beards and carried scrolls and tablets in their arms. Perhaps they were Romans. The only thing he knew for sure was that he had never sailed on any ship with the likes of them. He looked above the carvings and saw the three fat men in judge's robes and white-powdered wigs sitting behind the bench. None of them looked even vaguely familiar to Israel, at least not with their wigs on. He looked about, surprised at how empty the court was. There were but four or five other men in the room, most going about their own secretarial duties, largely ignoring the new prisoner. *There will be plenty more waiting at the gallows,* Israel told himself.

A tall, thin man in a fine silk suit stood in front of the judges at the bench and studied Israel with disdain. He motioned to the guards to bring him forward and pointed to a single chair in the middle of the room, a safe distance from the bench. A safe distance, Israel figured, for the guards to recapture any prisoner so inclined as to charge the robed men in the powdered wigs. He limped over to the chair and, for the first time, considered his crippled limb to be an asset to him, given the particular circumstances.

Israel peered over his right shoulder and saw a prisoner having his shackles removed by a magistrate. Although he could not understand the man through the sobs of joy that poured out of him, it was easy to see, and hear, that he'd had his freedom restored to him. Israel recognized the man as Sam Odell, a fellow who had come up the river with him and the others. The man had cried his innocence all the way up the James, and Israel was a little sorry to see him released. Such a man who would cry in the company of other men did not deserve mercy, let alone life itself. *Well,* Israel thought, a sardonic smile stretching his gaunt lips, *maybe it's a good thing; maybe these judges are in a forgiving mood.*

A muffled argument at the bench brought Israel's attention back to front and center. The man in the middle seemed to be attempting to quell the rising temper of the man on his right. The chief judge, Israel speculated, as he was sitting in the middle and seemed a bit more elevated than the two on either side of him, was red-faced in his efforts to quiet the man. The skin began to crawl on the back of Israel's neck when he heard the lower judge mention him by name. He dropped his eyes to the floor so as not to meet the judge's angry glare and tried to stir some recollection of how he might have injured this man. Despair seeped back into Israel's heart as he realized that the number of possible accusations of committed offenses was endless. He hung his head low and prayed to the devil to deliver him from justice.

A wooden gavel struck its sound block three times and brought silence to the room. The man in the splendid suit strutted like a peacock in front of the sole prisoner seated at a safe distance from the bench.

"Oy-yea, oy-yea, oy-yea. The vice-admiralty court of the royal colony of Virginia is in session. His Excellency, Alexander Spotswood, royal governor of the colony of Virginia, presiding. The case against one, Israel Hands, on the charge of"—he paused and looked down at the broken man before him and, with scarcely concealed joy, levied the charge against him—"piracy."

"Mr. Hands," Governor Spotswood began, "you have heard the charge against you. How do you plead, guilty or not guilty?"

Israel held up his empty palms in a questioning manner; the words he sought eluded him. Months of inactivity and the lack of societal intercourse left Israel's mind as feeble as his limbs. Spotswood saw the hopelessness in the man's eyes and allowed himself a small, self-satisfying smile.

"Very well. You plead guilty and desire mercy from this court. Let us consider the testimony that you provide and seek to find the merit in your words that may warrant the mercy you desire from this court."

Israel wiped the streaming pus from his eyes with the back of threadbare sleeves and nodded in submission to the governor's decision. He knew that he could only hope for mercy by going along, as far as possible, with the wishes of the prejudiced body.

"Please stand and state your name," crowed the barrister, strutting before the bench in full feather. Israel struggled to his feet, still suffering the effects of the cold on his aging joints.

"Israel Hands," he said and sat down heavily, but not happily, as the tremor of his landing resonated through the whole of his aching frame.

"Israel Hands," Spotswood repeated. "Also known as Basilica Hands?"

"Aye," Israel replied.

"Yes, *your lordship!*" the barrister shouted. "And you are to stand when you address this court!"

Israel faltered. This was not going as he had hoped. Again, Israel struggled to his feet. "Beg pardon, your lordship. Yes, your lordship. I have been called Basilica Hands." Israel dropped to the seat again.

"And Hezekiah Hands?" Spotswood continued.

Israel groaned with the stiffening pain of regaining his feet. It was a game to them. "Aye, er, yes, your lordship. I have been called Hezekiah as well." Israel shifted his weight and felt something tickle his belly.

Then the angry judge, seated to Spotswood's right, asked a question that truly unnerved him.

"And Ezekiel Hands. Would that name sound familiar?" The corner of the judge's mouth turned up in a contemptible grin.

Israel remained upright on ever-weakening legs. "Yes, your lordship. But that was my father's name, not a name that I ever answered to." He waited for the next dagger to be thrown. He didn't have to wait long.

"Oh yes, your father. Sadly, condemned as a witch in Salem in those dark days long ago, was he not?" The evil in the room was palpable, but it was hard to say from where its true source was flowing.

"Aye, sir." Israel slipped intentionally. "Unjustly accused, and from what I heard, died unjustly from a beating he received in jail!" Then he stated mockingly, "Your lordship." Both men locked eyes. Spotswood remained silent, watching the prisoner and searching intently for condemning evidence that he might divulge in the heat of the courtroom argument.

The angry judge pursued the lead Israel had left for him. "I would know something of a father who died from an unjust beating,

Mr. Hands. For my father died at the hands of a murderer who was never caught—and so never punished. Perhaps you might remember my father, Mr. Hands. He was nothing more than a simple innkeeper, but he was the only father I would ever have. His name was Seth Barlow." The judge stood behind the bench, leaned toward Israel, and sprayed his words at the crippled killer before him. "How does your memory serve you now, Mr. Hands?"

Israel stared blankly at the man whose father he had killed so many lifetimes ago. How did this man know it was he? Israel suddenly felt something heavy move down his hip. He dropped again to his seat, oblivious to the pain that rattled his bones.

"Stand up, Hands! Do not dare to offend this court with your acts of contempt!"

Israel had no choice. He stood up slowly, and while doing so, tried to control the tension on his belt. But a sharp jolt of pain from his injured knee caused him to lurch to his left, and the ring slipped from under his belt and rang out as crisply as a ship's bell on the polished wooden floor.

Twenty eyes stared as the heavy metal object spun like a child's top on the courtroom floor. Crimson beams of light fired out from four rubies as the light refracted in the jewels and sparkled on the faces of the mesmerized court. The bejeweled silver ring came spinning to a loud stop on the highly polished floor, echoing in the silence of the courtroom. A black onyx cross amid the field of red sat in the center of the ring and stared malevolently back at those who would do its master harm. The barrister approached it cautiously, still unsure of what lay before him. He picked it up slowly and studied it appreciatively as the perfection of the ring touched his magisterial spirit. The spell was broken by the booming voice of authority from the bench.

"Mr. Kimball, bring that item to the bench, if you please."

"Yes, certainly, my lord." Kimball walked slowly to the bench, still admiring and assessing the value of such a resplendent ring. He begrudgingly handed it over to the governor, who continued the assessment that Mr. Kimball had begun. Spotswood's eyes widened as he appraised the treasure in his hand. He entertained a private conversation with Lord Salter, the judge seated at Spotswood's left elbow, who nodded thoughtfully as the governor spoke. When he was finished, Spotswood turned to his right and continued the muffled dialogue with Lord Barlow. After reaching consensus, Governor Spotswood turned to Israel and the other men who occupied the space of the courtroom. He cleared his throat.

"We are truly blessed to have at the bench two of the most esteemed legal minds in the realm today. Lord Salter, from Philadelphia, in the Commonwealth of Pennsylvania, is, by experience and reputation, the leading authority on British common law and its application in the British colonies of America." Looking practically bored, Lord Salter nodded his head, ever so slightly, toward the governor, in acknowledgment of his kind, but hardly overstated, introduction of the jurist from Pennsylvania.

"To my right, Lord Barlow, from Boston, Massachu—" The governor was interrupted by Barlow, who placed a gentle hand on the governor's wrist and whispered something in his ear. Spotswood nodded and continued. "Lord Barlow, from Marblehead, Massachusetts Bay Colony, and the foremost expert on maritime law in the colonies.

"After conferring with my lords, it has been determined that this item, this ring, will remain the property of this court until its true ownership may be determined. In the meantime, Lord Barlow will serve as the protectorate of this item until said determination can be made."

Israel's heart sank; his fate was now clear. *That's it, then,* Israel conceded. *Barlow has stolen my ring, and with it, my life.* Through the mind-numbing blur of swirling reality, he smiled weakly to himself as he realized that, in the end, even the devil had betrayed him.

"Israel Hands," Spotswood began, "are you prepared to render testimony to this court, as to the actions you have taken while serving as both master and first mate under the command and flag of one Edward Teach, also known as Blackbeard?"

Israel looked up through murky eyes and spoke the only words that came to him. "Aye, Captain."

The three judges stared disconcertedly at the man swaying unsteadily before the bench. Detecting no contempt in the man's meaning, they shared a sideways glance with one another and decided to let the odd response pass without rebuke.

"Did you, Israel Hands, as master of the sloop *Adventure*, serve alongside Captain Teach and, by your own free will, take part in the blockade of the port of Charleston?"

"Yes, your lordship," Israel answered with regained composure.

"And during that blockade, did you not commit piratical acts against nine vessels total, including the *Crowley*, from which you held as prisoners some fourscore men, women, and children against their will?"

Israel fought back the panic ebbing inside him, as the questions themselves carried certain condemnation. "It was not my ship that took the *Crowley*, your lordship. It was Teach; it was the *Queen Anne's Revenge*."

"Oh, I see. Then to show your loyalty to the king, you fired upon the *Queen Anne's Revenge* to save the *Crowley* from capture by Captain Teach?"

"No, your lordship."

"No, indeed, Mr. Hands. You may correct the court in matters of factual error as they may appear to you, Mr. Hands, but to declare yourself innocent while in command of a pirate vessel does gravely insult the integrity of this judicial body. I am certain that is not what you desire. Am I correct, Mr. Hands?"

"Aye, er, yes, sir . . . your lordship."

A condescending smile curled the lip of the governor. "Mr. Hands, after looting the nine vessels in the port of Charleston and bringing your guns to bear on that city to threaten, abuse, and intimidate the citizenry, did you separate yourself from the company of Captain Teach in defiance of his malicious and unlawful practices?"

"No, your lordship, I did not."

"No, indeed, Mr. Hands. For shortly thereafter, you came upon two merchantmen off the coast of Bermuda, and you did commit piracy against those French ships, seized one and all its cargo, and either killed, or released to the other ship, the crew of that vessel. Did you not, Mr. Hands?"

He was trapped. To answer directly would admit to either piracy or murder, or both. "We killed no one, my lord. The French crew was released unharmed to the second ship."

"Ah yes," Spotswood acknowledged as he reviewed some unknown collaborator's written testimony that lay beneath the governor's eyes. He looked up at Israel, tapping his index finger on something in front of him. "Without food. Without water. Praise be to merciful God that they were but a day out of Bermuda." The last remark drew solemn "Amens" from the sanctimonious jurists flanking the governor. "They were truly fortunate to be the beneficiaries of your charity, Mr. Hands." Spotswood wore an expression of heartfelt concern. "I pray that the mercy you have shown your fellow man may be expressed in kind by the ruling of this court."

Israel stared at the judges. He was tiring of their game. "You can but to aspire, my lord," Israel said in open contempt.

Spotswood flinched but maintained his composure. "If the prisoner has any further testimony to provide, the court will hear it now."

"Nothing further, my lord," Israel remarked offhandedly, having learned early in the proceedings that the verdict and sentence were but foregone conclusions. But just as Spotswood was about to pass judgment, Israel lifted up a pointed finger, as if something had just occurred to him. "Oh, there is one thing, my lord."

The battle was lost, but the fight was not yet over. It was time to come about for one final volley across the enemy's deck. Spotswood looked suspiciously at the prisoner but bid him continue.

"My lords, I just wish to say that I have lived a life of piracy and murder." Israel looked each man in the eye as he spoke. "I bless every villainous moment I have lived. I have butchered hundreds of swine that weren't fit to live. I sailed with the best of men and fought beside the only ones who I could truly call friends. You speak of God and country? I found my god between the thighs of a whore and at the end of a cutlass. My country is the sea that has no border but covers the world. You call yourselves men? I curse you for the skullduggery maids that you are. You stand behind a law that allows you to steal what you're not even willing to fight for yourselves. I spit in the face of this court, and I damn you all to the devil himself! Go on now! And kiss the ass of Ol' Scratch in hell!"

"Israel Hands," Spotswood shouted, wide-eyed, "this court finds you guilty of piracy on the high seas!"

Israel began singing, almost shouting, defiantly drowning out Spotswood's cries.

To the mast nail our flag it is dark as the grave,
Or the death which it bears while it sweeps o'er the wave,
Let our deck clear for action, our guns be prepared,
Be the boarding-axe sharpened, the scimitar bared."

"Israel Hands, you shall be taken to a site determined by this court!" Spotswood shouted. Israel continued singing over the pronouncements, to the astonishment of all in the room.

"It shall never be lowered, the black flag we bear.
If the sea be denied us, we sweep through the air.
Unshared have we left our last victory's prey;
It is mine to divide it, and yours to obey."

The pirate's blood coursing through Israel's veins came back to life as he sang. Red-faced with anger, Spotswood meted out Israel's sentence in a loud cry. "And hanged by the neck until you are dead!"

But Israel sang even louder in his contempt and defiance.

"I fight, 'tis for vengeance! I love to see flow,
At the stroke of my saber, the life of my foe.
I strike for the memory of long-vanished years;
I only shed blood where another sheds tears.
I come, as the lightning comes red from above,
O'er the race that I loathe, to the battle I love!"

"And may God have mercy on your soul!"

CHAPTER TWENTY-TWO

Suspension

Saturday, June 26, 1999

Nate Ingersoll stretched his neck up as high as he could to see the button of his shirt collar. He made another unsuccessful morning attempt to fasten the unfastenable, to button the unbuttonable. His thick, stubby fingers once more proved ineffective against the massive fold of flesh that rolled generously over the collar of his mint-green shirt.

The weight-watcher commended himself for having recently shifted his loyalties from butter to margarine. It wouldn't be much longer before he could finally have a party and have both sides of his shirt collar meet. Until then, he'd continue to cinch them as closely together as possible with a snug slip of his tie. Today's color selection was aquamarine. Nate took a step back and inspected himself in the full-length mirror anchored to the back of his bedroom door. He originally had plans to take the mirror down when he'd first moved in. "What use do I have for a mirror?" he'd asked himself. But he expected big things from this new diet and was very close to getting that collar buttoned. Showing the mirror a complete profile, Nate turned from side to side. He thought he seemed a tad slimmer. His belt seemed a little looser to him today. If he were really serious about losing weight, he should get a bathroom scale, he told himself. "What use do I have for a scale?" he asked himself. "About the same as I have for a mirror." He flashed the mirror a coquettish smile and threw in a wink for good measure before tossing his sport coat over his shoulder.

In the kitchen, Nate slung the jacket over the back of one of the dinette chairs, opened the bread drawer, took out four slices of Wonder bread, and filled all the available slots in the toaster. He could have four slices, he reasoned, now that he'd switched to margarine. Nate picked out four eggs from the refrigerator door and removed the already-open package of Oscar Mayer bacon from the meat compartment.

It would not have been unusual for Nate to fry up a full pound of pig strips, but he decided to hold fast to his new regimen of no more than half a serving every morning. He eyed the remains of the package and gauged that there was about half a pound left, maybe three-quarters of a pound, which was close enough. What was he to do? Leave a few measly strips in the wrapper to go bad? That would be an unconscionable waste.

The pile of bacon and scrambled eggs was disappearing fast from the plate that sat in front of Detective Ingersoll. He sipped gingerly from the piping hot cup of coffee and looked sheepishly at the large bowl of fruit on display in the center of the table. A plump yellow grapefruit stared back, as did the neglected oranges and peaches, as another mouthful of bacon slid down his gullet. Nate had invested in the fruit on his last trip to the market but had yet to sample its goodness. Every attempt was being made on his part to improve his dietary habits, and as he'd seen grapefruit on every heart-smart menu at the restaurants he patronized, he made the healthy choice. *Think heart smart, Nate,* he reminded himself.

After retrieving a steak knife from the silverware drawer, Nate placed the grapefruit on his empty plate and began to cut. His unskilled technique in the portioning of a grapefruit left his fingers wet with juice that Nate licked clean. He grimaced at the tart, citric snap that bit his tongue and reached for the large sugar dispenser in front of him. For the next few minutes, Nate would taste and pour until the proper balance of sweet and tart was finally struck. When the fruit was gone, Nate picked up the grapefruit half and sucked out the last of the fruity sugar water that lay puddled at the bottom. He once more licked the sweetened juice off his fingers and pushed himself away from the table.

Standing tall, he felt like a new man. This was the new Nate Ingersoll, he told himself. The Nate Ingersoll he always wanted to be. The Nate Ingersoll he always knew he *could be.* He lifted his keys from the kitchen counter and locked the door behind him as he left. The morning air was crisp and clean. The humidity was down a notch from yesterday. That was good. Nate checked his coat pocket for his metered-dose inhaler just the same. His asthma could hit at any moment, no matter how fine the air quality might be. The doctors had said that his reactive-airway challenges would be significantly reduced with weight loss. *Well, don't look now, Doc, but I'm on my way. Pretty soon, you won't even be able to recognize me.*

The driver's door to the Cavalier grated open on rusty hinges. Nate positioned himself with significant effort behind the wheel of his '93 Chevy and buckled his seat belt. He winced as a rolling bubble of stomach acid burned its way up his esophagus and was expelled in a deep-baritone belch. Nate opened the unused ashtray and removed a small packet that lay among the pennies and nickels nestled in the little black bin. He tore the waxed-paper edges of the Tums wrapper away from the last two tablets, popped them into his mouth, and turned the key in the ignition. The four-cylinder engine woke up with a muffled car fart and a plume of blue smoke. "Starts first time, every time," Nate said to himself, relieved to find that his faithful vehicle had lived to see another day.

The chief of police was peering out his office window when the Cavalier balked to a smoky stop in the employee parking lot behind police headquarters. Shaking his head at the pitiable scene, he turned to his guest seated across from his desk.

"He's here."

Nate waved a friendly good morning to Sergeant Greg Boychuck, who sat behind the bulletproof glass of the communication room that looked out into the small lobby.

"Chief needs to see you in his office, Nate," the sergeant said through the small louvered speak hole in the glass. The statement stopped Ingersoll in his tracks.

"What's up?" he asked with a churlish grin. "Am I in trouble?"

"Not a clue," Boychuck replied with a shrug of his shoulders. "He buzzed me and said you were to see him as soon as you came in." With that, the sergeant turned to the radio console and responded to an incoming call. Nate stood motionless for a moment, looking down at the floor yet staring into space. The sound of the door buzzer brought him back around. He turned the handle and forced himself through the door.

Standing outside the closed office door of his commander, Nate took a deep breath, held up a nervous fist, and knocked. From inside, he heard the one-word command: "Enter." Nate opened the door, not certain what to expect, and he became even less certain when he saw Lieutenant Drew Kenealy sitting across from Chief LaFontaine.

"Have a seat, Detective," LaFontaine said without looking up from an open file on his desk and pointing an assigning finger to the chair next to Lieutenant Kenealy. Ingersoll shoehorned himself into the narrow, low-backed chair, accompanied by the embarrassing squeaking he often experienced when wedging himself into vinyl. No one else in the room seemed to have noticed. For the moment, at least, the chart in front of the chief of police held his full attention. Nate strained his neck against the pressure of his double-Windsor knot, trying to read the name on the file folder tab. He speedily sucked his head back into place when Captain LaFontaine shot an upward glance at the curious man wedged in a cup of black vinyl.

LaFontaine was a tall man with coarse brown hair and a commanding voice that made Nate think a little of James Earl Jones. Impeccably dressed at all times, whether in a suit or his official police uniform, LaFontaine had the bearing of someone who was about to announce his candidacy for some high public office. Firm but fair as an administrator, those who came before him could count on one of two things. If you had done your job to the best of your abilities, he would be your staunchest ally. If, on the other hand, you had committed some breach in law enforcement ethics or protocol, the man would grow horns and spit fire, and you would soon be praying for the earth to open up and swallow you whole. Still, no one spoke to Nate, and he couldn't imagine what he had done to warrant this meeting.

"Ingersoll, you're the detective who headed up the LaCava case?" LaFontaine asked. Nate stared dumbly at his superior, not knowing whether his query required an answer or was merely establishing a fact. The chief held his eyes steady until Nate's silence provoked another question. "Well?"

"Oh, I'm sorry, sir. Yes, that was my case," Ingersoll sputtered. Nate felt his jowls jostling on the front of his skull, rendering him a quivering human Jell-O mold. In that moment, Nate Ingersoll hated himself. He hated himself for being less than the man he really was, for quivering in front of a man whose respect he desired and, in fact, felt he deserved. But this was more than a meeting; that much was already clear to Nate by the few brief words that were spoken. This was an inquisition. And he was acting guilty before he even knew the charges. And *that* was why Nate Ingersoll hated himself now.

"I'm glad to hear you say that it *was* your case. Shows me that you understand that the case was closed. Death by natural causes, wasn't it?"

What the hell is going on? Nate wondered. *He knows damn well it was. Why the cloak-and-dagger routine?*

"Yes, sir, natural causes. Mr. LaCava died of a massive myocardial infarct."

"Well, then, maybe you could explain to me why someone would continue forward with an investigation on a case that's been officially closed. Would you be able to shed some light on this subject for me, Detective Ingersoll?"

Nate shot an instinctive glance to Lieutenant Kenealy, who sat at his right hand and looked straight ahead, past the chief and out the window beyond him. Drew turned his head as he felt a pair of desperate, pleading eyes upon him. He looked to the chief, who in turn rendered an approving nod.

"Nate," Drew started. The chief of police pointedly cleared his throat. "Detective Ingersoll," Drew said, correcting himself. "I was called to Stonecroft Inn last evening by the owner, Tom Stone. Yesterday, they'd received numerous calls from the people who held guest reservations for the summer. It seems they had been contacted by someone who felt it was their duty to inform them of the unfortunate death of Vince LaCava. And although the caller never said Mr. LaCava was murdered, it was apparently inferred." Drew paused and searched the blank stare of Detective Ingersoll for any sign of the guilty squirms, not that Nate had the room to squirm in his chair, Drew realized. "Within twenty-four hours, every one of them, except for a Mr. Timothy Buckley, who happens to be a personal friend of Mr. Brean's, canceled their reservations, leaving Mr. Stone's new business devastated."

"It was a call from Mr. Buckley that alerted Mr. Stone and the Breans to the subversive activity," Captain LaFontaine added, putting the last piece of the puzzle in place for the detective.

Nate shook his head in commiseration. "Terrible," he muttered, "terrible." He looked up quickly, a new alarm seemingly sounding in his brain. "But what's that got to do with me?" Through the eyes of the innocent, the question might appear harmless enough, but Nate sensed that his question drew a line in the sand between him and his superiors, a line between those on probationary status and those whose tenure bought job security and a lifetime membership in the good-cop club. The tension in the room thickened in the span of a single breath. A large lump formed in Nate's throat. He forced a swallow, hard and dry. A shared look flashed between the captain and the lieutenant. A steely edge rose in the captain's voice—under control, but cold and sharp.

"I was really hoping that you might be forthcoming with an explanation for your actions. What was your motivation for contacting these people? Do you really have any concept of the damage that you've done to a new business owner in our community? His business will all but assuredly fail because of your abuse of authority. And I've got to tell you, Detective, I find your nonchalant position on this issue as disconcerting as I do your behavior. Or should I say, your misbehavior?"

And there it was. He was being accused of errant police work, at best. A crime, at worst. "I . . . I . . . ," Nate sputtered, palms up to heaven, as if pleading for career-saving intervention from above. "I have no idea what . . . you don't think it was me, do you?" Nate tried to shift in his chair to square around to Lieutenant Kenealy but was so caught in its grip that the chair moved in its entirety, scraping noisily on the high-sheen tile floor. "You can't think I would do something like that, can you? I've worked so hard to get here. I would never do anything to undermine the welfare of the people of Marblehead, let alone compromise my situation on the force."

His head danced back and forth between the captain and the lieutenant, searching for the smallest glimmer of humanity that would direct Nate Ingersoll regarding onto which chopping block he should throw his head. It wasn't difficult finding the softer of the two hearts. And to that one he made his plea. "Drew, you know I couldn't do something like that. This is my life. This is all I've got." His voice grew thin and cracked with the strain. "Please, Drew, you gotta believe me."

"I wish I could, Nate. I wish I could. Give me a reason"—he offered an inferring hand to the captain—"give *us* a reason to believe you. In your investigation, you were in possession of the list of guests who had reservations. Let me ask you this: Did you, at any time, make that information available to anyone else, inside or outside the department?"

Nate's thoughts turned back to a near faux pas that his better judgment had averted.

"No," he stated with complete confidence. "Not one soul."

Drew shook his head. "You see the problem, then, don't you? The caller gave his name as Detective Nate Ingersoll, Marblehead PD."

"Well, it wasn't me, Drew. I mean, c'mon. You know that's a perfect setup line. I don't exactly fit in around here, you know. Some people have gone out of their way to let me know it too."

The challenge in Nate's tone was sandpaper on the already raw nerves of the captain. "Are you accusing one of your brother officers of committing a crime in order to set you up?"

"No, sir. Not at all, sir," Nate answered in a reassuring voice, and held up a gentle hand, trying to stem the surging tide of anger in his chief. "I'm saying that acceptance hasn't been easy, and I've done everything in my power to be an asset to the department. I know that in my investigation follow-up, I may come off as a hard-nosed pain in the ass. I'm very methodical. Everything is by the book, step-by-step. I'll admit, that makes me one helluva boring guy, but I can't afford to miss anything. If I do, either the bad guy gets away or, even worse, the good guy wears the black hat. I gather facts and draw conclusions. That's what I do. I can't afford to be wrong, and I can't afford emotions. So what's the result? An inaccurate belief that I'm some kind of loner, distant and aloof from the rest of the department, when that couldn't be further from the truth. I'm just trying to earn the respect of my fellow officers. And it's not easy. That's all I'm saying."

The captain studied the detective's face with perhaps more doubt about his guilt than before, yet still unmoved from the path he knew he had to take. He cast a look of regret at Lieutenant Kenealy and then squared around to Detective Ingersoll to deliver the fatal blow. "As much as I appreciate what you've said, it really doesn't address the issue of pursuing an angle of investigation on a case that's been closed and shedding a disparaging light on an innocent member of the community." The captain closed the file in front of him. "And with that, I have no other recourse but to place you on administrative suspension pending a complete investigation of the incident, the results of which will be reviewed by a committee, and then a ruling will be made."

"I'll need your gun and badge, Nate," Drew said in a near whisper. Nate stared dumbly at the lieutenant, who felt, although he couldn't exactly say why, guilty for what he had to do. The police-issued 9 mm grudgingly left the safety of its leather shoulder holster. The shield that Nate turned over next carried with it a much greater weight. A weight not felt when he held it but when he let it go. All his life, growing up with dreams of someday being a cop, the badge represented one thing to Nate: honor. Now, he had been stripped of even that. He felt as if he were in the middle of a cyclone. Dizzy, even sitting down, Nate's ears were filled with the tubular sound of being trapped in a wind tunnel. He felt dangerously light-headed and had a strange, almost detached, thought. For the first time since he sat down, he was thankful that he was wedged so tightly in the chair that it kept the blood flowing upward. It was the ice-cold voice of the captain that struck him like a slap in the face and brought him back around to full consciousness, and then only so that he could feel the full force of a kick in the balls.

"As you're still on probationary status as a detective, your suspension is without pay. However, I will review your situation with the committee; perhaps they may choose to waive it and reclassify your suspension to with-pay status. That, unfortunately, is not up to me. It's certainly not my intention to cause additional hardship, but in lieu of the facts—"

"Facts? What facts?" Nate said, cutting off his captain in midsentence. "Sir, with all due respect, you've made clear the accusation against me, but you certainly haven't supported those accusations with facts! What about caller ID? Some of the people who were contacted must have that feature as part of their phone service. Did you check that out?"

"Yes, we did, Ingersoll," the captain replied. "And we followed up with the phone company, and they verified the point of origin for the calls."

"Well? Where did they come from?"

Drew spoke up. "The calls were made from your house, Nate."

Nate Ingersoll turned as white as a ghost.

* * *

Paris Quicci listened intently to every detail divulged by the sobbing man who stood in his office, hat in hand. "Nate, what in God's name were you thinking? I thought we decided it would be a greater injustice to compromise the livelihood of a *possibly* innocent man than to remain mute and not notify those guests of what was merely a strange and unfortunate occurrence. Now, correct me if I'm wrong, but didn't we both agree to that?"

"Yes, Paris, we did. And I don't know who made those calls. I didn't give that list to anyone." Nate hesitated. "You didn't make those calls, did you, Paris?"

The anticipated verbal barrage didn't come. Instead, Nate received only compassion and understanding from a serene countenance. "You know I didn't, Nate. But I understand why you had to ask. Never give up, my friend. We'll uncover the truth soon enough. And God help the low-life sonuvabitch who left you holding the bag." Quicci strode the floor of his stately office, hands on hips, shaking his head in disgust. "You need to dust your phone for prints—that's what you need to do. Did you think to do that yet?"

Nate nodded. "Actually, the department already ordered it." He looked at his Timex. "They're probably done with that by now."

Quicci continued to roam the floor, still digesting the facts as they had been relayed to him. He stopped at the window and looked out over the parking lot. Patti Dickens strode into view as she walked back to her car, having completed her ATM transaction. Her sculpted body told of great genes and countless hours at the gym. She had an ass that just wouldn't quit and legs that went on forever. Paris Quicci had a name for her. He called her "Next."

He shifted his gaze, which regrettably fell upon Nate's aging chariot in one of the far spaces near the low retaining wall that held back the sloping embankment of well-manicured grass and colorful perennials. Quicci could almost smell the oil that was spilling out onto his parking lot and eroding his asphalt. He forced himself to push the thought aside and tend to the business at hand. "So it's fairly certain, then, that Mr. Stone's business can't recover from this?"

Nate sat heavily on the leather couch and rested his furrowed brow in the palm of his hand. "That's what they say," Nate moaned as he considered the piecemeal dissolution of a man's dream with which he was being saddled. "Oh God, Paris, what the hell happened?" he asked into cupped hands. "What can I do to fix this?"

"Oh, I wouldn't worry about that, old friend. If you ask me, this thing's already been fixed."

"What do you mean?" Nate asked, looking up from the hands that cradled his head.

"Hey, you're the cop," Quicci said with a shrug. "But it seems pretty clear to me that you've been set up by one of your buddies down there at the station. I mean, who else has the ability to get into your locked files and get into your house when you're not home? Even if you came home while they were there, they could say they were driving by and saw someone running out of your house. But chances are, they knew where you were, and it would be damn difficult for you to prove you couldn't have stopped at your house to make those calls, right?"

The question swam around loosely in Nate's head until he finally shrugged and let out a soft, "Yeah." He shifted his weight on the couch. "But a number of people could get into my house if they wanted to. There are a few people even outside the department who know where I keep a spare key," he added matter-of-factly.

Quicci considered him with utter loathing. It took every last bit of his abating patience not to pick up the letter opener sitting on his desk and plunge it into the fat man's throat, stopping only when it struck the front of his cervical spine.

"Well, now, you see, with so many possibilities, they could easily shake off any suspicions with that type of information. If I were you, I'd keep that under my hat. Don't provide them with the opportunity to falsely accuse someone else now," Quicci advised him. Nate nodded. *Sound advice.* It was information that, for the time being, best be kept quiet lest the guilty use it to accuse the innocent.

A busy silence sat in the room with the two men—a single question gnawing at one and a list of endless possibilities scrolling through the mind of the other. Nate felt his airways begin to clamp down and sat up straight on the couch, making the most of his diminished lung capacity. Legs spread slightly apart to allow the prominent belly to hang unimpeded, taking all possible pressure off his lungs. Nate reached into his pocket and pulled out his inhaler. He took two metered puffs and waited for the miracle to happen. Within seconds, relief poured over him as a cool rush of air filled his expanding airways. Quicci could always tell when the worst had passed because Nate stopped that annoying squeaking noise.

"Not the most pleasant way to die, believe you me," Nate said with a nervous grin. He wiped the sweat from his soggy brow with the palm of his hand.

A twisted Mona Lisa smile appeared on Quicci's face. "Maybe not the most pleasant, but certainly effective."

The banker sat down at his desk, his mind now on a completely different matter. He opened a folder that waited in the center of his desk and perused its contents. He yearned to be free of the albatross that sat wheezing and sweating on his couch and loudly cleared his throat.

Nate sensed his agitation. He took another hit off his puffer. "Say, listen, Paris," he began, wiping clammy hands on the front of his pants, still searching for the words that might move his friend to compassion. "This thing. This, uh, this false charge. They really got me over a barrel here, you know?" He stumbled over the tail end of his statement as the words struck him with the full impact that comes when a desperate situation is finally fully realized. "I'm in a pretty bad way, financially speaking. If I can't get clear of this thing fast . . . well, your friend Nate Ingersoll is pretty much a dead duck." Nate managed a nervous smile. "There I'll be, a dead duck, floating on the pond, wishing like all get-out that someone will have the heart to pull me out of the water."

I doubt you'd float, Quicci thought behind unblinking eyes.

Nate absentmindedly rubbed the seasoned leather arm of the couch. Every nerve in his body was singing in discordant vibrato. The light breakfast from this morning now congealed into a brick in his stomach. Nate needed to connect with Quicci; that much was certain. But as was so often the case, finding where the banker's head was at was a dicey game. The man behind the desk was not unlike the moon, Nate thought, sometimes full and bright, at other times devoid of any light at all and colder than anything else he'd experienced on earth.

"Paris, what can you tell me about my loan? Now, Paris, I've been patient on this, and I know you've been working on it," Nate said, forging ahead and gaining a child's portion of confidence. "You said I'd be approved by the end of the week, remember? Well, it's Saturday. It's the end of the week, past it, rather. I need that money, Paris. I need it now. Today."

The expression Quicci wore told Nate he'd jumped in the wrong sandbox. An unemployed cop doesn't come in and tell the vice president of the bank to give him money. Not when the banker had bent over backward to help him in the past. Not when his car was leaking oil out in the bank parking lot. And not unless the cop had a gun, which, of course, he didn't. The tone of Nate's voice softened. The look on Quicci's face did not.

"I'm sorry, Paris, that was wrong of me. It's just that I've got nothing to live on. It's the end of the month. I just finished paying my bills yesterday."

"Well, then, you ought to be good for another few weeks, right?"

"Oh, Paris, come on," Nate implored. "I've got one hundred and thirty-three dollars in my savings account. That won't last a week. What am I going to live on? I've got to buy food, gas, and my asthma medication," he said, pulling out his puffer and holding it up as if it were kindergarten show-and-tell. "I don't have prescription coverage. And there are other expenses as well."

There it is, Quicci thought. *Groceries alone must run him close to a grand a month.*

"Paris, didn't you say Mr. Forlini would be back this week? Is he here today?" Quicci saw where he was going.

That's fine, he mused. *It's time we wrap up this sad charade, anyway.* He posted a challenging smile that dared an answer before he even asked the question. "Why do you ask?"

It was an emotional leveler that Nate hadn't seen coming. And although Quicci seemed to have slammed the door in his face, Nate Ingersoll's existence was on the line, and he couldn't afford to let any question go unbegged. "Paris," he uttered in a deflated whisper, "I was hoping that you could get him to sign off on the loan today. That was all you were waiting for, wasn't it?" Nate's voice was weak. His humiliation complete. His hope abandoned.

Paris held up his hands as if pleading for help. "Hey, what about me? You put me in one helluva spot here, Nate. I go to the mat for you on this loan, when nobody in this place thinks you're good for it, and I tell them that you're a man to be trusted, a man of honor. Then you get yourself thrown off the force and come and tell me that I need to have the bank president sign off on a loan for an ex-cop who may not be able to pay his debts because he'll be in jail." Quicci stared hard at the quivering lump of flesh crushing the springs of his leather couch. "I was wrong about you, Nate. You're no man of honor," he said, almost spitting with contempt. "Now, if you don't mind, I've got a lot of work to do."

Nate Ingersoll forced himself off the couch, a trembling hand for a crutch. Eyes that moments ago were filled with moisture now spilled tears freely. The man in front of Paris Quicci had been reduced to something quite grotesque. He had been stripped of the one thing that defined a man in the first place. A man could carry on without money, without love, without any material possessions, and still be a man. But Nate Ingersoll had been stripped of his dignity.

He made his last stand. "I've got nowhere else to go, Paris. I don't know what else I can do. Isn't there anything you can do? Maybe a smaller loan, huh? What about that? Just something to get me by until I can clear my name?" Nate looked into the cold eyes of Paris Quicci, who seemed to be considering the possibility or simply looking for the right words.

Quicci took a deep breath before he spoke. "No can do, my friend," he said with an edgy smile. "Face facts, Nate. You're a bad risk."

CHAPTER TWENTY-THREE
Battle Stations

Sunday, June 27, 1999

With every strike of the hammer, chips of mortar flew from the beveled edge of the chisel and ricocheted off the safety goggles that sat securely on the bridge of Tom's nose. The first half hour had passed without issue or challenge; many of the stones were already loose in their station and were easily removed. The second half of the hour had required significant deliberation and patience. Anxious for a quick return on his labor investment, Tom struck the chisel with an overzealous hammer, threatening to bring the stone structure down in a mountain of rubble.

From that moment on, slow and steady became the project mantra, turning the stone-removal project into an archeological dig, which, Tom reasoned, was really what it was, after all. And if the ring had been buried somewhere behind one of the stones, he further surmised, then a change in the color, consistency, or condition of the mortar would signify a different time period in the house's history. Hence, a careful hand and a watchful eye were the truest means of following this theoretical road map. He had extracted over twenty stones from the face of the fireplace, but no map had yet been revealed.

"So tell me again, Indiana Jones, what makes you think it's buried behind the rocks?" Jake asked, having come from the sitting room, cup of coffee in hand.

Tom set the hammer and chisel down and observed his friend through white-speckled safety lenses. "If the ring is anywhere in the house, it would have to be in part of the original structure."

"What about the floor here?" Jake lightly tapped his foot. "Isn't this original too?"

"Yeah, but there's nothing under there, just dirt."

"Oh, yeah, good point," Jake replied, nodding his head in mock enlightenment. "Nobody would ever think of burying treasure in the dirt. What the fuck could I possibly have been thinking?"

Tom gave Jake a hard look. "As strange as it may seem to you, covering up a small space behind a stone with a flash of mortar would be a lot easier than tearing up planks the size of elephant legs just to hide something as small as a ring beneath them."

Jake narrowed his eyes and considered the statement. *Man's got a point.* He conceded with a small but earnest nod and noted the look of smug satisfaction plastered on Tom's face.

"You don't look cool in those safety glasses, by the way," Jake informed him. "I thought you should know." He took a sip of coffee. "In case you were wondering."

Tom hoisted the chisel back up to a loose patch of mortar and struck lightly with three easy taps of the hammer. Searching for a weak spot, the bevel of the chisel was continuously on the move. Jake took a seat at the foot of the table and watched the search continue. His ability to watch in silence lasted only as long as it took to finish his coffee. He stood to get a refill.

"So tell me again. How old are you?"

Tom turned away from his work and looked at Jake. "You saying this is a waste of time?"

"I'm saying that you shouldn't even be in this house now," Jake replied, abandoning his humor. "And you sure as hell better not be planning on being here tomorrow night. We ought to pack a toothbrush and stay at Bishop's for the night."

"What? The competition?" Tom joked lightly at the notion. But the smile faded quickly as he laid his tools on the hearthstone and plopped down in the chair next to Jake. "Look, Jake, I'm not taking this thing lightly. I know you think I am, but I'm not. I'm glad Marie's staying at Bishop's, and you should too. But I can't. This is all I have. This is what I'm committed to, and I'm not about to pack up and go. Not just yet, anyway. I've got to find some way to get rid of this bastard," Tom said, shooting a cursory glance at the painting. "He's not going to kill me, Jake. I won't let him."

"Tom, what good is staying here when almost all of your guests have canceled? We should be focusing on advertising—coordinating a marketing blitz and trying to get some new interest in the place."

"What good is that going to do if I've got a dead guy walking around here who doesn't like visitors?" Tom argued. "Don't you think he's the one who needs to leave?"

"This guy doesn't want to kill the visitors, Tom," Jake reminded him. "He wants to kill *you*."

"Yeah, well, people in hell want ice water," Tom said, standing in defiance. "And I'm staying."

Jake knew Tom well enough to know that there was no changing his mind at this point. Jake simmered in a perfect blend of frustration and admiration for his friend. He watched as Tom once more took hammer and chisel in hand and began to chip away at the gritty cement. *Good hunting, Dr. Jones.*

* * *

It seemed to Tom that if someone were going to take the trouble to plant something valuable behind the stones of a fireplace, there ought to be some kind of reminder to indicate its position. He took a step back and searched for a landmark. Nothing stood out, so Tom stepped back to the middle of the room, but still, no pattern could be discerned, no clue revealed.

"It wouldn't be on the corners," Jake said, rising from his chair and joining the fight. "It'd be too easy to spot if someone had been messing with a cornerstone." He paused. "Don't you think?"

Tom considered Jake's statement as he studied the stonework. "Yeah, you're probably right. But we could second-guess ourselves all day long. I think I'm just going to keep on going, all the way across and then to the layer beyond that if necessary. Maybe the clue lies just behind one of the stones we're looking at." The two men stood and stared at the fireplace.

"Got another chisel?"

Tom reached into his oversize gray toolbox and produced a chisel the size of a crowbar. "Sorry, this is the only other one I have."

"No problem," Jake said, smiling as he held the much larger tool. The joke was too easy, so he let it go.

"Do you know when Drew's coming by?" Tom inquired as he went back to work. There was a knock at the door.

"Right about now."

"It's open!" Tom called out, unwilling to break the hammer's rhythm. His back was to the door as it slowly creaked open. A lot of WD-40 had been invested in the door, yet it still sounded three hundred years old. Drew poked a dark face around the corner and bid the two men a somber good morning. His expression changed when he entered and saw the ensuing deconstruction of the fireplace.

"What in God's name are you doing?"

"Tom's got a bug up his ass about that ring," Jake said. "So he decided to tear the house down. It made perfect sense to me."

Another shadow followed fast behind Drew. Rebecca beamed with excitement at the activity. "Need some help?" she asked as she marched to the middle of the growing quarry. Tom was encouraged, albeit a bit surprised, to find such enthusiasm in Rebecca. Her question served more as a command to carry on and spoke to the question he still couldn't answer for himself: Was he nuts? She rummaged through the toolbox and pulled out a flathead screwdriver.

"How about if I try to find loose spots with this? It might help us find it faster."

"OK, but you don't want to go too fast," Tom warned. "My main concern now is that we don't weaken the entire structure so quickly that half the wall comes crashing down. If we remove a stone, we have to be as sure as possible that the stones around it are secure."

Rebecca was taking in every word Tom said with the utmost seriousness. Even Jake, to Tom's surprise, was paying close attention to the instructions he'd already received.

"If you take a stone out, place it on the floor in a pattern that will allow us to reconstruct the fireplace when we're done. Again, if this wall comes crashing down, we'll have one helluva time putting it back together again."

"Wouldn't you want to hire a mason to do that?" Rebecca asked.

"Well, we'll see when we're done," Tom muttered.

Rebecca turned when Jake tapped her on her shoulder. "Tom hasn't had the best of luck with masons," he whispered. Rebecca winced at the reminder.

Drew stood back in amused circumspection as the others dug into their treasure hunting. The smile on his face was erased by the robotic chirp from the two-way radio holstered on his hip. "Go ahead," Drew said to the yet-unknown caller.

"Drew, the chief needs you to call him here at HQ." Drew recognized the voice as belonging to Sergeant Boychuck, in dispatch.

"Sure, Greg. I'm just wrapping up some business. I'll give him a call in a few minutes," Drew said with the leisure that comes from living in a small, tight-knit community.

"Lieutenant, you really want to make that call now."

Lieutenant? He never calls me that.

"Copy that, Sergeant. I'm not in a secure location. I'll call from my vehicle." The cover of the radio clapped shut with a plastic snap. *Uh-oh,* Drew thought. *Something brown and stinky has hit the fan.*

He looked up to inform his friends that he'd be leaving but saw by their upturned faces that they had heard the cryptic message. "I've got to step out to make a call," Drew announced. "I doubt I'll be back anytime soon," he added as he regarded Rebecca with a regretful smile. The three nodded in unison, their imaginations running wild with possibilities. But not one of them was even close to guessing what had actually happened.

"Good luck," Jake said.

They were still staring in his direction when Drew shut the door behind him.

* * *

Drew waved at the officer blocking the driveway. The police barricade was removed, and Drew pulled up close behind a Marblehead police cruiser. He had never been there before and took a moment to familiarize himself with the grounds. The front porch was awash with investigative personnel. Drew smiled at the sight of an old friend. "What brings the state in on something like this?" Drew inquired as he approached the house.

"The kind invitation of your chief," replied Sergeant Cipriano of the Massachusetts State Police.

Drew Kenealy and Tony Cipriano met each other in a fistfight, in the fall of their sophomore year of high school. Although they'd bloodied each other, neither had the edge in a scrap that was readily broken up by Mr. Schneider, the gym teacher and head football coach. Hot tempers, in time, turned to a cool respect, and by the spring of that same year, a friendship was forged on the JV baseball team. The friendship grew as fast and strong as young muscle. Years later, the two found themselves still standing side by side, each having been the best man at the other's wedding.

"Good to see you, Tony," Drew said, smiling in spite of the purpose of their reunion.

"Back at ya, buddy. How come we haven't heard from you in so long?"

Drew shrugged. "I've just been really busy—that's all."

"Well, just to let you know, Joanie thinks it's because you've got a girlfriend. When I tell her I saw you today, she's gonna ask if she was right. What should I tell her?"

Drew smiled.

"You son of a gun!" Tony said through a broad white smile. "You're gonna have to tell me all about her. Hey, why don't you bring her to Dylan's birthday party?"

"I really don't know if that's such a good idea," Drew said with a pained look.

"What? You're not coming to your godson's birthday party? Man, you really know how to break an eight-year-old's heart."

"Of course I'm coming to the party."

"Then what's the problem?"

Drew glanced over his shoulder, on the lookout for curious ears. "It's my girlfriend. She's a . . . well, she's a witch."

Tony was a bit startled by how his friend described the girl he was dating. He looked Drew straight in the eye. "Hey, listen. I know you've been out of the game a long time, and I'm glad you're getting back into the groove of life, but you can't go around telling people that the woman you're dating is a witch. Dump her if she's no good. Believe me, there's plenty of other fish in the big blue pond."

"No, you're not following me," Drew said, shaking his head. "She's a *real* witch."

"What?" A quizzical look crossed Tony's face. "You mean like the Wicked Witch of the West in *The Wizard of Oz*?"

"No, she's a great lady. Nothing like your notion of a witch. You watch too much TV."

"Oh, OK. I gotcha. So she's more like Glinda, the Good Witch."

Drew gave up. "Yeah, Tony. Exactly. You can't tell 'em apart." He shook his head and pointed at the front door. "What do we have?"

Tony tore his thoughts away from his friend riding on a broomstick built for two and opened the door. "Let me show you." The two walked into the foyer of the house, Tony leading the way, both men methodically and instinctively looking up, down, left, and right, making mental notes of the overall condition of the surroundings. Tony took a left turn down a short, narrow hallway, with Drew close behind. Flashes of light popped from the room at the end of the hall, and Drew could see the profile of a busy photographer he didn't recognize. Drew thought he was ready for what was beyond the door. Later he would realize that what he had told others so many times in the past was true: you're never really ready.

The scene was macabre; Drew's thoughts, bizarre. For as horrific as the sight was, Drew could see only the uncanny resemblance to Jabba the Hutt. The large, dusky face with bulging eyes, almost bursting from a skull too small to retain so much mottled flesh, was accentuated by a black tongue sticking thickly from the open mouth. But it wasn't Jabba the Hutt. At the end of the rope hung the lifeless body of one Nathaniel Benjamin Ingersoll, late sergeant of the Marblehead PD.

Drew could tell he'd been dead for some time. Blood settled relatively fast. He knew that if he took a peek, he'd find black feet and ankles as well. The blood that had been refused return by the pressure of the noose took final refuge in the immense apron of flesh that spilled over the dead man's hemp collar. Drew took a few minutes to allow the shock of finding a fellow officer who had recently danced the air jig settle in his mind. He thought of the suspension that Ingersoll had endured only a day earlier and the role he had played in that suspension. Bringing the issue to the attention of the chief was the right thing to do. Drew had no regrets, no second thoughts about what he'd done. But why would a man kill himself over a suspension before he had his hearing? It didn't make sense to Drew. Not unless Nate really *was* guilty. If that were the case, criminal charges would have been filed. But it didn't feel right to Drew. Nate was not that kind of man.

"Did we find anything?" Drew asked any of the half-dozen law enforcement personnel in the crowded room who might be listening. "Did he leave a note?"

"Yes, sir," answered the uniformed officer who had discovered the body. He had called on Detective Ingersoll to deliver some personal belongings that the chief thought the suspended officer might need. The car was in the driveway, and the front door was unlocked, but no one answered when the officer had knocked. Becoming suspicious, the officer had entered after announcing his intentions to the silent house, his hand on his service weapon. Then he came upon the body.

"Do you have everything you need, Tony? Can we get him down from there?" Drew asked his friend, disgusted by the sight. Tony looked at the other state investigators, who nodded and left the room, along with the photographer. He'd be back later for another photo shoot once the "talent" was carted out of the building.

Tony hailed the paramedics to bring in the gurney and enlisted the aid of the two remaining uniformed officers as pallbearers to respectfully handle almost 250 pounds of deadweight. When the tension was taken off the rope, they lay the dead man on his back within the open black ziplock body bag. Only the eyes settled back into their sockets, and even then, they didn't settle in completely. Dead was dead, and dead didn't allow for much movement. So the eyes still bulged, the tongue still protruded, and Nate's face was still a dusky palette of red, black, and blue. Drew wished for Nate's sake that he could have gone out looking a little better than a bloated purple frog.

A deep sigh escaped Drew's chest as the paramedic crew rolled the gurney's burden out of the room. Drew recognized the crew as the same team that had responded to the call when Vince LaCava died, and he sincerely hoped he wouldn't be seeing this duo again anytime soon. He looked down and read the note the uniformed officer handed him.

Not without honor

* * *

When Drew opened the front door to Stonecroft, he found the trio sitting amid the dusty rubble of a day's work, looking both worn out and unsuccessful. Rebecca beamed beneath a thin veil of cement dust when Drew gave her a tired smile.

"My guess is that you didn't find anything," Drew said, mildly amused by the scene.

"No, but we sure as hell learned something," Tom said without taking his eyes off the mountain of rock at his feet. Drew's smile broadened in anticipation.

"We learned that when you remove support from beneath large rocks, they fall down."

"And when they fall, they can break the things they land on," Jake added from his dusty nook.

"What did they break?"

"A couple of the slate hearthstones down here," Tom answered, pushing two large fieldstones aside with his foot to reveal the large cracks in the gray slate slabs. "No big deal—just one more item on my to-do list."

"Item number seven hundred and twenty-one," Jake added, "rebuild the house."

Tom shook his head in disgust. Rebecca lifted herself from the chair and began dusting herself off. She looked at Drew and read something sad in his eyes. "I hope you had a better day than we did."

"I'm afraid I didn't," Drew replied in a voice that carried a message of melancholy deeper than the words themselves and so drew the attention of Tom and Jake as well. "Nate Ingersoll killed himself last night."

The occupants in the room stared at Drew and waited for him to continue. Even the last floating particles of cement dust seemed to settle in to listen. "They discovered his body about nine thirty this morning. An officer stopped by to return some personal items, found the door unlocked, went in, and saw him swinging from a rope."

"Damn," Jake murmured.

Drew looked at Jake. "Yeah." He nodded. "I'm afraid he was a better man than I knew."

"Look, Drew. I don't want to appear insensitive," Tom stated, "but there are a lot of questions that will never be answered now."

Drew looked at Tom and thought for a moment. "You're right, Tom. The same thing crossed my mind. But"—he hoisted his shoulders up in surrender—"there it is."

"No, no, Drew. What I mean is . . . are you sure it was a suicide?"

"Well, we found a note that would indicate it was a suicide," Drew confirmed, a hint of doubt still lingering in the air. "We'll analyze the handwriting; that's routine. We'll also continue to search for evidence that suggests foul play, but I didn't see any signs that would lead me to suspect anything other than a man who took himself to the edge of the abyss, then jumped."

Tom turned away from the group and began to pace the floor, shaking his head. "No, no, no, no, no, no, no. Not again."

"Tom, this has nothing to do with what we're dealing with," Rebecca inserted, cutting Tom off at the pass before he got too far down the highway of guilt.

"Hey, Tom, as terrible as this is, the guy obviously had issues," Jake added. "I mean, do you remember what he looked like, for cryin' out loud? He was on the fast track to a sudden death at an early age. Besides, he was the one who tried to ruin you. So he gets a serious case of the guilts and hangs himself. Now, I'll admit, that was an unfortunate way for his conscience to express itself, but that was his doing, not yours."

Tom said nothing but looked to Drew for affirmation. Jake was a dear friend, and Tom knew he'd say just about anything to help keep him afloat. Drew, on the other hand, seemed to care more about what was right than whose feelings he might hurt, with the possible exception of Rebecca's. Tom locked eyes with Drew, who nodded in agreement with the others.

The day turned grumpy. The humidity climbed, and when the air could hold no more moisture, the clouds let go, and the rain came down in chunks. The wet heat drained what remained of the strength from their limbs and, mixed with the news of the suicide, served as a sedative with unpleasant side effects. Jake sat back and mindlessly wiped at the dust that coated the stones. The moisture in the air had caused it to stick to the stones, and in places where the dust had accumulated in some quantity, Jake imagined it could be used as mortar once again.

"Tom, I'm gonna take advantage of this rain and get these stones outside and wash them down before the cement dust hardens on them."

"Good thinking," Tom replied, grateful for Jake's infusion of energy. Hopefully it was contagious. "I'll mop up the floor behind you."

"Let me do that," Rebecca offered.

"I did over twenty years in the navy, Rebecca. I know how to swab a deck," Tom quipped. "Are you any good with a mop?"

"Well, I do my best work with a broom," she smiled. "But I think I can handle a mop."

Once the cleanup began, the tension broke as easily as a toy made in China. The rain stopped suddenly, much to the consternation of Jake, and the windows were opened throughout the house. The humidity dropped, the barometer hopped, and a stiff breeze came in from the sea and stirred the stagnant air. It was delicious. Jake laid the stones out on the back patio and, when the rain abandoned him, turned the hose on the crusty rocks and scraped off all the mortar residue he could. Inside the house, Tom and Drew stood by as Rebecca worked her magic on the floor. The guys were impressed to the point of embarrassment with the muscle that Rebecca put into her work.

"Can we help?" Tom asked, ill at ease watching someone else clean up his mess. "Do you need anything?"

"All I need is for the two of you to stay out of my way," she ordered good-naturedly. As Rebecca swabbed the deck in front of the fireplace, Tom could see the water seeping down a large crack across the middle of one of the slate hearthstones.

"Watch where you step!" Rebecca shouted a few minutes later when Jake came in the back door, his Docksiders soaked through and squishing with every step. Rebecca, Drew, and Tom sat huddled at the table.

Jake halted on the mat just inside the door and slipped off his saturated loafers where he stood. "I'm just going to run up and change real quick," Jake said as he studied the suspicious-looking trio. "Looks like you guys are planning something special, like a jailbreak," Jake suggested. "I want in."

"We're trying to develop a plan to save your friend's life," Rebecca said. Jake looked at the faces at the table. There were no smiles now.

"Hold that thought," Jake said anxiously. "I'll be back in one minute."

Had anyone been timing him, they'd have known Jake was gone only fifty-seven seconds. Still pulling a T-shirt over his head, Jake slid a chair away from the table and joined the strategic planners. "OK, who's calling the shots?" Jake asked, barely able to contain his excitement that something was being done.

"Rebecca has some ideas that she's been going over with us." Jake could hear in Tom's tone that he wasn't sold.

"Sorry to be a Johnny-come-lately, but could you fill me in?"

"Sure, Jake," Rebecca said, pleased to have another chance to get her point across to Tom, although she now had to convince Jake as well. "First, I want to shield him in a protection charm and provide him a white-light pentacle. Also, black Ethiopian resin stops enemies, natural or supernatural, in their tracks."

Jake looked at Tom. "Do you have any black Ethiopian resin?"

Tom shook his head.

Rebecca frowned at the untimely joke. "I'll bring it. It would also be wise to surround you with sea salt." She quickly added, "I'll bring that too."

"Sea salt? What will that do to a killer from the sea?" Tom questioned. "This man was weaned on salt water."

"If he's purely spirit, the sea salt will keep him off you. If he's taken on flesh, as you say he has"—she looked around the table—"I don't think there's anything we have that can stop him."

"Are you reading the Bible like Marie and Father Al told you to?" Jake asked.

"Yeah, I am." The sincerity in Tom's eyes spoke as loud as his words.

"Good. I don't want to have to lie to her when she asks me."

"Can I make a suggestion?" Drew asked. He paused a moment before continuing. "Tomorrow's the full moon, and I think we should all get here early. Let's have everything in place and review every possibility well before this first mate shows up." He looked at Tom. "He comes at midnight, right?"

"Yeah. Well, that's been the pattern so far," Tom conceded.

"Great," Drew continued. "We take every precautionary and protective step we can think of." He made a point of nodding to the woman at his side. "Including measures Rebecca has already discussed." Rebecca waited for objections from Tom or Jake, but none came. "Tom, if this thing is flesh and blood and takes steps to harm you," Drew concluded, "I'll be here to bring him down."

The testosterone in Drew's voice stood in stark contrast to the friendly Officer Drew they had come to know. The men liked the new Drew. So did Rebecca. But something ate away at Tom.

"Wait a second, Drew. I appreciate what you're suggesting, but I don't think it's a good idea for us to throw a party here tomorrow night. Two men have already died because of this business, and I don't want any other names added to that list. I'll be here to show this thing that I have no intention of leaving, and that will be that. You'll see." He wanted to believe he was speaking the truth but knew he wasn't. Those around the table knew it too.

"Are you nuts?" Jake asked, rising in his chair as he spoke. Tom could tell his buddy was more than a little pissed. "You stupid fucker. You're completely unprepared to face this thing, especially on your own. That monster's coming to kick your ass tomorrow night, whether you want to admit it or not." Jake tried to quell his rising anger the only way he knew how. "I hope you don't think I'm going to miss that." Jake's point was made. There'd be no tolerating any refusal of assistance, or any other lunatic notion, on the part of the innkeeper.

"You're going to have company, Tom," Drew said in an eerily even voice. "That's just the way it's gonna be."

Tom tossed up two hands in surrender. "Fine. Suit yourselves."

Rebecca sought to regain control of the conversation as the testosterone now seemed to be flowing a bit too freely. "OK, then, I'm going to work on a protection charm for Tom tomorrow as well as bring the items I've mentioned. Drew, you'll be here, armed, I'm afraid, in case the first mate is more than just phantom, Goddess forbid."

"She's serious," Drew said to the guys.

"So am I," Jake returned in kind. "As a matter of fact, I'll go a step further. I think this house ought to be burned to the ground. Tom, I think you ought to sell it, and we ought to get the fuck outta here. Tonight." Jake leaned in. "Don't you see? This isn't even a house anymore. It's a battlefield. It's a place where spirits that won't go to hell come to live. It's nothing more than a demonic weigh station. And you own it!" He slapped Tom lightly on the shoulder. "Congrats, buddy."

Jake paused only long enough to take a breath. "Do you know that when I think of this place, I think of it as Stonecroft? Just like the sign out front. Can you believe that? I used to just think of this as your house. Stonecroft Inn was just a catchy name to lure tourists. But this isn't your house anymore, Tom, at least not in my mind. Even your would-be guests have been chased away. It's Stonecroft—a cold and hard structure of stone and wood. Evil is the real mortar that holds this place together. And you? You're nothing but its caretaker. Needless to say, the charm is gone. The polish is off the proverbial apple. I don't know what rules over this house, Tom, but it sure as shit ain't you.

"And you, Drew," he said, turning to the cop. "If the ghost has lived here for three hundred fucking years, do you really think a bullet's going to stop him?" Drew didn't meet his gaze, so Jake turned it to Rebecca.

"A protective charm? You yourself said what matters is not what *we* believe but what *he* believes. How is your charm going to help?" He let his concerns hang in the air for some time. He felt his emotional dump was therapeutic. But Jake knew there was only one way to bring about real healing. "The only right move is to get out of here. Tomorrow at the latest. Before the sun goes down."

A weary smile spread across Tom's face as he studied Jake, still squirming in his chair. "I'm sticking, Jake. And I'd sure like you at my side when we beat this guy."

Jake leaned his head back and stared at the ceiling. "Yeah, sure. What the hell. I mean, why not, right?" Jake mumbled in sarcastic resignation. "I'll bring the fucking garlic."

Smiles edged the lips of the others.

A refreshing gust of cool, dry air drove through the gathering room of Stonecroft Inn. Rebecca walked to the back door and looked out the window. Stars began to glimmer in the early dark of night. The clouds continued to run from an approaching moon rising over a sparkling sea. She allowed herself a moment to connect with her power source. She closed her eyes and drew down the moon. Every night when she found the moon in the nighttime sky, it seemed so fresh to her, so exciting. As if turning around and finding a forever lover once again. But darkness bent the light, and a faraway thought rose to the front of her mind and bore a weight as it came forward. Tomorrow, Rebecca knew, evil would rise with midnight's moon.

She turned suddenly. As if suffering from a sudden chill, she wrapped her arms around herself. "I'm tired, Drew. Could you please take me home?"

"Sure," Drew said, and he was up as if a springboard had released beneath his seat. He pulled the keys from his pocket and looked uncertainly at the group. "So then . . . what time tomorrow?"

Tom looked at Rebecca. "Ten o'clock?" she suggested.

"Good." Tom nodded. "Ten it is."

Tom walked Drew and Rebecca to the door. Jake did not. He remained in his own world, mulling over his thoughts and wondering how they'd all survive.

"Good night, Jake," Rebecca said as they were leaving the room. Her voice seemed to startle Jake.

"Oh, sorry, Rebecca. I was lost there for a minute." Standing, Jake shoved his hands deep into the pockets of his shorts. "Good night, and"—he hesitated—"sorry if I went a little batshit on you guys. I just want to do what's best."

It was Drew who waved him off. "Don't worry, Jake. You said things we all needed to hear. Frankly, I'm not sure I was taking this seriously enough. You made some good points."

Rebecca nodded from over Drew's shoulder. "We'll see you tomorrow night."

Tom shut the door behind the couple and turned back to Jake.

"Is your Bible upstairs?" Jake asked.

"On my nightstand."

"Go get it." Jake looked Tom dead in the eye. "It's time to start cramming for finals."

The Return

July 1719

His black woolen cloak billowed in the midnight wind. Silhouetted against the rising moon as it crested the Atlantic horizon, he appeared as a raven poised for flight against the onrushing breeze. A great horned owl, perched deep within the embrace of a venerable oak, stood sentinel over the silent hill and inquired as to the identity of the mysterious visitor. He moved cautiously among the dead. The headstones grew from the cemetery soil as a felled forest of pine stumps.

The light of the moon was more than sufficient to show the larger, flowing lines of the death's-head insignias at the top of the stones but not enough to read the names of the dead. Israel leaned over and squinted with troubled eyes at a large headstone along the outer rim of Burial Hill. With a taloned hand, he followed the flow of letters along the face of the smooth slate. He couldn't tell what the name was, but he was certain it was too long. He thought he counted out twelve letters in the dead man's name. The name Barlow had only six. Too many, he thought, unless, of course, the first and last name were so close together that it would seem as one. Israel counted the letters on the gravestone once more and arrived at a different number. Ten. It could be Seth Barlow. Still, it was impossible to tell for sure in the pale glow of the night moon.

Israel pulled himself back up with the aid of both the gravestone and his walking stick. The task of straightening himself up from a seated or crouched position was becoming more difficult and painful every day. He panted heavily as he leaned on his walking stick, catching his breath. He peered across the growing cemetery. So many markers; some large, some small. But it was the occasional footstone that threatened to trip him that he feared most. There simply wasn't enough light for a safe and fruitful search. His fingers tapped anxiously on the skull of his walking stick as he took a deep breath and resigned himself to the fact that his mission would have to wait until morning.

Israel had spent the earlier part of the day on the wharf in Salem. Although it had been a lifetime since he'd lived there, he was cautious to avoid conversation with anyone who might remember his name and his inauspicious beginnings. The village of his youth had changed significantly, Israel reflected, while Marblehead, on the other hand, had changed very little.

He stood on the dome of the hill, alone with the dead, and glimpsed the last of the flickering lights go dark in the town below. His day had been long, and after a noisy stretch of his creaking joints, Israel sought repose. He spied a large headstone that looked as if it would hold up against his leaning back and found respite in the cool night and the comfort of a grassy bed. He watched the moon as it floated high into the New England sky and pondered his good fortune. It was not so long ago that the noose of the hangman was about to be tightened around his neck. But the ring, which had been stolen by a vengeful Judge Barlow, must've, while still on Israel's finger, had enough magic to reach across the sea to England and grant Israel a royal pardon on the day he was to hang. He, Israel Hands, was the only one, out of nineteen condemned pirates, to receive the pardon. He had to get that ring back. His whole existence depended on it. Israel drew in the night through grateful nostrils. *Ah, the sweet New England air.*

He watched the gravestone shadows shorten until the moon hung directly overhead. He looked across the field and wondered which stone was the marker of Seth Barlow, the first man he'd ever killed, and also stood as the monument to the single act that set him on his murderous path. Israel yawned and shifted his gaze to the surrounding woods. He desired no surprises and searched the shadows for uninvited company. Remembering an old sea ditty from his youth, he smiled as he sang quietly to the dead. In time, Israel fell asleep.

The dawn's light, warm and golden on his eyelids, roused him gently from his slumber. He opened his eyes slowly, allowing all his senses to take in the new day. In the pines not far away, a turtledove cooed a love song to the morning. Israel felt the warm embrace of the sun on his face. Sea air filled his lungs, and the distant smell of woodsmoke made his stomach growl. Breakfast would have to wait.

Israel rose stiffly but with a sense of purpose that bordered on exhilaration. He stretched, dusting the cobwebs from his bones, his spindly arms and fingers moving in the air like a dead tree blowing in the breeze. A loose cough produced copious amounts of thick white sputum, which Israel retched out onto the ground as a matter of his natural morning routine. Wiping the spittle from his chin, he studied the tree line, wary of any curious watchers granted safe harbor by the woods.

A soft haze clung to the morning, and he knew the moisture in the air would give bite to the heat in the coming hours. Israel tossed his cloak over the large gravestone on which he'd been leaning all night and began his search. It would probably be small. An innkeeper was not likely to have the means for an elaborate memorial, but he took no chances. He checked every one, the tall and the small, being especially careful to uncover any ground stones that had been concealed by earth and grass. His search was laborious and took him through the morning and into the afternoon. The heat of the day pressed hard against his balding pate. He stopped frequently to wipe his brow and catch his breath. It was much more difficult for a man with one bad leg to move through tall grass than the deck of a rolling ship. *Maybe life as a sea cook wouldn't be so bad.* It was certainly superior to searching a graveyard for buried treasure.

Some of the headstones fascinated him. The elaborate carvings left Israel awestruck. The winged death's-heads, at least some of them, were perfectly accurate engravings of skulls, nestled between a pair of wings, spread in flight. *Aye, death takes flight, but which way will it take you, shipmate?* A wheezy laugh escaped moist lungs. He wiped the dripping sweat from his eyes with the back of his hand and shook his head in regret as he surveyed the ground he had just covered. Israel had to give up the search. The man was simply not there.

After shuffling back to the far end of the burial ground to retrieve his cloak, Israel rested for a few minutes and tried to make sense of it all. *Maybe he'd come to rest in the Burying Point at Salem. After all, the Barlows had originally been from Salem. Of course, he would be buried in the family plot!* Israel was angry with himself for not thinking of it in the first place. If he'd thought of it the night before, he might already be in possession of the ring. That is, if Judge Barlow followed a thief's logic and hid the ring in the one place that very few would have the nerve to search: in a dead man's grave.

Israel felt he was on the right path. Judge Barlow hadn't left Virginia until after he had learned of Israel's pardon. And as soon as he'd heard, Barlow, and the ring, had booked passage on the first thing that could float back to Salem. The judge had to know that Israel would follow soon after. Therefore, he'd have to secure the ring in a place where no one would look. *No one but me.* Israel smiled, grabbed his cloak, and slung it over his shoulder. But something tugged at the corner of his eye, pulling his gaze downward to the name chiseled into the marble headstone of the grave on which he stood. *Barlow.*

Israel dropped to his one good knee and stared dumbly at the stone. He brushed his hands over the writing, fearing his eyes were playing tricks on him, and fingered the lettering as he read the lines:

Here lyes ye body of

Seth Barlow

Who departed this life

September ye 25th, 1692

Israel slid his fingers down to the bottom of the stone and saw there was more writing covered by the tall grass. He grabbed the turf in clumps and tore it from the roots. With his heart pounding, he read the last of the inscription.

To he who hath expunged my life

To ye shall be eternal strife

Ye shall not lay in peace like me

But walk the world eternally

Ye shall know not but death alone

For ye shall reap what ye hath sown

Israel fell back hard, the words striking him as fiercely as any fist ever had. He held a shaking hand to his mouth as the curse began to take root in his mind. Barlow had waited almost thirty years to exact his revenge on him. His head spinning in confusion, he searched the grounds around him for the source of the sounds that seemed to come at him from all directions. A voice whispered to him from behind. Israel spun around on his knee and, with the agility reminiscent of the young pirate he once was, held his knife at the ready. There was no one there.

A strong wind came in from the sea, cooling the now-hot brow of the man down on his one good knee. Israel looked into the onrushing wind for the phantom that spoke to him. He searched the white haze for the black spirits he sensed about him, and he heard it again. Whispers among the dead. He scrambled to his feet and braced himself by the headstone of Seth Barlow. He kept his knife out in front of him, sweeping it from side to side to hold at bay any unseen foe. His lips curled in a trembling sneer that spoke more of fear than of contempt. He saw nothing, but heard voices on the wind weaving a tapestry of tales among the slate grave markers of the dead.

Israel tried to speak to break the spell, but what was intended as a thundering roar of defiance was but a frightened squeak of a motherless bird. It soothed his mind nonetheless just to hear his own utterance. The contrast of sound reaffirmed that he had not been swept away on the wings of death. Not yet. But the voices continued as the wind grew stronger. He grabbed his cloak and wrapped it around him to shield his body from the whipping gusts, then shrugged his back to the wind as it began to buffet his body like blows from a club. His thin gray hair swirled madly about his head. Israel remained anchored to the headstone of the man he murdered until a blast of air struck with such a force as to knock him off balance and send him tumbling to the ground.

Struggling to his feet, Israel steadied himself with his walking stick and slashed wildly with his knife at the empty space around him. A deep rumbling reached his ears. Israel cocked his head to try to block the noise of the wind. It was hard to place the sound, but he knew it wasn't thunder. It was low and even and getting louder, as if a hundred men had encircled him and murmured some unknowable chant as they drew closer to him. Israel knew he must flee to survive. He looked to the woods to the north of Burial Hill. The leaves of the trees hung limp on their branches, basking in the windless glory of the late summer day.

He strode toward the woods with all the speed of a horrified, one-legged man. He saw dark shapes and shadows move across the grounds behind him, where the unearthly voices cradled a warning. Keeping a watchful eye on the advancing evil, he stumbled several times over small footstones that lay unseen below the unkempt grass. His fear swelled as he neared the edge of the trees. Whimpers barked unchecked from his tightened throat as both the trees and the evil drew nearer. He looked to the silent woods that lay only a few tortuous feet away and felt a powerful hand take hold of his cloak. Without looking back, Israel grabbed a piece of the cloak with his open hand and gave one strong, swift pull, but he could not free himself. A familiar voice, calm yet firm, whispered into his ear. *"Memento mori."* The cloak was released instantly, causing him to hurtle forward in a violent lurch. He hit the ground hard.

Israel lay panting like a dog in the dirt at the edge of the woods. He looked back at Burial Hill, which now stood serenely in the settled peace of the day. Among the gravestones, there was scarcely breeze enough to bend a blade of grass. Whatever had pursued him had returned to its grave—or from wherever it had come. He gathered himself by bits and walked to the base of an old weeping willow, not far away, to rest and collect his thoughts. As he sat below the bowed branches and the pale-green leaves, he tried to make sense of what had just happened. The whispered message kept returning to him. *Memento mori?* He had seen it on some of the stones he'd read as he searched for the Barlow plot but had not considered the meaning. Now, it ate away at the last fleshy shreds of his moldering heart. *Remember, death awaits.*

Cupped hands topped the skull of his walking stick, stationed between his legs. He leaned his weary head forward, resting it against the back of his hand. A melancholy fell over Israel. Where had the boy of his youth gone? Once, he remembered, a long time ago, there had been hope. The possibilities of a good life in the new land had been within his grasp. Or so it had seemed. A very long time ago. Now, his only possessions were a failing body and a disappearing mind. He looked at what he held in his hands. *Oh yes, and a stick.* Israel lamented his poverty. It should not be this way. He examined the gnarled hands caressing the wooden skull and the place on his finger that once bore his god of silver, onyx, and ruby. The anger and hate surged once more and hammered away at a heart that was once purely human but had been fashioned, over time, into something quite the contrary.

Hunger gnawed fiercely at his belly and broke the spell that had strapped itself to his mind. He was free, for the moment, of the crippling despair in which he so frequently found himself immersed, and the spirit of the young pirate within was resurrected. Now, with retribution on his mind, the old sea rogue plotted. He sniffed at the hot, damp air and turned to the darkness of the woods.

Not long into his trek, he came upon an opening in the trees, a spot where raspberries grew full and ripe on the vine. Israel stumbled over himself to reach the fruit, abandoning his stick and hopping the last few yards to overtake his prize more quickly. Upon reaching the bush, he gorged himself, the red berries bursting sweetly in his mouth and providing much-needed ballast in the empty hold of his belly. He was still shoving the fruits into his mouth when the wind pushed itself through the trees. He turned and faced the wind with a red-stained face and an angry knife, but he sensed immediately that this wind carried no evil. This wind was the friend of every sailor on the sea, warm and steady. He enjoyed a rare relaxed smile. A full stomach of berries and a gentle breeze produced an easy calm, and Israel found his strength and energy renewed. He chose a soft spot in the shade of trees to recline and, resting on one elbow, began to assess his situation.

His plans had changed. Having found Barlow's grave in Marblehead, there were only two other places the ring could be, and it wasn't the Barlow family plot in Salem. It could be on the finger of Judge Barlow himself, Israel mused. But that thought was quickly discarded—the last thing the judge would want to do is set himself up as a target for the deranged and murderous Israel Hands. The smirk fell away from Israel's face. There was really only one place the ring could be. The Gold Crown Tavern. And it wouldn't be easy to reach. His skiff was tied up on Nogg's Head, almost a mile due north from where he now sat. He was closer to the tavern than his skiff, for the tavern lay not a quarter mile to the east, yet he couldn't descend on it from this position, as a formidable swamp lay between them. It was difficult enough for a lame man to walk on solid ground. Israel shook his head. He hadn't seen this coming. How could he?

He also couldn't afford to be spotted, that was certain. So under cover of darkness, he'd row from Nogg's Head to the northeastern point of William Peach's estate. Then, on foot, he'd hug the shoreline until he reached the tavern just south of Doliber's Cove. He shouldn't meet anyone along the way, but Marblehead had grown since he was a boy—he'd learned that from the size of Burial Hill alone.

It was a mile, maybe a little more, from where the *Hannah Grace* tugged on her mooring lines in Salem Harbor to where Israel's skiff lay hidden on Nogg's Head. It was almost that from Nogg's Head to Peach's Point, which meant it would be nearly a two-mile pull to reach the safety of the *Hannah Grace*. The tide would be with him, true enough, and although rowing was easier for Israel than walking, it would be a challenging night. His new escape route was long and arduous, but it was the surest he could devise. And what if the ring wasn't there when he reached the tavern? *It has to be there.* He refused to allow himself to think otherwise. Everything was at stake, and he would use that knowledge to push him onward. He needed to rest.

Israel slept.

It was evening when he awoke. The time of long shadows. He footslogged through the woods for more than an hour before finding the boat as he had left it, and he looked upon the small craft as a sleepy man might his bed. It was all Israel wanted or needed at that moment. He gazed at the twilight sky. It would be nearly midnight by the time he reached the Gold Crown Tavern. The black of night would be his closest friend and unwitting accomplice.

Israel pulled two oars out from under the cover of leaves, sprigs, and broken branches, slid them quietly into the boat along with his walking stick, heaved a stiff left leg over into the boat, and shoved off. He cast a nervous, watchful eye to the woods as he oared the skiff away from the beach of smooth pebbles and broken shells. At that moment, he felt vulnerable, at the mercy of anyone, or any*thing*, that lurked in the dark shadows just beyond the shore. Perhaps an unwelcome stray from Old Burial Hill longed to put to sea once more. *Just one more voyage; surely you wouldn't mind a shipmate, eh, Mr. Hands?* The thought made Israel shudder, and the first few strokes of the oar were the surest of Israel's life. As the world around him became more familiar to his nature and the land dimmed in his sight, Israel found his rhythm with the oars and hummed an old sea ditty.

* * *

King Richard watched the sun setting over the town from the deck of the *Hannah Grace*, steady at her moorings at Salem wharf. He walked the planks nervously, waiting for his friend to appear at the bottom of the gangway. Happy fortune had reunited the old shipmates on the streets of Salem only a day earlier. And even happier fortune would cast them together as shipmates once more. Israel said he had something to do and not to be concerned if he were to appear at the dock shortly before they set sail. Although the captain of the *Hannah Grace* bristled at this poor display of seamanship, he was already short two men, and he had a soft spot in his heart for those who had sacrificed life and limb in a ship's service. For now, he would overlook the slight, something that went against his general nature, and hoped that the performance of the new cook might compensate for this breach in protocol.

There was another concern that weighed heavily on the heart of loyal King Richard. His old friend was but a dull reflection of his former self. Once thought of as the most ferocious pirate on the seas, Israel Hands was now little more than a bent cripple, decayed in tooth and spirit. The clear, crisp sparkle in his pale-blue eyes had become the murky-gray squint of a man gone half-blind. The sure, lively steps that once bounded the bloody decks of burning ships now dragged a dead leg in tow. *All this,* King Richard thought, *from one pistol shot.* Leaning on the rail, he looked down at the black water of Salem Harbor and watched as the sea lapped playfully at the hull of the *Hannah Grace. No,* the Lionheart realized, *it had been much more than that; it was the betrayal of a dear friend.*

Across Salem Harbor, King Richard could see the ghostly outline of the Marblehead peninsula and wondered what mischief Israel had found for himself. A year ago, the entire crew would have fought to be at Israel's side just to be part of some midnight intrigue. Much had changed. King Richard felt only fear for his friend. The night smelled of blood, and his old friend was now his *old* friend, and he could not know the strength of the enemy Israel would face that night. All there was to do was wait—and watch. He looked up into the dawn of night as billowy clouds passed in front of the moon and painted the edges a bluish white. He heaved a wistful sigh for Israel and dropped his gaze back down upon the water. Illuminated by the lanterns at the head of the gangplank, he studied the water lines on the dock pilings and became more fearful as each barnacle vanished beneath the surface. He wondered if his friend would beat the rising moon as it tugged at the tide, bringing the Atlantic into the harbor to make ready the path that would take the *Hannah Grace* out to sea.

An ocean breeze crossed the deck, bringing with it the overpowering smell of pine sap that emanated from the cargo hold of the ship. Long pines were a premium product for the British Empire, and the tall, straight colonial trees made for perfect ship masts for the Royal Navy. The trunks had been treated generously with tar for the voyage, and King Richard knew the smell would send many a man to the rail for the first day or two at sea. Having a friend along would lessen the pain of the long, pungent passage. King Richard frowned as the breeze kicked up again. The tide was coming.

* * *

Having beached his skiff on Peach's Point, Israel hurried along the dark road, feeling the wind over his left shoulder coming in from the sea. The hour was late, and time was short. He would have to find the ring and make haste back to the boat before he lost the tide. It would take him about an hour to row across Salem Harbor, maybe a little more. His skiff rested five minutes behind him, and the Gold Crown Tavern lay a full sandglass ahead. Would that he could have put ashore closer to the tavern! For it was over a quarter mile from his landing to his destination. Ah, but there was too great a risk in that, he reminded himself. If he were to be seen leaving the tavern by boat, they could have a welcoming party waiting for him at the dock in Salem by the time he arrived. He must steal cleanly away. Any search would have to be on land, house to house. No one must see him head to the shore. Concealed by darkness, he would keep to the path alongside the woods, using them for cover if need be, head back to the skiff, then across the harbor to where the *Hannah Grace* lay restless, straining at her moorings.

Breathing heavily, he hurried down the road, dragging a dumb leg as quickly as he could, when an unsettling sensation came over him. Eyes were watching him. He could feel them. Israel stopped suddenly and peered into the trees that lined the road. "Who's there?" he demanded in a scratchy voice. He searched for human form among the shifting shapes of light and shadow but received no reply. The wind rose, and Israel felt a tightening around his neck. His cloak, in the firm grasp of the gusting wind, tugged at him and bid him onward. Turning his back again to the wind, he felt the fingers of his cloak loosen their grip around his throat.

The trees that lined the road grew as a canopy above the lane, and Israel peered into the dark tunnel that led to the tavern. With a determined, if canting, gait, he moved forward, his walking stick courageously leading the way, stamping the ground defiantly with every other step. The wind shifted with the bend of the road, and Israel held his cloak tightly shut so as not to be hanged by it. He searched the side of the road for those who travel the night but found no other company. He listened for voices in the air; if they were there, they held their tongues.

It wasn't until he was almost at the tavern that he heard a voice. "Who? Who?"

Initially startled, Israel raised a shaking finger of warning at the large owl perched on an oak branch that hung over the road. Israel caught his breath and answered his inquisitor. "'Tis I, my friend, Israel Hands. And you best not be putting such a fright into these old bones. You near scared life itself from me." He smiled and winked at the wise old bird.

The owl winked back and whispered, "Memento mori."

Israel reeled in a fear so intense it pained his chest. He ran, scraping the flesh from his dead foot as it was dragged without consideration along the rough road. With his chest heaving, Israel glanced over his shoulder to see the owl, unmoving on its perch, watching him. Up ahead, only one hundred yards away, Israel could see a dim light pouring from the roadside window of the Gold Crown Tavern. The tavern, which was to be his ship to plunder, now became his port in the storm. As the light grew brighter to his dimming eyes, Israel's breath came more easily. But he did not slow down.

Upon reaching the tavern, he leaned hard and heavy against the frame of the front door and looked back up the road. All was quiet. The owl had not pursued him, nor did the woods surrounding the tavern reveal any hint of impending doom. He swallowed air in gulps until his lungs were satiated and waited for calm to still his trembling hands. In a few minutes, his wits restored, Israel wiped the sweat from his palms on his tattered cloak, canted across the closed door, and peered into the window. A dim fire burned unattended in the fireplace. There was no sign of anyone in the home, certainly no visitor to the tavern. But surely someone was there.

Israel placed his hand lightly on the latch. He depressed the thumb lever and pushed, but the door would not budge. It was barred from the inside. Israel took several steps away from the tavern door and studied the upstairs windows, but no glow of candle flame could he see. He looked back up the dark road from whence he came and grew fearful of what might be following.

Israel gained the boldness born of necessity. With the head of his walking stick, he began to bang at the tavern door. The startling clamor from clubbing the door increased the sense of alarm burgeoning in his own heart. His eyes struck up the road once more, sure that the noise would wake and alert the demons he sought to escape. He was certain they would hasten their attack now. Soon, he would look up the lane and see them galloping, or slithering, or flying, or whatever demons do, toward him.

Israel received no response from his banging and grabbed his stick with both hands at the base. Pulling the stick back over his shoulder, he swung into the window of the tavern, shattering the glass and announcing his arrival. He reached in through the shards and released the wooden bar that locked the door. Tossing it aside, he entered the tavern and just as quickly put the bar in place once more. He backed away, staring at the door, hoping against hope to be free from the evil that traveled the night.

The flickering of the fading fire caught his attention, and for a lingering moment, he fell under the spell of the flagging flame. A small pop from the dying embers woke him from his trance. He looked to the side of the large fireplace and saw an ample supply of dry hardwood and began tossing the heavy logs carelessly into the pit. Soon Israel noticed that his placement of the wood served only to smother the last of the diminishing flames. Setting his walking stick aside, Israel took the iron dog hook from its holder and stirred the flames back to life. The simple distraction released his mind from his fear of the night. It wasn't until he heard the floorboards creaking upstairs that the fear rushed in on him again.

Israel peered over his shoulder at the narrow staircase, swallowing hard. He gripped the dog hook with both hands as another creak came from the top of the stairs. Israel's nerves steadied with the realization that anything that makes a floor creak must be flesh and blood. It might, in fact, be Judge Barlow himself. Would that be the case, Israel might be wearing the Devil's Kiss that very night. Hope now returned and burned as brightly as the fire he'd brought back to life. He cleared his throat for command. "Who walks about topside?" he asked in a voice forceful enough to please him.

"Who goes about downstairs?" a timid voice responded.

"Come down here, man, and let me speak to you," Israel demanded wearily. He watched as a barefooted, small-framed man in a nightshirt stepped cautiously down the staircase, every other step creaking as he did so.

"Who you be there, little man?" Israel asked, setting the dog iron down in its fireside perch.

"I'm Sims, the caretaker. B-b-beg your pardon, sir, but who are you?"

"A fit and proper question," Israel conceded. After all, he'd just broken into the house. "I'm an old friend of the Barlow family, come back from years at sea in service to His Majesty, King George." Israel looked back at the broken glass on the tavern floor. "I'll be begging your pardon for the window, but when no one answered when I thundered on the door, it seemed that there might be something amiss. And fearing for the safety of my dear friend, well, I bargained it wasn't the time for prudence," Israel said with a benevolent smile. "Now, last I heard, this here tavern still belonged to my old friend, Judge Barlow. I'd be very disappointed if it weren't the case."

"Oh, no, sir. This is the Barlow tavern. I tend to the business and live above. The judge, of course, lives in town." The man did not appear to be frightened of Israel but looked about the room as if expecting to find someone else.

"Of course," Israel said, comforted by the answer but uneasy at the caretaker's curious twitching and odd behavior. "You seem to be a might distracted, Mr. Sims. Is all fit and proper hereabouts?"

"It's the sounds of the night, sir. I thought you might have been someone . . ." An embarrassed shrug ended the man's statement.

"I've a question, Mr. Sims," Israel inserted, ignoring the man's response. "I left a precious family heirloom in the custody of the good judge before I put to sea. It's a shame you can't trust a shipmate nowadays," Israel lamented. "A very sad thing, indeed. Maybe the judge keeps it here for my return? It's a pleasant ring, made of silver. There be a cross of black stone in the middle, surrounded by four red stones in the corners. Maybe you've seen it?"

The caretaker's eyes grew wide. "Aye," Sims admitted, "I have knowledge of such a ring."

"Ah, you've put the wind in the sails of this old salt, Mr. Sims," Israel said, forcing himself to remain calm. "Perhaps you can help me locate it?"

"The Devil . . ." Sims's eyes grew wide with fear.

"Aye, the Devil's Kiss! 'Tis what it's called. But don't let that put a fright in you. It's just a name, and by all rights, it's mine. Would you be willing . . ." Israel stopped, becoming irritated by the increasingly odd behavior of the caretaker. He'd never liked caretakers. *So strange.*

Sims stared, wild-eyed, past Israel, toward the broken window at the far side of the room. Without a sound, he began quaking violently, unable to speak. Israel grabbed him by the breast of the nightshirt and shook him to regain his attention. "Where's the ring, Mr. Sims?" Sims's head rocked loosely on limp shoulders. "Where is my ring?" All efforts to bring Sims around were useless as his legs gave out from beneath him and he fell hard against the staircase wall. His eyes remained locked on the opposite side of the room, to which Israel had turned his back.

His anger brimming over, Israel bent down and picked up his walking stick, which lay on the floor near his feet. The skull of the stick struck the low ceiling as Israel raised it in a threatening posture. "Where's the ring?" Israel demanded, his eyes wide in a state of madness. Sims clutched his chest with an agonizing groan and slid down the face of the staircase wall. As his final breath left his lips, the caretaker slumped over on his side, his head lolling to the left until it hit the floor with a muted thump, all the while seeming to hold his gaze on the broken window.

"Damn you to hell, man!" Israel roared. *To be so close to finding my ring only to have this weak, worthless man die before me? Where is my ring? Where is my justice?* Israel seethed through clenched jaws.

The clock that stood in the corner at the base of the stairs began to chime. Israel counted, although its face was in plain sight. It was midnight, and he had to return to Salem or risk missing movement of the *Hannah Grace*. He had only begun to think of what that would mean when he turned around.

Beneath the shattered window, slumped against the wall in a position mirroring that of the caretaker lying across the room from him, was the bleeding corpse of Seth Barlow. Israel fell back against the wall that supported the lifeless Mr. Sims. He stared in disbelief as the blood poured freely from the neck wound, the marlin spike quivering in the chest of a man who had been dead for nearly twenty-seven years. Spellbound by the impossible sight, Israel wondered why the spike vibrated as it did. Moments later, he realized the dead man was laughing. A subtle, malignant chuckle that escaped the throat of the murdered man grew to a howling, mocking laugh.

The laughter suddenly stopped, and the only thing that Israel could hear was the thunderous pounding of his own trembling heart. He looked at the still figure of Seth Barlow—eyes closed, chest still, bleeding stopped. He quickly surveyed the rest of the room. All was as it should be, that is to say, with the exception of the two dead bodies that bookended the room. Israel took a tentative step toward the door, then paused. Nothing. He loosened his grip on his walking stick, then reapplied his stranglehold around its neck and took another timid step.

The eyes of Seth Barlow opened in a flash and locked on to those of Israel Hands. Blown pupils of black crosses lay anchored amid the blood-infiltrated sclera. His lips slowly parted, the corners stretched up and back, drawn as if by some invisible grasp into an obscene smile. Barlow's eyes moved down and gazed upon his hand.

The Devil's Kiss encircled the first finger of Barlow's left hand. Israel couldn't control the shuddering gasp that forced its way between his lips. He gaped in horrid fascination as the prize he held so dear lay but a few courageous steps away. Confusion owned his mind. The very thing that would protect him from evil wrapped the finger of evil itself. And if it weren't Ol' Scratch himself bleeding on the tavern floor, it was certainly one of his pawns. Whatever it was, it didn't appear to be in a giving mood.

The door burst open with startling ferocity as a foul, violent wind forced its way in and pressed Israel hard against the stone fireplace. The stench was unbearable. Israel pressed his nose and mouth into the crook of his elbow to breathe without gagging. Barlow threw his head back and laughed with the unbridled ecstasy of one returning from the dead. Israel sensed another presence that entered with the wind—a familiar presence, yet out of place. Regardless, it was there now, and Israel couldn't bear another minute more in its company.

He abandoned any thought of snatching the ring from the hand of the laughing thing on the floor in front of him. It was a trap. Israel sensed that's what the thing wanted him to do, and he could not bear to think of the dark embrace that awaited him were he to make such a foolish mistake. His only hope was to pass through the door before it shut, imprisoning him in a manner that, he was certain, offered no hope of escape.

Holding his stick out in front of him as if a talisman, his face still buried in the angle of his elbow, Israel inched closer to the door. He felt the heat of the fire against his back as he shuffled over the hearthstones and beyond the pit. Barlow's laughter ceased abruptly as he watched Israel move ever closer. Israel was only six feet from the open door when it began to close. He shot a fearful look at Barlow, whose eyes widened with excitement. In a single moment of clarity and reason, Israel hurtled himself through the closing door. It slammed angrily behind him, as if it had thrown him out.

Israel scampered to his feet and raced up the road as fast as one good leg could carry him. In his flight, he thought that perhaps the evil had left him. He began to slow his pace, looking back every few steps to ensure he was alone. His breathing calmed slowly, along with his nerves. Then he heard it. Whispered names on the air around him. Some of the names he knew; most he did not. Names of the men he'd killed mixed in discordant harmony with other names. Names he had heard in stories or used as blasphemies. They were the names of demons.

Israel snapped his head around in every direction, trying desperately to find a human voice behind the whispers. Above, in the trees, the great horned owl fixed wild eyes on the doomed Israel Hands. Terror stricken, he ran. He felt the blackness of evil fast approaching and did not look back so as not to be consumed by it.

Whether on impulse or instinct, Israel broke for the shore that lay unseen through a section of dense, unforgiving woods. The gentle slope off the side of the road put him off balance, and he stumbled wildly through the brush. His feet could not stay beneath him, and he tumbled down a steep and sudden drop until he came to a painful stop, his head landing hard against the trunk of a fallen tree. Israel shook his head loosely to clear his mind. He took one shivering breath and looked up. When he did, the evil was there, and it fell upon him.

CHAPTER TWENTY-FIVE

Battle

Monday, June 28, 1999

The day passed quickly for Tom. He'd braced himself for a day of anxious idleness, a day of clock watching, finger twiddling, and nail-biting. But something quite the contrary had happened. Many of the jobs he'd meant to finish for weeks now had been crossed off the list. By evening, an almost eerie feeling of calm swept over him as he took a final tally of the day's achievements. He rewarded himself with a cold Bud Light and, after a quick twist of the cap, took his first swig of the day. He stood at the kitchen window and looked across the narrow strait to Brown's Island. The sun had set, and the early twilight tinged the evening air with the delicate shade of a pale rose. Even the green copse of trees on the island blushed in the waning light of day. *Beautiful,* Tom thought as he peeled the label from his beer bottle.

Had he not already had plans for the night, Tom wondered if he might have, for the first time in a long time, taken himself out for the evening. Perhaps there were more people out there like him—growing tired of being alone and growing in their awareness of the ephemeral joy of being alive. Tom smiled. He was happy, and he couldn't say why. It certainly wasn't due to what they had planned for the night. Maybe it was because he knew he wouldn't be facing it alone. He didn't know. But he couldn't shake the sense of well-being that had come over him, and frankly, he didn't want to shake it.

The diver's watch felt heavy on his wrist, and he glanced down for a time check: *9:05 p.m.?* Tom drained the last of his barley pop and bounded up the ladder for a quick shower. He never really got used to daylight saving time, Tom pondered as he entered his room. At least not until it was time to go off it again. Everything's going to be all right, he told himself as he walked into the bathroom. The Bible was sitting on his nightstand as twilight entered the room.

* * *

Paris Quicci sipped his single malt from a monogrammed crystal whiskey glass as Vivaldi played behind him. The garden was much to his liking. Although not a complete Japanese garden, it was certainly well on its way. *The early returns look very favorable.* Gardens were not a particular passion of Quicci's, but it was something to have. A way to show others that one is connected to the earth without having to connect with it at all. And if it were the garden of the new bank president, which was officially announced earlier that day, then it should be a garden of true distinction.

As he marveled at the curious hand of fate, Quicci thought of the extraordinary accomplishments he'd achieved already, and all before the age of thirty-five. As with any measuring stick, there's always somebody on the other end. The people who, for whatever reason, just can't seem to make the cut. Those who don't have what it takes to make the team. Yesterday's suicide report came directly to mind. He took another sip of eighteen-year-old scotch and slowly shook his head in wonder regarding the sad, pathetic man. "Ah, Nate, you poor fat slob," Quicci said to the sky above him. "Here I am, hanging out in my garden, and there you were, just hanging." He giggled. The scotch was good, and dammit, he was happy. "Here's to you, Nate," he toasted in hollow honor of the fallen. He looked upward as he raised his glass when something remarkable caught his eye. He smirked as he shook his head. "The freaks over in Salem are going to have a field day with this."

* * *

Rebecca finished her charm as she always did, with the request to the Goddess that her magic be correct and for the good of all. Standing in the small bay of her apartment, she stared with closed eyes out the north-facing window at the gathering darkness. The last of the incense burned in its place on the altar before her, fragrant smoke wafting delicately into the space of the small bedroom. Here she felt complete—her life, enchanted; her magic, powerful. Before her stood her altar, set up according to her tradition. Wand and pentacle in the middle, with the incense burner just beyond the pentacle. A black beeswax candle and goblet to the left of the pentacle, with a white beeswax candle and her athame, the ceremonial dagger, balancing on the right. One more item completed the altar setting, a protection potion for the safety of the witch.

With a deep, cleansing breath, Rebecca came out of her alpha state. She looked around the room. She was forgetting something that did not want to be forgotten. It was as if a small voice was whispering to her from across a large room. She looked to her book of shadows that lay on the nightstand by her bed. Was it her book that was calling her? It often had in the past when she had overlooked some important detail or was about to enter into harm's way. She sat down on her bed and rubbed a loving hand over the dark cover of the leather-bound book. She opened it and immediately went to dates where she knew she had made notes that had to do with Stonecroft Inn. She went back to the time of her vision of the first mate and the entries she'd made when she captured his essence on canvas. But there was nothing there that she had not remembered. Something still eluded her, but she just couldn't put her finger on what it was. She decided to let it go for the moment, knowing it would likely come to her as soon as she stopped thinking about it.

A hard knock on the door bounded through the living room and into the white-lace and ruffle-adorned bedroom where Rebecca sat wondering. She consulted the digital clock on her nightstand and smiled. *Nine thirty. He's right on time. I like that in a man.* She looked through the small viewer in the door to ensure that it was her intended visitor. You could never be too certain. There were a lot of nuts in the world. She opened the door to the man who would protect her from all that.

"Hi," she said in a coy whisper.

His heart leaped at the sight of her. "Hi," Drew managed to return. So many good things had come his way since he'd met her, or maybe he just saw the good where he hadn't noticed it before. Nate Ingersoll swinging from a rope was, of course, not one of them. He stepped inside and gave her a light hello kiss. "Ready to go?"

"Yeah, just about," Rebecca said as she gathered up the sea salt and black Ethiopian resin from the kitchen table. "I have a feeling I'm forgetting something." She stared at Drew for a minute as if she could draw the answer from his face.

"Oh, that reminds me," he said. "Have you seen the moon yet?"

"No, but I know it's full," she said distractedly. "That's the whole point of us being there tonight."

"That's not what I mean. It's red. The full moon is red."

Rebecca spun around to face him, eyes wide. She started to speak, but no words came out. She darted to the kitchen window and threw up the sash. The moon was rising over the Atlantic Ocean beyond the brick building in front of her but was still too low on the horizon for her to see. She raced past Drew, who decided not to follow, knowing that she would be back before the minute hand of his Mickey Mouse watch would indicate nine thirty-five. He looked out the same window and saw her race across the street. He saw her stop when she reached the end of the three-story apartment building and stare out at what he knew was the moon. Mickey's big hand clicked to the next minute mark when he heard footsteps ascending the stairs. Rebecca burst through the door with great excitement, out of breath.

"I didn't write it in my book of shadows," she cried. "It was a dream. I recorded it!"

"What are you talking about?" Drew called out as she dashed past him into her bedroom. She was opening her top dresser drawer when he reached the doorway. He could hear the sound of thin plastic snapping as Rebecca's hands and eyes ransacked the small space.

"Yes!" She held up a microcassette tape in triumph, then quickly moved to her nightstand and pulled out a small tape recorder, all the while ignoring the man darkening her bedroom doorway. She fumbled to open the tiny door of the cassette recorder, then snapped the tape into place. Only then did she look up from her seated position on the bed and acknowledge the mystified man's presence. Still trying to catch her breath, she began to explain.

"I knew there was something important I was missing. Something about what is now Stonecroft but from long ago. I thought it was a premonition that I'd had, so I searched for my entry in my book of shadows. Well, I searched and searched and searched, but I couldn't find it. And I couldn't remember what it was, what it said. It wasn't until you said the moon was red that I remembered. It wasn't a premonition. It was a dream. I keep this tape recorder by my bed to capture the remnants of dreams. Well, this is it," she said, shaking the recorder at him. "I mark it by date and with some associated word or catchphrase to remind me of the dream."

Drew moved closer and stood at the foot of the bed, his eyes growing larger as he listened to the story. Finally, he said, "Play it," as he sat down beside her.

In a very deliberate manner, Rebecca pressed the button, and the two listened and watched as the mechanical wheels of the tape recorder began to turn. A hollow, scratchy sound told them the tape was about to speak.

"Ooh, ooh, turn it up," Drew demanded. Rebecca thumbed the volume wheel ever so slowly until they heard the sound of someone clearing their voice. They held their breath.

> *"When the moon rises red in the twilight sky*
> *The keeper of the inn will die*
> *Upon the croft in Barlow's Crown*
> *Above the graves of those not found*
> *Not in the hour when witches fly*
> *But when the darkness owns the sky*
> *He shall return to kill unless*
> *Ye bestow to him the Devil's Kiss."*

The hollow, scratchy sound continued for another ten seconds or so, then shut off with a sharp click. "That's it?" Drew asked. "What does that mean?"

Rebecca didn't answer. She found the reverse button and listened to the tape again. Her face was devoid of color after she listened to it for the third time. "When the moon rises red in the twilight sky," she said in a voice that bordered on panic, "the keeper of the inn will die." She paused and looked at Drew, who showed no signs of catching up. "Drew, a red rising moon is a sign of diabolical murder. It even says who is going to die. The innkeeper, Tom."

"Well, we knew that was the threat already, didn't we?"

"Yes, but listen to the second half of the message. It says the only way to stop him is by giving him the Devil's Kiss."

"That's the ring you were looking for, right?"

"Yes, but listen," she said, straining to remain patient. "Not in the hour when witches fly," Rebecca recited. She broke it down for him. "Midnight has always been referred to as the witching hour. It's saying that's not when he's coming. He's coming when darkness owns the sky." Rebecca left her seat on the edge of the bed and referred to the chart on the sill of the bay window. "Moonrise was at nine eighteen tonight. It'll be completely dark at the end of what's called nautical twilight."

"What the *hell* is nautical twilight?" Drew asked with growing anxiety. He didn't like appearing stupid and liked actually *being* stupid even less.

"Twilight is when the sun is six degrees below the horizon and you see the last of its brilliant light. That ended at eight fifty-nine tonight. After that, it's nautical twilight, and nautical twilight ends when the last of the sun's light has gone completely. In other words, when darkness owns the sky."

Drew looked at his watch. "It's nine thirty-seven now. When would nautical twilight end?"

Rebecca consulted her chart once more. She looked up at Drew with frightened eyes. "About two minutes ago."

"Let's fly," Drew said to the witch.

* * *

Tom stepped out of the master bath, combing back his salt-and-pepper hair. There seemed to be a lot more salt than there was just a few short weeks ago. This depressing sight forced him from the bathroom mirror and sent him back into his room, where the glass didn't look back at him but, rather, out to Brown's Island and the sea. He gazed out at the coming of night and saw the early glow of the rising moon behind the trees of Brown's Island. Tom stepped away from the window and into a clean pair of jeans and pulled a fresh T-shirt over his head.

He scanned the floor for his shoes. In the darkening room, he moved toward the door to turn on the lights. As he reached for the light switch, he saw that the white walls were reflecting a pinkish hue. Tom sensed a rising dread as he returned to the window he'd just left. Something was amiss. He'd seen the moon before in various shades of orange and yellow. But he'd never seen the moon as it was tonight. No, in all his travels around the world and in all the climates and conditions he'd experienced at sea, he never saw the moon shining bright red. Not like this. *Never like this.*

The chiming of a ship's bell tore his attention away from the sanguine moon. The sound triggered a visceral response, and a cold sweat broke out across Tom's pale brow and greased the palms of his hands. He counted every threatening clang. *Six bells. The sailor's watch begins.*

"He's early," Tom said out loud to himself, noting the time on his nightstand clock: 9:35 p.m. He stared at the phone, sleeping in its cradle. Fearing the line might be dead, Tom walked tentatively to the nightstand and hoisted the phone to his ear. He had a dial tone and breathed a sigh of relief as he glanced at the number on the back of Drew's business card, which Drew had given him for just such emergencies. As he pushed the glowing buttons of the phone, Tom heard a strange noise coming from the receiver. He put the phone to his ear and almost immediately pulled it away. It was the sound of the sea, the roar of waves crashing on the shore, and the shouts of approaching men.

Tom slammed the receiver down. He bolted to his bedroom door, opened it, and peered down the hall. A silvery-blue light flickered from down below. He knew it was time. Taking a deep breath, Tom stepped out into the hallway and shut the door behind him.

* * *

Jake drummed his fingers nervously on the armrest of the wing chair he'd pushed into the corner. From the room where Marie was staying, he could lean his head against the wall and look out the window to view the lights of Stonecroft Inn, a hundred or so yards away. From his watch post, he could see that only the front and back porch lights, which were set on timers, were on. Soon, Jake knew, Tom would be turning on every light in the house. That was the signal Jake was waiting for. The sign that would tell him that Tom's nerves were riding the razor's edge. It was either that or the strike of ten, whichever came first.

He glanced at his wife, who lay on the bed, reading a novel that had lost the battle for her attention. She hadn't turned a page in the last ten minutes. The afternoon had been much the same, filled with mindless wanderings and nervous prattle. Most of their discussions had centered on all they would do to get Tom back on his feet and make Stonecroft Inn the premier B&B in Marblehead, yet they hadn't believed a word of what they'd said.

Marie had bonded quickly with Tom's friendly competitor and next-door neighbor. Although she never had to borrow a cup of sugar, their mutual love of plants and flowers allowed Marie to spend a few enjoyable moments with Julie Bishop, sharing gardening tips and comparing notes. By the time the situation in Stonecroft had become too precarious for Marie to stay, the women had become friends. Marie had even confided in Julie as to some of the peculiar goings-on next door. At first, this did not sit well with either Jake or Tom. But the concern was short lived, as both recognized Marie's need for friendship, to have another woman whom she could confide in and relate to under such an oppressive shroud of fear. She found that in Julie. It was Julie, in fact, who suggested Marie stay with her until all was well, and for that, Jake was grateful. He couldn't leave his friend, but he couldn't compromise his wife's safety either. Here, Jake thought as he looked out the window at the inn, his wife was safe. He checked the time on his watch.

"How much longer?" she asked, peeking at him over the top of her Jodi Picoult novel.

"About half an hour," he replied, still sporting a facade of nonchalance. He leaned against the wall to spy the lights of Stonecroft. The porch lights were out. The only light he could see was a throbbing, silvery-blue luminescence from the first-floor windows.

"Time to go," Jake said, fear tightening around the words as they escaped his throat. He wasted no time but stepped quickly to Marie and kissed her firmly on the mouth. He looked her in the eye. "I'll be back in a little while."

While she trembled inside, Marie offered a brave smile.

Jake turned and hit the door at a near dead run. The door slammed shut as Marie shouted a faint "I love you."

It was too late. Jake was gone.

* * *

Mickey's sweeping second hand had not made it once around the face of the watch before Drew and Rebecca were on Route 114, heading toward Marblehead. Drew handed Rebecca his car phone. "Call Tom. Tell him to get the hell out of the house until we're all there." Rebecca began to dial as Drew continued his instructions. "Don't go over the dream with him now. Just tell him to leave immediately. Tell him it's an order from the Marblehead Police Department."

There was a prolonged silence. Finally, Rebecca snapped the mouthpiece shut. "No answer."

"He's got to be home," Drew said, puzzled.

A relieving thought came to Rebecca. "Unless he's already out of the house. Maybe something started to happen, and he ran out of the house."

"Yeah, I suppose that's possible, but I don't really see Tom Stone running from anything," Drew said, both respect and regret tingeing his voice.

"I'll try him again in a few minutes."

Although in a desperate hurry, Drew couldn't make himself go more than 5 mph over the posted speed limit without lights and sirens. It drove Rebecca absolutely batshit.

"Will you please put some weight on the gas pedal? Someone's life is in danger."

"It won't help matters by endangering the lives of others," was the knee-jerk response from the safety officer.

"I'm driving next time," Rebecca murmured.

"The part of the tape that talked about the 'croft in Barlow's Crown,'" Drew said, changing the subject. "How did that go again?"

"'Upon the croft in Barlow's Crown, above the graves of those not found.' Remember, Stonecroft was originally called the Gold Crown Tavern by its owner, Seth Barlow."

"Yeah, yeah, yeah, I remember that," Drew said, sounding more irritated than he'd intended. "What about the second line, 'above the graves of those not found'? Does that mean there are bodies buried under the room where we sat and ate and drank and laughed?"

Rebecca winced at the thought. "I think that's exactly what it means," she replied, nodding squeamishly.

"Why didn't you report this after you had the dream?"

"Oh, right." Rebecca did a hack job of a ditzy Marilyn Monroe talking on the phone. "Hi, I'm a witch. I'd like you to dig up a house in town to see if there are any dead bodies under it. Well, because I had a dream about it, that's why. Is that a problem, Officer? No, I haven't been drinking. No, sir, I just say *no* to drugs."

Point taken. Drew was sorry he'd opened his mouth. He turned left onto West Shore Drive. Just another mile and a half to Stonecroft, but on the narrow winding residential streets of Marblehead, it was a long-ass mile and a half.

He risked another question. "Oh, you used a term earlier when I mentioned the moon being red. You said it was a sign of *diabolical* murder. I know this is probably gonna sound stupid, but to me, *diabolical murder* seems a lot worse than just saying *murder*. Or was that just a figure of speech?"

"It doesn't sound stupid, and it was no figure of speech. It means that the first mate is not alone. There's something else there with him.

Something that feeds his hate and makes him far more dangerous than some vaporous apparition. A foreign entity or intelligence."

"What, you mean like an evil spirit or something?" Drew snickered, trying to make light of what he couldn't comprehend.

"That's exactly what I mean."

Drew gave the news a minute or so to settle in. "So what do you think we can expect when we get there?"

Rebecca thought for a moment. "Bad things."

"Try Tom on the phone again."

* * *

Tom descended the ladder as boldly as any man could as he hit each step with a hard and heavy heel. He only hoped his heroic facade could hold. The lights shifted quickly and often, as if part of some preternatural light show. But these lights possessed form and substance. Some held emotion, others sound, and still others a physical presence. Tom realized, although he couldn't say how, that these emanations were not actually lights—they were men, or the spirits of men, and they did not put out a happy glow.

A beam of bright silver light sliced the air with a scream and drew razor-thin streaks of blood across Tom's bare arms. He learned quickly to stay away from the brighter lights and instinctively moved toward the dark. But there was melancholy, despair, and self-loathing to be found in the dark blues and purples, and although he couldn't see the bleeding, their attack turned Tom's mind inward and brought him to his knees nonetheless. Suddenly, the room was plunged into complete darkness.

A dim illumination began to glow at the far end of the room, as if a very weak bulb were being held behind a black veil. From its center, a small gray orb issued forth. As it moved, it turned, and Tom saw it was changing, growing, and assuming a familiar form. He'd seen this before. Recently. Tom remembered a fuzzy gray ball that grew in front of his eyes. He remembered . . . *The old woman. She's a part of this?*

The woman entered as might a long-forgotten and unwanted memory, emerging from nothing as a dark cloud, moving in and applying its intention to weaken the mind, destruction of its host being its ultimate goal. Tom fought the jelly in his knees, grabbed the railing at the foot of the ladder, and hoisted himself back up. The old woman glided through the gathering room like a mist, flying at ceiling height one moment, then slithering like a snake on the ground the next.

Unlike her first visit, she now seemed to have no interest in Tom, if she even noticed him at all. But if that were the case, Tom was the only thing she didn't see or touch.

She moved both high and low and made physical contact with every object in the room. Harsh and heavy was her touch. Candlesticks were thrown against the wall, the fruit bowl on the table was flipped in the air like a coin. Oranges, apples, pears, and plums were sent flying, landing black and desiccated as they hit the ground. The chairs were overturned or tossed aside as the old woman pushed through the sea of wooden legs, and the heavy oaken table shuddered and thundered as it was lifted off the floor and then recklessly dropped back down with an echoing crash. Even the painting of *The First Mate* was rocked on its moorings.

Once the entire room had been ransacked, the old woman hovered in the middle of that space and, for the first time, leveled a blank stare at Tom. Then, with a howl that shook the walls and cracked much of the remaining mortar on the fireplace, the old woman evaporated in an instant.

With the aid of a dim and rootless light, Tom took his first step off the landing and onto the gathering room floor. His feet disappeared in a sea of fog up to his knees. Silhouettes of men, or what might have been men, began to appear in the gloomy mist not far away from Tom, from the far side of the room, had the room been there. Walls, ceilings, and firepits were gone, hidden from the world in which Tom stood. The shadowy figures didn't approach any closer to Tom but appeared to be turning to one another and then back, as if looking at him.

He heard a low hum. The sound became bolder, deeper, stronger. Voices, distinct and rhythmic, were chanting. Their words were clear, but Tom couldn't make out what they were saying. He focused on one voice that seemed the loudest. Then he heard it. Names. They were chanting names. Some were in English with first and last names; others seemed to have only one name and often in a foreign tongue. Tom didn't recognize any of them. What he did recognize was the scent in the air.

It was Carol's perfume. Not how it smelled when it was misted from the bottle, but the fragrance that was returned when it mingled with her skin. He closed his eyes. He remembered the first time he kissed her, the smell so soft as to be merely a suggestion. She slowly tilted her head as he lowered his face to her neck. It was warm, inviting. He felt the moist warmth of her breath on his ear as he kissed the subtle hollow between her neck and shoulder. He heard and felt her breathing quicken to match his own. His heart was racing. He wanted her, and she, him. He swelled with desire and opened his eyes. And she was there. In his arms.

Her eyes were just as soft, just as brown, and filled with an undeniable love that washed away any doubt of her reality. But how could this be? It didn't matter now.

"Maybe I've died and gone to heaven."

"Oh, no, my love, you haven't died," she said, comforting him with the gentle stroke of her hand through his hair. "I've come to tell you that you can't die, Tom. You mustn't."

Tom had thought he could never love her more. Right now, he did. "I've missed you so much, babe. I swear to God I don't know how I've lived without you. Sometimes I just want to end it all."

A gentle smile creased her face. "I know, my love, I know. But it's not time."

Tom closed his eyes and sighed, helpless in her arms. Carol cleared her throat. Tom opened his eyes when she cleared her throat a second time. Her voice was raspy, hoarse, and forceful.

"Not until you tell us where the fucking ring is!" Her eyes rolled up white. Still holding her in his arms, he felt the warm softness of her body wither and sag. Shadows formed beneath her eyes, which were quickly reduced to blackened sockets surrounding sightless orbs. The smooth contour of her face, the softness of her cheeks, fell suddenly into itself as she assumed the form of a living cadaver. Her breathing, with thick sputum that bubbled within her bony chest, was difficult and sporadic. Her intoxicating scent of moments ago was replaced by a stench from her mouth and body of rotted flesh and human excrement.

Her eyes rolled back down, and she gazed at him through murky lenses. She fashioned an unnatural smile. "Kiss me, lover, or they'll kill me again." She spewed a guttural laugh so repellent to Tom's senses that it buckled his knees, and he fell hard to the hearthstones beneath him. Tom winced in pain and looked about. The room had returned along with the dead. She stood less than a body's length away from him.

"What the fuck is this?" His voice was a panicked cry. This was not what he'd expected, and this was not his wife. "What the fuck are you?" He pushed his back up against the crumbling stonework of the fireplace. He couldn't get far enough away from this abomination. But he couldn't run.

Beneath what might have been a hospital gown, she began to move her hips, rocking her pelvis back and forth. She moaned in contemplation of pleasure. "Come now, lover, surely you'd like a taste. Just a little taste?" Her visage changed suddenly, as if someone had just whispered a secret in her ear. The wraith leered at Tom. It drew closer and asked in the gravelly voice of a crusty old sailor, "When was the last time you had someone take to tugging on yer rope end?"

"Jesus!" Tom cried. "Get out of here! Get the fuck out! Get away from me, damn you!"

Dead Carol stopped immediately and smiled. It was a true smile, if a sinister one. It was the gleefully evil smile worn by the person who knows something is coming, something bad, that the other person doesn't. She stood motionless and slump-shouldered, her hands at her sides, and stared at Tom, smiling. She started to giggle. The giggling became incessant, as unnatural, perverse, and unnerving as had been the rest of the spectacle.

Tom drew a short breath to speak again when her head snapped to the right as quickly as if it had been yanked by a noose. She turned slowly, suspended off the ground by the unseen rope, her eyes open and searching. Suddenly, she was jerked upward as if through the ceiling and lost from sight when he felt a sharp burn in his thigh. Instinctively he grabbed his thigh and saw the knife buried to its hilt in his leg. He let out a scream as the heavy muscles began to spasm and cramp. He looked up to see his attacker and was not surprised.

Haloed by a darkness more perfect than the night, the first mate stood not more than ten paces away and tapped a finger on a second knife under his belt.

Tom knew the knife in his leg had to come out. Any movement would only cause more damage, and Tom had no intention of sitting still. He was bleeding badly, and his attacker had another weapon. Without another thought, he wrenched it by the handle with one quick, sure-handed move. Tom's head swam amid stars with the pain, but he didn't black out. He fell on his right side, his face lying on the cool, fractured hearthstone. Tom opened his eyes once more to find that the face of his enemy had changed.

An older man, leaner in muscle and dressed in shredded rags, glowered at him from beneath stringy gray hair. His face was not much more than skin-covered bone, but the blue of the eyes confirmed his identity. The man steadied himself on unshod feet with the use of a finely carved walking stick. From his position on the floor, Tom noticed the intricate carvings on the stick, heavily ordained with symbols of death. The gnarled fingers of the angry old man cupped the smooth crown of a skull. Without a word, the old man railed back with his stick and hurled it at Tom. The stick flew high and hit a stone in the fireplace just above Tom's head. He heard the now-familiar sound of stone shifting against mortar, and with a herculean effort, he pushed himself out of the stone's path as it came crashing to the ground, shattering the already-fractured slate hearthstone.

Tom struggled to get up, but his efforts were in vain. His leg was bleeding badly, and he wondered how long until the world around him would go dark. He struggled onto his right knee and supported himself on trembling arms. The stone that had crashed to the ground lay at his hand. It was too big to hurl as a weapon, but the broken pieces of slate beneath it were both small enough to throw and sharp enough to cause serious injury. That is, if the thing could be hurt at all. Expecting stubborn resistance, Tom heaved a sigh of relief when the heavy stone slid smoothly off the slate. When he looked up again, the old man was gone. The fiery murderer with one more knife in his belt stood menacingly in his place. Tom grabbed the largest piece of slate, the jagged edges digging into the flesh of his palms, and hurled it at his attacker. It struck the pirate on his shoulder and bounced harmlessly to the ground. Tom's strength was waning.

He reached back and threw another sharp rock with all his might. The fragments of slate were proving to be no more than a mildly inconvenient distraction to his assailant. Tom reached his hand down for another piece but found only a cold dirt floor below where the slate had been. He searched the floor quickly for some weapon he could brandish, but the knife and the walking stick that had been used against him had vanished.

His options exhausted, Tom quickly wedged his fingers between the next unbroken hearthstone and the dirt floor beneath it. The mortar was crumbling at the edges; he funneled all his remaining strength and hoisted the heavy stone up and over onto its back, cracking the slate into three large pieces. Tom worked the smallest of the pieces up onto an edge; it was very sharp but still much too heavy for the injured man to throw with any force.

Helpless to defend himself, Tom looked up into the pale-blue eyes of an indestructible beast as it stepped out from the blackness that surrounded him. Tom studied the shifting lines and curves on the face of the killer. He stared, transfixed, as the features changed before his eyes. A long, gaunt face, wrinkled with age and disease, began to tighten and fill with the healthy muscle of youth. The hair, once dull and gray, turned a dingy brown, then sparkled to gold in the brilliance of some invisible sun shining down upon him. But the faces stayed only moments. The man's image was ever changing, except for the lipid blue portals that were his eyes. The first mate moved slowly toward Tom with malicious intent. As death approached, despair gripped Tom's heart. "God," he murmured under his breath, "please, help me." The first mate smiled at Tom and reached for the second knife.

* * *

Jake had twice circled the house, searching for an entrance, when the white van scraped to a stop on the pebbled driveway. He ran toward it, relieved that reinforcements had arrived, but rarely did his eyes stray from the house as a deep rumble emanated from within. "I can't get in," he shouted to Drew in greeting. "I've tried the doors, but they're locked. So are the windows. What's more, I can't even break the windows to try to unlock them from the inside." Drew studied Jake through narrowed, doubting eyes.

"What's going on in there?" Rebecca called out as she came around the front of the van. A brilliant pumpkin hue shone from the gathering room windows. She ran to the house and peered into the window closest to the front door. "It's like someone is shining a bright orange light through wax paper," she said, frustrated. "I can't see a thing in there." She stopped to listen for a moment. "Jake, it sounds like a tornado's touching down in there—we've got to get in!"

Drew ran up to the door and cautiously placed his hand against it. "It's ice cold," he said, surprised at his findings.

"It looks like the place is on fire," Rebecca added.

"But there's no smoke, and there's no heat," Jake pointed out. "When I left Marie, I looked over here and saw the lights coming from these windows, but they were blue. By the time I got here, it was just as it is now. Like the place is burning, but there's no fire."

Drew couldn't stand idly by any longer. He bent down and picked up one of the large slate stones that made up the walkway. Holding it like a discus, Drew coiled back like a spring, the slate slab poised to fly. Jake and Rebecca stood clear as Drew swung the stone around and hurtled it into the window. The stone tore savagely into the wooden framework surrounding the paned glass, but the windows proved invulnerable to the attack.

"See what I mean?" Jake asked, feeling both vindicated and at a complete loss as to what to try next.

Drew ran to the van and hopped behind the wheel. He yelled out the window, "Clear the way!" Jake clutched Rebecca's hand and pulled her to relative safety behind a nearby silver maple.

"I hope he remembers one important thing," Jake said as Drew backed up onto the grass to help him achieve an adequate ramming speed.

"What's that?" Rebecca asked, eyes wide with fear.

"That the house he's about to crash into is made of stone."

Drew gunned the engine twice.

* * *

Tom watched the hand of the pirate as it crossed his midsection to the blade tucked beneath the wide belt. The large hand, sticky with drying blood, grasped the long knife and drew it from its leather berth. The noxious stench that came off the long-dead man accosted Tom, causing him to gag. He pushed himself farther away, into the all-too-shallow recesses of the cold firepit. Supporting himself on one arm, he watched in horror as the second knife was lifted high.

Tom's arm strength gave way, his hand slipping off the hearth-stone and into the shallow hole he'd dug in order to remove it. His hand, sliding down the sharp edge of the broken stone, was sliced open from the palm to his lower wrist. He cried out as the pain ripped into his brain, and the first mate roared with evil delight at the sight of the bloody accident. As Tom's injured hand struck the bottom of the hole, a small rock touched his fingers, and he instinctively latched on to it and brought it up to throw. One final act of defiance in the face of his invincible foe. But it wasn't a stone at all.

As the dirt fell away from it, something shimmered in the light. It was bright—and silver, black, and red. Even before he saw it, Tom knew what he had found. The Devil's Kiss sparkled in Tom's bleeding grasp. The eyes of the first mate grew wide with excitement. He slowly brought the knife down to his side. He studied the face and movement of the possessor of the ring, uncertain of what would happen next.

Tom hesitated, more relieved from the stay of execution than from the thrill of the prize in his hand. The two locked eyes and searched the other for a weakness. Slowly, the first mate extended a bloody hand out to accept from Tom what he'd sought for almost three hundred years. An evil, knowing look spread across the face of the first mate, and from the corner of his eye, Tom could see the pirate's grip on the knife tighten once more. This time, Tom smiled.

Suspicion shadowed the eyes of the first mate as a waxing confidence came over Tom. Before his attacker took another foul breath, the ring was on Tom's finger. The first mate screamed in impotent fury. The skin, again, drew taut and white against its skull. The defeat was total. Flashes of light struck Tom with the impact of a fierce and sudden wind. A baleful dirge went out from the fading specter that decried the fate of the damned. And as on the wings of inexorable evil the first mate had come, so he now departed. The last thing Tom heard before he lost consciousness was the melancholy echo of an old woman sobbing.

* * *

Jake was first through, shoulder bared to the door. Expecting to meet with brute force from the other side, the complete lack of resistance caused Jake to spill clumsily onto the floor. Drew, who had decided not to ram the stone-walled house with municipal property, stumbled in just after Jake but kept his balance. The police officer held his department-issued 9 mm out at the ready. Jake was up almost as fast as he went down and darted to his unconscious friend.

Rebecca had been ordered to stay outside until Drew had determined it was safe for her to enter, an order that Rebecca considered both flattering and infuriating. The absence of the sound of gunfire told Rebecca that all was well, or that, at least, Drew hadn't seen anything he could shoot. She stuck her head around the corner as Jake came to kneel at Tom's side.

"This doesn't look good," Jake said to Drew, who stood nearby, surveying the room. Despite the puncture wound in the thigh, it was the slow, steady bleeding of the laceration on Tom's hand and wrist that concerned Jake. "Rebecca," Jake called, bidding her to enter, "there's a first-aid kit under the sink in the kitchen. Get it for me, would you, please? I need it, quickly." The last Jake said with a note of urgency, causing Rebecca to hurry her pace to a near run.

Seeing no evidence of any unwelcome visitors about the place, Drew holstered his weapon. He took a deep breath and turned to check on Tom's condition. Rebecca already had the gauze out of the first-aid kit when she reached Jake and was searching for the tape when Jake grabbed the tin box from her hand. He rifled through the kit, removed a small plastic tube, and dispensed a beaded line of antibiotic ointment on a Telfa pad. Holding the pad firmly against the laceration, Jake wrapped the rolled gauze tightly around Tom's hand and wrist. He looked up at Drew. "We've got to get him to a hospital."

"I'll take care of it," Drew said and flipped open the mouthpiece of his phone.

"He'll be all right, won't he?" Rebecca asked with hopeful concern.

Tom groaned but remained on the verge of consciousness. His left hand, which had not been injured, reached for his wounded leg.

"He found it!" Rebecca shouted as she pointed to the large lump of silver on the middle finger of Tom's hand.

Jake looked up at Rebecca and smiled. "Then I guess he'll be all right."

"The ambulance is on its way," Drew said to ease the others. "And I made sure they sent a different crew tonight."

The statement struck Jake as odd. "What do you mean?" he asked as he tended the puncture wound on Tom's leg.

Drew waved a dismissive hand at Jake. "Never mind," he said with a smile. "It's not important."

You're right, Jake thought. *It's not important.* Nothing else mattered right now. They had their friend. He was bleeding and semiconscious, but he was alive.

King Richard's Lament

July 1719

King Richard watched as the distant lights of Salem and Marble-head grew smaller and smaller in the night. He wore a heavy heart for his old friend and couldn't guess what had kept him from one last voyage. He smiled. *Maybe a whore.* His smile fell away. *Maybe death.* He didn't know. But if he did die, he only hoped that his friend had died well. It was what he wanted. It was what he deserved.

The Lionheart allowed himself a few minutes to remember times long gone by, when their kind ruled the sea with the cutlass and the boarding pike. The rum, the blood, the whores, and the money that slipped through their fingers as if water. It was their way, right or wrong.

They were all gone now, but when they sailed, they struck fear in the hearts of all. He was lucky to have sailed with so many of them. Men whose fearlessness and ferocity in battle were matched only by their fellowship and loyalty to their shipmates. It was a life fit for few. And it was only by living that life that one was able to understand their way. That those who would be good must do the terrible. And those who would be great must be the worst.

In the eyes of the Lionheart, the greatest of these was Israel Hands.

Epilogue

Wednesday, July 28, 1999

Tom's hand and wrist had healed well, but he was still walking with a considerable limp, and his thigh began to cramp if he stayed in the same position too long. He received some relief from the pain meds he'd been prescribed, but he went easy on the pills during waking hours. The reduced range of motion in his leg made it difficult for him to help with many of the chores that needed to be done, and that bothered him almost as much as the injury itself. Today, the pain was exacerbated by countless trips in and out of the house, each of which required him to sit and rest afterward. Jake told him he was just being lazy. He'd been telling him that for the past four weeks.

It was a tough day to be moving so many boxes. The mercury had hiked to the grumpy side of ninety by late morning, and the humidity trailed close behind. "This kind of weather doesn't have many friends," Tom said as Jake passed him by, struggling with a box of books slung on his hip.

"Well, then, the two of you have a lot in common," Jake quipped. "You know, limping like that reminds me of one of those guys in that *Spirit of '76* painting," he added.

"That original painting is right down the street if you want to check it out," Tom said.

"No thanks," Jake replied as he deposited the box of books in the back of Tom's SUV. "I think my appreciation of 'paint on canvas' as an art form is pretty much down the shitter." Jake turned to see Tom struggling with a smaller box, shifting its weight for a better grip in his sweaty hands.

"Here, let me help you with that, Limpy," Jake said, relieving Tom of his burden.

Jake followed Tom back into the house for one last load. The cool felt good against hot skin and throbbing temples.

"Man, I'm gonna sit for a few," Tom said, starting to massage his leg before his butt even hit the chair.

Jake filled a paper cup with cold water from the kitchen faucet and returned with a bottle of Tom's medication.

"I wish I could," Tom said, waving him off, "but I can't take one of those before a long drive."

"Don't worry about it. You can ride in the car with Marie, and I'll drive your truck," Jake insisted.

"Nah. I appreciate it, but I think I'd like to drive myself."

"Leave under your own power, so to speak?"

"Yeah," Tom said quietly. "Something like that."

Jake set the bottle down in front of Tom and dropped heavily into the chair he'd come to think of as his place at the table. It seemed so normal now. That is, now that the eyes that had once watched him were no longer there. *The First Mate* had been burned in the cold fireplace into which he now stared, and he recalled the joy he felt watching the portrait go up in flames. He regarded the long, sturdy table that supported his tired arms. It was magnificent. A damn shame it had to stay. But the table and the chairs were a set, and they went perfectly with the room. It was only right that they remain. Jake lifted his gaze to the mantel and the surrounding stonework. The mason had done a fantastic job. All the masonry, inside and out, had recently been completed at the expense of the new owner.

Immersed in their own thoughts and allowing the cool of the gathering room to replenish their waning energy, the two sat quietly as the events of the past six weeks replayed in their minds over and over again. In the midst of their shared silence, Ol' Sentry began to chime. Tom jumped reflexively and felt the knifing pain shoot through his thigh.

"Relax," Jake said as the chiming continued, "it's just the clock."

Tom steadied himself on the table and slowly eased back down into his chair as the grandfather clock finished tolling twelve. Tom had not furnished the details of what had happened that night to anyone, not even Jake. So no one could possibly know why, like Pavlov's dog, every time the clock struck twelve, Tom damn near pissed himself. He took a deep breath and let it out.

"Eight bells," he said, turning to Jake. "My watch is over."

Over the last few days, as Tom began moving out, the new owner had been moving in. The owner had been very patient with Tom. Tom had agreed to terms that included immediate occupancy but was allowed to linger and move at a ridiculously leisurely pace. Due to his injuries, Tom was allowed to stay an additional ten days, which gave Tom until noon on the twenty-eighth of July. Ol' Sentry had just told him it was time to leave.

Marie stood just inside the front door. Jake looked over and nodded as she lightly tapped the face of the watch on her wrist before stepping back outside to take one last look at the promising garden she'd cultivated over the last month and a half.

"How's your leg feeling, champ?" Jake asked, smiling more out of compassion than humor. Tom stared mutely into the fireplace. After a prolonged silence, Jake stood. "I'll grab the last box and meet you outside," he said softly.

Tom nodded, his eyes never leaving the fireplace. Jake shut the front door behind him. He delivered the last box and tucked it in securely among Tom's other treasures.

"Where's Tom?" Marie asked.

"He's saying goodbye," her husband said somberly. Marie considered his statement, confused.

"He's saying goodbye to the house?" she finally asked.

"No," he said, shutting the Expedition's rear hatch. "He's saying goodbye to Carol."

A familiar shape on the driveway put smiles back on the couple's faces. Lieutenant Drew was coming by to wish his new friends a fond farewell. The snow-white vehicle, with "Safety Officer Drew" stenciled cleanly on the front quarter panel, rolled to a stop in front of the Breans' Bonneville.

"Whew." Drew whistled as he stepped out of his air-conditioned vehicle into the heat. "Looks like you picked a good day to leave," he said, gazing into the thick haze of summer. "Forecast predicts we'll set a new record high for today."

"Geez, there's a cause for celebration, huh?" Jake said as he took Drew's hand in greeting.

The passenger door swung open, and Rebecca stepped out from behind it.

"Hey there," Marie said, truly pleased to see her. The two women embraced, much to Jake's amusement—he still recalled the cold friction of their first meeting. With so much having passed between them over the last six weeks, today seemed like a day of parting between brothers and sisters in arms, a bittersweet goodbye that was as regrettable as it was inevitable.

A friendship forged by such bizarre circumstances would remain alive only in the memories of those dear and impossible friends. Oh, maybe Tom and the Breans would receive invitations to the wedding, if it ever came to that. But Jake doubted it. Although he did muse that such an event would be worth coming to see. It would make the front page of the *Marblehead Reporter. The witch and the cop? Hell, they could sell tickets.*

The front door opened, and Tom came limping out. He smiled sheepishly when Rebecca moaned in sympathy to see him walking with a significant limp—or a bent axle, as Jake referred to it. Tom was greeted with a hug and a handshake from the new arrivals.

"How are you feeling, stranger?" Rebecca asked. She took a step backward to have a better look at him. She'd stayed away from the house after that night, wanting to give Tom his space, knowing that time, more than anything else, was what he needed. She and Drew had visited him in the hospital, but it had been twelve days since his discharge from North Shore Medical Center, and she hadn't seen him since he'd returned home.

"I'm doing OK," Tom said, shifting the weight from his gimpy leg. "It still throbs if I stand too long," he reported as he looked down at his limb, reassessing his condition, "and it starts to cramp up if I don't do some light stretching every once in a while."

"What are your plans now, Tom?" Drew asked as he scribbled something on the back of a business card. He handed it to Tom.

"I'm gonna drop anchor with Jake and Marie in Connecticut for a short time, lick my wounds, and figure out what I want to do next," Tom replied, all the while studying the card just handed to him. "Drew, you already gave me a card with your number on it."

"That's Rebecca's number," Drew said with a subdued grin. "You might catch me there if I'm not home. Keep me posted on how you're doing, all right?"

"Sure, Drew. I'm gonna be fine."

There was nothing more to say, and the heat was pressing the day. Jake made a point of hoisting his wrist up to look at his watch. "Well, you about ready to go, there, sport?" he asked Tom, anxious to move from the heat and the house.

Tom slightly dipped his head. It was time to go. The hugs went around one last time as the group that had been brought together under the most extraordinary and tragic circumstances said goodbye.

Jake followed as Drew went back to his vehicle, turning to face Jake when he opened the car door.

"What's *he* doing here already?" Drew asked, motioning at the new owner's car in the driveway.

Jake looked over his shoulder and lifted his eyes to the upstairs windows. "It's his house now. I think he's still going through all the bedrooms."

"Looking for buried treasure, I'll bet."

"Well, if he's looking for treasure, I'm afraid he's too late," Jake said as he studied the grounds around the house. "But I'll bet there are other things buried here if he wants to find them."

He turned back to the lieutenant. "Have you heard whether he's going to authorize an excavation of the property?"

The question surprised Drew. "Didn't you and Tom ask him?"

"Yeah, but he's sort of the standoffish type, if you know what I mean."

"Oh yeah." Drew chortled. "I know *exactly* what you mean. Anyway, I heard he refused the town's request for a preliminary dig on account of there's no proof that anyone's buried here. He says it's just Rebecca's word, and that's nothing but a bunch of voodoo bullshit."

"I'll bet that really pissed her off," Jake said in a conspiratorial tone. Drew glanced over Jake's shoulder to spy his lady, still talking to Marie, and looked back at Jake. "Oh, you have no idea." The two shared a final smile.

Jake stepped away from the safety officer's van as Drew turned the key in the ignition. Rebecca slid into the seat beside him and shut the door as soon as the cooler air issued from the vents. She waved to Marie as Drew backed the van safely out of the driveway and headed toward downtown Marblehead, a quick toot of the horn marking their departure as they disappeared down the tree-lined street.

"Where's Tom?" Jake asked his wife as she waved to friends no longer there.

"Inside," she said, turning her attention back to the house. "He said he wanted to make sure he didn't leave anything behind and to let the owner know that we're leaving."

Tom stood at the bottom of the main staircase. "We're leaving now," he shouted up. He waited. Nothing. "Hello? She's all yours.

We're heading out." He waited some more. Still nothing. "I'm leaving my key on the table." Silence. Tom shrugged it off and set his key on the gathering room table.

He looked up the staircase as he opened the front door to leave. He thought about going upstairs to say goodbye to the owner but quickly decided against it. And it wasn't because of his injured leg—which was reason enough. There was just something about the guy that Tom didn't like. The door creaked on its well-oiled hinges as it slowly closed. As he stepped out into the heat, he heard the distinctive click of the latch bolt behind him. It now belonged to another.

The new owner of Stonecroft Inn looked down from an upstairs bedroom window and watched as Tom walked away.

Jake tossed Marie the car keys as Tom limped toward his truck and an unknown future. "Get her started and cool off, babe. I'll just be a minute." Marie reached over from the passenger seat and turned the ignition. Hot air blew from the vents, but it'd be cool soon enough. She kept her door open just the same.

Jake joined Tom at his truck, where he leaned through the driver's side window and turned the engine over, making sure the air conditioner was turned to high. He looked back at the house.

"Are you sorry you're leaving?" Jake asked as he followed Tom's gaze.

"No, I'm not," Tom replied, a quizzical expression on his face. "I thought it would kill me to leave this place, but I'm OK."

"Really?" Jake said, equally pleased and surprised.

"Absolutely," he replied with a comfortable grin.

Jake looked at Tom's hand. "So how long are you gonna keep that on?" Jake asked, pointing with a toss of his head at the Devil's Kiss wrapped around Tom's finger.

Tom held up the ring on his fisted hand and shrugged. "I don't know."

"Man, you've got to get that thing appraised. I'll bet you could easily get six figures for it."

Tom nodded in likely agreement as the light rebounded off the sparkling silver and the precious gemstones of onyx and ruby. "You might be right, but I think I'm going to keep it right here for a while."

Jake turned and looked at the house. Despite the heat, a shiver, as cold as steel, ran down his spine. "I think that's a good fuckin' idea, Tom."

"Language," Marie said from ten feet away and with the AC blowing full force.

Jake rolled his eyes and patted Tom on the back. "You keep that thing right where it is." Jake returned to his car and, before slipping in behind the wheel, extended a final message to his friend. "Try to keep up!"

Jake rolled slowly down the drive, the small stones spitting out from under the tires as he pulled out onto Beacon Street. Tom put his Expedition in drive but held his foot on the brake. He took one last look at the house he'd known but for a short while as Stonecroft Inn. It never saw a guest. At least, not one who paid. Tom glanced at his hand that crowned the steering wheel and the mammoth silver ring tightly gripping his middle finger, then took his foot off the brake.

Paris Quicci peered out from the northwest bedroom window. "That's it," he said out loud to himself, "turn tail and run."

A gentle roll of laughter tickled his throat as the brake lights came on, then off again, at the end of the driveway. "Adios, loser," he added with adolescent disdain. "Get the hell off my property."

He watched until the Ford Expedition rolled around the bend before he shifted his attention to the other window in the bedroom. He smiled broadly as he stepped over to the far side of the room and was met with a magnificent view of Doliber's Cove and Salem Harbor beyond.

He gazed out the window at the crystal-blue waters of the cove below. There were many things he liked about the property, and he had decided there were some aspects he wouldn't change. He liked the garden out front, and a quality landscape job is nothing to sneeze at. Like the house itself, as well as the views, landscaping says something about a man. Taken as a whole, his new home helped separate him from the chaff—the mindless, mouth-breathing masses he was forced to endure every day.

This was what he'd been waiting for. True, the style was not entirely to Paris Quicci's particular liking, but it was a piece of property he'd always desired. Some thought the purchase frivolous, but not the banker. That he desired it was reason enough.

Finally, he was alone in his new home. He had it all, and nothing more stood in his way. He smiled as he considered his world. There was no man he could not defeat. There was no woman he could not bed. There was, in fact, no object that he desired that he could not possess. Paris Quicci was well pleased with himself and all he had.

And then the window shattered. It was the damnedest thing he ever saw.

John Geerer is a U.S. Navy veteran. He grew up in Connecticut and now lives in Michigan with his wife, Chris, and their dog, Charlie. This is his first novel.